HALL OF MIRRORS

It is not often that a libel action involves a whole profession. But when Sir Thomas Gilling, one of the physicians to the Royal Family, a Fellow of the Royal Society and consultant to one of the great London hospitals, sues David Line, Professor of Surgery and head of the experimental unit at the Metropolitan Hospital, almost every figure of importance in the world of medicine finds himself involved.

Yet as the story progresses it becomes increasingly clear to both men that it is their own character, their own history, their own life that is the focus of attention. The case will, in the end, be decided on what the jury thinks of them as people. Is Gilling a widely experienced, highly capable doctor nearing the end of a deservedly successful career, or is he just an old buffer who wants to hold on to place and power? Is Line a brilliant pioneer, obstructed by mediocrities in entrenched positions, or is he an erratic exhibitionist, exploiting the opportunities offered by television and the popular press? We see them as they appear to themselves and to the women who love or once loved them; we see how life has made them what they are. Fascinating as the medical details involved in the case are, the real questions to be judged are those of character and personality.

The two aspects of this absorbing novel give full scope to John Rowan Wilson's unique combination of talents. As a doctor and surgeon who knows the world of medical politics at first hand, he is a thorough master of his materials at every point.

Martin Mackay
Hollingside.

JOHN ROWAN WILSON

HALL
OF
MIRRORS

COLLINS
ST JAMES'S PLACE, LONDON
1966

Author's Note

THE ACTION of this book takes place a few years in the future, for two reasons. The first is that it mentions existing institutions, such as the Royal College of Physicians, the Royal Society, the Ministry of Health, etc., and I wish to make it absolutely plain that all of my characters are totally fictional and bear no resemblance to past or present holders of office in such bodies. The second is that it deals with a scientific advance, the full development of which lies a little way ahead. The Brook-Halder machine does not refer to any existing machine, though prototypes of this kind of apparatus have been described and their implications discussed in the scientific literature. Their potentialities, limitations and dangers will be apparent to anyone who reads this novel.

I

Chapter 1

As THE CLOCK STRUCK SEVEN, Sir Thomas Gilling stirred gently into wakefulness. Usually, with him, sleep, as it retreated, left behind a curious sediment of apprehension. It was a distressing feeling which resisted any logical analysis. All his adult life, so far as he could remember, he had awakened each morning full of a vague, unspecified dread, as if something disastrous were in store for him during the coming day. He had often tried to banish its effects by speculating on its possible origin. It certainly bore no relation to his present life. He was a successful man, he was afraid of nobody, he was rich and secure, happily married, respected, influential. His health was good. Where, then, was the origin of this fear, this regular ten minutes of half-conscious early morning apprehension? Was it a relic of his childhood or a premonition of his future, a recoil of his unconscious self against the inevitability of death? Or was it just a physiological process, a fall of the blood-pressure as consciousness flickered and sleep receded? He could not tell. But like the experienced physician he was, he did not let obscurity about causation interfere with a search for a suitable treatment. He had found from experience that the best remedy for this particular malaise was activity. As soon as he felt the clouds of gloom descending on him, he threw off the clothes and got out of bed.

He put on his slippers and dressing-gown and padded over to the windows. A pull on the cord opened the heavy velvet drapes and let in some intermittent shafts of light spring sunshine. He felt better already. Out on the common the wind was blowing the clouds across the sky and shaking the branches of the great chestnuts; a girl was riding a horse, galloping, with her hair

9

streaming behind. Across the common, just visible through the trees, were other houses like his own, large, comfortable, opulent. To his wife, he knew, they were all slightly absurd, these pretentious upper middle class residences built about the turn of the century to house well-to-do stockbrokers and tea-importers from Mincing Lane. In the world she had inhabited before her marriage, there was something comic about Wimbledon. She concealed her amusement as much as possible, for she was a woman without malice; yet it was there, he knew. He did not resent it.

He moved along the corridor which led to his dressing-room and bathroom. For the thousandth time, he enjoyed the warmth and luxury and spaciousness of it all. At the age of sixty, after thirty years of prosperity, it was still a delight to him to be warm and cosy, to have unlimited hot water, servants, good food, and all the luxuries he could think of. It always seemed to him like something of a miracle, that anyone could have gained so much of his heart's desire as he had. For many years, indeed, he had suffered from a secret terror that people would find him out, would say disgustedly that he was just an ordinary person and had no right to the honours they had heaped on him. He had felt a combination of gratitude and shame that the world had continued repeatedly to choose him in preference to others. What had he to offer to the rich and the powerful, to royal personages, to his hospital and his Royal College, that they could not so easily get elsewhere? But recently his anxieties had grown less. Among the great, he had found, inadequacy was the rule rather than the exception. His uniqueness rested solely in being conscious of it.

As he bathed and dressed he reflected on his programme for the day. It was Tuesday. That meant a teaching round at St. Vincent's from 9.30 a.m. to 11 a.m., then Wimpole Street until lunch time. Lunch at the Savoy with Sir Horace Trimble— what did *he* want? Gilling made a grimace. He wasn't very keen on Trimble and he wasn't very keen on lunching at the Savoy Grill, good as the food was. He always ended up by eating and drinking more than was suitable for the middle of the day. Then there were his out-patients at the North Essex. There was no teaching at the North Essex, and his registrar would have to do the lion's share of the out-patients since, Trimble being what he was, there would be no possibility of getting to the hospital on time. Well, he would do his best. He would try to be there for three o'clock, perhaps even a little earlier. He would be firm with Trimble.

When he went down to breakfast his wife was already sitting at her end of the table reading the *Daily Mail*. Two black labrador puppies scuffled around her feet, baring their fangs and biting each other's necks with mock ferocity. They looked up as he came in, eyed him indifferently for a moment, and then returned to their game.

His wife said, in her clipped, aristocratic voice, "I'm worried about Rob this morning."

Rob was the larger of the puppies. He had lost interest in his brother and was busy licking the polish off one of the legs of the breakfast table.

"He looks fit enough to me," said Gilling mildly.

"He keeps being sick."

"It's hardly surprising when you consider the things he eats. I found him chewing a doorstop yesterday morning."

She shook her head. "There's something very curious about his motions."

Gilling nodded as sympathetically as he could and helped himself to coffee. He had never been able to share her involvement in the detailed lives and habits of her dogs. His mail was lying in front of his plate. A bill, something from his insurance brokers, an investment circular. . . .

"What do you suppose it could be?"

He looked up abstractedly. "What?"

"Oh, really, Tom, you're no help at all. I should have thought you could have made a suggestion. What could be wrong with him?"

"My dear, I'm not a vet. I haven't the least idea."

He heard her give an exasperated sigh as he returned his attention to his letters. He could have taken more interest— been a little more sympathetic. Why were we so peevish and ungracious with the ones we loved, he wondered. It was ignoble, yet quite irresistible, and he could not bring himself to apologize. Besides which, he had quite genuinely no gift for diagnosis when it came to retrievers. He came to the last few letters. There was one in a plain, enigmatic white envelope. He opened it without emotion until he saw the heading on the notepaper. Then the apprehensions that had plagued him on waking returned with redoubled force. And this time they had some basis.

The letter was from his solicitors:

Dear Sir Thomas,

This is just to notify you that the hearing of your action for defamation against Mr. David Line has been scheduled by the Court for Monday, 16th April. It is likely that the hearing will last for at least several days and we hope that it will not be too inconvenient to you to keep yourself available during the week in question. No doubt you would care to call in to my office some time and have a talk about final arrangements. If so, perhaps you would give me a ring and make an appointment at some time convenient to you.

Yours sincerely,

L. Perrin

It was ridiculous to be so upset by it, he told himself. He had known it must come soon. And yet somehow he had managed to put it to the back of his mind and live as if the whole wretched affair had been disposed of. He had been like a man with an incurable disease, who is lulled by some merciful faculty for self-deception into believing that this time Nature will make an exception and that death, in some unexplained way, will forget to call for him at the appointed time. He looked gloomily at the breakfast congealing uneaten on his plate, and then at his wife. He had a faint hope that she might see from his face that something was wrong. But she was still preoccupied with the dog.

"I've wormed him times without number," she said. "It can't be that."

Gilling said, "There's a letter from Perrin."

"Perrin?"

"About the case. It's scheduled for Monday, 16th April."

"Oh—well, you were expecting it, weren't you?" She spoke abstractedly. He could see that she had no conception of his anxiety.

"Yes."

"I expect that dreadful fellow Line will be shaking in his shoes," she said with lofty contempt. "He probably expected you to back down."

"Perhaps."

"Of course he did. Shifty little scoundrel."

"I don't think he's a scoundrel."

"You're too trusting. He's dishonest. I can tell by his face. Associating with street-corner reporters—it's disgraceful. But they're all mad in that family. His father was just the same."

"His father?"

"Yes. He came to Marlowe once for a weekend when I was a girl." For a moment a wild, absurd hope fluttered in Gilling. Was this a possible way of putting pressure on Line? Could it be that Marlowe might help him in this crisis, as it had done before? The hope died almost as soon as it arose. Line's father was dead, he knew. She was talking of something that happened forty years ago.

"He was well-known to have a screw loose," she said reminiscently. "He was a classics don at Magdalen, and he had an idea that there was a hidden city in Delos. He spent all his own money and a good deal of other people's digging for it. He never got a penny out of father, I'm glad to say."

"Did he find anything?"

"Not a sausage. Stop it, Prince!" She slapped hard at one of the puppies. "He's disgusting—he likes to lick the inside of my slippers. What they both need is a damned good run on the common."

"I expect so." He got up from the table.

"Going already?"

"The car's outside."

"So it is." She put up her face to be kissed. "Will you be home to dinner?"

"No. There's a meeting at the College. I'm dining with Maxfield at the Athenaeum."

"Don't be too late," she said perfunctorily. He smiled and shook his head. He never was, but in any case she would be in bed when he returned. She liked to retire at ten o'clock and watch a television set which she had fixed to the foot of her bed. Frequently she would go to sleep with it full on. He would creep into the room and switch it off without waking her and then return to his own. He often envied her invulnerability, her passionate absorption in her own fads. To have had so much, so young, seemed to have left her completely immune to the normal competitive pressures of society. The currency of distinction had been devalued for her. There was something rather magnificent in the way she never compared herself in any way with others. Dowdy, grey-haired, in her baggy tweed skirt and brogues, her spare figure strode across the common each day, accompanied by her dogs. She was always alone. Sometimes she could be heard singing discordantly to herself.

The housemaid helped him on with his coat and handed him his paper. He liked to read it in the car on his way to the hospital. Curwin had orders to drive slowly so as to cut down the vibration. As the Rolls moved sedately into Parkside he opened the paper and began to glance through it. One of the minor signs of advancing years, like pains in your joints and wanting to pass your water more frequently, was an increased interest in *The Times*. It was (it made no bones about it) a paper written for Top People, about Top People, and very probably, for all he knew, by Top People. Once you became a Top Person, you became willy-nilly identified with it. So many of the news items seemed to refer to your friends.

Or to you. At the bottom of page four, a headline struck him with a jolt: "Royal Physician in Libel Suit."

The story under it was short and discreet, Times-fashion. There was nothing to which one could take exception. It said little more than that the action had been brought and that it would come up for hearing on the 16th April. This was nothing, he told himself; he would have to get used to a great deal more than this during the next week or so. "Royal Physician!"—that would presumably be the angle. You couldn't blame the journalists. Anything to do with royalty was news. A little of the magic rubbed off on everyone connected with it. He remembered when he had first visited a royal personage. A frail, rather fussy old lady, with a habit of champing her false teeth as she spoke, but she had made him feel as if his finger-nails were dirty and his fly-buttons hanging open. It was like being suddenly precipitated on to a stage in the middle of a show. The figures

14

around you were unreal, they were not of your world. Even now, though familiarity had bred a less reverential outlook, there was still an undertone of awe in his dealings with them. Perhaps that was why they liked him so much.

St. Vincent's, like so many of London's teaching hospitals, was in a dark and sooty part of the East End. The slums which had once surrounded it were now replaced by office blocks of hardly more attractive appearance. The old façade of the hospital still remained. Enormous Doric columns, pitch-black, like a photographic negative of the Acropolis; behind it, an entrance hall, a few of the old corridors, and then the new building, erected piecemeal, on a multitude of levels; wards, laboratories, animal houses, Nissen huts, operating theatres, boiler-houses, sheds. The corridors wound aimlessly, in labyrinthine fashion, from building to building, sometimes ducking underground, sometimes emerging into the open air, high up, on ramshackle structures resembling a fire escape or a ship's bridge. Here and there, dotted irregularly between the buildings, were damp, squalid little courtyards, populated by coal bunkers and dustbins. Lines of flagstones, which steamed gently on cold days, masked the course of the hot pipes close beneath the ground, and here sat rows of cats, warming their furry backsides at the expense of the National Health Service. As with many British institutions, sporadic modernization had been going on in such an unco-ordinated fashion over a number of years that any kind of total reconstruction now seemed out of the question. The hospital contemplated its many architectural excrescences with a mixture of dismay and resignation, like a man past middle life looking at his physique in the bathroom mirror. The flat feet, the varicose veins, the pot belly are there for good—he no longer has any hope of curing them. The most he can hope to do is to cover them up.

The head porter came out of his glass enclosure behind the front door and took Gilling's coat—it was a service he reserved for senior members of the staff. His expression was impassive but infinitely knowing. Had he read *The Times*? Almost certainly. Head porters always knew everything. Well, everyone must know sooner or later. They had got used to him being one sort of celebrity, now they would see him as another. It would be a great topic of conversation for the students and the house-men. He could remember his own youth well enough to know that they would not have any real sympathy with him. In his position, he was above sympathy. They would want him to win, he hoped, because he believed they liked him, but they would not really visualize that he could be hurt, or embarrassed, or afraid. They knew nothing of those dreadful moments after waking, or the sick feeling in his stomach when he opened his solicitor's letter. The price you paid for greatness was that nobody was ever sorry for you. But then, why should they be? Greatness was notoriously overpaid, not only in money but in privilege and respect. Whatever you might lose would only bring you a little nearer to the rewards you really deserved.

But he would not lose, he told himself. It was out of the question. Quite apart from the cold legal merits of the case, he knew himself and he knew Line. The jury would see them both in the witness-box and he had little doubt of the impression they would both make. After all, that was his stock-in-trade; that, more than anything, had got him where he was today. A reason-able, thinking, balanced, tolerant gentleman—that was the image he had presented successfully to the world for thirty years now. Like all public images it was not the truth, but it was a simplified version of the truth. It had some basis. Could a jury find against him? Would they shoot Santa Claus? Surely not.

He spent the first hour in the hospital teaching the students. He still enjoyed teaching. Many of his colleagues, he knew, grew tired of undergraduate teaching and dodged it whenever possible. The committees and the private consultations seemed more important to them, and also they began to be a little nervous in their old age that their medical knowledge was going rusty. They found it hard to keep up with advances in general medicine among all their other activities, and they feared the knowing looks of the students as they were ruthlessly compared with the younger members of the consultant staff. Gilling was well aware that he was regarded as a little old-fashioned and he made a slight cult of it. He believed in first principles and a down-to-earth approach, and he was pleased to see that attendances at his teachings were still as high as they had ever been. He looked round the students benignly. Always the same assortment of faces—they changed very little really, over the years. The earnest boy who took notes all the time, copying down each triviality you uttered as if it were Holy Writ; the bored rugger player looking furtively out of the window or grinning at the staff nurse; the ambitious poseur who aped the consultants in manner and dress, with a bow-tie one year and a bowler hat and umbrella the next. And there, too, the type he liked the least, the self-conscious, dapper, clever young man with a copy of the latest monograph tucked under his arm, listening in a slightly condescending manner as if he knew everything you had to say before you said it. Maxfield must have been like that as a student, he thought suddenly. That was the dreadful thing—you couldn't really prevent them succeeding.

After the teaching he did a short ward round, had coffee with his registrar and house physician, and set off for Wimpole Street. When he got to his rooms he handed the letter from Perrin to his secretary.

"You'd better add that to the file," he said. He paused for a moment. She knew perhaps more about himself and his feelings about the action than anybody. "It's down for Monday, 16th April. We'd better keep the whole of that week free."

"You already have a few appointments." She looked at his book. "Nothing that can't easily be changed."

"All right—change them, will you?"

Mrs. Dobson scribbled a note on her pad. She was a middle-aged woman with a lined, humorous face and a personality which remained indomitably cheerful in face of whatever disastrous circumstances life might have in store for her. Widowed at the age of twenty-four when her husband had been killed at El Alamein, she had succeeded in bringing up three children on an Army pension and her earnings as a secretary. Now that they had grown up and left her, she had turned her talents for organization and evidently inexhaustible store of devotion over to Gilling. She was perhaps the person he admired most in all the world. She was on close terms with his wife, and once a fortnight visited the house at Wimbledon for tea, a feminine function to which he was not invited. Charlotte called her by her Christian name, and had done so for years, but for some reason he had never been able to address her as anything but Mrs. Dobson.

She read the letter. "He suggests you might like to see him. Do you want to?"

Gilling nodded. He was suddenly very anxious to see Perrin. The truth was that he was in a slight panic. There was no getting away from it now; unless something dramatic occurred at the last minute it was really going to happen. He would have to go down to the Law Courts and give evidence and be cross-examined and photographed and have his replies splashed all over the daily papers. "Royal Physician in Box." It would be horrible, even if he won—which, of course, he was bound to. Line had no chance, everybody agreed. Just the same it was frightening, and he wanted to see somebody with a cold, clinical approach, who would tell him unemotionally that everything was going to be all right, that there were cases of libel every week of the year and his was nothing exceptional. A professional, who would reassure him from the depths of long experience and laugh at his fears. . . . Somebody, in other words, to do for him what he did so often for others. He was the patient now.

"I'd like to see him today," he said.

"You've got Sir Horace Trimble for lunch."

"I know. After that."

The North Essex would have to go, once again. He felt a pang of guilt. But he really must see Perrin. He would make it up some time. "Tell Kennedy I may not be able to make it this afternoon." He looked at his appointment book. "Who have I got to see this morning?"

"Mrs. Mulholland at 11.30. Then the Bishop of Bognor at twelve. Mrs. Mulholland's already here."

"She always arrives on time. It's getting rid of her that's the problem."

"I'll ring through as soon as the Bishop arrives and you can use that as a hint." She looked away from him for a moment. In a slightly over-casual voice she said, "A reporter from the *Mercury* rang this morning. He wanted to know if you'd give him an interview."

"About the case?"

"Yes. I told him no. I take it that I was right."

"Of course." With sudden bitterness, he said, "Tell him to ring up Line. He's the man who talks to reporters."

Hatred sounded strange from his mouth. It was like a man talking in a foreign language. She frowned anxiously. "This is going to go on for a long time, you know," she said. "You must try not to be upset."

"All right." He smiled at her. "You saw *The Times*?"

"It's in all the papers. You'll have to get used to it. From now on, everybody knows."

Everybody. The hospital porters, the students, the members of his club, his servants, the tradesmen who supplied his home, his patients, Mrs. Mulholland, the Bishop of Bognor. From now on, he was not just simply a distinguished physician, he was a public performer, a prize-fighter, a matador. His personal agonies would be served up to the people of England to compensate them for the tedium of their own existence. And the more he squirmed under the spotlight, the more entertained they would be. It was a time for strong nerves.

His two patients were finished by half past twelve. When he got to the Savoy, Trimble was already there, sitting at a table in the bar. He was a remarkable figure, well over six feet tall and enormously fat. His great red baby face was like a rolling landscape of hills, rivers, gorges, cliffs, and valleys, while his white, tufted eyebrows stuck out from his forehead like trees rooted precariously on a mountainside. His hair was luxuriant, a forest covered with snow. His body was swathed in yard upon yard of expensive worsted, cut and fitted by a tailor who regarded bellies such as his as the kind of challenge which made his craft worth while. His enormous, podgy hands clutched a dry martini of comparable size.

He heaved to his feet as Gilling entered. "A drink, Thomas?"

"No thanks. I'd prefer to go straight in, if you don't mind."

"Excellent, excellent." Trimble's voice boomed across the bar. He had the plummy, self-satisfied intonation of an archdeacon. He swallowed the remains of his drink at a gulp and signalled to the barman to put the cost of it on to his restaurant bill. As always, he made Gilling feel stunted and rather dusty. He was an eighteenth-century figure. You could imagine him in a full-bottomed wig, bowing and scraping ironically around a Hanoverian court, dispensing patronage, bribing and receiving bribes, buying pocket boroughs, riding to hounds by day and drinking his bottle of port every evening. Gilling himself wasn't very keen on the eighteenth century and was always slightly uneasy with Trimble—the Puritan artisans in his ancestry recoiled from all this easygoing corruptibility. Also, Trimble had a curiously un-English habit of constantly touching you. He had none of the usual inhibitions against physical contact. He would pat you on the back, put his hand on yours to emphasize a point, without the least embarrassment. At this very moment, as they walked into the restaurant, Trimble stooped down from his enormous height to talk confidentially to Gilling, and gripped him by the elbow. Gilling moved awkwardly forward, holding himself stiff, like a marionette.

He said defensively, " I'm afraid it'll have to be a short lunch. I have an appointment at half past two."

"Out-patients? Get your registrar to do it."

"No, it's not that. It's . . ." He stopped himself. He had an inhibition against mentioning the case. On the other hand, of course, when you came down to it, Trimble was one of his most important witnesses. "It's my solicitor," he said.

"Ah," said Trimble with ponderous comprehension, "I thought it might be. Still, we mustn't talk shop yet, must we? Not till we've ordered." He settled his bulk into his chair. It was the table in the alcove they always kept for him. Trimble sat down at a dining-table with the ease and confidence of a professional. He was like Bradman taking guard at the wicket, like Casals drawing the bow across his cello for the first note of the solo part in the Elgar. He picked up the menu and regarded it benignly. Most of it he knew by heart; his eye searched rapidly for any variations designed to tease a jaded palate. The waiter hovered helpfully.

"There's a beautiful saddle of lamb on the trolley, Sir Horace."

"Mm." Trimble was unenthusiastic. One could have saddle of lamb at home. "Let's see. Moussaka à la Grecque. Rognons au Porto. Canard pressé. How about you, Thomas?"

"Something light. I don't eat much at lunch time."

"Nor I. But one might as well have something interesting. Anything in the fish that takes your fancy?"

"I'll have a sole, I think."

"Excellent. How would you like it? Normande? Cubat? Walewska?"

"Just grilled."

"You're sure? Very well. And to start with? Some oysters? I had a dozen excellent Whitstables here the other day."

"Yes. That would be fine."

"Good." Trimble folded up the menu and handed it back to the waiter. "I'll have oysters too, then lobster cardinal. Not too much brandy on the lobster."

"I'll tell the chef, Sir Horace."

"And some wine. Now let me see . . . Thomas, would a Berncasteler Schlossberg be too sweet for you?"

"Anything you say. I'm sure it'll be excellent. But just a glass."

"I think," said Trimble firmly to the wine waiter, "that we can manage a bottle." He eyed the man balefully. "And don't swing it about. I've seen chaps like you handling bottles like Indian clubs. It bruises the wine."

The wine waiter half closed his eyes, but his lips still smiled. "I'll take good care of it, Sir Horace."

When they were alone, Trimble said, "Well now, to business. How do you feel about the case?"

"I'm not exactly looking forward to it."

"Nor I." He tore a roll in half with his great fingers and proceeded to butter it. "It's a devil of a business. Of course, we've got to show him——" He hesitated. "There's no question of backing down now. But it's certainly a devil of a business." He crammed a piece of bread into his mouth. "It's going to do a lot of harm to the profession, you know."

"That's hardly our doing."

"Of course not. But we suffer. That's the devil of it. He drags us down to his level—win or lose."

The oysters appeared and Trimble examined them with bulging eyes. Finally satisfied, he squeezed lemon and sprinkled pepper on each one and began to eat them. Gilling applied himself abstractedly to his own food. Trimble always had a depressing effect on him. He was a man who never did anything without a purpose and it was always rather unnerving waiting for the purpose to appear. He was reminded of that memorable time when Trimble had taken it into his head that he ought to be a Fellow of the Royal Society. What a time they had all had then! The trouble was that, unhappily, he had no qualifications for election. He had no record of worthwhile research; nor had he a list of second-rate publications which could be represented as research. He had even neglected to arrange for his name to appear as a co-author of research carried out by others. This difficulty had been explained to him, first tactfully, and then with increasing brutality, but he refused to see it. To Trimble, the Royal was just another club for which his eminence entitled him to membership. He was, after all, a past president of the Royal College of Physicians, he was senior adviser to the Ministry of Health on almost every subject under the sun, he was the chairman of innumerable committees, he was a knight and would, God willing, become very shortly a baron. If White's and the Athenaeum and the Carlton and the Beefsteak would have him, what was so wonderful about the Royal that they should dare to blackball him? It had become an obsession with Trimble. With an ordinary man one could just have said it was impossible and left it at that. But Trimble was different. He made everybody's life a misery. And he was powerful. Before you knew where you were, the Minister was involved, trying to put pressure on Maxfield; Trimble himself and various protégés of his were making difficulties in all kinds of ways. He had friends in the City and in industry, whose readiness to give donations for various purposes depended to an alarming extent on Trimble's advice. It was all extremely awkward.

Maxfield had got to the stage where he was almost ready to give way to pressure. It would have been just possible to get Trimble elected a Fellow, by pulling every string available, by whipping together the whole medical group in the Royal Society, keeping them to heel by either bribery or threats, and using them as a lever to persuade the other Fellows. It would have been just possible, at the risk of making the Society itself ridiculous. Gilling had opposed it. Finally, when deadlock was reached they had decided to take the matter to Old Fred for arbitration.

Old Fred (otherwise known as Frederick, first Baron Sandray) was over eighty now. But for ten years before his retirement, he had virtually managed the profession single-handed. All the spheres of influence, now divided between Maxfield, Trimble and Gilling—the Royal College, the Medical Research Council, the Committee on Distinction Awards, the foundations, the special advisory positions in the Ministry, the key committees— had been dominated by Old Fred. Every office had been held either by him personally or by some nominee who could be relied upon to do his bidding. Every important appointment had been in his gift. It had been an unprecedented situation which could only have arisen in exceptional circumstances with a man of exceptional industry and personality. It had aroused a good deal of resentment at the time, for all Fred's admitted genius, and after his retirement his empire had been broken up by common consent. Old Fred had taken no active part in medical affairs for almost ten years. He was rarely seen in public and reputed to be falling gradually into senility. Yet his name still held magic and he could be used as a final court of arbitration for certain vital issues on which no agreement could be reached. Maxfield and Gilling had taken Trimble's case to him for an expert opinion. His aged quavering voice had delivered a final judg- ment, as cruel, lucid, and decisive as those for which he was renowned in his days of power. "You can put Trimble up for anything else," he had said. "But not the Royal." With a spite- ful, senile grin, he had added, "You might just as well make him Admiral of the Fleet." That had been the end of the matter. Before the voice of the master, even Trimble was silent.

Trimble had finished his oysters and was busy mopping up the juice with a piece of brown bread. "I was speaking to the Minister this morning," he said. "He's a little concerned about the possible implications."

"In what way?"

"Well——" Trimble paused and sucked at a hollow place in one of his teeth. "One can't be too precise. He has the good of the profession at heart, you know."

"Has he?" Gilling spoke dubiously.

"Yes. I really believe he has. I know you have reservations about him, but personally I think he's one of the best Ministers we've had. Efficient, no-nonsense, knows what he's after."

"What *is* he after?"

"Well, if you want it in one word—co-ordination. He wants

everyone to work together in an organized framework. We've
said for long enough that the Health Service was in a stupendous
muddle, and I believe he's seriously determined to set it right.
He's a hundred per cent in favour of the Academy of Medicine
plan, and Ministry support isn't to be sneezed at, you know. He's
afraid that this libel action—well, it's obvious that it's not going
to make co-operation any easier, is it?"

"Perhaps not." Gilling became suddenly impatient. "What
are you trying to say? Are you trying to convince me that we
shall all suffer horribly from the action? You don't have to.
I know it. It'll be bad for me and for Line, for anybody else
who's involved, for the profession, for the Health Service. It may
even, as you say, be bad for the Minister and his future plans.
What of it? We were all agreed, weren't we, that I had to
bring it?"

"Oh yes, of course."

"Well, here it is, we've got it. There's no turning back."

The lobster cardinal was placed in front of Trimble. He sniffed
it suspiciously. "I believe they *have* put too much brandy in the
sauce. It takes away the flavour of the lobster." He took a piece
in his mouth and his massive face suddenly folded up into a
gratified smile. "No, I misjudged them. It's perfect. Is your
sole all right?"

"Excellent, thank you."

"Not dry, or anything? Good." He took a draught of wine.
His face became thoughtful again. "I must say it never entered
my head that Line would refuse to retract. I mean, how on
earth could you be held responsible for Kincaid's death?"
Gilling shrugged helplessly. Trimble went on, "Once the editor
of the journal who published the letter had apologized, I thought
it was all over bar the shouting."

"Line's an obstinate man."

"And I'm quite convinced the *Post-Telegram* would have given
in too, if they hadn't had Line behind them."

"Perhaps."

"One vain, fanatical, self-important man—and he can do all
this damage to a great profession. It makes me feel sick." Trimble
swallowed another large piece of lobster. "He'll ruin himself in
the process, of course. Does he realize that?"

24

"I should hope so. Plenty of people have told him."

"Mm." Trimble pondered for a moment. "You don't think he's bluffing?"

"I don't see any reason to suppose so."

"He must know how awkward a court action would be for you. He might be gambling on your giving way at the last moment."

"I doubt it somehow. From what I hear from people who know him, he's not a particularly calculating man. Rather rash, if anything."

"Don't be too sure," said Trimble. He spoke from a lifetime of experience of people who, whatever façade they presented in the first instance, almost always turned out in the end to be interested in the main chance. "Look at Gandhi," he said obscurely.

Gilling spoke with slight acidity. "Even if he is bluffing, it doesn't govern my course of action. I've no intention of compromising. If he decides to give in at some stage, I shall of course be extremely pleased. But I can't say I consider it very likely."

Trimble shook his head. "Life isn't like that, Thomas. Other people aren't like you, with two clear alternatives in their heads. I'm prepared to bet that even you aren't so logical either, when it really comes down to it. All I'm really saying is this. You received a letter from your solicitor this morning. Right?"

"You know I did. I just told you."

"It said the action was to be held on 16th April. The court-room was booked, the judge was picked, the lawyers were lined up. It wasn't just a lot of stuff on paper any more. It was actually going to happen. Now, can you put your hand on your heart and say this didn't give you a very nasty jolt?"

"It was a shock," admitted Gilling.

"Even though you knew it was bound to happen." Trimble smiled triumphantly. "Now, think of something else. Line got one of those letters too."

"I suppose so."

"Since his chances in the action are so much worse than yours, it seems likely that the jolt to him might be even greater. Didn't you have a moment over breakfast this morning when you wished you could settle it somehow—on any sort of terms?" Gilling

25

nodded reluctantly. Trimble went on, "He may be feeling the same way. In fact, he almost certainly is. But he may not be able to bring himself to approach you and sue for terms."

"So?"

"So I think one ought to consider a final attempt at mediation. The Minister agrees with me. There's nothing to lose, after all."

"We tried very hard before, if you'll remember."

"It may be easier now. We're coming up to the crunch. And," Trimble said mysteriously, "there's another factor in the situation."

"What's that?"

"Rex Hartly. He got back from Australia yesterday. He might be able to do something."

Gilling told himself to be careful, not to be misled into false hopes. It was far better to expect the worst at the beginning of any struggle. There was nothing so destructive to morale as self-delusion and disappointment. Yet Trimble's suggestion had at least opened another avenue for exploration. Rex Hartly was the president-elect of the Royal College of Surgeons. He was due to take office next month but in the meantime he was a person of considerable influence, more so indeed than the present president, Sir Basil Frobisher, a garrulous, ineffectual man. They had tried Frobisher on Line right at the beginning of the case, but without any real hope. Hartly was a different cup of tea altogether. Fresh from a world tour, with a term of office as president in front of him, relatively young and reputedly energetic, he might be just the person to procure a settlement. No matter how unreasonable Line was, he could hardly refuse to listen seriously to the president of his own College.

Gilling said, "Would Hartly be co-operative, do you think?"

"I don't see why not. He'd hardly want to start his term of office with a storm like this. Whatever you think of Line, he's a prominent Fellow of the College. If he ruins himself in court, it's bad for the surgeons as a whole. And I happen to know that Hartly's as keen as mustard on this Academy of Medicine thing. If that flops, he stands to lose a peerage. It's in his own interest to co-operate."

"You make it all sound very easy," said Gilling. Trimble

26

loved this kind of thing, he knew, the manipulation, the intrigue, the bribes and rewards, the dispensing of patronage—it was both his work and his pleasure. Even when he said that matters were serious, he said it with a kind of relish, as if anticipating more employment for his special talents. He loved drama and excitement, he fed upon secrets as eagerly as on oysters and lobster cardinal. He was enjoying himself enormously in his own way. Gilling said, "What do you suggest?"

"The Minister suggested a little luncheon party on Friday. Myself, Maxfield, Hartly, Maclaren from the Ministry—and you. To discuss the Academy project. I think we might be able to lead the conversation towards the action and make Hartly realise how much he has at stake. How about it?"

"It's very helpful of the Minister."

"He likes to get things done," said Trimble. "So I can tell him you'll be there? Twelve forty-five at the Ministry."

"Thanks very much." Gilling noted the time in his diary and looked furtively at his watch. It was already almost half past two. "I'm awfully sorry, I'm afraid I must rush off——"

"You won't stay for a dessert? Some fraises des bois? Goodness knows where they get them from at this time of year."

"No, thanks very much." Gilling was beginning to feel badly now. He was ashamed of all the evil thoughts he had harboured against Trimble. It was all very well to sneer at him, at his eating and drinking and love of money, at his intrigues and backstairs gossip, but he was a friend in need. It was true that his interests were bound up with yours and that by helping you he helped himself. Nevertheless . . . It was like the lunch itself, he thought, as he watched Trimble signing the bill. You knew that it cost Trimble nothing, that it would be entered into one of his innumerable expense accounts and be paid by some company he was associated with. It was true that you hadn't wanted the lunch in the first place. Yet it left within you a vague, ineradicable feeling of indebtedness which no logic could destroy.

He was bound to Trimble, he thought. Distasteful though it might be, there was no getting away from it. Power, like adversity, made strange marriages. Just as poverty trapped you among the poor, so power trapped you among the powerful, it restricted your friends to the important and the influential. Like all conspiracies, it tied you willy-nilly to your associates. He walked out of the restaurant in a mood of philosophic melancholy, the hand of his fellow-conspirator steering him gently by the elbow. As they reached the street outside, a gust of wind struck him and his head began to ache. In spite of all his resolutions, he had drunk too much moselle.

Chapter 2

LESLIE PERRIN, senior partner of Goldman and Mackintosh, returned briskly to his office in Lincoln's Inn after a light luncheon at the Garrick Club. He had just half an hour before his appointment with Sir Thomas and he was a man who liked to familiarize himself with the documents before interviewing a client. It always made a good impression to be sure of your facts rather than having to go rummaging through the file for them. As he passed through the outer office, he said to his secretary, "I'd like Gilling and Line."

"It's on your desk, Mr. Perrin."

"Good girl." He gave a thin smile of appreciation. He went into his own office, looking about the room with satisfaction as he walked over to his desk. Perrin was not a man who favoured the British cult of dust and disorder, uncleaned windows and moth-eaten leather-bound volumes. The furnishings of his office were elegant but discreet—a thick Persian carpet, heavy reproduction Chippendale furniture from Maples, polished mahogany, fresh flowers on the table, tidy bookshelves, and an enormous desk. He settled his compact, well-tailored figure behind the desk and stroked a hand across the top of his head. He was almost totally bald on top, but had formed the habit of brushing long hairs from the side over the patch to conceal it. He was aware that the effort at concealment was not only vain but also slightly ridiculous, but he could not somehow bring himself to abandon his scalp in all its nakedness to the public gaze. On windy days he lived in a constant state of apprehension.

He opened the file and began to read. It was, he reflected, a decidedly fascinating case. He was a man who specialized in the affairs of the great, and he had come by long experience to understand their special problems. He had a reputation, not only for judgment and discretion, but for a particular skill in keeping matters out of court when at all possible. Perrin disliked court proceedings and regarded an action fought to a finish as something in the nature of a defeat, even if his own side won. He was a man who loved confidences and secret knowledge. It was the files that fascinated him, the silent struggle of letters, replies, hints, innuendoes, private meetings and discussions. It was a delightful exercise to try to visualize one's opponents, what they were doing and thinking, what was going on on the other side of the hill. The file, if one read it with imagination and with the eye of knowledge, contained all the drama and the professional interest of the case. What happened in court, so far as he was concerned, was anti-climax.

The first entry was the basis of the whole action. It was a letter from Mr. David Line, F.R.C.S., Professor of Surgery in the University of London, Director of the Professorial Unit at the Royal Metropolitan Hospital, to the editor of the weekly journal, *Medical Science*:

Sir,

A recent tragic case much reported in the newspapers emphasises once again the uncertainty of conventional methods of diagnosis. The patient, a statesman of outstanding distinction, was first reported to be ill in mid-January. From the beginning of his illness he was under the care of some of the most eminent physicians in the United Kingdom, and it cannot be doubted that they exerted all their considerable powers and experience in an effort to arrive at the correct diagnosis. When the condition progressed in spite of treatment, surgical exploration was carried out. A rare fungus infection was discovered, which by this time had progressed beyond possibility of control, and the patient died.

It is at least conceivable that earlier diagnosis might have led to a more favourable outcome. The diagnosis was an outlandish one, and the condition exceedingly rare. Anyone might be excused for not considering it as a possibility. There are limits to the number of unlikely possibilities which the human mind can consider in any given circumstances. Mistakes of this kind are inevitable so long as we rely on fallible human intelligence.

But need we? There are machines available which are equipped to consider all alternative possibilities. One of these, the Brook-Halder machine, is in constant use in my unit. It is founded on the simple principle that diagnosis, in spite of all the mystique which has been built up around it, is based essentially on the analysis of data. What happens in an ordinary consultation is that the physician acquires information from the patient, first by asking him questions, then by examining him. He takes these facts and assesses their significance against his knowledge of the nature of disease. This background knowledge is essentially memory—the memory of disease as he has seen it, heard about it, and read about it. If the data fits into the picture of an individual disease which his memory is aware of, this gives him a diagnosis. More often the data from history and examination will fit several diseases. The physician's memory will then notify him of certain further investigations, such as X-rays, blood counts, etc., the result of which will exclude some of the possibilities. The ideal situation exists when only one possibility is left; that must be the diagnosis.

It is our belief that every one of these processes following the initial questioning and examination can be carried out more reliably by electronic machinery. It is possible to programme a modern computer with far more facts about the relation of symptoms to disease than any man can possibly carry in his head. They remain in the machine's memory for all time. As any new disease or any new sympton is added to medical knowledge, it can be fed into the machine, which becomes in due course the repository of the collective knowledge of innumerable people. The machine cannot forget, it cannot grow tired, it cannot have an off day. If you feed into it the symptoms and signs of a particular patient, it will notify you of the possible alternative causes of these. It will also tell you what investigations are required to give a further exclusion of alternatives. When the results of these investigations are fed into the machine, the alternatives remaining are notified by the machine. This goes on until the final diagnosis is reached.

Theoretically, within its terms of reference, it is impossible for the machine to make a mistake. If the basic information on disease is correct, and the basic data about the patient is correct, it must connect the two. And indeed, this is confirmed in practice. In my unit at the Royal Metropolitan we have used such a machine for three years. We have compared its diagnostic powers with a very great number of purely clinical assessments of patients, and there is no doubt that it is more reliable than even the most experienced individual diagnostician. This machine was offered for use in the important case mentioned above. Unhappily this offer was refused.

It is this kind of experience which makes one wonder if the few great men who decide our research policy are capable of taking a completely dispassionate view about this important discovery. The machine is admittedly expensive, and to supply models of it widely throughout the Health Service, which we believe should be done, would cost the Government a great deal of money. It also has the effect of diminishing the mystique of the clinician, which may be considered a disadvantage by some of our older colleagues. Yet we would submit that the good of the patient comes before all self-interest. We cannot afford to risk the lives of men, whether eminent or obscure, by clinging on to obsolete methods.

I am, etc.,

David Line

There was a lot to be learnt from a letter, thought Perrin, as he looked at the momentous document, covered with thumb marks, scribbles and corrections from the sub-editor's pencil. Did Line know, when he wrote it, how dangerous it might be? Was he trailing his coat? It was always important to know, from the point of view of a settlement. A man who had nerved himself to write a deliberately provocative letter was obviously less likely to compromise than a man who had written an unintentional libel in a fit of irritation. He personally was inclined to believe, in spite of subsequent events, that Line had not anticipated the possibility of legal action. The letter was on hospital notepaper and probably if Line had been trying to provoke an action he would have written from his private address. The letter had been typed by Line's secretary at the hospital. Had it been dictated, Perrin wondered? Half the trouble he came across was caused by the fact that men imagined they could dictate lucid prose straight out of their heads to their secretaries. In his experience, this was almost impossible—such letters always ended up full of ambiguities and *non sequiturs*. Line's letter was rather too well co-ordinated to have been dictated; he had probably scribbled it down on paper first. All this seemed to show that it was not done on impulse. Yet Line was known to be a man with a fixed idea. People of that kind were rarely able to imagine how other people would react to a situation. It seemed likely that Line felt strongly about his machine and strongly about the Kincaid case. In all probability he had never tried to imagine how Gilling would take the letter. The storm which he had aroused might have come as a complete surprise to him.

Next on the file was a cutting from *Medical Science* which showed they had published the letter in full in their issue of April 8th. After this was a cutting from the *Post-Telegram*, a popular newspaper with a circulation of over three million. It was dated April 9th:

WAKE UP, MR. CURTIS!
by Raymond Marsh,
Our Scientific Correspondent

When is the Minister of Health going to wake up? For three years now the greatest development in medicine since the discovery of penicillin has been going on under his nose and he refuses to do anything about it. It's the Brook-Halder machine, an uncanny computer-like piece of apparatus which can remember more facts about disease than all the Fellows of the Royal College of Physicians put together. You feed in a list of your symptoms, coded on to punch-cards, and the machine juggles them around inside its electronic circuit until it finds the correct diagnosis. With no more time, trouble, or fuss than a Speak-your-Weight machine, it tells you accurately and completely what's the matter with you.

It works. I've seen it and tested it up at the brand-new up-to-the-minute surgical unit headed by Professor David Line at the Royal Metropolitan Hospital. It told me about my hammer-toe and the stiff hip I got from a parachute jump at Arnhem in ten seconds flat. It solved a whole battery of medical teasers which had been sent in specially from hospitals all over the world, selected to try and trip the machine up. They didn't succeed.

"Try it," said Professor Line, "just give it a chance. That's all I'm asking anyone to do." He's been asking for some time, without success. The trouble is, I'm informed on good authority, that the Old Guard of medicine don't like the idea of it. The moth-eaten pundits of the Royal College of Physicians and the Medical Research Council have turned up their collective noses. Medical prima donnas don't like the idea of their personal prestige being diminished by getting their answers from a machine that any Tom, Dick, or Harry could use—it takes away the magic. What's more, our Minister of Health, Mr. Francis Curtis, has taken their advice and never even bothered to see for himself. It's time somebody told him to wake up. The time is coming when there ought to be machines like this in every major hospital in the country—whatever the cost.

Two weeks ago John Kincaid, the most brilliant political brain this country has seen in the last twenty-five years, died in hospital, with two knights and a peer at his bedside— undiagnosed. Nobody can bring Kincaid back now. But surely we can commemorate his death in a suitable way. The *Post-Telegram* proposes to start a John Kincaid Fund, the money from which will be used to finance research on diagnostic computers like the Brook-Halder machine. Already a donation has been received of over £10,000 from Lord Frampton to start the Fund.

That's what *we're* doing about it. What are *you* going to do about it, Mr. Curtis?

Following this was Perrin's own report:

34

It is our opinion that both these publications are libellous of Sir Thomas Gilling on various counts:

Line's letter:

1. There is sufficient information given at the beginning of Mr. Line's letter to make it clear to any thinking man that he was referring to the illness of Mr. Kincaid. Mr. Marsh, in his newspaper article, names Mr. Kincaid specifically.

2. It was well-known to all readers of the newspapers that Sir Thomas Gilling was in charge of Mr. Kincaid's treatment.

3. It is made clear that, in the opinion of Mr. Line, a mistake was made in not making use of the computer. It is not necessarily defamatory to say Sir Thomas made a mistake. However, it might be, if the mistake in question was an easy one to avoid.

It is very defamatory to imply that Sir Thomas was negligent or that he deliberately refrained from using the machine because of prejudice against it. This would imply that Sir Thomas was acting with a lack of skill or integrity which is not worthy of the high position he holds.

Is this implication present in the letter? In our opinion it is. It is stated fairly clearly (1) That Gilling should have used the machine; (2) That Kincaid might well have been saved if he had; (3) That Line believes that the leaders of the profession have resisted the machine from discreditable motives.

There seems little doubt to us that an informed person reading the letter would interpret it as saying that Gilling was vain, obstinate, and old-fashioned, and that his omission to use the machine on Kincaid was attributable to this. This we consider to be a serious libel.

Marsh's article:

The statements here bear a considerable resemblance to those in Professor Line's letter, except that they are differently expressed, and more explicit.

Mr. Marsh implies that failure to use the computer may have been responsible for the failure to diagnose Mr. Kincaid's condition.

The reference to two knights and a peer, taken in conjunction with the Kincaid case, identifies Sir Thomas Gilling fairly clearly.

The inference that the machine is being pigeon-holed for reasons of personal vanity is fairly definite here. Whose vanity is not specifically said. However, the part of the article concerning Kincaid so obviously indicates Sir Thomas Gilling that a reasonable man might take it for granted that he was being referred to.

We believe that this article is defamatory of Sir Thomas Gilling in that it is stated or implied that he:

(1) For reasons of personal prestige or vanity deliberately prevented advancement of an important piece of research.

(2) Negligently failed to use this device in the treatment of Mr. Kincaid.

These suggestions may be calculated to do serious harm to Sir Thomas's professional and personal reputation.

CONVERSATION WITH SIR THOMAS GILLING

Monday, April 10th

Our opinion on the letter and the article was given to Sir Thomas. He said that he was very anxious to avoid legal action and would be satisfied with a full apology and retraction from Line, Marsh, and the editors of *Medical Science* and the *Post-Telegram*. He said he felt sure he had considerable personal influence with the editor of *Medical Science* and could make him see the necessity of printing a retraction. A form of words for this retraction was prepared by us for Sir Thomas so that he could submit it to Dr. Gale, the editor of *Medical Science*.

CONVERSATION WITH SIR THOMAS GILLING

Thursday, April 13th

Sir Thomas informed us that Dr. Gale had accepted our terms in full and that the retraction would appear in a prominent position at the beginning of the editorial page of the issue of *Medical Science* of April 22nd. If this were done, Sir Thomas was prepared to close the matter so far as *Medical Science* was concerned. It was suggested to Dr. Gale by Sir Thomas that he should get in touch with Professor Line and arrange for him to be a party to the retraction. Regrettably, Professor Line has refused. Sir Thomas has therefore referred the matter to us to take further steps.

The "further steps" were fairly routine and Perrin skimmed more rapidly through the rest of the documents. There was a formal communication from Sir Thomas, protesting to Line against the letter. It was phrased with deliberate moderation:

Dear Line,

I was very shocked and surprised to read your letter in *Medical Science*. As you know from our previous acquaintance, I am not a man to object to fair and reasonable comment, but your remarks and inferences in this letter go far beyond the ordinary give-and-take of medical controversy and amount to a personal attack on myself. I am informed by my legal advisers that in their opinion parts of your letter are highly defamatory and give strong grounds for legal action. I have discussed this with John Gale, who has expressed his great regret that his Journal inadvertently published such a letter. He is proposing to insert a full apology in the issue of April 22nd.

I must also request you, as the author, to agree to the publication of a similar apology on your behalf, together with a withdrawal of the damaging statements made. The details of this apology are in the hands of Dr. Gale, and I believe he has been in communication with you on the subject. I am naturally reluctant to bring an action for libel against a colleague if this can be avoided, and if you are prepared to make amends in the same way as Dr. Gale it may be possible to consider the whole unfortunate business at an end. However, if no apology is forthcoming I shall obviously have no alternative but to put the matter in the hands of my lawyers.

Yours sincerely,
Thomas Gilling

The reply from Line was short and non-committal:

Dear Sir Thomas,

Thank you for your letter. John Gale did ring me up and say that you had taken strong exception to my letter and demanded a printed apology. I told him that I could not agree that an apology was indicated, either on his part or mine. I'm afraid I still haven't changed my views on this point.

The idea of a legal action between colleagues is as repugnant to me as it is to you, but I obviously cannot be expected to withdraw statements in which I sincerely believe, solely to avoid unpleasantness.

Yours sincerely,

David Line

After that there was a letter to Line from Perrin himself, summarizing the reasons for regarding the letter as libellous, and asking once again for an apology and retraction. There was a letter from Line's solicitor, Anthony Bradwell, of Bradwell, Fairburn, and Oakshott, formally refuting their allegation. There was a cutting from *Medical Science* of April 22nd, showing the editor's official apology. There was the opinion of counsel, Sir Frederick Groom, who agreed with Perrin about the defamatory nature of the letter and was obviously prepared to do battle with enthusiasm and a considerable degree of confidence.

Then there was the Statement of Claim, a detailed document prepared by Perrin which set forth Gilling's case in detail for the Court, and Bradwell's reply for Line. There were minor letters and records of conversations between himself and Bradwell on points of detail. It all took a great deal of time. It was almost two years now since the beginning. That was probably a good thing in this type of action, Perrin thought—it gave everybody time to cool off and reflect, to ask themselves what they were really trying to achieve. It gave them time to realize how quickly the world forgets. At the time an insult was offered, it usually seemed to the victim that the sting of it would last for ever, that he would be an object of contempt and ridicule for the rest of his life as a consequence of it. After nine months or so, he was frequently surprised to discover that the world in general had forgotten all about it and that even he himself, in the face of other preoccupations, was finding it difficult to maintain his indignation at fever heat. The progress of a libel action was shaped like a drama, with moments of excitement and confrontation and alternating periods when the tension was low. It had the peculiarity that at any moment the play might be stopped. However, there were certain points in the action when the possibilities for ringing down the curtain were particularly high. This was one of them.

The telephone buzzed gently. It was his secretary. "Sir Thomas Gilling has just arrived."

"Show him in straight away, will you?"

He went to meet Sir Thomas at the door, took his hat and coat, handed them to his secretary to hang up in the cupboard in the outer office, and finally deposited the old man in the arm-chair across the desk from his own. He regarded Sir Thomas with approval. He was the kind of client in which Goldman and Mackintosh specialized. He was not only rich and distinguished, but there was a reassuring air of stability about him. He was cool and determined, and knew his own mind; yet he had the kind of courtly charm which would go down well in the witness box. He was not the kind of man to let his legal advisers down.

Gilling caught Perrin's sharp appraising glance and moved uneasily in his chair. He was not accustomed to being assessed in this fashion. Usually it was he who sat behind the desk or stood beside the bed, the detached professional confronted with the baffled, frightened, dependent person who had come for his opinion. One of the most unpleasant features of this lawsuit had been the feeling of having entered a situation, indeed, a whole world, where he was inexperienced and consequently at a dis-advantage. He had even felt himself growing emotionally dependent on Perrin, regarding him at one moment with a quite excessive confidence, and at another with suspicion. He reminded himself now that he must not expect too much of Perrin or Groom or any of his legal advisers. They were professional men doing a job, just as he was. They would do their best for him. They were no doubt highly competent, but they were not infallible.

He said, "So they've fixed the day?"

"Yes. I hope it's relatively convenient."

"It wouldn't have been convenient, whenever they'd chosen," said Gilling. "But it's as good a week as any other. I've arranged to cancel all other engagements."

"Good." Perrin looked down at the file on his desk. "I thought you might like to come in and have a chat, because this is quite a good time to review the situation. A good number of actions are settled at this point, when one side or both really get faced with the fact of jumping into the icy water on a specific day."

Gilling nodded hopefully. "Trimble was saying much the same thing at lunch time."

"Was he?" said Perrin indifferently. He was not much in favour of amateur lawyers, no matter how distinguished they might be in other spheres. "Mind you, I wouldn't like to hold out any extravagant hopes——"

"I can see that. But there is a new factor in the situation." Gilling began to describe Trimble's plan about Rex Hartly. He had been thinking it over in the car on his way to Lincoln's Inn and he could not help feeling optimistic. As the names rolled off his tongue—Hartly, the Minister, Maxfield—it seemed impossible that anyone could resist such pressure. "I really think there are possibilities here," he concluded.

Perrin was thoughtful. "He resisted Frobisher."

"Frobisher is a cipher, really, in spite of his position. Hartly's a different proposition altogether. He's a personal friend of Line, and he has a great incentive to use all the persuasion he can bring to bear." Gilling stopped himself from going any further. Confidences with one's solicitor were all very well, but there was a limit to how much anyone outside the small group who controlled the profession should know.

"Well, then, let's hope for the best," said Perrin. "If Sir Rex can make any progress, you know I'm here to help in any way I can." He thought for a moment. "Were you thinking of making any concessions yourself?"

Gilling looked at him in surprise. "I? What concessions could I make?"

"Well, of course that's a matter for yourself. I know you have so far refused to consider any, but——"

"All I'm asking Line to do is to withdraw his allegations that I sabotaged his research and killed Kincaid by negligence. Obviously I can't go back on that if I'm to keep any reputation."

"Oh quite, quite."

40

"It seems little enough to ask. I'm sure Hartly will understand."

"I'm sure he will. Of course—it's Line who represents the problem."

"Yes." As he thought of Line, Gilling's confidence began to weaken a little. A spasm of rage passed over him and he told himself sharply for perhaps the thousandth time—he must not hate Line. He must not. Because if he once began to hate him he would somehow have lost irretrievably, no matter how the case went. He steadied his voice and said mildly, "He's an unpredictable man."

"Evidently." Perrin fished gently. "I take it he regards himself as a man with a mission."

"A whole series of missions. Have you ever met him?"

"No. I've seen him on the television." Perrin added dryly, "As I recollect, he spent most of his time protesting about undesirable publicity."

"Yes, I remember that." Gilling brooded. "I've met him on and off at various functions but I only had dealings with him on one occasion. That was when he operated on the Duke of Leicester." A shadow passed over his face. "We had trouble with him even then." He did not go into details. "One of the maddening things about Line is that he represents himself as the leader of a sort of new wave in scientific medicine. In fact, when you come down to it, he has practically speaking no research background at all. I don't criticize him for that—not everybody has a talent for research. But it's perfectly monstrous for him to go round as he does, criticizing a man like Lord Maxfield, who has a magnificent record of discovery in neurophysiology and was in the Royal Society before he was thirty." Line was in the habit, as Gilling knew, of referring to Maxfield as the Vicar of Bray. Whether Maxfield himself knew of this he was not certain. Maxfield was not the kind of man one could easily ask. "It's quite disgraceful. And the journalists swallow it hook, line, and sinker. I suppose it's good copy for them."

"I thought you had some rather severe rules about personal publicity?"

"We have. I may say he's steered very close to the wind on a variety of occasions. He's had unofficial warnings. He always swears that it's no doing of his. But it always happens to the same people, doesn't it? Frankly," said Gilling, "I think he might have been in trouble before this if it hadn't been for the position he occupies. To have had a man with a chair at the Metropolitan up on an ethical charge would have made the sort of scandal that everyone tries to avoid. Probably we should have done it just the same. Now it looks as if we're going to get the scandal anyway. Of course, the Metropolitan should never have appointed him. That was when the real mistake was made."

Gilling pondered regretfully over what might have been. If only they had foreseen this! It was in Old Fred's day, and he could certainly have stopped the appointment. But the truth was, Old Fred had always tended to discount the surgeons. He visualized them as a pack of blood and thunder, cut and thrust, bombastic dunderheads, too lacking in intelligence to constitute a danger to his own system. In his eyes they were the cavalry officers of medicine, dashing and romantic, useful to impress the simple-hearted, but totally unimportant when there was any serious business to be done. He had outwitted the surgeons all his life and regarded them with scant respect. If Line had been a physician he would have been tamed years ago.

"You don't think there's a possibility," asked Perrin tentatively, "that Line could be looking forward to the publicity of the action?"

Gilling frowned. "Oh, surely not. I mean—well, he's not insane."

"Some people have a pathological craving for public attention, you know."

"Yes, but just the same——" He shook his head. "Favourable publicity, even of the most vulgar type, is one thing. But this—squabbling with a colleague in open court—he couldn't want that. No, I really can't believe that of him."

Perrin looked pensively through the file. "I hope you're right. If that's the case, we still have a chance to settle. But there are one or two slightly disturbing features about his attitude. He's made no attempt to deny that he was referring to you. His defence is that the statements were true and that they were fair comment on a matter of public interest. This turns it into a kind of reversed action. Instead of you trying to prove that he libelled

42

you, he has to prove that you are the sort of person he said you were. He acts as a sort of prosecutor, with a heavy financial penalty if he fails to make his case. In effect he's putting you, and the leadership of the profession, into the dock."

"Yes," said Gilling gloomily. "I appreciate that."

"It makes it difficult for him, of course, since he has to take on the burden of proof. But it leaves him free to stir up a lot of mud if he feels so inclined." Perrin paused and then said delicately, "There isn't any personal element in the case you can think of, is there? Something I haven't heard about?"

Gilling pondered and shook his head. "No, honestly I can't think so."

Perrin said, "A pity. It looks as if we may be dealing with a man of principle. They're always a problem in law."

There was a short silence and then Perrin said, "You're quite happy about all the details?" He turned over the pages of his file. "This later point of Line's in his answer to your Statement of Claim—where he says that after Kincaid was dead he fed his clinical data into the machine——"

"There's not much in that. He got eight alternative answers. Hardly an impressive performance, I would have thought." Perrin smiled and closed the file. Gilling said suddenly, "Incidentally, for your information, I didn't kill Kincaid."

"My dear Sir Thomas, of course——"

Gilling put up his hand. "No, please. I'm serious. I've been in practice for nearly forty years and I've killed quite a number of people in my time. Sometimes through inexperience, sometimes through ignorance; even, in one case, I'm ashamed to say, through carelessness. It happens to all of us. But in the case of Kincaid, my conscience is clear."

"I never doubted it for a moment."

Gilling frowned, recognizing the routine tones of reassurance. He was angry with himself for indulging in self-justification before Perrin. He changed the subject sharply. "How about the *Post-Telegram*?"

"I should forget about them for the time being. Your action against them comes on separately at a later date. Naturally, they're sitting tight to see what happens to Line. If Line loses, they'll almost certainly settle."

"I see." Suddenly there seemed nothing more to say. Gilling was overcome by a great weariness with the whole affair, a sense of grievance that a man of his age, who had worked hard and conscientiously and tried to do his best all these years, should be tormented in this fashion. He said, "So all depends now on Hartly."

"It looks like it."

Perrin got up and showed him out of the room, helped him into his overcoat and saw him downstairs to his car. The old man carried his years well, Perrin thought. He was spruce and sharp and erect—his bright eyes missed very little. Would he be the same man in two months' time, if the case went through? It was usually the proud men, in his experience, who were broken by the law. He walked pensively back up the stairs to his office. Automatically his hand moved to the top of his head, to make sure the wind had not disarranged anything. Did Gilling really understand, he wondered, what he was risking? Probably not, though one had tried to make it clear to him. For himself, he had his instincts about a lawsuit just as Sir Thomas had his about a patient; and in this case they filled him with unease. It would be a good thing for everybody, he thought, if Sir Rex Hartly was successful.

Chapter 3

THE MINISTER OF HEALTH had a secret vice. He liked to lie in his bath and compose his own obituary notice. He was a methodical man and allowed himself exactly twenty minutes each morning at this slightly shameful pastime. He washed himself thoroughly and always in the same order, starting at the neck and working his way down to his toes; sometimes, when he was feeling below his best, he became prey to an illogical anxiety for fear he had left some part out, and he felt compelled to start all over at the beginning. Meanwhile, as he soaped and scrubbed and rinsed, the sonorous, appreciative phrases thundered through his head. In these fantasies he abandoned all false modesty . . . "The imaginative sweep of his ideas, which occasionally left his contemporaries gasping, was equalled only by his administrative brilliance in bringing them to fruition . . . From his earliest years his talents marked him out as a candidate for the highest honours. . . ." Then something more personal. "A flashing intelligence and mordant wit, tempered by a warmth and charm which made him loved by all who could penetrate below the surface." No, that was a little clumsy somehow. "A sympathetic, humane man, with a sly sense of humour . . ." And a peroration to wind up with; something to place him in the stream of history. "Over the years since his retirement his stature has grown rather than decreased. Not since the days of the younger Pitt has the personality of one man had such a profound influence on the future of Great Britain."

Yes, that was more like it, he thought as he dipped beneath the water and washed off the soapsuds, thereby calling a halt to another morning's daydreaming. It was time to get out now, to lay yet another stone laboriously on the foundations of greatness. He dried himself carefully, sprinkled talcum over his bony, rather hirsute torso and made his way back to his bedroom. He took out clean underclothes and a shirt, then picked out a suit from his wardrobe. There were twenty of them and he liked to arrange them always in the same order, black at one end, then blue, then brown, then grey, growing lighter and less formal as he went along the row. He selected a discreet clerical grey worsted, and dressed carefully. Before putting on his jacket he brushed his hair. He used ivory-backed nylon brushes and gave precisely thirty-five strokes.

He left twenty-five minutes for breakfast and the newspapers. He was a man who liked to watch his weight, and breakfast each day consisted of a boiled egg, one thin piece of toast, and an apple, with one cup of white coffee, unsugared. He skimmed through *The Times*, the *Telegraph*, and *The Guardian*, confining himself to the political news.

"Another speech by the P.M.," he observed. His wife gave him a noncommittal smile and poured out coffee. "Usual stuff, Principle of what the Party stands for. Great figures of our past. Onwards and upwards towards broader horizons." He shook his head. "That's not going to do much good with the floating voter."

"Poor man. He has to speak so often."

"He ought to speak less, in my opinion. And when he does speak, say something. Make an event out of it. He's getting garrulous."

"He's always very nice to us. And most helpful with Roger."

Roger was their son. He had just been adopted for a fairly safe seat in Dorset. Patton sighed. Would he ever be able to persuade Muriel that there was more in politics than personal likes and dislikes? "Just the same, he's losing touch with the electorate. He's thinking in terms of the last ten years, not the next." He turned back to his paper. "Curtis has made a statement about transport. Rather a waspish leader in *The Guardian*. They say it reads like the hashed-up left-overs of his predecessor." He chuckled. "Frank won't like that. Especially after the way they took up my Oxford speech."

He was silent for a moment, savouring the memory of his

46

triumph. His Oxford speech had been, by his standards, daring. It had gone so far as to consider certain facts that the public had been aware of for years but that both parties had been afraid to say—that England's problems were nothing much to do with either social justice or imperial greatness, but were purely commercial. He had made some rather rash comparisons with present-day Sweden and Gustavus Adolphus. There had been frowns in the lobbies but the Press, particularly *The Guardian*, had taken it up and saved him from serious trouble. The P.M. was so pleased to see one Minister in good odour with the newspapers that he was prepared to forgive almost anything.

"It serves Frank Curtis right," said Muriel, "he's always been jealous of you."

"Well——" Patton was quickly tolerant. "He's a politician." He spoke as if he himself were not. And, indeed, in a sense, he despised politicians. He was at heart an administrator. The House, with its sloppy inefficiency, its obsession with tradition, bored and rather repelled him. But since you could not be an administrator on the highest level without going through the political mill he had steeled himself to endure it.

He liked to get to his office at the Ministry in good time. He arrived there punctually at nine o'clock and settled down to work. He enjoyed the routine of his day, the files, the discussions, the conferences. He was convinced that he had made a big difference to the Ministry since he had taken over from Curtis a year ago. Things had been left in confusion. In a few months he had straightened them all out and now everything went like clockwork. He flattered himself that his civil servants liked and respected him. It was true that he was not a man of very creative or original thought, and when he had first taken up his post he had had no ideas at all about his future policy. This had not worried him. He had found from experience that the pigeon-holes of Government departments are loaded with plans of every conceivable kind. The Minister's job was not really to think of new ideas—it was to go through the old ideas, pick out one or two, dust them off, set them in motion, and advertise them to the public as his own. So far this had worked very well. He had also consulted a public relations firm about his personal image. They had advised him that there was room for improvement. He lacked warmth, there was nothing sufficiently singular about him to attract Press interest. He was not easily cartoonable. They advised him to take up some slightly off-beat recreation without any controversial or snobbish overtones (he eventually settled on bird-watching) and to have some informal, eccentric habit at work. He had even consented, with some reluctance, to be photographed at his desk in shirtsleeves with red, white, and blue braces. But somehow he had a suspicion that this had been going too far. People had laughed, rather unkindly. As a stunt, it hadn't really come off.

This was the day for his lunch with the doctors. Somehow they were to be induced to stop quarrelling among themselves, to accept a little organization. What group of 60,000 men had such a bewildering variety of representative bodies? Not only an Association and a Union but five Royal Colleges, one each for physicians, surgeons, gynaecologists, pathologists, and general practitioners. It might have been all right in the old days, but with a central Health Service you needed to know who you were dealing with. The Association was all right—fortunately the Secretary was a good friend of Trimble's. The Medical Practitioners Union was too small and political to carry much support. It was the Colleges that caused the trouble. If you could tie them all up in one big Academy of Medicine, with a strong president who understood the facts of political life, you would have developed a really effective organizational machine. You could plan, you could govern, you could impose solutions. You would be getting near the ideal form of negotiation, which was negotiation with one man. It had worked like that once, for a short period of time, years ago, in the days of Old Fred. Old Fred had come to dominate the profession by charm, by guile, by brilliance of intellect and force of personality, but his position had had no constitutional basis. With his retirement, fragmentation had occurred. Authority founded on one man died with the man. It had to be built in to the organizational pattern.

And now, confound them, they had started quarrelling again. This idiotic libel action! It was the kind of thing that happened when you had wealthy, independent men, cocks of their own dunghills, bowed in and out of hospitals by nurses and house surgeons, throwing their weight about in operating theatres, pontificating at dinners. They became utterly independent. They forgot that they were part of a State Service, paid out of taxes. They accepted public money but considered they were immune from the loyalties and discipline accepted by civil servants. They put their personal feuds before the public good. They ignored or even publicly attacked the government and the minister, they bit the hand that fed them. What had Aneurin Bevan called them? Prima donnas. It was true. Something would have to be done about them.

The luncheon was scheduled for one o'clock. Trimble was the first to arrive, with Rex Hartly. As the oldest member of the Ministry club, it was Trimble's job to introduce new members. Hartly was an Australian in his middle fifties, heavy featured and thickset, blue jowled and with thick black hair. He had been a famous scrum half for the Wallabies in his younger days, with a reputation for quick thinking and pugnacity. He concealed an extreme self-confidence beneath an air of quiet affability. Everyone who met Hartly for the first time expected him to try to dominate them, and were surprised and relieved to find him easy in manner and at times almost deferential. Because of this he had acquired the valuable reputation of being a modest, unassuming man.

Just now, he was working hard to give Trimble the impression that he was slightly overawed by his first contact with the fountain head of ministerial authority. In fact he was not impressed in the least. In the early years of his career he had for a while nourished the delusion that each ascending level on the climb to greatness held men of superior capacity to those lower down. Now he knew that this was not so. He had never yet met anyone he considered more able than himself and he did not anticipate doing so. His election to the Presidency of his Royal College introduced him to another level on the climb. He anticipated with some confidence that it would be populated by men not noticeably better or worse than those he had met farther down.

"Consommé Julienne and lamb cutlets," Trimble was saying mournfully, "and a piece of mouldy Stilton—that's what we're in for. You mark my words. There's a puritanical streak about the Minister, one can't deny that." He took a glass of sherry from the waiter and handed another to Hartly. "Apart from that, he's a really first-rate man. We're lucky to have him." Trimble added solemnly, "He's very anxious to meet you."

Hartly tried to look flattered. "I gather he's a great supporter of the Academy of Medicine?"

"Yes indeed. So are we all. It's high time the Colleges got together. Indeed, we were ready to go ahead and start making plans last year. And then—Frobisher——" He threw up his hands. "What got into him I don't know. He seemed to be incapable of making his mind up about anything." Hartly smiled noncommittally. Trimble put a hand on his arm and beamed confidentially. "Frankly it'll be a great relief to all of us when you take over. Charming fellow, Frobisher—I had a great personal regard for him. But—with all due respect to a colleague—he was hopeless—hopeless."

Hartly smiled again. "He was a very useful fellow if you had a stone in your kidney."

"Yes—yes——" Trimble's voice was slightly uneasy. Could Hartly be laughing at him? "And, of course, I agree, that's the main thing. We're all clinicians, first and foremost," he said sententiously. "Just the same, he was a poor president. Too indecisive. The College was paralysed during his tenure of office. I'm sure you're going to make a great difference to it."

Hartly shrugged his shoulders modestly. He thought so, too. He intended to do a great many things, some of which might not suit people like Trimble at all. He reflected with a certain amusement that the time might come when Trimble looked back nostalgically to the good old days of Frobisher. "It's a great challenge," he said. "And rather intimidating. But I shall certainly do my best." Trimble squeezed his arm benignly and Hartly suddenly tired of this pantomime. There was a limit to how much one could stand. He changed the subject. "Who else is coming?"

"Gilling and Maxfield—you know them. And Archie Maclaren. He's an old Ministry workhorse. He's watched a dozen Ministers come and go. Sound fellow, but limited. Graduated from Public Health and he's still a bit of a sanitary inspector at heart. He'd like a Service full of full-time salaried officials like himself, neatly arranged in order of hierarchy. But he doesn't cut very much ice with the Minister, policy-wise. Patton's assured me personally that he thinks full freedom for the clinician is the cornerstone of medicine. He's really very enlightened for a politician. Ah, hallo Gilling. Maxfield—my dear fellow. Have a glass of sherry. You both know Rex Hartly."

He smiled at them benignly. Someone had once said that Trimble was the best man at every wedding and the chief mourner at every funeral. Whatever the gathering, he had a tendency to take on the character of host, and was renowned for making introductions between people who had known each other all their lives. Despite his efforts the conversation immediately stiffened a little, as it always did in Maxfield's presence. Gilling, who had entered with him, noted the fact and wondered what exactly it was that was wrong with Maxfield. Superficially, he was incomparably the most brilliant man present. He was a man of wide interests and great intellectual capacity, who could undoubtedly have achieved outstanding success in any career where analytical intelligence counted. He could have been a great lawyer or economist. As a student his academic record had been startling. He had obtained his higher qualifications with ridiculous ease. Then he had looked around, as if not quite certain what he should do. Ordinary clinical medicine hardly seemed enough. The intellectual side was too simple to be stimulating—the more indefinite, human side called for qualities of sympathy and understanding in which he was noticeably deficient. It was inevitable that he should choose research. At first all went well. On the basis of some very useful discoveries in neurophysiology he was elected F.R.S. and began to be talked about as a scientific prodigy. Then, in his early thirties, the well suddenly ran dry. He found it hard to think of satisfactory projects. When he did decide on a project, it came to nothing. It appeared that the creative energies he had enjoyed had been shortlived, perhaps a mere function of the vitality of youth. The great mind, of which he was so proud, was once more unemployed. He had returned to clinical medicine. Inevitably he had succeeded, achieving all the honours available one by one, the knighthood, the honorary degrees, the professorship. Now he was a peer and the President of his College. The great intellect was still there, still frustrated, inadequately stretched, wasted . . . And Maxfield himself, in his human contacts remained curiously detached, as if he was perpetually distracted by some insoluble problem within himself.

It was only a minute or two later that the Minister came in through another door, followed by Maclaren. Patton was brisk and affable, though his smile was wintry. He had had a slightly exasperating morning. He had accused his personal assistant of losing a document and then found it in an inside pocket of his overcoat. His secretary had been slow in anticipating his wishes before she was told and had inconsiderately disappeared at a moment when he wanted her. He had played a favourite game of his, of asking three different subordinates to do the same job, and then found out they had foiled him by working in collusion. He was a man who liked to make work for other people and it always annoyed him when they found means of avoiding it. In addition to which he was constipated. It was incomprehensible when he considered the trouble he took with his diet. Lots of roughage and a three-mile walk every day, his doctor had said. He followed the regime religiously, yet he was still in trouble. Yet his wife, who ate as she pleased and slacked around the house all day, was as regular as clockwork. Incomprehensible. He must have a chat to Trimble about it one of these days.

Maclaren stood a little behind the Minister as he greeted the doctors. His face betrayed no shadow of emotion. He was a large, shaggy white-haired man, almost ready for his pension and his garden in Thames Ditton. Whatever was decided now would not affect him personally. Once when he was younger he had dreamed, like the Minister, of getting the profession and the Health Service tidily organized. Time, and the discouragement involved in working for a series of masters differing wildly in temperament, industry, and political philosophy, had cured him of that. The ministers came and went at the rate of one every two or three years. Mostly they were glad to go, yearning for one of the more spectacular jobs which carried weight in the Cabinet. Patton was full of ideas now, but he would either leave or lose interest long before there was any chance of carrying them to fruition. It was all too complicated, there were too many people involved, and none of them really strong enough. In Fred Sandray's time it had been different. He had combined, not only the influence, but most of the qualities of the men in the room today. Almost as clever as Maxfield and as worldly as Trimble, with Gilling's charm and Hartly's determination, he had the power, and sometimes even the desire, to get things done. He had explained this to Patton. Now Patton was trying to be clever. He wanted the Academy of Medicine so as to centralize the consultants. Then the President could be invested with something of the influence and mystique of Old Fred. If you had him, you (theoretically anyway) had them all. The details had been agreed. Patton wanted Maxfield as President. Hartly would have to be made Vice-President to bring the surgeons in. Gilling would be the other Vice-President, and Trimble would be on the Council, with the leaders of the gynaecologists, pathologists, general practitioners, psychiatrists and anyone else who needed to be placated. There would be a peerage or two and a sprinkling of knighthoods to stifle criticism. Patton was going to press for a long term for the president, perhaps five years. Then Maxfield, according to Patton's logic, would become Old Fred. Except that, of course, he wasn't Old Fred and never would be. Patton was misled by forms and also by the fact that Maxfield impressed him—he was Patton's sort of man. But to Maclaren's experienced eye, there was something vital lacking in Maxfield —he would never carry the profession with him. He was a lost man and you cannot lead others when you are lost yourself. He looked around the others and his eye picked out Hartly. If there was to be an empire at all (which was doubtful) he was the man who would eventually succeed to it. He was, after all, still relatively young. He would be prepared to let Maxfield have a few years of pomp, so long as it was agreed that he should take over afterwards. That was the reason why he was so interested in the project. As for Gilling and Trimble, they would be finished by then.

Trimble had predicted correctly about the luncheon. The Minister ate slowly, chewing each mouthful with considerable care. He himself never drank anything but water, but a rather thin St. Emilion was served to his guests. Hartly, as the new member of the club, was seated on his right. Throughout the meal he was sounded out on various points. His views on the main issues were known, but it was necessary to confirm them and amplify them on points of detail. Yes, he was strongly in favour of the Academy. Could he carry the College of Surgeons with him? He was fairly confident. There was a group of back-woodsmen gathered around Frobisher who might be difficult but they were old and losing influence all the time. A few honours, perhaps, or at least a promise of honours, a seat on the Council for Frobisher himself . . . It could be arranged. What was more (though Hartly did not say this aloud), Frobisher had con-trived to get the College finances into such a mess during the past two years that something would have to be done, and done quickly, to prevent it going bankrupt. The Academy would be a perfect opportunity to go to the millionaire drapers and property tycoons for further benefactions—also it was·rumoured that the College of Physicians had a very respectable surplus, some of which they might be prepared to share. There was certainly the basis for a deal. Present power for Maxfield, future power for Hartly, ascendancy for the physicians, money for the surgeons, knighthoods and peerages, new multicoloured fellow-ship and council robes, pomp and circumstance, dinners and symposia, maces and chains of office, gold-headed canes, a sense of taking part in the historical process—there was something for everyone.

"The question of finance," said the Minister primly, "is obviously of some importance. While we at the Ministry would like to help in any way possible, it would obviously be unde-sirable for an institution of this kind to be dependent on public funds. I imagine we're all agreed on that?"

Maxfield and Hartly nodded vigorously. Maxfield said, in his beautiful, dead voice, "I have confidence that the money can be found. A yearly levy on elected Fellows would be an obvious source of income. The Colleges would make a contribution. At the moment the various Colleges are spending a good deal of money on overlapping services. They will save that when the Academy is set up and those funds could be made available to the Academy. The initial cost of the building is in a different category. That will require a large capital sum. However, we have reason to hope that this problem may be soluble. A pro-visional suggestion has been made by one of our more far-sighted industrialists——"

"Miles Plant," said Trimble to the room at large. "I've been working on him for some time." He saw Maxfield wince slightly at the vulgarity of the expression, but carried on without embarrassment. "He's at last beginning to accept the fact that he can't take it with him. Also some of his friends have been telling him that, for the sake of millionaires as a class, he ought to start giving something away. He owns a magnificent house in Regent's Park which he doesn't know what to do with. If he gave us that, with perhaps half a million for extensions and modifications, we'd be well away."

"You think he will?" said Hartly.

"Between ourselves, he's ready to sign the moment we have the project properly set up. He insists, reasonably enough, that it's a sound proposition with the full support of the profession and of the Ministry. That seems to be fairly assured, from what we've heard today. However"—he paused—"there's another matter at the present time which is causing him a certain amount of anxiety." Gilling shifted uneasily in his chair. "This confounded lawsuit."

The Minister pursed his lips. "Most unfortunate. Most unfortunate."

Gilling said nothing. He could feel a faint atmosphere of disapproval. They had all agreed with him at the time that the action had to be brought; if he put the question to them now they would still agree that Line was entirely in the wrong, and that it was impossible to back down. And yet—the truth was, he had become associated in their minds with something tiresome which might upset everything, and it had imperceptibly affected their attitude towards him. There was nothing he could do about it, since they would never admit it. It was as if he were suffering from some unavoidable but rather embarrassing illness.

"I can't understand why Line doesn't withdraw," said Maxfield, with an undertone of petulance. "He must know he has no chance. He'll damage the profession and ruin himself. He's a brilliant fellow, by all accounts. He's young." He said significantly to Hartly, "Just the sort of man who could have a great future in the Academy, if he'd behave sensibly. Hasn't he any common sense at all?"

Hartly was thoughtful for a moment, then he shook his head. "You may have put your finger on it," he said. "I don't think he has. He has a great many other gifts, but not that."

"You know him well, I believe?" said Gilling.

"Yes. Very well." There was a sudden silence and he could feel their eyes on him. They were asking him, silently, a crucial question—are you one of us? Whose side are you on? Are you prepared to act as a member of the power club, to make your knowledge and your abilities available to us, for the strength and glory of the great ones? Are you worthy to rule, are you prepared to put the requirements of ruling above your personal preferences? Are you, in other words, Line's man, or ours?

I am my own man, thought Hartly, neither Line's nor yours. I will do what I think fit. He repeated emphatically, "I know him very well."

It was over twenty-five years ago, in 1944. The July sun in Calabria was like the draught from an open furnace. The fields were parched and the roads were covered with a thick white dust. The advance had slowed up and they had run into casualties. It was a disappointment after the walkover in Sicily and everyone was edgy. He had been in charge of a temporary field hospital near Cosenza. One day the brigadier had called on him unexpectedly. He was a man of thirty-five, only a few years older than Hartly himself, tall and lanky as a stork. He had sprawled in a canvas chair in Hartly's office drinking beer and looking unhappy.

"I thought I ought to explain personally," he said. "We're sending you rather a ticklish sort of case. A Lieutenant Line. He's been in the hoosegow for the last week."

"What for?"

"Disobeying orders. Mannion turned him in. All very emotional. A flagrant case. Mutinous dog. Fifty lashes, Mr. Christian —all that sort of thing. And quite right too, by the book. He had disobeyed orders."

"What sort of orders?"

"He was told to occupy a village. The wops had pulled out but they had it covered from the hillside and it was a fairly dodgy assignment. Line took a platoon up there, lost a few men, and

56

then turned back before he got into the village. He said he'd met a wop civilian who was looking fairly seedy and told him there was typhus in the village. Then he'd nipped off and got away before Line could bring him back for questioning. None of the others could confirm the story, unfortunately, because Line was the only one who spoke Italian. He's a sort of educated type, by the way. Well, Mannion tore a strip off him for coming back, told him it was all rubbish about the typhus and he'd better take his finger out and go right back. Line said he thought the medics and the sanitary boys ought to go too, so as to take the proper precautions. They had an argument and both lost their tempers and the next thing you know Mannion had him bang to rights and clapped in irons. All perfectly in order according to the book. Unfortunately——" He halted suddenly and began to scratch between his shoulder blades. His bush jacket was damp with sweat. "Prickly heat," he exclaimed apologetically. "Roll on winter."

"Unfortunately——?"

"Line was right. They found the wop a couple of days later in a field, covered with spots and in bad shape. He *had* got typhus. Now Mannion says—and of course he's right—that doesn't affect the matter. Ours but to do or die and so on. But personally I can't quite swallow that. Also some war correspondent seems to have got hold of the story, we don't know how. So it's been a little sticky. However, this morning we had a stroke of luck. Line threw a faint on the way to the lats and caught himself a fourpenny one on the side of the head. So we whipped him in here. I thought it might solve our problems. Frankly I'm very anxious to avoid a court martial."

"How?" said Hartly.

"Trick-cyclist," said the brigadier briefly. "If you want the diagnosis of an amateur who'd like to get on with the job of fighting the enemy rather than his own men, I think he's got battle-fatigue and ought to be flown back to the U.K. for urgent treatment. Do you think O'Connor would play?"

O'Connor was the psychiatrist. Hartly grinned at the brigadier and poured out another bottle of beer. "It sounds a deserving case," he said.

'Good." The brigadier was thoughtful for a moment. "I'd

be interested to know what you think of Line," he said. "He impressed me—in spite of myself."

When the brigadier had gone, Hartly telephoned the officers' ward. Line was ambulant, he was told, and refused to go to bed, contending that nothing was wrong with him. One of the junior M.O.s had already seen him and could find nothing abnormal. Hartly gave orders for him to be brought to his office.

When Line was shown in he was rather surprised. He had been expecting someone dark and sulky, a man with an obvious sense of mission and a chip on his shoulder. Instead he saw a fair, gangling young man with a long, eager face and a tentative lop-sided smile. Line settled himself awkwardly in the cane chair when requested to sit down. He accepted a beer but refused a cigarette. As he raised the drink to his lips, his hand was trembling so much that he spilled a little on to his uniform. He seemed unaware of this. He drank from the glass and put it down, with eyes fixed all the time on Hartly. He was tense and wary, a curious mixture of aggressiveness and timidity. Hartly had experience of fear and he knew that Line was frightened to death. Frightened by the situation, by his own rashness in bringing it on—and yet at the same time fascinated by it.

"How are you feeling?" Hartly asked.

"All right." Line shifted nervously in his seat. "I shouldn't be in here at all, you know. There's nothing wrong with me."

"Perhaps not." Hartly watched him take another drink at the beer. This time he brought his face down towards the glass and quickly jerked his hand up to conceal the trembling. The glass banged against his teeth. Hartly said, "Beer all right?"

"Fine." Line put the glass down. He was a little easier now. The sweat had broken out on his brow and he took out a handkerchief to mop it. "How do you do it? Ice cold drinks at this time of year."

"They gave me a special fridge for the penicillin."

"There's something to be said for the R.A.M.C."

Line laughed nervously. There was a short silence. Then Hartly said, "I've just had the brigadier in. Talking about you." Line looked at him warily. Hartly went on, "He's a good fellow."

"Is he?" Line smiled thinly. "I wouldn't know. He's above my social level." He looked out of the window. "Do you know Colonel Mannion?"

"Yes."

"What do you think of him?"

Hartly considered for a moment before replying. "He's a shit," he said judicially.

Line sat up in his chair, his eyes shining. "That's most encouraging," he said.

"Don't try quoting me on it. I shall deny every word. And in any case it doesn't really matter what I think of Mannion or what you think of him. It's not relevant to the situation." He saw disappointment on Line's face. He was really very naïve, thought Hartly. He had imagined for a moment that he had gained an ally. He said, "I think you have a somewhat over-simplified idea about authority."

Line shrugged his shoulders. "If I have, the army gave it to me."

"Maybe." Hartly changed direction abruptly. "It seems you were right about the typhus."

"Yes." Line laughed shortly. "Unforgivable."

"So far as the brigadier's concerned, he doesn't want either to condemn or forgive. His idea is to get on with the war. And he has my sympathy."

"Very Olympian. What did he arrest me for then? I didn't ask to be arrested."

"So far as I can gather, you did."

Line said sulkily, "I suppose you're going to say now that I was in the wrong."

Hartly leaned forward impatiently. "Can't you see that I'm not interested in who's right or who's wrong?" He sat back again. "They tell me you're a bright boy. You came to us from Oxford. What were you reading?"

"Greats."

"What's that now? Philosophy? Logic? Classics? Aristotle and Plato? All that kind of stuff?"

Line said, "If that's how you like to refer to it——"

"That's how I do refer to it," said Hartly. "I'll be frank with you—to me it's just a load of junk. When I was at Cambridge I met the men who taught it and the men who learnt it. None of them seemed to be any more philosophical or logical or useful for having had it. They've been arguing about philosophy for over two thousand years and they're no further than when they started, so far as giving people something worth living for. All they do is to turn out chaps like you who spend all their time worrying about who's in the right and who's in the wrong. Science is worth something, because you can test your hypothesis by experiment, prove it or disprove it, and then move on to something else. Philosophy's like psychiatry—speculation, theories, wind. It has no application. Would Mannion be any the less of a bastard if he'd read Aristotle?"

Line grinned. "Now *you're* being speculative."

Hartly was disconcerted for a second. Then he laughed. "Think it over. Someone has to do the world's dirty work. People like me and the brigadier. He has to capture the next point on the line of advance. I have to take a piece of stone out of the inside of a man's skull. We do what we can in our small corner." He paused for a moment and then said abruptly, 'I'm asking you to co-operate."

"In what?"

"There's nothing you can do out here any more except to waste everybody's time court-martialling you. The brigadier recognizes you were right about the typhus and nobody likes Mannion. Just the same you'd be convicted." He saw a secret smile flit across Line's face. "Yes, you would. In spite of your pal with the Press card." Line looked at him warily. "It was you who told him, wasn't it?"

Line said, repeating Hartly's own words, "If you quote me on it I shall deny it."

"Of course."

"Do you blame me?"

"There you go again," said Harlty. "You think of everything in terms of yourself. You think the world was put there to give you a few moral problems to solve. I don't blame you. It may have been the right thing to do. But it was a calculated thing. So don't go round behaving as if you had a private line to Jesus Christ."

There was a short silence. Hartly looked thoughtfully at the young man opposite to him. Was there anything there? Or was he just a prig, with an exaggerated idea of his own significance? That was the trouble with British education—he was twenty-one and still he seemed like a boy, adolescent and unformed. You didn't know what they were going to turn into. He was clever, obviously. He had a sort of courage—or was it mere impulsiveness? Which was the real force in his character, the arrogance or the diffidence, the serious action or his coltish, adolescent reaction to it? How afraid was he really? How great was his conviction? How much of his action was founded on a childish rebellion against authority? How much did he feel that, whatever happened, nothing really serious could happen to him?

Hartly was still young himself, but he had discovered certain things. He knew that many of a young man's characteristics are not really his own at all—they belong to youth itself. As he grows older, they are taken away from him again. Gaiety, courage, humour, imagination, they might all seem to be inherent in a man's character—and then you found out later he had them only on loan, as it were. It was hard to tell what part of a man's personality would stay with him into middle age. He wondered idly what Line would be like as an older man. He would never know, of course. The army was full of transient contacts like him. One never met them again.

Hartly said, "This is a tiresome situation for everyone, and no good can come out of it. If it comes to court-martial the army will have to convict to support its own rules. You might get a mention in the newspapers but it wouldn't last. There's too much happening just now. Mannion would stay where he is. You couldn't really hurt him. The army won't victimize an officer for keeping to the rules and he wouldn't be getting any promotion anyway. So what's the point?"

Line said, rather contemptuously, "From your point of view, none."

"Okay," said Hartly cheerfully, "I got the sneer. I'm just a simple-hearted nutcracker with a Colonial background. But give it some thought. If you're determined to sacrifice yourself, you might as well sacrifice yourself *for* something, don't you think? That's unless the sacrifice appeals in itself, of course. Some people go through life yearning to be a victim."

61

"Before I think about it," said Line coldly, "perhaps you'd tell me the alternative?"

Hartly picked up Line's medical record sheet and ran his eyes idly over it. "Repatriated on medical grounds. Action outside Cosenza a momentary aberration due to ill-health. The brigadier suggested a trick-cyclist, but I notice here on your card you have a soft functional murmur over your heart. Said at the time to be quite harmless but you never know with these things. I propose to play it safe."

He closed the folder. After a short silence Line said, "Do I in fact have any choice?"

"No, not really."

"Then there's nothing more to be said, is there?" He tried to conceal the relief in his voice but it was there. Hartly thought, there may be something to him after all. He doesn't really want to be a martyr.

A few days later, Line was invalided home. In the excitement of the Italian campaign, Hartly forgot about him almost completely. Then one day he received a short letter. It was on the notepaper of the Metropolitan Hospital Medical School. Line wrote that he had now been discharged from the army. Somehow he hadn't found it possible to go back to Oxford. The episode of the typhus epidemic had made him feel that life was only tolerable if you could do something useful. He had decided to study medicine "and perhaps become a rough, extrovert butcher like you." It ended, "You were right about Aristotle."

Hartly read the letter again and shook his head. He could not quite see Line as a surgeon. Like most ambitious men, he equated the qualities necessary for success with his own characteristics.

When the luncheon was over, Gilling gave Hartly a lift in his car. As they sat together in the back of the limousine he said diffidently, "It's very good of you to offer to help in this very delicate matter."

Hartly said, "I only hope I can do something."

Gilling hesitated. Then he went on, "What I did want to say to you in private was that——" He paused. "Well—I hope we haven't tried to influence you too much. I wouldn't want you to approach Line if you had any doubts in your mind."

Hartly turned to Gilling and smiled. There was something about the old man, he thought. He was the sort of person you couldn't help liking. Like that brigadier at Cosenza—whatever had happened to him? He spoke with deliberation. "I've studied the case very carefully. I think you're absolutely right and Line's wrong. I think he should retract and I'm going to tell him so. I should have done so anyway, quite apart from what was said today. Good enough?"

Gilling smiled back. He suddenly felt something for Hartly which he had never felt for Trimble or Maxfield or the Minister. It was a kind of respect, founded not on any particular ability or talent but on the man as a whole. "Good enough," he said.

Chapter 4

LANDAUER stopped the rehearsal with a snap of his fingers and scribbled a last note on his clipboard. "We've gone as far as we can today. Ten o'clock tomorrow morning." As the cast began to wander off the stage he said, "Susan."

Susan Cranmer turned and looked at him questioningly. It was a great little face, he thought. The body was not bad too. Long legs and big breasts and plenty of vitality in the movement —but it was the face that would really pick her out and give her individuality. It didn't just carry expressions, it actually projected them. If she was elated or unhappy, you could feel it right down at V for Vinegar. It was fine if she knew what she ought to be projecting. If not, it could be terrible.

"How was it that last time?" she said. "I thought it worked better."

"Not bad at all." He wasn't the kind of director who went in for easy superlatives. "Not as good as we shall get it, mind you. There's still a certain flatness. At the point where you say 'See, I am not crying . . .' The audience has got to feel you're crying inside. You can't do that by thinking about it. It's got to be down here." He banged himself violently in the stomach. Then he laughed and kissed her on the cheek. "Stop trying to work it out. Just go away and be unhappy somewhere."

She collected her coat and handbag and walked out into the chill sunshine of the Waterloo Road. It was all very well for him to talk. How could she go away and be unhappy when everything was going the way it was now? Not that he meant it seriously, of course. She could tell when Landauer was satisfied with her. There were still rough bits in the performance but she felt confident now that she could fix them before opening night. Not like that dreadful time at the beginning when nothing had gone right. She had been excited when he suggested she should play Nina and yet when she tried it just wouldn't work—she was outside, watching herself, all the time. The juice simply wasn't on. Now she felt at ease in the early parts—and the last act was coming, it was just a question of working it out. But she could never have done it without David. Not that he took much interest in her work—it wasn't that, it was how he treated her, how they felt about each other, the context of their whole relationship. You couldn't really act like a mature woman until you were thinking and living like one. It was as simple as that.

She hailed a taxi, "Metropolitan Hospital." She was a little late but that wouldn't matter. His work as well as her own made accurate time-keeping impossible, though tonight was a little more formal than usual. She was supposed to be meeting two of his assistants. Who was being shown off to who she wasn't quite sure, but it was obviously that sort of occasion.

The public house was just opposite the front gate. She went through the saloon bar, across a corridor and saw a door labelled "Snug." As she opened it she heard David's laugh. There was a note in it which reminded her of Landauer, and indeed of other powerful men she had known. It was the laugh of a star performer, very confident and very sure of his reception. It was followed by less dominant and more self-effacing laughs from others, and a buzz of appreciative conversation. Line was sitting at a corner table with two other men. She observed him for a moment before he saw her. The first impression he made was one of almost indecent youthfulness. Though he was forty-five years old, he could have passed without difficulty for thirty. He was tall and slim, with slightly rounded shoulders and very fair hair which tended to fall untidily over his face. He had the knack of wearing rather shabby clothes with an air of distinction. His cuffs were fraying and there was a button missing from his shirt.

As she came to the table he rose and introduced her to his two companions. One of them was a sallow, dark-haired young man with a beaky face and a nervous manner. "This is Sam Brook." He gripped her hand in a moist, bony palm. The other was stocky, with large glasses and hair cut so short that it appeared as little more than a black shadow on the top of his scalp. Line said humorously, "And this is Frank Halder. Hair styles by Alcatraz."

They all sat down at the table. The landlord came in and hovered around as Line gave their order for drinks. He said sympathetically, "A big list today, Mr. Line?"

"Not so bad." With a rather mechanical modesty Line said, "My assistants do most of the work, you know. That's when they're not telling me what to do."

The landlord went out and Susan said, "How did it go?"

Line rubbed a hand across his face. The facetiousness of his reply to the landlord had now left him. He suddenly looked very tired. Curiously, the tiredness did not make him look older but indeed almost younger. He was like a small boy who had over-exerted himself in a football game. He said, "I don't know—it's too early to say. It was fairly heavy going." His voice was full of weariness. "We got in, we got it done, we got out. But it was a battle all the way. Not one of our most carefree incidents." He looked up and saw the puzzlement on her face. "Sorry, I'm talking about the operation. It's a modern cliché that the operation is just an incident in the course of surgical treatment. The real headache starts afterwards."

Halder said, "Do you think he's going to make it?"

"I doubt it. His blood chlorides are shot to hell as always. Macpherson's trying to sort them out at the moment." He said gloomily, "Sometimes I wonder if this whole business of organ transplants is just a blind alley."

"They thought that at first about a lot of things."

"Sometimes they were right."

The landlord came back with the drinks. Line searched his pockets for money. He dropped a handkerchief and a bunch of keys, retrieved them and felt in his breast pocket for his wallet. "Damn," he said, "I've left my money somewhere again." He turned rather helplessly to Halder. "Frank, do you think you could lend me a couple of quid?" Halder smiled and handed over the notes. "And for God sake, Frank, please don't let me forget to pay you back."

The intervention of the landlord seemed to have broken the

sequence of Line's depression. He said to Susan, "Cosy little place this, don't you think?" She nodded. Line went on, "That landlord's remarkable. He knows as much about operative technique as my theatre sister. He's been serving drinks to the staff of the Metropolitan for so long that they call it the annexe." He was seized by a momentary sense of social obligation. "How was the rehearsal?"

She smiled diffidently. Somehow their conversation made her preoccupation with the theatre seem trivial. It was hard to turn from matters of life and death to a discussion of lighting problems and the reluctance of Dorothy Gorer to come in on cue. She said, "Much better today. I think it's going to be all right."

Brook said with interest, "I hear you work at the National Theatre?"

"Yes." She added quickly, "Don't think you have to pretend to have heard of me. I'm still quite obscure."

"What are you playing in?"

"Nothing at the moment. I'm rehearsing *The Seagull*."

Halder spoke unexpectedly. He said, "What part?"

"Nina."

He said, hardly able to conceal his surprise, "But that's a big part."

"Too big perhaps," she said. She couldn't help sounding apologetic. "It's the policy at the moment to give obscure people like myself a chance. Sometimes it works. Sometimes we fall flat on our faces."

An abstracted look had come on to Line's face. "I'm sure you'll be a great success," he said. His mind seemed to move away from the subject. He drummed his fingers on the table and then said to Halder, "You did remember to speak to Sister about the transfusion?"

"Yes."

"I'm sorry to fuss about this. But you know what happened last time. They don't seem to understand that a block for only ten minutes can make all the difference."

Beneath the words she caught a suggestion to Halder that he should go over to the hospital and take another look at it. Halder replied stolidly, "She understands. It's taken care of."

"I'm sure it is." Line appeared to retreat, to accept Halder's

67

rejection of his hint. "I'm not criticizing Sister, we all know she's first-rate. But she can't improvise."

They began to talk amongst themselves about the case and their work. She was once again forgotten. She noted this with amusement rather than offence. It was so very like the theatre. Line could well have been a leading man worrying about the timing for his big entrance. This was another closed world such as she herself lived in. There was all the self-absorption, the pride in being part of the special world with its own rules and hours, the endless talk of technicalities, the obscure private jokes, even the pub across the way. The landlord took telephone messages, picked up the jargon, gave them little privileges until he also almost became part of the world himself.

They talked for a while and then Line looked at his watch. Evidently the object of the meeting had been accomplished. "I must go now," he said abruptly. She noticed that his glass of vermouth was hardly touched. He had a curious aversion from drinking. Why then, this weekly gathering in the public house after his operation? Presumably, like so much else in medicine, it was a matter of ritual. It was typical of David that with increasing eminence he hadn't grown too important to sit around informally like this and get to know his staff. "I've got Hartly coming," he explained. He said reflectively, "I wonder what he wants. The last time I saw him was at one of those bloody dinners at the College. White tie and decorations. Frobisher's last stand as President. I got my shirt stuck in the zip of my fly and turned up half an hour late." Brook and Halder laughed. "There's really no need for you chaps to leave."

Halder said, "I'd like to take another look at that transfusion." "Would you mind?" Line's face brightened—Halder had evidently said the right thing. He turned to Brook. "I don't know about you, Sam—are you busy? Because I have a feeling that Macpherson could do with a bit of help."

Brook and Halder left them on the pavement outside to walk across to the hospital. Line hesitated for a moment. He showed her into his car and then said, "Would you mind very much—I think I'd better pop in with them for a moment, just to have a look at the patient. Could you possibly wait two minutes?"

"Of course."

She settled down in the passenger seat of the car. It was a Bentley of uncertain vintage, with a high, lordly view of the road; an old-fashioned town carriage. Everything, she reflected, with a mixture of pride and amusement, had to be done with style. His appearance, his car, the atmosphere he created, his relations with his subordinates. And most of all his work. It was work of such tremendous dignity that it made all vanity and pretensions unnecessary. It was also, she was beginning to learn from experience, not subject to minor restrictions of time. His two minutes prolonged itself into twenty. When he did come back, his apologies were no more than perfunctory.

"Sorry about that. We ran into a little bit of difficulty."

"Is it all right now?"

"Relatively," he said. "Though frankly I don't give very much for his chances."

She was not yet so involved in the conventions of hospital life that she could accept this kind of remark without emotion. For a moment she saw herself in the position of the patient, being casually written off as hopeless by a man on his way to a dinner engagement. He noticed her distress and said apologetically, "One has to try these things. Nothing else helps, so you haven't much to lose. But it's depressing when they keep dying. It seems to come in runs rather."

"Deaths?"

"Yes, God knows why," he said, "Halder contends it's mathematics. Just like a roulette wheel. There are so many chances against you, but in the nature of things you get a run when they come up together. I suppose he's right, but it's hard to keep believing it in the face of repeated failure. You begin to think you may be doing it wrong somehow. You lose confidence. At other times, of course, everything goes your way and you think you're bloody marvellous. I'm not sure which is the more dangerous state of mind."

He was silent as he drove west through the traffic. He was a flashy but not always accurate driver with a rather absent-minded technique. He had a tendency to ride the wheels over the corners of the pavement as he turned the corners. He said, "Where shall we go for dinner?"

"What's wrong with home?" she said.

He smiled at her. "I like it when you say that."

"What?"

"Home." They had only been living together for two weeks and it was still new enough to be exciting. "But I don't think we've got much in the way of food."

"Are you hungry?"

"Not very."

She said hesitantly, "I could give you an omelette or something."

He laughed. "Or something." He made an adventurous dash round Hyde Park Corner. "You seem happy tonight."

She sank contentedly back into the deep cushions of the Bentley. "I am."

"Any special reason?"

"Oh, lots." She said reflectively, "Nina, for one thing, she's really coming through at last."

He laughed. "You sound like a medium."

"Well—it's a bit like that, you know. You can't do it just by thinking about it." She thought back to those dreadful early days when she had seen Landauer wondering whether it had all been a mistake—whether there was still time to take her out before she wrecked the production. "It was terrible at the beginning. Like trying to make love when you don't really feel anything. Then——" She put her hand affectionately on his knee. "It was you really, you know. You did it for me."

"Nonsense."

"It's true," she said seriously. She remembered how worried she had been. She had known that she couldn't afford to fail. At this point in your career, they were looking for your range. A part like Nina was a kind of test. If it worked, you were really an actress—if not, just another nice hard-working girl and a pretty face.

Part of the trouble was that until she had met David she hadn't really known what life was about—hadn't *felt* anything, not about serious matters. She had had affairs with students and actors but it was puppy love, fun and games really. Nothing you could translate into Nina's love for Trigorin, which was something serious and big and tragic.

"What's the story?"

"It's about a young girl who falls in love with an older man.

A writer. He's touched and attracted by her but he's too involved with his own freedom. He treats her very badly."

He grinned. "Do I treat you badly?"

"Of course."

Not that he was very much like Trigorin really, she reflected. He was far too strong, for one thing. No one could accuse David of weakly, charmingly flowing with the tide. He was not trying to fit a picture of himself into the world around him. He was actually controlling that world. He was active and dominant. He made things happen. You couldn't imagine him trailing round at the skirts of that ghastly Madame Arkadin. Though he had a wife, of course, somewhere in Suffolk, whom he didn't like to talk about. According to rumour she was an alcoholic American heiress he had picked up in New York.

The flat was in a mansion block overlooking the Brompton Road. It was a comfortable but characterless place which he had rented furnished because it was convenient for the hospital. Susan promised herself that when she was really established she would make a few changes. The rooms were not a bad size and with some different lighting and one of those interesting French wallpapers . . . However, she mustn't interfere just yet. He might think she was taking too much for granted, trying to manage him.

When she looked in his refrigerator she remembered she had forgotten to buy any eggs, so thank God she wouldn't have to make a shot at an omelette. But there was some smoked salmon and brown bread and she made sandwiches. They sat together in the kitchen and ate them. It was all very exciting. She had never actually lived with a man before. She said seriously, "I liked your two assistants."

"You did?" he said reflectively. "Yes, they're nice boys." It seemed odd to her to hear them referred to as boys. They must have been thirty at least, ten years older than herself. "Very promising, too. They've done wonderful work together. In character they're totally different. Halder's a playboy. He's a rich bachelor and he likes parties and drink and women. Brook's just the opposite. He has a devoted wife and two children and gets home whenever he can——"

Susan nodded. She could see Brook hurrying home to his mousy wife in the suburbs, a troubled frown on his long sensitive

71

face as he worried about school fees and electricity bills and whether one of the children was sickening for chicken pox. She smiled. "Domesticity in Golders Green," she said.

A shadow passed across his face. "Why did you say that?"

"Say what?"

"Golders Green."

"Well, why not? I mean——"

He broke in. "There's nothing wrong with being a Jew, you know."

She looked at him, completely at a loss. "But I was just thinking of a suburb—any suburb." She was ruffled at the assumption behind his remark. "Why the hell should I care about his religion?"

He replied, "Some people do."

"Well, I'm not 'some people,' " she said angrily.

He became suddenly contrite. "I'm sorry if I misunderstood you. It's just—I feel this prejudice against Brook. He's brilliant —a most remarkable brain. He really is." There was something extraordinarily intense, almost plaintive, about the way he said it. Her momentary indignation left her—she realized now that his first reaction had had nothing to do with her at all. It was some very deeply felt emotion. But what? He could surely not be Jewish himself? Quite apart from his appearance, no Jew would ever have reacted so violently.

"Really?" she said.

"Yes indeed. The most brilliant man on the unit." He said it like a man reciting a lesson he has taught himself. Line went on, "He's carried out one of the most valuable pieces of research in this country—he and Halder together. But they're having the greatest difficulty getting recognition for it. Brook tries to pretend it doesn't matter, but I know it's a terrible disappointment to him." There was quite a long silence. Then he said with apparent irrelevance, "Did I tell you that I was involved in a lawsuit?"

"No."

He laughed, with the air of a man about to embark on a good but not very serious story. "It's stupid really. You'd hardly believe it. Have you heard of Sir Thomas Gilling?"

The name was familiar to her. "You mean the man who's

72

always photographed outside Buckingham Palace, saying there's no grounds for anxiety?"

Line nodded. "He's bringing an action against me."

"Why?"

"Well——" He gave her a short account of the events leading up to the action. At the end she said, "It seems crazy. Surely it won't come to court?"

"No," said Line confidently, "I shouldn't think so. Gilling was probably annoyed by my letter and he's trying to bluff an apology out of me. You've no conception of the arrogance and vanity of these old men. They're used to cracking the whip and waiting for everybody to stand to attention. When he finds it doesn't work he'll probably change his tune. I should imagine he'll drop the whole thing."

"You don't seem very concerned," she said. "I should be worried to death."

"Oh, there's nothing to worry about," he said. "I just thought you might find it amusing."

There was something in his tone that precluded further discussion. He got up from the table and, as if at a signal, she stood up and waited for him to come to her. It was curious, she thought, how not only his every expression but his every action held meaning for her—it was a secret language between the two of them which made speech unnecessary. As he approached she was conscious of his natural grace of movement—though impulsive and spontaneous, he was never clumsy. Always he seemed to generate a curious atmosphere of excitement and tension. His skin smelled faintly of antiseptic, and his hands were still a little dusty from the powder of his surgical gloves. He kissed her, at first very gently, and it was she who opened her lips and strained against him. As he began to touch her breasts she slipped her hands inside his shirt and ran them down the side of his chest. His body was hard and lean, with none of the flaccidity of middle age. When she touched him she could imagine that he was no older than herself. She felt the muscles tighten under her fingers and he said, "There's an hour before Hartly comes. If you want——"

She pressed her hands into the small of his back. "You know what I want."

Chapter 5

Line stretched out an arm towards the bedside table to take a look at his watch.

"My God, Hartly's due in a quarter of an hour."

She lay back and regarded him with affectionate amusement. His life was made up of such startled announcements. In the way of unpunctual people he liked to involve others in his last-minute attacks of panic. She could see that he was slightly put out by her lack of response. He got out of bed and began to dress furiously.

"Aren't you going to get ready?" he said.

"There's no need for me to hurry. I'll slip out of the flat when you two are talking business in the living-room."

He said, "I'd like you to meet Hartly."

"Not tonight."

"Why not?"

"Because I shall be an irrelevance," she said. "For a man in Hartly's position to make an urgent appointment means he has something important on his mind. When I meet someone for the first time I like them to be thinking about me. Not waiting for me to leave." What's more, she thought, I'm not anxious to be produced as a kind of demonstration—this is my mistress and I'm not ashamed of it. With a man like David there was always the danger of losing your individuality—of being regarded, perhaps even coming to regard yourself, as merely an appendage of his life. If David had taught her something about Nina, perhaps Nina had taught her something about David, too.

"All right," he said. He picked his way past several articles of underclothing which she had dropped on the floor on her way to the bed. "It's just as you like."

She asked, "Have you any idea why he's coming?"

"I think so." He took a letter out of his jacket and handed it to her. It was from his solicitor announcing the date of the lawsuit. "The case is due for hearing in three weeks."

"Where does Hartly come in?"

"Everyone comes in—or will do if Gilling doesn't see sense in time." He explained, "Hartly's the new President of the College. If the case comes to court it will be a frightful embarrassment to him. Also he has larger ambitions which depend very much on people like Gilling. Naturally he doesn't want the old man to make an ass of himself." He knotted his tie rather carelessly in front of the mirror. "I expect Gilling got a similar letter to mine. Now that they can see it actually coming into court they'll all be piddling their pants. I was expecting them to make an advance about now. Symons was getting a bit panicky but I told him to hold on." He said confidently, "Barristers are like all other experts—their advice is useful just so far. But you have to take the big decisions yourself."

There was something rather frightening about his self-assurance. She remembered how he had spoken about the problems of a surgeon. "One day you think you don't know how to do it—and the next day you feel you're bloody marvellous. I don't know which is the more dangerous of the two." She had the feeling sometimes that he regarded his own life in the same half-fascinated, half-terrified way—it was simply a gamble like his work, but on a much larger scale. But if you gambled with somebody else's life you could lose and start again. Was he coming to need the more desperate thrill of finality, the ultimate stimulus of total disaster?

Yet beneath her anxiety there was a certain admiration. If this was neurosis, it was neurosis on the grand scale. While she acted out her dramas on the stage, he incorporated his within the framework of his life. She knew that he would never really take seriously the world of make-believe in which she lived. His occasional efforts to express interest in it were obviously no more than mere politeness. She had tried introducing him to Landauer, but it had not been a success. They had circled round each other like a pair of dogs, bristling slightly, each demanding ascendancy, each resentful of any area of existence which he was unable to dominate. She was prepared to accept this restriction of interest; even rather admired it. It was appropriate to his position as a great man, engaged in great affairs. She also derived a curious pleasure from the contrast between the passive, almost feminine role he played when making love and his autocratic demeanour at other times. She was fascinated at the way he seemed to put on dominance, as it were, with his clothes. It gave her a feeling that a secret man existed, known only to her. Whatever happened, she thought, as she watched his face gradually set into an expression of determination as he brushed his hair, however it might turn out in the end, this was like nothing else that had ever happened to her.

The doorbell rang. Line pulled on his jacket. "That's Hartly now," he said. "I'll have to go."

He leaned down over the bed to give her a final kiss, his body fully clad against her nakedness. There was something exciting in the touch of his jacket against her skin, in the contrast between his business-like preoccupation and her own lethargy. But she knew that his mind was on other things. He was already preparing what he was going to say to Hartly. The bell rang again.

"I really must go," he said.

"All right. Don't worry about me. I'll find my way out in my own time."

Then he was gone. It was pleasant to lie there in his bed, alone. She put her hands behind her head and gazed up at the ceiling. Soon she would get up and have a leisurely bath, dress herself, and go home. There was no hurry. There was no need to rush anxiously here or there, looking for life. Life was here. She was content.

Hartly peeled off his overcoat and dropped his lemon-coloured pigskin gloves on the table in the hall. Seen against Line, he looked very small and square and dark and determined. His hair had turned quite grey. He said, "I'm sorry to call at such short notice."

"That's all right. We're very informal here." Line looked with amusement at the overcoat and the gloves. "You've forgotten part of your uniform. Improperly dressed. Where's your homburg hat?"

Hartly laughed. "I bought one once, but it made me look like a rabbi at a funeral." He walked past Line into the living-room.

"Drink?" asked Line.

"Whisky and water, please. No ice." Line poured a drink for Hartly and a much smaller one for himself. Then he sat down and waited in silence. He made no attempt to open the conversation. It occurred to Hartly that this wasn't going to be an easy interview.

There was a short silence and then Hartly said, "I suppose you've guessed what I'm here about."

Line's gaze rested on him momentarily and then moved quickly to a Chinese figure on the occasional table slightly to the right of him. He said softly, "Say it, Rex. You mustn't expect me to say it for you."

"All right," said Hartly equably. "This affair with Gilling. Don't you agree with me that it's gone far enough?"

"Of course. But aren't you at the wrong house? After all, this is Gilling's action, not mine."

"I know that." Hartly was not disturbed by this initial response, which was more or less what he had expected. He looked at Line, wondering which was the best approach. That sulky obstinate expression was only too familiar to him. He had seen it the first time he and Line had met at Cosenza. It was the expression of a boy awaiting blame for some action, fortified by a solemn conviction that he was in the right. Line's attitude now would be, as it had been at Cosenza, an adult version of the schoolboy cry—"It wasn't my fault—he started it." He noted with interest that Line was still obsessed with this immature preoccupation about who was in the right. In Hartly's world this was a very minor factor in any situation. Motives were complex, the initial cause of any quarrel was hard to find, and usually both sides were to some extent wrong and to some extent right. Even in the rare cases where blame could be clearly fixed on one party or another, it usually had little bearing on what was to be done. Hartly had the preoccupation of the administrator with future action—he cared nothing for the past, he thought only of what to do next. He was very conscious of this quality and proud of it—it seemed to him a sign of maturity, a qualification for power and leadership. He had not yet realized that it might also be a source of weakness—that in an irrational world, the irrational had constantly to be taken into account. A man might destroy himself from an excess of common sense.

It was going to be a heavy job talking sense into Line, but he thought he could do it. He sipped at his whisky and then said, "It's no use going over the history of this thing. It's been a string of disasters and misunderstandings."

"Has it?" said Line with polite interest.

"Well," said Hartly stolidly, "I don't think you wrote that letter with the deliberate idea of provoking Gilling. Or did you?"

"Of course not."

"Well then." Hartly made the gesture of a reasonable man cutting through red tape. "Who wants this action? Who gains by it?"

"Search me." Line was equally reasonable. "I didn't ask him to sue me."

"Yes you did." He interrupted Line's protest. "Unintentionally, I admit. You're so bloody self-absorbed you didn't think at the time that you were putting him in an impossible position. It never entered your head to put yourself in his place. At least that's my interpretation."

Line said, "Have you read my letter?"

"Of course."

"Then you know as well as I do that it was true from beginning to end. The machine works. It might have helped Kincaid. That was all I said." His voice rose in exasperation. "So that old lunatic sues me."

Hartly shook his head sorrowfully. "Oh really, David——"

"For Christ's sake stop being so statesmanlike. I'm giving you the facts."

"No, you're not. What about that newspaper article?"

"I'm not responsible for what they print in the newspapers."

"You knew about it beforehand," said Hartly with certainty.

"Is that a crime?"

"He didn't get that stuff out of his head," Hartly said significantly. "Gilling wouldn't have taken action just on your letter."

"You mean he thought I put them up to it?" Hartly nodded.

78

"Oh, that's absurd." Seeing the scepticism in Hartly's face he said vehemently, "I swear to you I had nothing to do with that article."

"The views were yours," said Hartly reasonably. "Gilling knew they were. What was he supposed to think?"

"Why didn't he telephone me? I'd have given him my word——"

"Perhaps he should have done. But thinking what he did, it's really understandable that he didn't feel so inclined. Few people behave entirely sensibly in times of crisis."

Line suddenly grinned at him sardonically. "Except you, Rex."

Hartly replied quite seriously, "Unfortunately I was away at the time."

Line got up suddenly from his chair and began to pace across the room. He said, "How you must despise us, being involved in such an untidy situation! I suppose if you had been here you would have advised me not to write that letter?"

"I think so."

"And if you'd been in Gilling's shoes——"

"I'd have advised him to ignore it. It would all have been forgotten in a week or two."

Line said, with an engaging smile, "And everyone knows I'm a bit of a nut case." The smile suddenly faded from his face and he said sharply, "Still, it's not too late. Gilling can withdraw any time."

"Do try to understand his difficulty," said Hartly earnestly. "It's not just your letter—it's the newspaper article. You must agree that it was monstrous. They practically accused him of killing Kincaid. He can't back down without appearing to admit it."

Line shrugged his shoulders with an appearance of indifference. "All right. So nothing can be done."

Hartly went on patiently. "I should like to think there were other possibilities. Something between unconditional surrender or utter disaster—for both of you. Because that's what it means if it comes to court." Maddened by Line's expression of apparent unconcern, he said violently, "You do understand that, don't you?"

Line stopped pacing and came to a halt in front of the window. He looked out of it, his back to Hartly. He said, "I'm not so foolish as you sometimes think."

"I'm sorry," said Hartly coldly. "I was misled by your behaviour."

"I'm not surprised you find my behaviour difficult to understand," said Line. There was something particularly exasperating to Hartly in his tone of voice. It reminded him of their first encounter during the war. He went on. "It's founded on principle. You've been associating too much with politicians, Rex." He shook his head gloomily and gazed out of the window. "I find all this very depressing."

Hartly was startled. "Why?"

"Sending you here like this. The president-elect of the Royal College. Just to get themselves out of a hole. It's disgraceful—disgraceful."

Hartly kept his temper with some difficulty. He was determined not to be provoked. "Nobody sent me here."

"Ambition sent you," said Line with maddening superiority. "You want to be a great man."

There was a short silence. Hartly realized, with relief and not a little pride, that he was not angry—the insults had not hurt him. Why was that? Perhaps it was the fact that Line still remained with his back to him, looking out of the window. It was really impossible to insult a man effectively if you could not bring yourself to look him in the face. On the other hand, he wasn't getting very far. The important thing, he decided, was not to allow Line to turn the affair into a melodrama. He said casually, "Don't be an ass, David." There was a short silence. Then Line suddenly turned round and looked at him. He said, "Do you remember Cosenza?"

Hartly nodded. So it had been in Line's mind as well as his. "Of course."

"You conned me then, all right. Very nicely done, it was. It was months before I realized how clever you'd been." There was bitterness in Line's voice. "I was in the right all the way and you conned me out of it. Of course I was young then."

You're still young now, thought Hartly. He said, "We've come a long way since then."

80

"I suppose we have." Line regarded him speculatively. "You don't look very much different to me."

"Nor you to me," said Hartly. "I suppose that's fairly common. When we look at people we see an attitude. So long as they preserve that attitude they seem to stay the same age. Once they change it they begin to look old."

Line thought for a moment and then said abruptly, "We're not making much progress. Did you have some definite proposition you wanted to make?"

Line was not a fool, thought Hartly. The mention of Cosenza had been deliberate, to put him on the defensive, to remind him that the same trick would not work again. He said, "Nothing really specific. I wanted to find out your attitude of mind. Most things can be negotiated if people want to negotiate them. Otherwise it's all a waste of breath." He lit a cigarette and settled back in his chair, crossing his short legs and displaying at the top of his socks an inch or two of rather hairy calf. He said, "Gilling and you have three weeks to decide whether to destroy each other. You've each managed to get yourself stuck in a sort of far-out position. I can't believe there's no way of making some kind of settlement."

"What about the newspaper article?" said Line. "You say that's the real libel and that's nothing to do with me. Any settlement on my part wouldn't cover it."

"We have reason to believe that if we could get a satisfactory settlement between yourself and Gilling, the newspaper wouldn't present too much trouble."

"You mean if I gave way, they'd be out on a limb?"

Hartly shook his head. "Let's not talk in those terms. It's not a question of giving way."

Line was unimpressed. "Tell me how else you can make a settlement."

He spoke almost triumphantly and Hartly had a sick feeling that things were going to go wrong. There was an unhealthy eagerness about Line's tone of voice, which seemed to indicate a desire to embrace the disastrous possibilities of the situation rather than to avoid them. His apprehension made Hartly a little impatient. He said, "Damn it, we've all killed a number of people in our time. But it isn't customary for people to write to the papers about it."

Line became equally impatient. He waved his right hand angrily and almost upset an ash-tray. "You know the facts as well as I do. This was no ordinary mistake. In fact it wasn't a mistake at all. It was a disaster caused by a deliberate policy. A policy which I begged him to reconsider. He wouldn't." He went on violently, "It's a policy which is still in operation."

"You mean Brook's machine?" said Hartly. Line nodded. "Not everyone has the same confidence in that contraption as you have, you know."

"You've used it yourself on occasions."

"Yes," agreed Hartly. "I think it has possibilities. But Gilling doesn't have to agree with me—or you."

A dogged uncompromising look came on to Line's face. He said, "It's never been given a fair trial. It's been turned down without proper examination." He brooded for a moment, and then said bitterly, "It's a matter of prejudice."

"Against you?" Line shook his head violently. "Well, what then?"

"Against Brook." Hartly suddenly felt hopelessly out of his depth. He had no idea what Line was talking about. Line went on angrily, "Oh, yes, we like to believe it doesn't exist, don't we? The war knocked all that out of us. Very shocking. It can't happen here. But you know better."

Hartly looked at him in astonishment. "You're not suggesting that this is all due to anti-semitism?"

Line shrugged. "Just try looking at his record." When Hartly said nothing, he added with an undertone of menace, "You might as well. You'll have to, if it comes to court."

Hartly said wearily, "David, we all know what London teaching hospitals are like. I don't know whether what you are implying is true or not. Maybe it is—I don't know. But where does it lead us?"

Line was very emotional now. He said, "I met Brook in America and he's worked with me ever since. He's an outstanding man. Yet since he's come back here he's had nothing but obstruction. Difficulty and delay in getting papers published, trouble with grants, difficulty in getting patients to use the machine on. He was put up for the Royal Society and black-balled."

Hartly said acidly, "What you really mean is that he didn't get elected?"

Line shrugged his shoulders. "Call it what you like."

"This all sounds like absolute nonsense to me," said Hartly. "Quite apart from being hopelessly beside the point."

Line said forcibly, "It *is* the point. If scientific advance is going to be hamstrung in this way, if men are going to be blocked and penalized and discouraged——"

They were getting a long way from the sensible discussion of practical possibilities which Hartly had envisaged. He said, "If the boy's had a bad break, I'm sorry for him. But you must see that we're not going to get anywhere discussing all these old grievances."

"I'm giving you the background," said Line obstinately. "You can't understand it until you know what we're up against. That letter wasn't an irresponsible attack. We didn't want to publicise the matter. We tried every other way and it was no good."

"Even so," said Hartly doggedly, "I can't believe it was intended as a personal attack on Gilling."

Line said impatiently, "Of course not. Not as such."

Hartly thought he saw a ray of light. In his eagerness he jumped up. Then, realizing he was several inches shorter than Line, he sat down very quickly. "So there *is* a misunderstanding. What we have to do is to clear it up without going to court. After all nobody cares about your disagreement on the use of this machine. It's purely a question of whether Gilling was negligent."

"Which he was," said Line maddeningly. "I know it, you know it——"

"Please let me finish," snapped Hartly. He gripped the arms of his chair and went on, "If we could agree on some kind of public statement in which you said there was no personal reflection on Gilling—after all, your point about the machine would still be valid. You could make that clear."

For a moment he was hopeful. Line seemed to consider the suggestion seriously. Then he shook his head. "Impossible."

"But why?"

Line replied very slowly and deliberately. "I meant every word I said in that letter. I still do. If I make a statement like that everyone would think I couldn't substantiate it and have had to withdraw it. But it was the truth." He turned towards Hartly and for the first time seemed to look him straight in the eyes. His brow was furrowed in thought and the expression on his face contradicted the finality of his words. It occurred to Hartly that Line's mind obviously worked in quite a different way from his own. He himself had come to this meeting with a precise idea of what he wanted, what he was prepared to suggest, what he felt about each issue that might be raised, what he would be prepared to agree to. Line had no such plan. His mind oscillated to and fro as the conversation progressed, dominated by violent and unpredictable emotional impulses. When he did reach a conclusion upon which action could be based, it would be as much a surprise to himself as to everybody else concerned. He said, "I'm not going to go back on what I believe, to avoid unpleasantness. Even if I wanted to, I couldn't let my juniors down. I have a duty towards them."

Hartly said delicately, "Have you asked them?"

Line shook his head. "I can't put the responsibility on them. I must decide."

"All right," said Hartly, "so you won't come half-way to meet us. Have you any proposals?"

Line was silent for a while, and then he said, "It's up to Gilling."

It was getting dark. They sat there together for several minutes without speaking. Then Hartly said, "This could be very serious, you know." Line did not reply. Hartly went on, "You've been very lucky all your life. You've survived a lot of risky situations by the skin of your teeth. Sometimes just by luck, sometimes because people have helped you. It doesn't have to last for ever."

"Yes," said Line, "I know."

Hartly looked at him, assessing him. In some ways it was the same Line whom he had dealt with at Cosenza. He was still excited by himself, by his own daring, his own principles, his own determination to make a stir and not to be bought off. He was still scared by himself, as he had been then, but less so.

Success had bred in him a kind of confidence, a confidence not at all like Hartly's, stolid and careful and broad-based, but febrile and precarious, and only half sure of itself. Was there anything one could do with him? Was there any bribe one could offer him to persuade him to abandon this piece of insanity? Almost anything would be cheap at the price, but what could he be induced to accept? Certainly it would be absurd to offer him a knighthood or any conventional distinction. What else was there? A new unit? But that would be too obvious. Suddenly he had an idea. Hartly said, "This question of an F.R.S. for Brook. If there's been an injustice done there, it could probably be rectified."

Line said warily, "I'm delighted to hear it."

"As you know I'm not a Fellow myself but I know the P.R.S well. He's a reasonable man. And then there's Maxfield. He's very influential in the Society." He let it hang around in the air for a while.

Line said, "I take it this offer would be unconditional?"

Hartly said, "I should like to regard it as part of an overall settlement designed to settle outstanding differences." He grinned. "If you see what I mean."

To his surprise Line did not treat this offer of a package deal with indignation. He seemed to consider it carefully, without emotion. He was really, thought Hartly, a man of baffling moods. Eventually he said, quite calmly, "That sounds rather immoral to me. After all, if Brook deserves it, he should have it anyway."

"With a case like this coming up? My dear fellow, you know the Royal."

After a long pause Line shook his head. "I must say I'm tempted. It would make a big difference to Brook. But one can't do a deal on a matter of principle." He made this last statement almost as if it were a question, as if he wanted reassurance that one shouldn't in fact make such a deal. Hartly wondered whether to press it, and then decided it would be a mistake. He got up and said, "Well, you don't have to say definitely now. Give it some thought."

As he turned to leave, Line said, "There's just one thing I'd like to ask you before you go." He hesitated for a moment. "Why are you doing this? You're not really their sort of person."

85

"Whose?"

"Gilling, Trimble, Maxfield. That bloody awful Minister. What are you doing with them?"

It was a question which deserved consideration. But Hartly did not hesitate. He had considered it himself long before. He was never in any doubt about his own aims or his own motives. He said, "I don't like waste." He looked at Line challengingly. "I want good people to do good work and not spend their time ruining each other in law courts over a sentence in a letter. We're lucky in our profession. We have better work to do than this. We need all the men we've got and all the prestige we can raise to do it properly. We can't afford to throw it away." In a voice that was almost an accusation, he said, "Is that good enough for you?"

Line ran his hand anxiously through his hair. As always, he seemed to be thinking on his feet, working out his attitude as he went along. "No," he said hesitantly, "because I think it's probably humbug. What you really don't like is vulgarity." His voice gathered power as his convictions rose within him. "You don't mind waste so long as it's done with propriety. Brook and his machine can be wasted by prejudice and neglect, and you wouldn't care." Now he was quite confident, almost domineering. "I never knew what was wrong with this country until I went to America. Here we sneer at the Americans for extravagance. But all the time we're wasting the most valuable thing we have—the lives of our young men. If I can do anything to break that system, it's worth a little sacrifice of dignity."

Hartly put on his overcoat and fitted the fingers of his yellow gloves carefully round his thick strong fingers. "You won't break the system this way, David."

"No?"

"No. You'll break yourself—and Gilling too, perhaps. But the system will remain."

"What do you recommend, then?" Line looked with amusement at the trim dark overcoat, the polished shoes, the pigskin gloves. "Your way?"

"You could do worse," said Hartly equably. "After all, you're still a young man. In ten years' time I shall be on the way out. If you really care about doing something constructive rather

than making an exhibition of yourself, you might consider that.'
He halted as he came to the door. As if it were an afterthought
he said, "Incidentally, I suppose you've considered the cost to
yourself of an action like this?"

"We've been into that," said Line. "My reputation——"

Hartly interrupted. "I wasn't thinking of your reputation,"
he said as he went out of the door, "I was thinking of the money."

Chapter 6

BRADWELL looked across his large cluttered desk and smiled benignly at Line. His pale blue eyes shone with idealism, his battered face held the deep lines of innumerable struggles in the cause of the right, his big heavy head and mop of white hair were impressive to the point of theatricality. His tie was rather too full and his collar too soft for a completely practical attitude towards life. In fact he had never desired to be a solicitor, and in his youth he had yearnings towards the world of letters. This was the origin of his interest in defamation, and he was much consulted by authors and publishers. He had stood unsuccessfully for Parliament as a Liberal and then as a Socialist, restlessly changing his allegiance as his convictions developed. His interest in law centred largely on its reflection of the social conditions and beliefs of the times, and he was active in the fields of obscenity, capital punishment, police violence, and wrongful arrest. He had taken to Line from the start. He recognized in him the qualities he most valued—a passionate resentment of injustice, suspicion of established authority, and a determination to carry the possibilities of protest to their ultimate extreme.

Line had respected him for the same reasons. When one was associated with Bradwell, it was almost impossible to doubt that one was acting from the very highest of motives. This Line had always found reassuring. It was only now that it was beginning to occur to him that certain rather sordid points of detail needed clarification. He moved around awkwardly in his chair, writhing slightly in embarrassment. He said abruptly, "There's something I forgot to ask you before. Perhaps one ought to go into this before becoming totally committed." Bradwell raised his bushy brows and waited. Line said jerkily, "How much is a case like this liable to cost?"

Bradwell frowned and pursed his lips. His expression showed plainly that he hoped Line was not developing cold feet. "Do you mean if it comes to court?"

"Yes."

He hesitated. "Not too easy to say. Depends on how long it lasts, of course."

Line waited. Surely this could be no more than an introduction. But Bradwell seemed in no hurry to proceed. Line became exasperated by his vagueness. It was a slightly unsuitable quality in a lawyer. He said rather shortly, "Well, how long is it likely to last?"

Bradwell shrugged his shoulders. "It might be three days. Might be a week. If it lasted a week that would almost double the costs."

Line said irritably, "Surely you must be able to give me *some* figures."

He was beginning to develop the first signs of an attitude which Bradwell had experienced before in other clients. It was as if he were beginning to suspect that Bradwell was altogether too casual about the actual financial details involved—was perhaps, indeed, so anxious to fight a test case on a matter of social importance that his client's own financial interests might become submerged in the process. Bradwell knew from experience that when this point was reached, even with the most idealistic clients, further hedging was useless. The more you procrastinated, the more suspicious they got.

"Well," he said reluctantly, "if we take the barristers first, Symons will want about three hundred guineas to get on his feet, and a refresher of one hundred and fifty a day. Say about a thousand for a week. Then there's the junior, Carter-Jones. He has to get two-thirds of that, so there's another seven hundred or so. Then there are our fees, of course, and the previous work that's gone into it. What with one thing and another it might knock up to three or four thousand." Noticing the look on Line's face he added hastily, "But of course if you win, Gilling will have to pay most of it."

"And if I lose?"

"Well, that's bound to come more expensive, of course. You'd have his costs to pay, which would almost certainly be more than ours, since Groom is leading. And then there would be the question of damages." His voice trailed away and then he said in an effort of reassurance, "But I don't think we should go looking for trouble. You have a good case."

Line ran a hand nervously through his hair. He said slowly, "Let me get this straight. I need to know what I'm in for. If it's a long case and I lose it, it might cost me ten thousand pounds, apart from damages. Is that right?"

"It's an outside figure," said Bradwell. "I don't think it will go anywhere near a week."

Line said resentfully, "I don't wish to be critical, but I think perhaps it would have been helpful if you had mentioned this before."

"I did try, you know," said Bradwell rather vaguely. "Much earlier on, if you remember."

Line made a baffled grimace. It was, he supposed, quite possible that Bradwell had tried to raise the question of money earlier, but that the details had not really registered. Like a great many impractical men, his attitude towards financial matters oscillated between an unjustified optimism and moments of blind panic. At the moment he felt himself moving very rapidly into the second stage. He blurted out, "You might as well know that I haven't got ten thousand pounds—nowhere near." Bradwell frowned at him incredulously. He had always visualized Line as a rich man. Line went on, almost apologetically, "I'm a full-time professor, remember. My salary is only five thousand a year and I have a wife and two boys."

There was a silence. The lines of Bradwell's face deepened. He said heavily, "Well, as far as our fees are concerned, you can be sure that we'd be reasonable——"

"That's very good of you," said Line. "But if I lost, your fees would be one of the smaller items, I take it."

"I suppose so," said Bradwell reluctantly.

Line said, "Supposing I couldn't pay. What then?"

Bradwell sighed audibly. Plainly all this was very distasteful. "Well—I suppose they *could* put you into bankruptcy. But really, I don't think one ought to look too much on the black side——"

"That's all very well——"

"Naturally," said Bradwell, "I appreciate your anxiety. On the other hand, I think this is a case of fundamental importance. I feel very strongly that you are in the right in resisting this action. The law isn't here to protect privilege and discrimination and obscurantism, and it's iniquitous to try, as Gilling is doing, to use it for such a purpose. I've admired your stand on this matter and I think it would be a tragedy if you felt you had to call the case off. On the other hand, the final decision is of course always yours."

Line nodded gloomily. He felt the most painful pressure of all, that of being trapped within somebody else's high estimation of him. He said, "Gilling sent someone to see me last night." He added, with some bitterness, "An old friend of mine." He paused. Bradwell waited expectantly. "He offered me a bribe, and a threat. Also the suggestion of a compromise."

"Yes?"

"I turned it down." He felt the warmth of Bradwell's approval, but was it quite enough? He added restlessly, "But that's all very well. I can't guarantee to win. If I lose I can't pay up."

Bradwell said, "You have no—other source of funds?"

Line shook his head. He said, as if to himself, "I have my children to consider."

"Naturally."

Line looked up at Bradwell and recognized that there was nothing more to say. It was no use talking to Bradwell any more. That massive leonine head, that furrowed face, they were fine to look at, but they could not solve his problem for him. He got up suddenly. "As you say, it's my own decision. I only came here to ask the score. Many thanks."

As he left the solicitor's chambers Line found himself feeling a little dissatisfied with Bradwell. There was nothing actually wrong with him, nothing you could put your finger on. Yet Line had not found him sympathetic. His principles and his honesty and his sense of purpose were undeniable. And yet . . . His interest in the case seemed to be impersonal, as if he were a general and Line was a regiment to be sent over the top, to be massacred in a just cause, if necessary. He did not seem to be sufficiently concerned with Line's personal predicament. It was rather unnerving to be treated as cannon fodder by one's own solicitor.

Line realized that he was being unjust. Bradwell had not really tried to persuade him to fight the case. He had gone in to see Bradwell determined to fight to the last ditch and Bradwell had appreciated his point of view, had backed him to the hilt. Yet it would somehow have been more reassuring if Bradwell had been less enthusiastic, if he had tried to restrain Line's eagerness instead of encouraging it, if he had been more concerned to point out the dangers of the position. After all, he, Line, was going to have to make any sacrifices that were necessary. He was preparing to risk irretrievable ruin. If the worst came to the worst, no doubt Bradwell would be concerned. But how concerned? What would he actually do? Write a letter to the *New Statesman* about it?

This question of the money, which he had managed to forget about for so long, had now become a source of alarm to him. He was vague about the implications, but in his present mood they seemed infinitely menacing. He ought to discuss them with someone. But who?

Well, there was his wife. Indeed, he thought, with a stab of conscience, there was no doubt that he should have spoken to Brenda about this before. But how could you discuss anything satisfactorily when all true contact had long since been lost? How it had been lost he couldn't exactly say. It had been a gradual process, a succession of arguments and squabbles and misunderstandings, with every attempt at conciliation ending in a fight more disastrous than the one before. As time went on he had made his work the excuse to spend an increasing amount of his time at the flat, while she stayed at their country home with the boys. Nowadays sometimes weeks went by without their seeing each other.

However, it was plain he couldn't shirk it any longer. When he arrived home he telephoned his house in Suffolk. Brenda herself answered. He heard the familiar voice, still retaining the remnants of an American inflection. "Hello," she said, faintly accenting the last syllable.

"David here." He asked awkwardly, "How are things going?"

"Oh—fine." Her voice was noncommittal.

"And the boys?"

"They're great. Mark got his house colours."

"Football?"

"No," she said, "running. Don't you remember, he was running in the inter-house cross-country?"

"Oh yes—yes." He had a vague memory of this. He really ought to pay more attention to the boys, he thought uncomfortably, but there were so many things, his work, Susan, now this lawsuit. "We'd better congratulate him."

"I just did." Was there reproach in her voice? He couldn't tell. He was a man who hated talking on the telephone. Without the intimate interplay of facial expression and gesture he was lost. He found himself turning awkward and stiff.

"I thought I'd like to come home this week-end. Is that all right?"

"Of course. It's your home."

"I mean," he spoke defensively, "if it's not convenient——"

"I'm not so busy as you," she said. "I've got time on my hands." She paused for a moment and then asked, "When are you coming?"

"This afternoon, if that's all right. I'll be driving out."

He arrived at the house about teatime. It was an old rectory with grey walls and a paddock, and a large overgrown garden which smelt of spring. As he saw it from the road, he wondered why he didn't spend more time in the country. It was a shame to be always shut up in the flat and the hospital. Characteristically, his active and restless mind began to make detailed plans for a change in routine. Why should he not go up to the rectory every weekend? He could drive up in the evening, the only problem was his Friday afternoon operating list, and he could let Brook finish that—well no, not Brook, really he wasn't good enough with his hands. Macpherson? He had promise, but he was young . . . Well, maybe he would manage somehow. The main thing was to have two days' peace, or pretty near it. Rest, relaxation, country air. See the boys, play games with them, get to know them better—except that they were away at school, of course. Well, anyway, he would get down more often. It was worthwhile making an effort.

Brenda was out riding, the housekeeper said. She seemed to

93

ride a great deal these days. He could not help feeling a stab of illogical resentment that she was not there to greet him. After all, he had driven for three hours. He unpacked and then came down and sat in the drawing-room on a chintz-covered sofa, listlessly turning the pages of *Country Life*. After half an hour's boredom he became restless. Why did she have to be so long? Was she being deliberately offhand? It was really too bad. He turned back to his magazine but the articles on gun-shy setters or pig-farming seemed to say nothing at all to him. After a while he fell into a troubled doze.

When he awoke she was standing in front of him.

"Were you asleep?"

"Just for a moment."

She peeled off her riding gloves and began to tidy her short black hair in front of the mirror. She looked well in breeches and cream silk shirt. She was very spare and physically fit, a well-preserved, athletic woman of early middle-age. By contrast, still recovering from his uncomfortable sleep in the chair, she made him feel frowsty and crumpled.

She said, "I'll tell Mrs. Bradshaw to make you some tea. I'll be down myself in a quarter of an hour."

She left him. When she returned, in almost precisely ten minutes, she was dressed in a blouse and skirt. Soon afterwards Mrs. Bradshaw came in with the tray. As they sat drinking tea, she said, "How are things in London?"

"Things?" he said vaguely.

"The hospital."

"Well—we keep going." Somehow he could never bring himself to talk about his work to her. At the beginning, he remembered, she had made repeated efforts to draw him out about the hospital. But it sounded altogether artificial, far too much like a policy dictated by the advice in one of those American magazines for women that she read. If you want to keep your husband, become involved in his work, share his interests. No, he thought suddenly, that was unfair. She *was* interested, in a way. The fault was really his—he did not want to share his work with her; perhaps not with anybody. And he had become maddened by her persistence. She would not accept his reserve on this subject, as an English woman might have done, as a manifestation of male eccentricity. She wanted to find out why, to talk the thing out. As he resented her intrusiveness, she began to accuse him of being secretive. They had endless arguments before she had given in. But in a sense she had never given in. She had accepted that he could exclude her if he wished. But she continued to resent it.

However, there were certain matters that could no longer be avoided. He dreaded her interest in the lawsuit, the questions she was liable to ask, the opinion she was likely to give. Like a man taking an unpleasant draught of medicine at a gulp, he said abruptly, "I was talking to Bradwell this morning."

"Bradwell?"

"My solicitor," he said rather sharply. "Surely you remember him."

"Why should I? He's not *my* solicitor."

It was going to be worse than he thought. "He's acting for me in this libel action." He waited for her to respond but she said nothing. "It's getting pretty near. They've fixed the date in three weeks' time."

"Yes?" Her voice showed polite interest, nothing more.

Unreasonably, he resented her pose of detachment just as much as he would have resented an excessive interest. He said, slightly exasperated, "I don't know whether you realize it, but my whole life and career depend on this action." She remained silent. He said angrily, "You're not really interested?"

"What do you want, David? Another chance to shut me out?" She said helplessly, "I just don't know what you want." After a moment's thought she went on, "I never have. When we were first married I worshipped you. I thought you were the greatest and most worthwhile person I had ever met. I didn't mind your dedication to your work—I admired it. I was prepared to sacrifice myself to it willingly. All I asked was that you should share a little of that part of your life with me." She shrugged her shoulders. "Well, so you didn't want it. You slammed the door in my face." She saw the frown on his face and her voice rose a little. "Can you deny it?"

He said, "Was it so essential for you to be involved?"

She said indignantly, "What else had you to offer? You'd given your life to your work—all right. I was even prepared to give my life towards it. But at least I wanted to know what it was I was giving my life for."

It was turning out just the way he had feared. The wretched hashing over of old issues. He said, "This gets us nowhere."

But she was already in her stride. "A blank cheque was what you wanted. Isn't that right? Unquestioned support for everything you did. No questions. Keep my mouth shut. Because anything you did was so vital—so important——"

"It *is* important."

"Important to you, perhaps. Why should anybody else care?" she said bitterly. "This lawsuit you're so anxious to see me about. I first heard about it from the newspapers."

Suddenly she stopped. Her anger ebbed away. She walked away from him to one of the windows and looked out into the garden. If she could blot him out of her sight and consciousness for a moment, perhaps she would have a better chance to understand. It was stupid to argue, stupid to quarrel. The quarrel had been long ago. Since then, she sometimes thought, she had spent far too long thinking about David, trying to make some reason and sense out of the contradictory elements of his character and mind. Relationships with him tended to force you into a position of constant character analysis. The task was rendered infinitely more difficult because he himself had no clear idea of his own character or why he did things, or what was the basis of his own feelings. Action in David sprang from deep complicated underground springs, which were as much a mystery to himself as to others. His intelligence was combined with naivety, his tenderness with occasional callousness. Each day incidents occurred which had to be analysed and explained. Some tentative attempt had to be made to fit them into a pattern. But it was an unrewarding activity, since in the end all one's ideas were no more than theories and their results in terms of one's actual relationship with David tended to be disappointing. It was rather like trying to achieve an understanding on a political level with a government whose system of working and basic assumptions were so different from your own, that eventually you came to wonder whether the effort of understanding was really worthwhile—or whether a simple programme of achieving a balance of forces was not in the end more satisfactory.

Unfortunately, it was not possible to adopt such a policy unless it came to you naturally. She knew that she would never cease to struggle at the impossible task of understanding him. Perhaps this in itself antagonized him. Perhaps he felt a sense of suffocation as a result of her interest. Or did he simply find her dull? She didn't even know that. And so perhaps it was a judgment on her. She left her first husband for David because he was dull. Now perhaps she would be abandoned for the same reason. But then all the world became duller as you grew older. It was part of his immaturity that he had never learnt to accept that.

She spoke now in the voice she used to Mark when he spoke of his house colours. "So the case is to come on in three weeks? Are you going to win?"

"I don't know." He added rather dramatically, "I don't know if there's even going to be a case."

She could tell, knowing him so well, that he was moving towards something. The thing was not to express interest. If she did he would shut down on her. "Really?"

"I think I may have to compromise."

"That doesn't sound like you."

"Unfortunately I'm not the only party concerned."

"Who else?"

He hesitated for a moment. "The boys——"

She became suddenly wary. He could attack her, that was one thing; but not the boys. She said, "How do they come into it?"

He spoke, as he sometimes did, maddeningly, as if explaining something to a child. "A lawsuit can be a very expensive thing."

She said irritably, "I know that."

"While I'm assured that my case is a good one, and I shall probably win, I can't be certain. If by any chance I don't win, the costs will take everything I have, and probably more. I shall have difficulty in keeping the home going and the boys at school . . ."

She felt herself once again gradually losing control. She paced up and down the room in great agitation. "David, if you want to settle out of court, do so. But don't try to put it on to me, or the boys. I won't have it, do you hear?"

At last she had struck home to him. His face flushed violently.

She went on, without giving him a chance to protest. "What am I expected to say? To sympathize with your problem? To help you work it out? It doesn't exist." She stopped in front of him, her brow furrowed with the effort of obtaining some form of communication. "The money you pay me doesn't keep this house up or send the boys to school. It doesn't go anywhere near it. I don't mind—why should I? I've got more than enough money of my own. I never wanted an allowance, but you insisted. Otherwise I suppose you'd lose face. But if you stopped it tomorrow the boys wouldn't suffer in the least. So you can forget about them." She felt him on the defensive and the desire to press home her victory was too much for her. "In fact you can forget about money altogether. If you lose I'll pay your costs for you. How's that for an offer?"

His anger was lost in humiliation. He said, "You like being rich, don't you?"

She said sadly, "It's all I have. I should be dirt under your feet if I had no money."

"You can be assured of one thing," he said. "Whatever happens, I shall never come to you for it."

It was the answer she had expected. He could indeed hardly have said anything else. The desire to force him to see the reality of his own actions and his own motives, which had been the root of so many of their savage quarrels in the past, could not be restrained. If he had been content to deceive himself, she thought, it would not have been so bad, she might have been prepared to let it go. What outraged her was that he used artificial situations, built up on his own self-deception, to put her in the wrong. She said slowly, "There's one thing I ought to say right now. You're a man who had—I thought you had anyway—great things to do. I don't think this lawsuit's one of them, but you didn't ask me. You never asked me about anything. Now you're in it and you know it can break you, I think you're scared. What's more I believe you know in your heart that it's all a pointless, stupid fight over nothing. It won't help anybody and for all I know it may kill some poor devil because you're too tied up in your own affairs to do a good job at the operating table." His hand was over his face, he was not looking at her. He said nothing. She went on, "So I'd advise you to settle. But if you do, settle honestly and face the real reason. You made a mistake. You should never have written that letter—or, once you had, you should have withdrawn. There's nothing to be ashamed of there. But don't tell yourself that you're settling because of the boys. That would be nauseating."

Line said wearily, "I suppose I was a fool to come here."

"What did you expect?"

"I don't know—understanding——"

"Understanding!" It was really too comic. The one thing he'd always resisted, the one thing she'd tried to give him for years and been rejected for. A sense of outrage led her into unintentional cruelty. She said, "Don't you get that in London?"

His voice was suddenly ice-cold. "You're being obscure," he said.

She was herself a little alarmed at what she had done. Her voice trembled slightly. "You know what I mean." She walked over to a side table and poured some whisky into a glass. "Drink?"

"No, thank you." He watched coldly as she mixed the drink for herself. Then he said, conversationally, "That's rather a large one, isn't it?"

She recognized this as an opening shot in one of their final, terrible battles, in which no holds were barred, and anything could be said, anything, that is, which might hurt or lacerate. From now on it would not matter how small the advantage obtained, how brutal the weapon used. The attempt to hurt would be total. The important thing was not to show too obviously when a blow had landed. She laughed artificially. "It's traditional in the circumstances. Americans always drink in times of emotional stress."

"And when there isn't any emotional stress they find life flat and uninteresting——"

"So they drink then too. Right. We're a nation of drunks. As for the British, they sit there with pursed lips, balancing on the edges of their chairs sweating in their furry little suits——"
She was suddenly disgusted with herself, with both of them. "Oh Christ, do we have to talk this way? If you think I'm an alcoholic, have the guts to say so. Don't narrow your eyes like a spinster in a private hotel in Bournemouth and say"—she

mimicked him viciously—" 'that's rather a large one, isn't it?' "

"Go ahead and drink," he said. "After all, it's your whisky—bought with your money——"

She grinned viciously at him. "That's what really hurts, isn't it? The money. But hell, David, you can't be that impractical. What do you earn? Five thousand a year? Do you really think you can keep a country home and a town flat with two boys at boarding school, a wife, a mistress——"

"I am not keeping a mistress!"

"O.K., so you're going dutch. What's the difference." She added wearily, "Oh what the hell does it matter! You'll get tired of her. Or maybe she'll get tired of you. I left my husband for you because you were young and vital and he—well, he seemed to be dying on me, I could see his life right up to the end just the way it was going to be—and mine too. Then when I left him I could see from the look on his face that he wasn't dying any more—he was dead. While I stayed with him he could fool himself he had something left, but now he knew the truth. So it's a judgment on me really, isn't it? Well now, here are you at forty-five, at the top of your career. But where does one go from the top?" Line did not reply. "On the other hand she's just beginning." On an impulse, maddened by his lack of response, she walked to the bureau and took a photograph out of the drawer. Looking at it she said, "She's striking, I grant you, but I was prettier at her age. You'll never believe me, but I was. And she's not really up to playing Nina. They brought her on too fast."

He jumped up and snatched the photograph from her hand. It was a picture of the two of them coming out of the stage door of the theatre. He was holding Susan's arm affectionately and they were talking, looking at each other. There were other people around, but the photograph had been enlarged and the others cut out. He searched his memory to try to remember the occasion when it had been taken. But it was impossible. He had passed that door with her on many occasions and there were often people on the pavement outside waiting for autographs. One never noticed their faces.

He said, "How did you get this?" She did not reply. There was really no need. He said, with studied calm, "You're a strange woman. Not only do you hire people to spy on me. You want me to know it."

Suddenly he did not know what to do with the photograph. He knew she had showed it to him for one reason only—to poison the memory of the time he had spent with Susan, to make him realize that all the time he had been watched, photographed, reported on. It was unbelievably squalid. Seeing the look on his face, she turned away from him and made herself another drink. He said, "What is it you're after? A divorce?" She shook her head. "Well, what is it then? You must have some proposal? You couldn't have done a ghastly thing like this for nothing."

Suddenly she was wretched. Why had she done it? She hardly knew. The whisky was taking effect and she spoke without thinking. She said, "It's very lonely here."

He looked at her in astonishment. "This isn't exactly the time to play for sympathy."

"I don't want sympathy. You asked me to explain something. I was trying to explain. It may not make much sense to you, but I can't help that." She saw him deliberating, working out the appropriate method of response to what she had said, and it maddened her. She would almost have preferred physical violence. At least it would have been an indication of spontaneity. There was something exhausting to her in his endless controlled deliberation. She felt a violent impulse to shake him out of it somehow. She shouted at him. "Oh for Christ's sake don't just sit there! Hit me or scream the place down or pour yourself a drink, or go back to London—or something. Don't just sit there trying to think of something to say which fits in with your own picture of yourself."

It was of course useless. His response was to get up from his chair, to walk out of the room without looking at her. She heard him walk along the path to his car and then drive off to London. She sat down in one of the easy-chairs, ashamed and exhausted, rocking her drink to and fro like a baby between her hands. God, she thought, why was she such a bitch. Why—why?

But she wasn't always. It was David—he had made her like this. He had made her like this—and now he put her in the wrong.

Chapter 7

LINE DROVE FAST on the road back to London, his hands clutching the wheel to stop them trembling. He kept on repeating to himself snatches of the nightmare conversation in which he had just taken part. The more he ran it over in his mind the more appalled he became. Was she going mad? What had he done to make her hate him in this way? And what was to happen in the future? They could not go on like this. But what were the alternatives? Divorce with Susan named as co-respondent? Then marriage to Susan? But would Susan want it? Did *he* want it, if it came to that? The truth was that he had never considered it in these concrete terms. It came to him that his life was totally out of control. He had become so preoccupied with a mass of day to day crises and problems that he had not considered these larger issues, or if he had he had merely hoped vaguely that circumstances would somehow point a way to satisfactory action. What with his work and the lawsuit and Brenda and his sons and the sheer problem of getting through the ordinary responsibilities of the day, he had no time or energy to consider the possibilities of future situations or the pitfalls which might suddenly appear in his path. He was like one of those statesmen or civil servants who had immersed himself so much in the detailed administration of his job that he had no time to think ahead, so that every new development took him by surprise and caught him unprepared.

He recognized this danger, and yet at the same time recoiled from it. The problems were so intangible, they contained so many aspects over which he had no control that he could think of no way of attacking them. He felt a sense of outrage that he should be burdened with them at all. The only way, he thought, with one of his rare but enthusiastic ventures into an efficient analysis of his difficulties, was to deal with one thing at a time. What, after all, was the immediate problem? There was no difficulty in answering that. The money. He had not solved his financial problem yet. Nor indeed, he thought hopelessly, had he any idea at all how he might do so. Perhaps the answer was that it was insoluble. He cheered up a little at this. Remote dangers had never terrified him as much as they terrified most men, perhaps because his life had rarely been free from the possibility of such future catastrophes, and for the most part they had never developed into anything disastrous. He had a vague hope that something would turn up.

He went home and took a hot bath. At a distance of eighty miles from Brenda his natural resilience began to return. But he found himself at a loose end. Susan was away for the weekend. He felt the need of company and went across to the hospital. There was nothing much to do but he was able to chat with the ward sister. She was used to him wandering over aimlessly in this fashion and gave him a cup of coffee in her office.

As they were talking, a probationer nurse came in and said, "There's somebody on the telephone, Sister. For Professor Line."

He went outside and picked up the telephone.

"Professor Line?"

He recognized the voice of Marsh, the scientific correspondent of the Frampton Press. He had known Marsh for some years and had been in the way of handing him occasional stories, including the one which had caused the present libel action. The Frampton Press had expressed its gratitude by making generous grants for laboratory equipment. Line said amiably, "How's Fleet Street?"

"Not so bad." Marsh's voice was wary. "Can you talk freely?"

"Well—moderately."

"I imagine you've received notification of the date of the court hearing?"

"Yes."

"Of course our case will come on afterwards." Marsh paused. "Lord Frampton's taking a great personal interest in the whole thing."

Line was amused at the reverence with which he spoke. "Is he indeed?"

"Yes. But he's beginning to get a little worried. He's heard rumours that the other side may be pushing for a settlement." He paused as if waiting for a comment, but Line said nothing. He went on. "He's anxious that you shouldn't be forced to give in——" He paused with the sentence unfinished. "By circumstances," he added finally.

"That's not very likely," said Line cautiously.

Marsh said, "It's bound to be a very expensive case." The words hung in the air for a while. "Lord Frampton thinks it would be in everyone's interest to get together. He'd very much like to have a talk with you."

"When?" said Line.

"Now," replied Marsh rather apologetically.

Line felt a distinct reluctance to go instantly at Frampton's call. He said, "I'm rather busy——"

"I know. But he'd really be most obliged——"

There was anxiety in Marsh's voice. It occurred to Line that Marsh might be in trouble if the invitation was refused. And he really hadn't anything else to do. "All right."

Marsh said with relief. "Wonderful. He'll be sending a car around."

As Line put down the telephone he wondered if he had made a mistake. He had never met Frampton, but Marsh spoke of him with considerable awe. He was a hereditary rather than a self-made press lord, with a reputation for remoteness. He was not seen very much in public. He was said to be independent of political pressures and to have a kind of eccentric integrity. He was also extremely rich. It was possible, thought Line, that this might be a solution to his financial problems.

Frampton's limousine called for him at the hospital fifteen minutes later. He was taken to the new and particularly hideous skyscraper just south of Fleet Street where the Frampton Press had its headquarters. Murals representing such subjects as Progress, Responsibility, and International Co-operation covered the walls of the lobby. He was led to a small private lift which took him to the top of the building. Then he was taken through a series of corridors to Frampton's personal suite. He was finally shown into a large living-room, built on two levels. The level on which he entered was several steps lower than the main level, on which Frampton was seated with his three henchmen, so that he had the sensation of going upwards in some royal presence. One wall of the room was taken up with an enormous picture window looking out over the south and west of London.

Frampton himself was tall and thin, a well-preserved man in his early fifties, with greying hair and a mask-like face which looked as if it had been exposed to too much sun and too much care and attention. It succeeded in preserving a superficial appearance of youth from a distance. Yet as one approached closer it was apparent that he might have done better in the end to have allowed himself to age in a normal way. Frampton's mouth was rather small and lop-sided, his expression discontented, his smile unconvincing.

"Professor Line?" He had a curiously high-pitched, metallic, rather toneless voice. "It's very good of you to come." He made a perfunctory introduction of the other three men in the room. "You know Marsh, don't you?" Marsh nodded to him. As on every other occasion when Line had met him, he looked very anxious and his clothes needed pressing. "Mr. Bewdly." He pointed to a battered, careworn, melancholy man in a shiny blue suit. "And Tony Cawthorn, my personal assistant. Tony, a drink for Professor Line."

Everybody, thought Line, seemed to be trying to get him drunk these days. "Nothing, thanks," he said.

"Sit down, sit down." said Frampton. He was evidently used to people who didn't sit down until they were told to do so. "Now, first I'd like to say that I'd been hoping to meet you for some time, Professor. Mr. Marsh will tell you that I have taken a great interest in this case from the very beginning." Marsh and Bewdly nodded with some solemnity. "I admired your letter and I think Marsh wrote a great story. I was very pleased when I heard that you'd refused to back down under pressure. A great gesture."

"It was more than a gesture," said Line.

Frampton gave no sign of having heard him speak. "A very great gesture indeed. And I want to say that we are proud to be associated with you, and to be fighting this thing together as it were. You can rely on us, Professor. We won't fail you."

It was the sort of speech which seemed to count on some dramatic response. Line wondered whether he was supposed to wring Lord Frampton by the hand and say God bless you, my Lord, or something of that kind. He sensed a distinctly patronizing note in Frampton's voice. He was prepared to consider some degree of co-operation, but only on a basis of equality. He tried to make this plain. "I'm not exactly intending to rely on anyone——" he began.

Frampton looked at him in a glazed fashion. He said, "In union is strength. We shall not fail."

It was really essential to get this straightened out. Line persisted. "You may have misunderstood my position——"

Frampton interrupted, bulldozing Line's protestations aside. He had the common characteristic of the compulsive talker which lies in treating anyone else who tries to get a word in as if he is rudely interrupting. "And we must have confidence in each other. We must be frank. We are fighting against something evil and pernicious. The suppression of opinion. Freedom of speech—we must protect it. You in your way, I in mine. It's the general principles that count, Professor. We must stand by them, come what may. And we shall—we shall." He made a curious braying sound which he used to keep the conversation open in those moments when he was momentarily at a loss for words. "Ahhh. Science—you represent science. And that's progress. I believe in science, Professor. Methods have to be changed. The old thrown out of the window, the new welcomed. I've recently issued an instruction to all my executives here to have yearly check-ups. Not just stethoscopes and blood pressures and stuff like that. But true scientific investigation. Blood cholesterol, electrocardiogram, barium enema. A very dangerous area, the large bowel. Don't you agree?"

"Not entirely."

Frampton looked at him approvingly. "I'm glad, I'm glad. Ahhh. This country's future depends on science. You've got to push it, encourage it, I tell all my editors, encourage the scientists, it's the policy of my publications, without the scientists this country's dished and done for. Ahhh. When this case came up, some of them were for backing down——" He looked balefully at Bewdly. "The lawyers scared them. The lawyers can't scare me, Professor. They didn't see the principle, you see, they thought it was just another defamation case. They soon saw when I explained it. So we're all united now. Ahhh. I have some news for you. I promised you news, and when I promise news I come through with it. That's my success as a newspaper man. I didn't bring you here just to encourage you. I've had the Minister himself on the line."

"The Minister of Health?"

"The Minister of Health." Frampton nodded solemnly. "Strict confidence, of course. Wanted to know if anything could be done. He said it was all a great pity. Medical men damaging themselves, great government schemes in jeopardy, all a misunderstanding. That was his line. Arrangements could be come to, satisfactory to all parties. Was I prepared to talk, persuade you to see reason? So on and so forth. I told him: I said, I can see your point of view, but you've missed the point. Ahhh. I could see that to him it was just an ordinary dispute." He wagged an instructional finger. "He hadn't seen the principle, you see."

Somehow Frampton's enthusiasm for science actually seemed to make science itself ridiculous. Line wondered if he could possibly be as fatuous as he sounded. He had the reputation of being an able man. Despite his constant experience of being disenchanted with the great, Line could not help feeling disappointment. There was a temptation, in spite of all the evidence, to imagine that successful men must have *something*, that their position and achievements could not be the result of mere chance alone. Yet one knew that this was most frequently the case. Why did he find himself recoiling from it? Was it that the reality was too grotesque to contemplate? Did he simply lack the fortitude to admit that the whole structure of power in society was a meaningless accident, that the game was so ridiculous that it was not worth playing? Power, when all was said and done, was like money—men spent their lives working for it, craving for it, sacrificing themselves, their families, their integrity for it. Yet this same power was received by others as a gift, by inheritance or by pure chance.

Was it, on the other hand, not so much that idiots so frequently gained power, as that power made men into idiots? He listened

107

to Frampton talking and was presented with the picture of a man driven by excess of authority into a state bordering on insanity. He talked to the wind, and the wind alone would listen. His long continued association with those subservient to his will had robbed him of conversation, of human contact. No one communicated with him because no one dared. And so he ended up like a schizophrenic, talking in a way that lacked sense or co-ordination. The schizophrenic was separated from the world by his disability, the tycoon by his position. They both lacked the necessary discipline of contact with the society they lived in, they inhabited a world of their own, where what they said need only make sense to themselves, since no one else was ever really really there—hence these jumps in thought, this jerking from one subject to another, the appearance of abstracted concentration. With the tycoon, as with the schizoid, it was as if there was a screen of plate glass between him and the outside world.

Suddenly his mind slipped back to what Frampton was saying. ". . . and you need have no fears, no anxieties. I shall be responsible for all that. Everything you require. I've given instructions."

My God, what was all this? He hadn't been listening. What on earth was Frampton talking about? Responsible for what?

Frampton waved a hand generously. "Don't thank me. It's the least I can do. You have to bear the brunt of the case. The personal strain. The risk to your reputation. It's only fair that you should be relieved of financial anxiety."

Line jumped up from his seat in alarm. Evidently, while he had been looking out of the window, dreaming, Frampton had been promising to pay his costs and evidently thought he had agreed. He had anticipated some kind of leisurely discussion on which he would be able to make it absolutely plain where he stood—that while he could visualize Frampton (or better, his Foundation) accepting some liability for his costs, this could only be done on the basis of a written agreement which exempted him from any obligation in return. Even then he might have trouble getting it past the Board of the Metropolitan. Any other way, he would be hopelessly compromised. Frampton's pocket professor.

For the first time he began to realize the special dangers which might beset a man who couldn't pay his debts. Appalling as the thought had been of being indebted to Brenda for the means to fight his case, it was nothing to the possibility of being beholden to this megalomaniac who sat opposite to him now. The unnerving thing was that Frampton seemed quite oblivious of any possibility that he might refuse. He was still talking. It seemed impossible to establish any kind of communication with him. Whatever you said, he just crushed you into the ground, with that inhuman, unearthly voice. A kind of panic struck Line. The situation was so extraordinary that he began to act in an extraordinary way, waving his hands and crying feverishly.

"No! No, I won't accept it!" He became suddenly conscious that this was rather an offensive reply to a generous offer. He qualified it a little. "It's very kind of you, but no." He shook his head violently. At this point, to his intense relief, Frampton at last stopped talking. He brought the flow of words to a halt, a puzzled frown on his face. Anxious that there should be no ambiguity at all, Line said vehemently, "Out of the question." To soften the refusal he smiled.

Frampton was suddenly silent. The frown on his face grew deeper and it was possible to see a change from puzzlement through suspicion to something almost like anger. The silence became oppressive. Thunder seemed to gather in the air. Bewdly, Cawthorn and Marsh began to squirm uneasily in their seats.

Line, looking at Frampton now, was conscious that he had given bitter offence. He realized that the violence of his refusal must have sounded deplorably offensive and he felt a certain shame about this; but what on earth was he to do, if Frampton wouldn't listen? He made an ineffective attempt to patch things up. "Really," he said, "it's very kind of you to offer this and don't think I am ungrateful. I've certainly no wish to be rude about it. It's just—if I might explain my position——"

Frampton did not look at him. He did not listen to the explanation. He simply said, interrupting in the middle of what Line was saying, "Just as you please." Then he nodded curtly and made a gesture to his subordinates. They all rose to their feet. Evidently the audience was at an end. "Cawthorn will see you home."

Frampton turned and walked out of the room. It seemed curiously, almost indecently empty without him. The four men stood in silence. Bewdly lit a cigarette. He handed one to Marsh, whose hand was trembling slightly. Cawthorn smiled nervously and mixed himself another drink.

"A pity about that," said Bewdly. His voice sounded like a whisper after Frampton's. He scrutinized the glowing end of his cigarette. Then he said to Cawthorn, "We should have told him."

He was obviously referring to Line. Line became exasperated. There was something humiliating in the way they stood there, like four schoolboys when the master has stormed out of the room. They seemed almost afraid to talk. And here was he, a professor of surgery, a man distinguished in his own right, afraid of no one, standing ignominiously with them. It was an outrage. To restore his self-respect he barked irritably, "Told me what? What's wrong with the man? Is he mad or something?"

Bewdly shook his head. "No," he said. "As a matter of fact he's deaf." He frowned at Marsh. "Somebody should have told him."

"If he's deaf," exploded Line, "why the devil doesn't he wear a hearing aid?"

Bewdly shrugged his shoulders. "He doesn't choose to, I suppose."

"But how does he manage? I mean——"

Bewdly said, "You've seen him managing."

Line rose from his seat. "This place is a madhouse."

"Sit down and take it easy," said Bewdly. He seemed quite unruffled. "We've got to think of some way of changing his mind."

"What do you mean?"

"Well, he got under your skin, didn't he? It's understandable. But you still need the money. What's more, we need you, because if you cave in, we're out on a limb and have to settle. And that means trouble for me personally——"

"I can't see why. Frampton said it was his idea to fight——"

"It's his idea if we win—mine if we lose." He turned to Cawthorn. "What do you think, Tony? What's the best way to handle it?"

Line interrupted. "You can forget that. I don't want his money."

"Now don't be like that. You don't even have to see him again——"

"I'm not interested."

"You've no alternative," said Bewdly gently. "Listen, Line, we know your financial position——"

"Don't call me Line!" Suddenly he felt a great sense of relief. He had indeed no alternative. It was not worth while considering the dangers of his position since there was now no question of withdrawing. "And don't worry about your own skins. I'm not going to settle. You can tell Frampton I'll fight without money if I have to." He added contemptuously, "Write him a letter about it."

When he had gone, Bewdly mixed drinks for the three of them. Cawthorn said with some disgust, "What a load of bull."

Marsh shook his head. "I know him better than you. My guess is, he'll do it."

Bewdly nodded agreement. "He wants to suffer," he said sadly. "But at least he has a choice, which is more than you can say for the rest of us." He drained his glass. "Take your seats for the crucifixion."

II

Chapter 1

SIR THOMAS'S LIMOUSINE drew up outside the Law Courts. There was already a small crowd waiting and he heard the click of cameras and the buzz of excited interest as he got out of the car. For a man in his position it was a fairly familiar sensation and he put on the kind of noncommittal face he used for such public occasions. Lady Gilling, oblivious as always of the outside world, strode on ahead of him. She was wearing a tweed suit of antiquated design.

Perrin met them and took them inside the building. Gilling recognized the atmosphere immediately. This was Victorian Gothic architecture at its grandest and most inconvenient. The outside was built to look like a monastery. Inside there were tortuous passages, courtyards, cold courtrooms with high ceilings, and a wretched lack of essential accommodation. It was full of dusty pomp and circumstance, symbolic ornaments and comic opera clothing—the whole familiar ponderous machinery of an antiquated professional organization.

In an alcove off one of the corridors Groom was waiting for them. He was a thin, dried-out man of Gilling's own age, with a wrinkled skin and an air of permanent scepticism. He seemed to view the whole world with a kind of weary disgust. It was the first time that Gilling had seen Groom in a wig, and the absurd headgear seemed to dehumanize his lizard face even further. He greeted them all with cold courtesy and looked at his watch.

"We have plenty of time," he said. "We shan't get through a lot today. We're late starting. There's the jury to swear in and various other formalities. After that I shall make my opening speech, which will be fairly short. Then I shall call you as my first witness. I don't suppose for a moment we shall get through all my direct examination of you before the court rises." He looked at Gilling rather in the way of a dyspeptic naturalist who has just gathered a new specimen from under a stone. Was it really of any value? Was it really worth keeping or wasn't it? Only time would tell. "I shall take the whole thing very quietly and very gradually. My first object is to build up a picture of you, of your background and your general position in life. That's very important—we want to make the jury realize in the first place how unlikely it is that you'd be negligent, and secondly how damaging an accusation of negligence could be. Then we go on to the Kincaid affair. We want to get your story clearly established in detail because there's where the cross-examination is likely to be concentrated. That leads us to the publication of Line's letter and what happened afterwards." There didn't really seem to be very much more to say. He was not a man who liked to engage in a great deal of unnecessary conversation with clients. In his experience the less a counsel did of that the better. They grew alarmed, they misunderstood things you said, they raised hypothetical issues. It was far better for them not to think about the case too much, to let him worry about the problems. The witness's task was to answer questions simply and clearly, and if possible to project a sympathetic personality to a jury at the same time. Most of them found even this more than they could manage. He said, "The great thing is to be clear and brief and let the facts speak for themselves."

Gilling understood perfectly what Groom had in mind. It was very similar to the way he spoke to patients. He was determined to be a good client and to trust his professional adviser. Nevertheless, he was nervous. The talk of cross-examination had alarmed him slightly. He did not like the thought of being subjected to hostile questioning. It was all very well for people like Groom to say that if you had a good case and told the truth you had nothing to fear, but it was not so simple as that. The issue here was whether he had treated Kincaid in the best possible way. But anybody who knew anything about medicine realized that it was full of guesses and mistakes and changes of mind and things done today which you regretted tomorrow. Anybody's treatment of any case, particularly an unsuccessful case, could be made to look careless or incompetent. No man in his senses would welcome cross-examination on the subject. If it came to that, one's whole life was worked out on the same rough and ready basis. One did the best one could. But who would like to have his life dissected by a clever counsel, intent on proving him either a rogue or a fool?

He said, "What's the opposing counsel like?"

Groom had been expecting the question. They always asked that. "Symons? Quite young. Only took silk four years ago." He spoke in a casual off-hand manner. It was his policy not to build up his opponent. "Made a name for himself in industrial cases. Rough sort of manner, but said to be very able."

In another part of the Law Courts Symons and Bradwell were waiting for Line to arrive. Symons was a thick-set man with an incipient paunch and rather irregular teeth. He had a northern accent which he was at great pains to preserve. He said, "Are the troops in good heart?"

"Yes." Bradwell spoke shortly. He had never been able to like Symons.

"Just as well. It's going to be a rough few days." Symons shook his head. "Doctors," he said wonderingly. "Can you credit it? They must be out of their minds."

Bradwell said acidly, "I'm sorry you think that. In my view this is a very serious and important case. There are vital principles——"

"Principles my arse." It amused Symons to be vulgar with Bradwell. He knew that Bradwell was theoretically in favour of a rough proletarian approach but was exasperated by it in practice. "Shall I tell you what I think about libel actions? They're like breach of promise. It's a pathological form of litigation. Either it's a financial try-on, or one of the parties is nuts—perhaps both. If both parties are honest and sane they should be able to settle out of court. Who cares a damn now what Line wrote about Gilling two years ago? Whoever read it in the first place will have forgotten it—until they see tomorrow's paper, of course." He gave a slightly menacing laugh. "What Line said about Gilling then is nothing to what I shall have to say about him now."

Bradwell said tartly, "I'm surprised you took the case on."

"Why shouldn't I? I'm a barrister—that's what I'm for. And

I'll do it as well as I can, you know that. But our client hasn't exactly made it easy for me. Admitting everything and standing on fair comment and justification. I'm not defending him, I'm prosecuting Gilling. Corruption, negligence. Practically murder."

Bradwell looked at him uneasily. There was no doubt, if one looked at it dispassionately, that it was a wild, risky action. That was one of the reasons why they had chosen Symons. For all his personal uncouthness, he was known to be a savage fighter. He said, "You'll manage it all right, I know that."

Symons guffawed. "Don't be too sure." He thought for a moment. "Really it all depends on Line. Do you think he's going to be a good witness?"

"First rate," said Bradwell. "Obviously honest, nice chap, charm, sympathetic manner. Reasonable and clear-headed. Knows what he thinks. What more could you want?"

Symons said dubiously, "Yes, all right. But—I don't know—there was something about him . . . He seemed a bit—fragile to me."

"Fragile?"

"Yes. A sort of tense, racehorse look about him." A slight note of contempt crept into his voice. "Sort of an Oxford type, if you know what I mean."

"No I don't," said Bradwell. Really, Symons was insufferable. "I suppose I'm an Oxford type myself if it comes to that."

Symons nodded meaningfully. He went on, "Do you think he's going to have the balls to stick it out?"

Bradwell felt himself on the verge of losing his temper. "This is the age of inverted snobbery," he said. "Just because he didn't have the privilege of spending his formative years in a miner's cottage at Allerton Bywater——"

He saw Symons grinning at somebody over his shoulder and turned round. Line was standing there behind him. He pulled himself together and managed a frosty smile. "Oh hallo, Line."

It was true, once it had been called to his attention, that Line had a nervous, delicate look, like a racehorse waiting for the race to start. He was cheerful but obviously tense. They talked in desultory fashion for a while, and then Line asked the inevitable question, "What about this chap Groom? What's he like?"

"Pretty good," said Symons. Suddenly he was quiet and shrewd and his voice had lost a good deal of his Northern accent. He had stopped fooling now. He was a professional talking on a professional level. "He's a very good cross-examiner. He doesn't like talking so much and he's a bit too arid to go down very sympathetically with the jury—but he's very good at asking questions." Line warmed to him. It was reassuring to be given a genuine assessment instead of platitudes. He began to feel that perhaps he had had the luck to engage a really able man. Symons went on, "With some counsel you have to warn the witness not to underrate them. With Groom, if anything, it's the other way round. He hasn't got an easy and ingratiating personality and he knows it. What he has got is a knack for making ordinary people feel about four feet high. It's not that he says anything offensive. But he has a sort of manner like a schoolmaster who's just come into a room full of boys when somebody's let off a stink bomb. Before the witness knows what he's doing, he's blushing and stammering, even though he hasn't anything to be ashamed of at all. After a while he gets indignant. He asks himself, who does this old bastard think he is? Somehow that makes him sound guiltier than ever. If Groom is really in luck the witness answers back and loses his temper. Then Groom looks back at him in astonishment. He looks at the jury. What on earth can be the matter with the witness? Why is he getting so excited?" Symons shook his head in reluctant admiration. "He does it well."

"You make him sound frightening," said Line.

"Not if you keep your head. The effect wears off. Actually Groom has one or two serious deficiencies. Juries have never liked him much—he's much better in front of a judge. And although he's very painstaking and intelligent and aggressive, his intelligence is entirely destructive. He's a spoiler. He finds it difficult to make a really positive impression. He's a dull speaker and arouses no sympathy. He failed as a politician largely because he could always see a perfect case for doing nothing." Suddenly he smiled at Line. It was a very large smile, baring a most regrettable set of teeth, and there was something reassuring about it. It was the smile of a warrior. He said cheerfully, "As a matter of fact, privately he's a nice old chap, very fond of his wife and family, and with a rather dry sense of humour. Remember that if he tries to get your goat. Remember he's just acting."

It was fairly late in the morning when Groom got up to make his opening speech. He said:

"My Lord, members of the jury, this is a very unhappy case and nobody is more conscious of it than my client Sir Thomas Gilling. The last thing he wished to do was to bring a legal action against a professional colleague for whose work he has the greatest admiration and respect. Unfortunately, as I shall show you, he has had no honourable alternative. A grievous wrong has been done to his reputation. An imputation has been made against his conduct which could have a disastrous effect upon his practice as a physician. He has been publicly accused, by implication, of jobbery, conspiracy, incompetence and negligence.

"The subject of this action is a letter which was written to a medical journal in April two years ago, and which contains the gravest reflection on my client's management of a most important case—that is to say, the treatment, in association with other doctors, of the final illness of Mr. John Kincaid. The medical journal in which this letter appears has a world-wide circulation of over one hundred thousand doctors, all of whom might reasonably draw the inference that Mr. Kincaid's death was attributable to the neglect of certain modern principles of treatment by Sir Thomas Gilling. Now Sir Thomas, as you all know, is one of the leaders of his profession and his name is world famous. It was well-known to everyone who reads the newspapers that he was in charge of Mr. Kincaid's illness. I do not have to labour to you the damage inflicted on such a man by such an accusation, made in such a place. Even more damaging is the fact that it was made, not by some nonentity, whose views could be easily disregarded, but by a man of distinction and eminence in his own right, whose views were bound to command attention. However, the libel did not stop there. Professor Line's letter became the basis for a further publication——"

Symons interrupted. "My Lord——"

The two counsel moved towards the judge and began a protracted legal argument about the admissibility of evidence regarding the article in the *Post-Telegram*. Gilling soon lost interest. He wished this preamble would soon be over. It was rather like when he had played cricket as a boy. He had been a sound, careful, methodical batsman, slow in scoring but with a good defence, and he had always been sent in first to take the edge off the bowling. He had often envied the more dashing performers who had gone in later when things were easier, to push the scoring along. He had always been nervous beforehand, as he was now. He remembered sitting in the pavilion with his pads and his gloves and that awkward triangular box between his legs to prevent him being knocked out by a ball in the testicles. He had waited glumly and mutely, not wishing to chaff with his friends, or to receive encouragement from the coach, just to be left alone with his apprehension. The captains went out to inspect the pitch, the umpires fixed the stumps. There were some manipulations of the sight-screen; cricket, like the law, was a leisurely game with complicated rules and elaborate ritual. Usually, he recollected, confidence had gradually returned to him after the first few balls. Perhaps it would be the same today.

He looked round at the court-room. Every seat was filled. Some of the journalists in the press box were scribbling away furiously, others were lounging or whispering to each other; one was drawing on a piece of paper. The public gallery was crammed. There had been a queue since early morning and a great number had been turned away. There was a perceptible atmosphere of tension and excitement in the court. A *cause célèbre*. It was unfortunate, but they had all known that it was bound to happen. The public excitement was not so much on account of him, though he was moderately famous as the court physician—or even because of Line, though his public appearances on television had made him even better known. The true celebrity was a man who was not present, but whose name and whose fate would dominate the trial: Kincaid.

Suddenly he was overcome with something like panic. How, in God's name, had he worked himself into this ghastly predicament? What doctor in his right mind would precipitate a situation in which he had to defend, in open court under hostile cross-examination, the management of the most unhappy and disastrous case of his career? Yet at no point had he been able to see the satisfactory and dignified way out. Line had never demanded anything less than capitulation. Gilling's nature, his whole life, precluded capitulation. Nor would the system of which he was an integral part admit of it. Line was not attacking him personally, he knew that, Line was attacking the system, the hierarchy. So far as Line was concerned, he was just a useful symbol, like one of those frock-coated capitalists one still saw in left-wing political cartoons. The system would fight Line to the end, through himself in this case. It was the price it exacted from him in return for all it had given him.

He looked at the rows of seats where the witnesses sat, the participants in the combat. Trimble, vast and double chinned, a symbol of fleshy Georgian grandeur. Maxfield, all brain and no heart, infinitely withdrawn from his fellow-men, inscrutably, coldly vain. John Gale, of *Medical Science*, an amiable anxious man, who believed in the importance of important people. And there, at the other end of one of the rows, was Line. He hardly knew Line. He looked at the tall, gangling figure in perplexity. He seemed such a pleasant, earnest, rather impractical man. How could he be capable of so much hate? What lay within that apparently innocuous frame that led him to court professional and financial suicide, merely to destroy another man he hardly knew?

Gilling had met him only three times. The first was at a dinner, a purely superficial social contact, the second on that occasion when Line had accosted him in the Royal Society of Medicine, the third on that last, appalling occasion which he could hardly bring himself to think of. Even on that occasion it would never have entered his head that Line would ever be able to damage his position. He had been shocked and outraged but never afraid. That was because one assumed that people followed the rules and behaved with common sense. One couldn't bargain with people who were prepared to destroy themselves.

Line must be mad, he thought; it was the only possible answer. It was a bitter thing, at the height of his career, to be struck down by a lunatic. Yet, as he looked at the other man, he found it surprisingly difficult to hate him. There was a certain grandeur about his action, a grandeur which was missing from

Trimble or Gale or Maxfield or the Minister—the grandeur which had been present in Kincaid too, in spite of his faults and his weaknesses. It was the quality of sacrifice.

His attention was drawn back to the proceedings of the court. The point of law had been decided and Groom had resumed his outline of Gilling's case. He was plodding on about the damage done by the letter and the efforts, which had proved unavailing, to get Line to withdraw it. Then suddenly he brought his speech to a close. The innings, thought Gilling, with a momentary feeling of nausea, was about to begin. The opening batsmen were due to walk to the crease. Sir Thomas suddenly wished that he had thought of going to the lavatory beforehand, but it was too late now. The usher said, "Sir Thomas Gilling."

"You are Sir Thomas Gilling?"

"Yes."

"You are senior physician at St. Vincent's Hospital?"

"Yes."

"Sir Thomas, how old are you?"

"Sixty-two."

"How long have you been qualified as a doctor?"

"Thirty-nine years."

"And you have been in continuous practice in medicine ever since?"

"Yes."

Groom then went through his career laboriously by question and answer. He took him from his early years at Graftondale Hospital, detailing the distinctions, the prizes, the examinations successfully passed, the move to London as a lecturer in medicine at St. Vincent's, the war service. It was an impressive record and it gave Gilling confidence to go through it. He began to feel more at ease. As a climax to this Groom began a cumulative recital of his offices and decorations.

"You are the senior physician to the Royal Household?"

"Yes."

"And a Fellow of the Royal Society?"

"Yes."

"And Vice-President of the Royal College of Physicians?"

"Yes."

"For the benefit of the jury, could you briefly distinguish between the Royal College and the Royal Society."

"The Royal College of Physicians is the professional body which represents consultant physicians, in the same way as the Royal College of Surgeons represents the surgeons. The Royal Society is a purely scientific body, founded by Charles II for the encouragement of science. Any scientist can be elected to the Royal Society if he is thought to have carried out original work of the standard which the Society accepts as sufficiently distinguished. Scientific work within medicine will qualify a man for election in the same way as research in physics, chemistry, biology, and so forth."

"So you were elected on the basis of scientific research?"

"Well, there isn't any other basis for election."

"I see. Now are you the author of a number of scientific papers?"

"Yes."

"These have appeared in important medical journals?"

"Yes."

"I have copies of these available for the jury. According to my information, during the last ten years you have published some sixteen original papers."

"Yes."

"The most recent being in *Medical Science* of three months ago?"

"Yes."

"Do you teach students, both undergraduates and postgraduates?"

"Yes."

"Are you an examiner for the Royal College of Physicians?"

"Yes."

"Are you a member of the Medical Research Council?"

"Yes."

"Would it be possible for you to carry out all these activities—Vice-President of the Royal College of Physicians, Fellow of the Royal Society, teaching, examining, sitting on the Medical Research Council, if you were not very well informed about the most recent advances in medicine?"

"Obviously not."

"Would it be possible for you to treat your many distinguished patients adequately if you used out-of-date methods?"

"No."

"Sir Thomas, has anybody ever, until now, accused you of negligence?"

"Never."

"Has anyone, until Professor Line's letter was published, accused you of being reactionary or behind the times?"

"Never to my knowledge."

"What was your reaction when you first read Professor Line's published letter?"

"I was dumbfounded. I could hardly believe my eyes."

It was true enough. That had indeed been the most salient feature of the case from his point of view—the unreality of it. Medical men on his level, and on Line's level, simply didn't attack each other in public. It was a violation of the code, the great unwritten law that the profession, whatever squabbles might occur within it, always presented an unbroken front to the general public. Quite apart from whether he was right or wrong (and he believed implicitly that he was right) he knew that he would carry with him the support of the profession against Line, who had committed this unforgivable offence. The code might be restrictive, it might conceal inefficiency and jobbery and nepotism, but it was the shield of the profession. Anyone, he felt sure, from Maxfield himself down to the most junior general practitioner or school medical officer, would agree with him about that. Lay interference was the one evil which could never be tolerated. Whatever the cost, the profession must stick together.

Line knew the law and he had deliberately violated it, just as he had deliberately violated the law about personal publicity by his television appearances. He had got away with it then, largely because he was important and celebrated and nobody wanted an unnecessary fuss. Perhaps his success in ignoring the code in one respect had made him bold in another; or perhaps he was so unbalanced that he did not realize the implications of what he was doing. It was impossible to tell. Only one thing was certain about Line, Gilling thought—the death wish, the impulse to self-destruction. He would go down, eventually, if not this time then on some other occasion. He was born to melodrama and disaster. The only question was—who would he drag along with him?

He went on answering Groom's questions mechanically—a modest, successful man, giving under gentle pressure an account of an impressively successful career. He was fairly confident that he was making the right sort of impression on the court. He was a person of eminence, yet without pomposity or pretension, obviously baffled at having been involved in an affair utterly outside his experience. The shorthand-writer scribbled, the journalists yawned, the court seemed to be going quietly to sleep. There was no excitement in this—the cross-examination was what they were waiting for. The inside story of the death of Kincaid. Finally, in the middle of his examination, the clock struck five, and the judge adjourned the hearing.

There was a crowd outside as he left. He heard the click of cameras as he and Charlotte made for the car. As they drove away she said, "You were good—very good." He nodded his thanks but he was only mildly encouraged. It had been nothing today. He felt like an actor who had given an adequate performance in an unimportant early scene of a play—the real test would come later. When they got home his wife had to take the dogs out on the common for an hour while he sipped a glass of sherry and waited for her to return. When she returned they had dinner and talked in a desultory fashion about the case, about the judge and Groom and the way things had gone. Then, soon after dinner, she went up to bed. He was left in his armchair with the *Evening Standard*. There was a certain amount about the case—mostly excerpts from the earlier part of Groom's speech, which was all they had been able to report before the paper went to press. He was surprised at the odd things they reported—many of them, to his eye, were not important at all, while the really vital matters in the case seemed to be hardly mentioned. Also he was confused by their habit of putting what they regarded as the most interesting pieces of news first, instead of working through it in the proper sequence, as *The Times* would have done. It all seemed quite unlike what had really happened in court. But then, he thought, the account of his life and career which had been given in the court, though true enough from the point of view of the facts, had borne very little relationship to what really happened. A polite, respectful biographical note, all very simple and organized, a logical sequence of events, in which he always behaved in a reasonable, honourable, competent fashion. There was no agony and no conflict. It was only when you heard your own life detailed in that fashion in court that you realized what nonsense most biographies were. What did any of them know of his life?

Chapter 2

THERE WAS that episode of the boots, for instance.

It had happened a long time ago, when he was a schoolboy at Thorpe Hall. By rights he should never have been at Thorpe Hall, his parents were the wrong parents, they were of the wrong class with the wrong income. His father was a master craftsman in the Graftondale Copper Works, a conscientious, quiet, unambitious man, much respected by his employers and workmates. He was the type of man you thought of if you claimed that British craftsmanship was the best and most reliable in the world. He was loyal and irreplaceable and consequently he earned what in those days was the unusually high wage of five pounds a week, six with overtime. He lived in a council house, smoked four ounces of Erinmore Flake every week, bought a new suit at the Co-op every two years, and was a staunch socialist and trade unionist. He made no secret of his political views, which indeed were regarded sympathetically by his employers. They reasoned, wisely enough, that, if you had to have a trade union movement, sound reliable fellows like Ted Gilling were the right people to be in charge of it. He read a good deal out of the public library. He had no secondary education, but he had educated himself industriously and knew the works of Marx and Kropotkin and Tom Paine and H. G. Wells, and Sidney and Beatrice Webb. He was a great believer in W.E.A. evening classes. He marched behind banners every May Day and had once stood, unsuccessfully, for a seat on the Town Council. He did not believe in privilege or Christianity or private education. All his beliefs were held reasonably and placidly, without passion, and he sympathized with those who disagreed with him. He recognized their point of view and thought that they were just as likely to be right as he was himself. He recognized that he was not a person of any outstanding ability or importance and never would be. It did not upset him in the least.

Mrs. Gilling was a plump woman of dynamic energy, who cared less than nothing for Marx or Kropotkin or socialism or social welfare or the inevitable assumption of power by the working class. Nor did she take her husband's beliefs at all seriously. To her, socialism was just another crank sect, like spiritualism or vegetarianism or the Seventh Day Adventists. If Ted cared to amuse himself with it, she was tolerant, but it had nothing to do with life or the family. Certainly it had nothing to do with the obsession of her life—her only son Tom. From his earliest childhood she took complete charge of Tom, as if his father, like some amiable well-meaning drone, had performed his sole duty with the act of fertilization—the rest was up to her.

Mrs. Gilling had no principles at all except a rough family morality which she referred to vaguely as "Doing the right thing." She also believed that if you didn't look after yourself nobody else would look after you, and regarded her husband's life as an illustration of that principle. Her job was not to look after the world, but to look after her beloved Tom. Tom must not dedicate his life to an equality that nobody believed in but him, a movement that wanted to keep brilliant boys like Tom down to the level of ordinary common or garden lads on street corners. It was her job to give him a start in life.

Her idea of a start was Thorpe Hall, a good, undistinguished private school not far from where he lived. It wasn't as grand as a public school, but it was a long way better than a council school, somewhere about grammar school level, and it took day boys. When Tom was ten years old she went to the headmaster of Thorpe Hall and pleaded with him. She had not the money to pay the full fees but she would pay everything she could lay her hands on. She would go on paying after he had left until she had discharged her debt. She would do anything.

Fortunately, Tom was unusually intelligent, and the headmaster was prepared to give him a chance. But even so there were problems. Mrs. Gilling had no sooner come to an arrangement about the fees which would enable them to manage, than she was confronted with the nightmare of the school uniform. It was impossible for her to afford the complete outfit, even if she robbed herself of food and clothing to do it. She could not buy the clothes from the official tailors. She did her best in cut-price shops to buy him something vaguely resembling the uniform, enough to pass the headmaster. But it looked undeniably cheaper and shoddier than the clothes of the other boys. His suit was thick and coarse and the boys laughed at him. That was bad enough, but it was just tolerable. Far worse were the boots. All the boys had to have one pair of black regulation boots. His mother had gone to a second-hand shop she patronized and here she had, to her delight, found a magnificent pair of black boots, just his size, of top-grade calf, with slightly pointed toes and little hooks for the laces. They had been specially made for some rich man who had died and had never worn them. At least, she thought, one article of clothing would be not only up to standard but actually better than that of the other boys. But when Tom wore them, he found to his dismay that to the other boys, all clad in their coarse, square-toed regulation black boots, his magnificent boots were the most ridiculous feature of his attire. They could not control their derision. His suit was forgotten. There had never been anything in the school so absurd, so contemptible as Gilling's pointed boots.

He stood it for as long as he could. He knew his mother's struggles and sufferings, he knew how proud she was of getting the boots, but he was only ten years old—after three days he broke. His parents listened to him as he described, through his tears, the humiliation to which he had been subjected. His father patted him on the back, consoled him, dried his eyes, and suggested a visit to the headmaster—the headmaster was a reasonable man, he would surely understand, he would tell the other boys to stop tormenting Tom. Tom listened to the kind, gentle, ineffectual voice. He was very young but he was already wise enough to know that his father's proposal was absurd and impractical and would only make things worse. He looked to his mother. She sat in silence, her lips contracted in a thin, determined line. He could see she had already discounted his father's suggestions. He knew she recognized, as he was always to do throughout life afterwards, that you had to do your fighting in terms of the situation as it was. It was no use complaining about cruelty and injustice. Protests to headmasters were like marches behind banners on May Day, they were gestures, nothing more. She was not looking at Tom. She was looking at a chair just behind him. It was a family treasure, a light, delicate mahogany piece with carved legs, left to her by an aunt years ago, and generally regarded as rather too precious to sit on. It was the only piece of valuable furniture in the house. After a while she walked out of the house without looking at Tom or her husband, and without speaking to either of them. The next day Tom found a rough, square-toed pair of regulation boots at the foot of his bed. When he came down for breakfast his aunt's chair was missing from the dining-room.

He started to speak but his mother interrupted him.

"Eat your breakfast," she said roughly. Then she smiled. When she smiled at him, she looked curiously young and shy, almost like a girl with her lover. It was a way in which he had never seen her smile at his father. It was almost as if there was a conspiracy between the two of them against the rest of the world. "The trouble with those boots, they were too good," she said. "It's even worse than not being good enough." As he opened his mouth to speak again, she said, "And watch out for that bacon fat."

It has been said that all the really important things are learnt before the age of sixteen. Gilling was an eager, ambitious boy. He was not rebellious by nature, he did not resent the world or desire to change it as his father did; he simply wished to learn how it worked. He knew that he was cleverer than the other boys and that he could beat most of them, given the chance. But this early episode taught him something else. Cleverness was not enough. To be exceptional was dangerous. The mob was always on the lookout for the nonconformist, to deride and persecute him. A man who wished to survive must at all costs, in all circumstances, wear the right kind of boots.

From that time onwards he took particular care to efface himself and draw as little attention as possible to his particular talents. He began to find life at Thorpe Hall tolerable, without ever being actually enjoyable. Always conscious of his poverty, sensitive about his Yorkshire accent and cheap clothes, he kept to himself and made few friends. His task, as he saw it, was not to enjoy himself but to work hard and justify his mother's sacrifices and her faith in him. As a day boy, he was not so dependent on the social life of the school as he would have been as a boarder. He worked hard, he had a quick mind and an outstanding memory. Soon the masters began to regard him as something out of the ordinary. He was strong physically and determined enough to stand up against the other boys, so that eventually they grew tired of trying to torment him and treated him with a certain aloof respect. He asked nothing much of them except that they should leave him alone. He took a series of prizes. He seemed to have a natural bent for science, and, on the suggestion of his headmaster, decided to go in for medicine. The medical school at Graftondale was world-famous. There were a number of scholarships available and he obtained one with ease.

The first year at medical school was just like school, only with more freedom. He went in each day and attended lectures in the same way that he had attended his school classes. He worked hard in the evenings. He knew that there was a social life at the university, enjoyed by the rich boys with their sports cars and the idlers who were just playing at being students with no chance of qualifying. Like most boys of his age, he had a vague dream in his head of a gay student life full of girls and dances, but he knew it was not for him. He had neither the money nor the clothes, and he was shy with girls.

In the second year the work was harder and more serious. Now the students were beginning to fall into groups. The wholly stupid or lazy or frivolous had dropped out. The rest of them were spread out like the field in a cross-country race ten minutes after the start. He was well identified with a group of students at the front of the field, with marks in terminal examinations always in the sixties and seventies. He was already marked as a prize performer and treated with interest and deference by the professors. It was no surprise to him. He was used by now to being treated as a prize pupil.

At home his mother made over to him the front room, the family shrine where nobody ever sat except when company came to tea. Every evening she brought him a bowl of tinned fruit and a glass of milk. She sat, as she had always done, on the edge of a chair, and talked to him for exactly a quarter of an hour;

and then went to bed and left him to his work. His father was quietly complimentary on his industry. He was happy to have a studious boy.

All the students lived for the day when they should pass the second M.B. and begin to walk the wards of the hospital. There was a big failure rate in the second M.B. and the hundred students who started the course were now down to about thirty. But a few others joined who had been to Oxford or Cambridge for the earlier part of their course and came on to Graftondale to do their clinical work. Gilling did not expect much competition from them, but to his surprise he found that he had underrated the opposition. In the clinical course hard work and a good memory, though still important, had to be supplemented by other, less tangible qualities such as clinical instinct and common sense. One had to learn manual dexterity and how to handle patients. Credit was given for sympathy, an easy manner, and a gift for self-expression. One was dealing with human material, which followed few rules and was baffling in its variability. The capacity to improvise and to face unexpected situations without jumping to conclusions, and yet to make quick decisions when necessary, were all of importance. It was easy for him to learn to be observant and methodical, but the more subtle attributes were difficult to acquire. And here he found that one of the Cambridge men, Arthur Benson-Grey, was at least his equal. Benson-Grey was a tall, soft-spoken boy, with a ready smile and an easy manner. From the first moment of appearing in the hospital he appeared to act on the assumption that it was no more than a matter of time before he became a member of the consultant staff. He had a few friends, but on the whole he preserved a distance between himself and most of the students of the year. On the other hand, he was on easy terms with the consultants. He appeared to regard them as human beings of his own world, but of a different generation. To almost all the other students they were Olympian figures of unexampled magnificence, grandees. As they drove up in the morning in their Rolls-Royces in their black suits with pin-striped trousers and homburg hats, pulling off their pigskin gloves and handing them to the porters, the students sat on benches outside the front door and gaped at them in admiration. This was where you might possibly end, if all went well. This would make it all worth while, the slogging, the midnight oil, the incessant examinations, the poverty, the years of sycophancy and servitude. Of course the chances weren't very high. For perhaps one in a hundred at the age of thirty-five to forty, this rich prize might at last be made available. But one could dream at any rate. After all, it had to happen to someone. And even the senior surgeon himself, the great Lord Roderick, had been poor once.

Not that it was easy to imagine Lord Roderick as poor or struggling. For if the others behaved like lords, Roderick was at least an archduke, so utterly intimidating that when he taught in the wards all but the most brash and self-confident students shuffled desperately to the back, for fear his gaze might alight on them and they would be forced, tongue-tied, into the lime-light.

Benson-Grey was one of the few students who could even make a semblance of being at ease with Roderick. To Gilling it was obvious from the start that he, with his awkward manners and ill-cut clothes, stood no chance of making an impression on the great man. It was a disappointment to his hopes. Surgery, under the domination of Roderick, was incomparably the most fashionable subject at Graftondale; in the 1920s the great surgical romance was at its height, the ritual and the rubber gloves were still relatively new, the ecclesiastical atmosphere of the operating room dominated the hospital. In twenty years the romance would turn into a tawdry melodrama, and in thirty it would be transformed into a technical episode in the course of medical treatment. But in 1924 the heart of every clever medical student turned towards it. For this supreme distinction Gilling knew that he had no chance. He could tell by the way Roderick looked at him that he had been rejected in spite of his academic performance. Benson-Grey had, equally obviously, been accepted. If he wished to succeed it was necessary to turn his attention to the less romantic physicians.

Here, in any case, he felt more at ease. It was a more placid, intellectual discipline, and more suited to his temperament. As for the senior physician, Christie, he was so different from Roderick that it almost seemed that the Board of Governors of the hospital must have chosen him for the purposes of contrast.

He was small and neat. His face was pink and babyish, his feet were tiny, and he wore shiny pointed shoes. He tripped along the corridors with small careful strides. His hair was worn long and brushed back in little greying wings behind his ears. This, and a pair of large horn-rimmed glasses, gave him a perceptibly owl-like look. He smiled a great deal and was noted for making oblique, malicious remarks about other members of the staff. He had a curious manner with the students—intimate and mocking, but sometimes quite unexpectedly cruel. He took a delight in embarrassing them in front of the patients. And yet he was a brilliant teacher. He had the knack of generating interest and excitement, of involving his audience in the subject he was teaching.

Gilling, as one of the brighter students, attracted his attention from the beginning. On one occasion when Gilling had expressed scepticism about the meaning of a symptom, he said, with a sardonic smile, "A sceptic in our midst—one T. Gilling. I take it your name must be Thomas?"

"As a matter of fact it is, sir."

There was a titter of laughter from the class. Christie was delighted. "All right, then, doubting Thomas, come along and see if I'm telling the truth."

Gilling came to the front of the crowd of students and stood beside the bed while Christie demonstrated some X-rays to him. Each time he drove home a point, he jogged Gilling's arm playfully with his fist. At the end he said, "Very well, Thomas, go and sin no more." He spoke amiably, delighted obviously with his little joke. When Gilling smiled back he received another kindly little punch on the arm. It was plain that he had made some sort of impression.

Afterwards one of the older students called Dixon grinned at him and said, "You made quite a hit with Little Jesus."

"Is that what you call him?"

"Didn't you know?"

Gilling shook his head. "What's he like?"

Dixon guffawed, "Padlock your flybuttons and you haven't a thing to worry about."

Dixon's innuendo about Christie did no more than confirm his own suspicions. His years at Thorpe Hall had given him a certain introductory experience of homosexuality and he was neither shocked nor frightened by it. A penniless, ambitious young man cannot afford to be too outraged by the behaviour of his elders and betters. Gilling found from inquiries among the older students that it was Christie's practice to pick out in each year one or two students whom he treated as his favourites. They were spoken to by their Christian names, attention was directed constantly towards them, sometimes they were praised, sometimes mocked, sometimes subjected to little pinpricks of humiliation. They were occasionally, if Christie were in a bad mood, made to look ridiculous in front of the patients and other students. One simply had to put up with this, if one was to retain favour. As time went on, Gilling would often find himself out in front of the class, with Christie's hand on his arm, being asked impossible and perhaps absurd questions. When he was unable to answer, Christie would wink at the patient.

"This is my cleverest student. He should know the answer to your trouble. Little doubting Thomas, we call him. Well, Thomas?" He would then pinch Gilling's arm. Sometimes gently, sometimes rather more painfully.

"Well, it's rather difficult——"

"Difficult problems are made to be solved, Thomas." A little punch on the arm. "Nothing venture, nothing gain."

"Well—I suppose it could be disseminated sclerosis——"

"It could be, Thomas—but it isn't, is it, Mr. Hargreaves?" Mr. Hargreaves, the patient, would usually grin delightedly. If you are a patient in a general ward, almost any entertainment is better than none. Christie would punch Gilling's arm again. "I'm going to punch you until you pull your wits together. Now Thomas . . ."

Gilling had to learn to control his irritation. This was one of the things he was going to have to put up with, just as Benson-Grey, searching for favour on the surgical side, had to put up with Roderick's sudden rages and interminable reminiscences about his own past triumphs. For, after all, the prize they were after was a very great one. Out of those in the year who would certainly qualify, less than half would be given jobs at the Royal. Two of these jobs were regarded as the first step to eventual distinction—the house surgeon to the senior surgeon and the house physician to the senior physician. Roderick's job and Christie's job. It was worth while putting up with a certain amount of spitefulness or megalomania to land one of these.

Gilling had no doubts that he would qualify when the time came, and qualify with honours. He didn't think he would get all the prizes, but he hoped to share most of them with Benson-Grey. Far more important was to become Christie's house physician. In the last year before his Final Examination he was always there when Christie taught, he did extra work on Christie's wards or in his out-patients. Everyone knew it and the other students laughed at him for creeping to Little Jesus. He didn't mind very much. In any case their laughter was muted by the fact that most of them had picked some other physician or surgeon with whom they were desperately currying favour. The consultants knew about it too. It was a yearly ritual which pleased and flattered them. Christie's teasing reached an almost excruciating level. Gilling began to feel that everything was going to be all right.

It was at that moment that his position was suddenly threatened by the general strike. It took Gilling completely by surprise. It was true that he had heard his father talking for months about the economic condition of the country and the war being waged by the Conservatives on the standard of living of the working class, but then he had heard this kind of talk all his life and neither he nor his mother attached any importance to it. His father's high, academic voice prophesying the doom of capitalist civilization had always been a sort of background music in the house, like a radio left on, or the rumbling of traffic on the road outside. It was taken for granted by Gilling and his mother that nothing that his father prophesied would ever happen. They regarded themselves as the practical ones, and they believed in leaving politics to politicians. "You and your old socialism," Mrs. Gilling would say affectionately. "Sit down and have your dinner. Socialism won't get the Yorkshire pudding out of the oven."

It was a shock when the national crisis which Mr. Gilling had predicted actually came to pass. At first Gilling did not realize its significance. He had little interest in politics. Why were those miners so wrong-headed? Why couldn't they get down to work day and night, slogging away like he did, instead of constantly making trouble?

When the strike became general, he was, like most of the medical students, divided between indignation at the impudence of the unions and a feeling of excitement that something extraordinary was happening. The breakdown in services was rather a lark. A special squad of students was being formed to drive coal lorries and buses. Gilling was tempted to join for the fun of it. When he came home and told his parents about it he was appalled at his father's reaction. It was, so far as he could remember, the first time he had ever seen him angry. His hands and lips trembled.

"These men are fighting for their lives. This is the only weapon they have." He struggled for words to express his emotion; there was something infinitely pathetic in the fact that his real agony and indignation could only express itself in the clichés of his faith. "They've been ground down by the bosses——"

"Come on, Dad," said Mrs. Gilling, with an elephantine attempt at tact. "Try grinding down some apple tart."

Gilling had seen him silenced in this way a hundred times before. Ordinarily he would accept it with good humour and carry on with his meal. But this time he shook his head and pushed the food away. "These are men who work day and night underground. Now the bosses want to give them less than they can live on. And there are others on the dole. Thirty bob a week. All they want is to live like human beings. Men who gave their lives in the pit——"

Gilling could not resist the opportunity to score. "Not the bus drivers surely," he said. Then he suddenly felt ashamed. Who was he to be flippant about his father's beliefs? Who was he to score debating points because of the better education which his parents had given him? His father's bookish socialism and public library economics might be absurd and unsophisticated but they were all he had—all he had been given the chance to acquire.

He was about to apologize but his father spoke first. "Young lads like you don't understand," he said, shaking his head sadly. Inevitably, like an incantation, the left-wing cliché sprang to his lips. "It's a question of working-class solidarity." He looked at Gilling earnestly. "I'm not a clever man and I can't argue with you. But I'd like you to try to respect my point of view. I wouldn't want to think of my son as a scab."

Then to everyone's astonishment, possibly her own, Mrs. Gilling said, "Your dad's right, Tom." Tom looked at her aghast. He could never remember her having agreed with his father before. As if it required urgent explanation she said, "There might be trouble. You might get hurt."

Gilling shrugged his agreement. He was not really very interested in the strike one way or another, and he was fond of his parents. He would not join the volunteers. But unfortunately when he arrived at the Royal he found that it was not so easy. Christie was holding one of his morning rounds. After half an hour he looked at his watch. "Well, I must be careful not to keep you gentlemen much longer. I believe the dean is taking the names of volunteers to keep up services during the strike, and I imagine you all want to enrol." His little mouth creased whimsically. "We shall enjoy seeing our Thomas dressed as a coal-heaver."

Gilling flushed. He felt a trap closing in on him. There was, of course, no compulsion at all to take part; there was no doubt that the dignified, independent thing to do would be to say quietly to Christie that he had decided not to join the emergency force. If the improving books were right, Christie, though perhaps a little angry at first, would later on come to respect Gilling for his independence and his principles. Unfortunately Gilling's experience, restricted though it was, had already taught him that all this talk about respecting independent opinions was so much nonsense. Men in positions of power liked young men to agree with them. They did not regard such agreement as sycophancy, as it mostly was, but as a sign of good sense. About Christie, Gilling had no illusions at all. Like most of the consultants, Christie wanted servility. And he would get it, if not from Gilling, from someone else. The ambitious young men were reconciled to this. They did not like it, but they would serve as long as they had to. This was just as long as it took for them in their turn to become consultants. Then, at last, they might safely turn on their patrons.

It would have been easier for him, thought Gilling, if it had been a genuine matter of principle. But the truth was that he cared nothing for the strike. If he defied Christie he might well damage his own career, perhaps seriously. Could he be expected to do this simply to avoid hurting his father's feelings? It really seemed an unreasonable sacrifice to ask. He thought of his mother and he was confident of the advice she would give him. For, after all, her interests were concerned too. If he damaged his career he would break her heart. She had given her life to make him a success and what, when all was said and done, had his father done? His father had not slaved for him to go to Thorpe Hall. His father had wanted him to go to the council school and end up as a sanitary inspector. If he owed anything to anyone, his mother must come first. He took his case confidently to this supreme court of appeal and knew immediately what the verdict must be. He remained silent.

Gilling rode the buses as a conductor, taking the fares, without telling his parents. Unfortunately, a few days later, there was a scuffle with some pickets. Gilling was too busy to notice the newspaper photographer in the watching crowd. When he went home that evening he found his father sitting alone in the dining-room in his old alpaca jacket, reading his paper.

Gilling said, "Where's Mother?"

"She's gone to see your Auntie May. She'll be back in an hour or so. Your supper's in the oven."

There was something strange about his father's tone. As Gilling passed by him he looked over his father's shoulder at the head-lines of the paper. It said, "Fight at bus station. Clash between students and strike picket." Underneath was his own photograph dabbing blood from his face and looking, he was taken aback to notice, distinctly pleased with himself. It was, he knew, a true reflection of his mood at the time. Every man has a secret fear in his heart—that he may be afraid of violence when it comes. When it does come and he finds he can face it, his main emotion is one of pride and relief. That is what showed in Gilling's face. But there was no way of explaining this to his father.

He said, "I didn't want to go, but I couldn't get out of it." His father said nothing. The silence was more oppressive than a storm of abuse. "I didn't want to go on the buses but I didn't have any option. I know how you feel and I'm sorry."

His father spoke as if he had not heard him. He had a curious remote way of speaking at times, as if he was not addressing a single person at all but some distant audience. "I've always been against violence of any kind. But violence against the struggling masses—against the working class—it's your own class, you know, Tom, whether you like it or not."

He would apologize, but this he wouldn't accept. He said forcibly, "It isn't. I'm myself, not just a member of one of your classes. You tell me you're all against the hereditary system. Well all right then, I don't want to inherit your class or your views. Why should I?" His father remained silent. Gilling ended rather weakly, "And anyway, I wasn't violent, they attacked us."

"You attacked them as soon as you stepped on those buses. You attacked their livelihood."

"I told you—I couldn't help it. Everyone was doing it. If I'd refused, they'd have had a black mark against me. I might never have got a job at the Royal. They'd have thought I was a Bolshie."

His father said bitterly, "It wouldn't have been so bad if you'd done it because you disagreed with me. Better that than just for a house job at the Royal."

He was outraged. What did his father know about the Royal? Or about success? If it had been left to his father he would have been a nobody. He said, with contempt in his voice, "God, you don't understand a thing, do you? *Just* a house job at the Royal! This is the key point of my career. If I miss my footing now it could take me years to get back. I might never get back."

His father considered his words with a calm dignity that made him ashamed of himself. Eventually he said, "Yes, I know. I understand all about that. And your mother would agree with you." You could see working in him his inherent reasonableness, that fatal capacity to see his opponent's view which had rendered him ineffectual all his life. "Your mother's done a lot for you, and you followed her way and I've never interfered. But just this once I would like to say something—before she comes back. Then you can forget it and never mention it to her, because it would only upset her and it wouldn't do any good." He seemed to be working out in his own mind, as he went along, something very important to him. "Your mother's a very fine and good woman, Tom. She's got tremendous energy and drive and she thinks the world of you. But she's not always right, remember. Because people are strong and self-confident and take charge of things, it doesn't mean they're right. She thinks about you and your career and getting on, and all that's very fine, but there's another side of life." His eyes became dreamy. He was looking at far horizons. "There's something to be said for living for a cause——" He added with dignity, "I've never done anything important, but I've had great comfort from the feeling that I was part of something bigger than myself."

"It didn't show much gratitude, did it, this cause of yours? I remember you telling me that you knew all the big labour leaders when they were young and nobody cared tuppence for them. Where are they now? They're sitting in Parliament, most of them—or Transport House. They never come here. They never found a safe seat for you—not even on the Council, never mind the bloody House of Commons——"

"Please don't talk like that." There was disgust in his father's voice. "You make me ashamed."

Gilling said defiantly, "It's true and you know it."

"They're big men now. What time have they to bother with me?"

"The working class is the same as any other class," said Gilling. "Only the big men count."

"And you want to be one of the big men?"

"I'll do my best."

Mr. Gilling shook his head sadly, "You'll destroy yourself." He spoke with great earnestness. "You're a clever boy, Tom, but you're not big enough; you're not rough enough. I've known big men in my time and I know you. It's not the right way for you."

To Gilling it was the final insult, the final blow to his pride and self-confidence. He no longer wanted to argue. He had no thought but to hit back. "What do *you* know about the right way?" He ran his eyes down the lined submissive face, the alpaca jacket, the cheap grey flannel trousers. "Look at yourself in the mirror."

As he stormed out of the house he knew that he had insulted his father irreparably. He had been provoked, he insisted to himself, yet in his heart he was ashamed. On an impulse he turned back and walked into the room where his father was. "I'm sorry, Dad, I never meant that——" Then he saw the tears on his father's face and bolted out of the door.

Next day Christie said, looking at his lip, "Violence, Thomas! I wouldn't have believed it of you." He turned jocularly to the other students. "We must be very polite to Thomas in future or he'll give us a punch on the jaw, like those strikers."

Now Gilling knew that he was certain of the job.

Chapter 3

"Dear boy," said Christie, looking at him thoughtfully, "I really think it's time we did something about your appearance."

Gilling blushed vividly. For the moment he hated Christie more than any man on earth. But he forced himself to smile. "Sir?"

"You're really not at all bad-looking, you know. But that rather unkempt student style doesn't really suit you, especially now you are qualified. I can't have my houseman looking like an undergraduate, now can I?" He paused for a moment at the front door to put on his overcoat. "Are you frightfully busy just now?"

"Nothing that couldn't wait." This was the correct answer. It showed that you were industrious, yet you were always able to make yourself available for the boss.

"Then come along with me to my tailor. One should always take the advice of a consultant on these matters."

Gilling was seized with something like panic. He had exactly four pounds ten shillings in the world. He had a terror of falling into debt. Christie's tailor would certainly be frightfully expensive. The other alternative was that Christie was intending to pay for his clothes—an even more disastrous obligation. He was on the point of stammering something which might give serious offence, but fortunately he kept his head.

Christie chuckled. "At times, Thomas, you hardly need to speak, your face is so expressive. I'm quite aware that you're not a rich man. But you'll be looking after my private patients and I can assure you that before Hamilton has finished cutting and fitting the suit you'll have enough to pay for it. It's just a question of controlling your expenditure on beer and boxing lessons." Since the strike episode Christie had kept up the fiction that Gilling was a keen amateur pugilist. It was becoming rather boring. "I can assure you that you'll find this a useful investment."

Gilling tried to remind himself that Christie was trying to be kind. He had to fight to remember this rather often. Christie had a curious way of being able to tarnish even his most generous gestures. Gilling was also embarrassed at the thought of the reaction of Christie's tailor to his present clothes. But he need not have worried. He found himself treated with the greatest of deference.

When the new suit finally arrived, Gilling was astonished at the difference it made, not only to his appearance but to his confidence. The comment it aroused in others was flattering but rather disconcerting, since it made him realize how unsatisfactory his appearance must have been before. He saw Benson-Grey looking at him with a kind of amused respect, as if for the first time he was beginning to realize that Gilling had potentialities beyond those of a mere bookworm. And gradually he found himself thinking that Benson-Grey was not quite such a snob as he had previously imagined. The two young men became drawn to each other by a kind of mutual curiosity. They were thrown into contact, since they had adjacent rooms and life for the housemen at the Royal allowed of very little time away from the hospital. The housemen lived a military kind of life, working all day and often at night, taking their recreation in visits to the hospital pub or in beer parties to which sometimes nurses were invited and sometimes not. They were very happy in this confined life. It was an enormous thrill to be qualified at last, to work "in the House," take charge of patients, to be able to patronize the students and flirt with the nurses; to be, in short, part of the élite. A closed communal life was entirely satisfying for the first six months or a year that they lived in hospital, and even longer for some of them. Living together in this way, they got to know each other very well. It occurred to Gilling, almost as a matter of surprise, after several months, that Benson-Grey was his closest friend.

This was only one of the factors which increased his confidence. Everything seemed to be going well. Christie had been as good as his word about the private patients and paid Gilling two guineas each for helping him to look after them—twice the going rate. Shortly Gilling found himself, by his modest standards, comfortably off. His suit and other clothes cost him less than he had feared and he was actually accumulating money in the bank. He counted his savings with pride and delight.

These first fruits of success augmented his determination to succeed. On the occasions when he was able to go home for an evening, he would sit in front of the fire, pouring into the eager ears of his mother stories of the hospital and the consultants, of Roderick and Christie and Benson-Grey. She never got tired of hearing even the smallest details of his life. She savoured each petty triumph, she grudged him nothing, she admired his new clothes and refused to take his money when he offered it. She never asked him to bring Benson-Grey home, because she knew it would be unsuitable and embarrassing—after all you couldn't invite a man like that to a council house. She wanted nothing more than to hear about it all. It was the only reward she asked for a lifetime of sacrifice.

Mr. Gilling sat at the other side of the chimneypiece, in his red plush chair, wearing his alpaca jacket. He said nothing. Sometimes he would read the paper, sometimes he would gaze sadly into the fire as if searching there for another and braver world. The general strike had failed, the Movement was crippled, his son and his wife had been right to support the big battalions. In his work, in his house, in his whole life, he was nothing, a man made to be ignored and abandoned. Gilling would occasionally pause in his narrative and look at his father—in these moments he was uneasily aware that he had killed something in this gentle, impractical man. His father had asked him only one thing in his whole life and it had been refused. Well, he told himself, it was inevitable. It would be hypocrisy to say that he regretted it. He would do it again. But it gave him a pang nevertheless. It was also another force which made it necessary for him to fight with everything he had for his own success. It was bad enough to break your father—it was inexcusable to break him for nothing.

After a while Gilling began to feel that he misjudged Christie. It became apparent that for all his peculiarities, he was a kind and generous man, who asked little from Gilling in return for what he did except thanks and appreciation. Gilling realized for the first time how hard it was to dislike a man who obviously liked and believed in you. Their relationship became more relaxed, and Gilling found that Christie was an intelligent and capable physician with a natural gift for teaching which did not stop at medicine. He seemed to take pleasure in enlarging Gilling's general education. Every two weeks or so he would invite Gilling to dinner, either to his house or to a restaurant. Christie's house was a huge stone edifice which had been left to him by his father, a prosperous iron-founder. He lived there in some state, in a household presided over by a gaunt tight-lipped housekeeper. It amused him to lay on elaborate dinners for himself and Gilling, and during the course of these Gilling learnt a great deal which he stored industriously in his memory.

Christie taught him first about food and wine; how to eat asparagus and oysters and caviare; how to order a bottle of claret, how to taste it, and when to send it back. He taught him the correct temperatures for serving it, not to heat the bottle in front of the fire, nor to chill a good Rhine wine in the ice compartment of the refrigerator. He taught him how to intimidate wine waiters, and not to carry a little card in his pocket to memorize vintages. He taught Gilling about period furniture, how to recognize Chippendale and Sheraton and Hepplewhite, that oak was at the present out of fashion, and that French polishing was considered vulgar. He discoursed on domestic architecture, a subject of which Gilling, in common with most of the inhabitants of Graftondale, was totally ignorant. He showed Gilling pictures of Bath and Cheltenham and Mayfair. Gilling was staggered to find that it was possible to live in style, not just simply without a front garden, but possibly even without a garden at all.

Sometimes after dinner Christie would play records, of which he had an enormous stock, mainly of Mozart and Brahms. Gilling, who had little appreciation of music, would stay upright in his chair fighting to keep awake, and thinking of himself and his own problems, and particularly his relations with this strange, rather lonely little man who sat opposite to him. He began to feel that he had achieved a new understanding of Christie. He thought of him now as a man who could not accept the thought of marriage, but who had a craving for a son whom he could instruct and upon whom he could lavish affection. It became apparent to Gilling that it was not enough merely to earn the prizes, he must turn himself into the kind of person who might be thought worthy to receive them. He could no longer afford to be the poor, ill-clad, hard-working scholarship boy. Gradually, step by step, in the same way as he learnt medicine, he learnt to laugh, to converse, to be easy in company and hold his own socially with anyone—well, almost anyone.

But the main aim was never forgotten. Social development was a weapon in his armoury, not an end in itself. He continued to work as hard as before. When his first six months at the Royal were over, Christie arranged a sinecure for him in charge of one of the hospital's convalescent homes. Here he could have peace and quiet to work for his higher qualification, the Membership of the Royal College of Physicians. He worked and passed. That was the end of examinations, but not the end of striving. There was a thesis to be written for his M.D. and papers to be written for the journals. After a year at the convalescent home he was back at the Royal as resident medical officer; here he found Benson-Grey following a parallel course on the surgical side as casualty officer. It was assumed by them, and by everyone else at the hospital, that they were on the first stages of an inevitable progress towards the Staff.

It was consequently a serious shock to Gilling when he ran, during his second year as R.M.O., into sudden and unexpected trouble. He was twenty-five now; he had completely disposed, or so he thought, of his Yorkshire accent; he had a hundred pounds in the bank; he knew how to dress and order a dinner and converse with social superiors. He had bought a small third-hand Austin car. He was, he knew, regarded with envy and admiration by his contemporaries, while to the younger members of the nursing staff he was an object of interest second only to Benson-Grey himself. He was flattered at being so much in demand, but his experience of girls was still fairly limited. So far he had been too shy, too poor, and too busy. Visits to the pictures on an occasional night stolen from his work, a little kissing and petting in the back of a friend's car or in a darkened side room at a University dance, was as far as he had managed to get. It was not until he had passed the Membership and finished writing his thesis that he found himself, for the first time in his life, with one or two evenings a week to be given over purely to enjoyment. It was at this particularly impressionable time of his life that he met, at one of Benson-Grey's parties, a tall, fair, and slightly enigmatic girl of his own age called Gwen.

Gwen was graceful in a lanky, athletic way, her legs were almost too long, her head a little too small, a greyhound of a girl, slim-hipped and small-breasted with blonde hair piled on the top of her head. When he was introduced to her she looked at him with a slight nervous laugh. "So you're Gilling. Arthur told me about you." He had no idea what to say, and he was determined not to say something obvious and inane, so he merely smiled and remained silent. He was intimidated by her, but he was shrewd enough to guess that she was equally ill at ease. She said, "Aren't you awfully clever or something?"

"Awfully." He grinned. "Can I get you something to drink?" He took her glass to where Benson-Grey was ladling a peach-coloured fluid out of a punch bowl. He looked at it dubiously. "What *is* that stuff?"

"God knows," admitted Benson-Grey with disarming frankness. "It started off with a gin base. But it grows more complex as the evening goes on. I think it's rather delicious just now. But a bit sweet." He emptied the remains of a bottle of French vermouth into the bowl, spilling a good deal down the front of his suit. It occurred to Gilling that Benson-Grey, in common with most of the people in the room, was extremely drunk. He took a glass of punch back to Gwen.

"Try this."

She sipped at it and raised her eyebrows in alarm. "Dear God, what is it?"

"Punch."

She accepted the statement dubiously. "Well, there's certainly rum in it somewhere." They drank and talked rather awkwardly for a while. Gilling noted that the room was beginning to clear; there was a gradual drifting off of couples to bedrooms. He wondered idly whether there would be "anything doing" with Gwen. The acquaintanceship was short but that was not necessarily a barrier at hospital parties. He was wondering how to broach the subject in a sufficiently delicate way when she said suddenly, "I think I ought to go."

She stood up with what appeared to be an unnecessary degree of determination. He noticed with alarm that she was swaying slightly. Under her make-up her face had turned grey. He said, "Are you all right?"

She hesitated, as if wondering whether to bluff it out, and then decided that things had gone too far for that. She shook her head. "No, not really." Defensively she added, "It was that last drink. I knew there was something wrong with it."

The usual unspoken question arose between them. What did she really need—fresh air or the ladies' room? She answered it immediately. "I feel sure I shall be all right if I can get outside."

He held her arm awkwardly as they passed out through the front door under the amused eyes of the night porter. Gilling felt slightly aggrieved. It was just his luck to find himself paired with a pretty girl and then have it turn out that she was feeling ill. Also, it was always very difficult to know what to say on these occasions. They were both of them awkward and embarrassed, and he wondered whether she would have preferred him to leave her alone. On the other hand it would look ungallant to abandon her in the circumstances.

They stood in silence on the terrace outside the hospital and smoked a cigarette. After about five minutes, Gilling said, "Feeling better?"

"Much better." He could tell by her tone that she was telling the truth. It was a distinct relief to him. Perhaps something might be salvaged out of the evening after all. She shivered. "It's rather cold out here."

"Do you want to go back inside?"

"Not really. I think I've had enough of that party. But you go back if you want to."

"No." The thought of returning to that smoky dilapidated room full of squashed cigarette ends and the smell of rum was hardly attractive. "Why don't you let me drive you home?"

She lived in one of the more fashionable suburbs of Grafton-dale, about six miles out of town. As they drove she said, "I feel badly about this."

"There's no need to."

"Dragging you out. I've done you out of your evening. You could be in bed with one of those nurses by this time."

"I think you have the wrong idea of the way we live."

She laughed. "I don't think so. You're all too much in demand. It's bad for you."

He wondered whether there was a slight edge to her voice or whether he was imagining it. He seemed to remember hearing that she was a one-time girl-friend of Benson-Grey. He said, "Have you known Arthur long?"

"A few years. He's good fun." She paused. "Except for this protracted love affair."

Gilling was startled. "Love affair?"

"With himself, I mean. It's rather indecent. An Englishman should have more reticence. And he's very predictable."

"I don't know." He was slightly taken aback to hear anybody talking in a disparaging fashion about Benson-Grey. He replied feebly, "I suppose we're all predictable to some extent."

"Not you. I don't feel I understand you at all."

"You haven't known me for long."

"I knew all there was to know about Arthur before I met him." She tried to settle herself more comfortably in her seat. The Austin was small and her long legs kept bumping up against the dashboard. "It's interesting. He has a sort of reluctant respect for you. He doesn't understand you, but you bother him. He has a feeling that you have something he hasn't, but he doesn't know what it is." Gilling felt sightly embarrassed. It was flattering to hear that Benson-Grey regarded him in this light, but he was unable to think of any comment to make.

She made no attempt to pursue the matter. He stopped the car at the end of the lane some distance from her house and said, as he usually did on these occasions, "You don't have to go home this instant." She said nothing, which was the normal convention for assent, and he turned in his seat and kissed her. At first her lips were cold against his, and then she responded. After a while they moved into a more comfortable position and he moved his hand gently on to her breast. She said, "Don't think I'm as easy as some of those nurses."

"You needn't worry," he reassured her. "You're quite safe

really. Sexual intercourse is impossible in an Austin Seven."

It was a matter of a few weeks before he was able to trade it in for a larger car, less reliable mechanically but more accommodating from other points of view. He was conscious, when he made the trade-in, that he was moving into a new and more dangerous situation. He was twenty-five and had never been involved in anything which might be called a serious love affair. His transient relationships with women had been little more than hurried amateurish scrambles at parties and dances, and he had been conscious always of the danger to his career of any permanent involvement. His eventual commitment was all the stronger for being so long delayed. He craved not only the satisfaction of physical desire, but also a female companion, someone who could give him light-heartedness and gaiety and a sense of play. He needed an outlet for affection, foolishness and sentimentality. Until now everything in his life had had a serious purpose; even his cultural evenings with Christie had been more concerned with education and the advancement of his career than mere pleasure. Now he derived a feeling of recklessness from pursuing his own immediate desires without caring too much where they might lead him.

Whether it was something in Gwen that inspired his recklessness or whether it was mainly suppressed desire to escape from the caution of his earlier years, he found it difficult afterwards to decide. From the very beginning, his emotion for Gwen was a complex one—the excitement and admiration she inspired in him was tempered constantly by a feeling of responsibility for her. She was a girl of strong moods, passionate and gay and amusing, yet with a way of falling quite suddenly into self-doubt and depression. She had a conception of herself, in these dark moods, as a person dogged throughout life by ill-luck. Every misfortune was counted and added triumphantly to the list to prove her point. At these times Gilling found argument useless—it was as if she found an enviable singularity in being pursued by fate in this remorseless fashion. There was no doubt that she enjoyed a sense of tragic drama. Her family history, she told him with perceptible satisfaction, was an unhappy one. Her father, a prosperous solicitor in Graftondale, was an incorrigible lecher. He flaunted his mistresses round the house and treated her mother with sadistic cruelty. There were terrible scenes in the house, frightening to a young girl; often both mother and daughter threatened to leave home. It was all very agonizing. When Gilling finally met Mr. Burgess he was rather disappointed to find a dyspeptic-looking man of well over fifty with a sallow complexion and a way of sniffing irritably due to some chronic catarrhal complaint. Mrs. Burgess was tall and plaintive and almost totally occupied with details of her appearance. It was hard to visualize the wild scenes in which they were credited to indulge.

It was apparent to Gilling quite soon that Gwen was falling in love with him. While he was moved and grateful for her passion, he was not sure how much he felt for her—certainly not so much, but then he doubted whether he was capable of such a violent emotion. Though his experience of girls had been necessarily limited, he had, like most boys who have had a very intimate relationship with their mothers, a natural sympathy for women and ease in their company. He was quick to learn the place of sexuality in a woman's life and was quite happy to come more than half-way to adapt himself to it. Gwen's pattern of love-making was one first of reluctance, followed by enthusiasm, followed in its turn by a kind of regret. All these emotions were, by his standards at any rate, over-dramatized, and he insensibly fell into a way of trying to restore them to balance, starting by overcoming the reluctance, then controlling the enthusiasm to within the bounds of prudence, and finally reassuring her afterwards.

She built up in her mind a somewhat enigmatic portrait of him. She liked to regard him as a mystery, a bland façade with a core of violence and ruthlessness beneath it. Sometimes, when she was angry with him, she would call him a climber and an opportunist. He could hardly deny it, since he knew it to be true, nor was he in any case ashamed of it. It was, after all, the only way he had of making a mark in the world. She was impressed by the width of his knowledge — she had expected him, like so many doctors, to have a mind trapped within the limits of his profession. For this distinction he had Christie to thank, as he well knew, but he could also take credit for his own efforts, built on the foundation which Christie had given him, Gwen's admiration was a reinforcement to his self-confidence. The image of himself which he longed to present included not only the brilliant careerist, but also the urbane distinguished man of the world. If she, an outsider from a family distinguished by Grafton-dale standards, saw him in precisely this light, he was reassured that the part was convincing. The costume was a good fit.

It was some time before he could bring himself to take her home. It was not, he told himself, that he was ashamed—no, that was a lie, he must be honest, he *was* ashamed of the council house and the cheap furniture, the way his parents spoke and dressed. He was not ashamed of his parents themselves. He knew that his mother, in different circumstances, could have been a great lady, his father a charming and distinguished eccentric; they were, very obviously, people of a higher and more interesting order than the Burgesses. He was ashamed only of their poverty, and he regarded it as his mission to put that right. He could see that Gwen was startled and disconcerted at first, but only for a moment. After that she sat down gracefully to her tinned salmon and strong tea, she flattered Mrs. Gilling and encouraged Mr. Gilling to talk about his early days in the trade union movement. She played up magnificently, in fact, and Gilling was both admiring and grateful for her tact. Afterwards he drove her home. Following their usual custom he stopped the car in a quiet little lane some distance away from her house. Without saying anything Gwen moved into her favourite position on the front seat of the car. She lay across his knees looking up at him, with her head pillowed in the crook of his right arm.

"Well?"

She knew immediately the question in his mind. "They're marvellous people, aren't they?" She said, almost sadly, "They make me feel like nothing at all." She was in one of her rather wistful moods, he thought. Her voice was slightly melancholy. "But I think they quite liked me."

"Of course they did. My mother particularly."

"Perhaps. Of course, I don't really mean anything to her as a person. No one does except you. I exist for her purely in relation to you. If I'm good for you—I may be all right. But if I'm not——"

He stroked her face. "You're good for me."

He kissed her and then they made love without saying anything more. It was a good answer to every awkward question.

Next week, when he visited his mother alone, he asked her, "Did you like Gwen?"

She nodded. "A nice girl."

Mr. Gilling said, "Very sensible. Well turned out." In his direct, inoffensive way he asked, "Are you courting her?"

Mrs. Gilling said sharply, "Don't be silly, Dad."

"What's silly about that?" asked Mr. Gilling equably. "Either he's courting her or he isn't. I just wondered."

"Of course he isn't. Are you, Tom?"

He hesitated. He had somehow grown unaccustomed to the direct way of looking at things which was expressed in his parents' conversation. "Going around" with girls meant nothing to them. There were certain realities in life. "Courting," getting married, having children, this they understood. And of course they were right—that was what the whole process was about. Even if the man tried to pretend that it wasn't, the girls had no such illusions. He would be foolish to imagine that Gwen was treating the affair as irresponsibly as he was. He could not evade the question for ever. Did he intend to marry Gwen?

He passed off the question with a joke, but later on his mother asked, "Have you been going with her long?"

"A month or so."

Her lips were tight, her face very thoughtful. She said, "I felt safer when I thought you had a lot of girls."

They were so close to each other that she had no need to say more. Her meaning was clear to him. While his mother had hardly spoken to him before about sex, he realized now that it came into the quite large group of subjects on which she had no moral feelings. Her preoccupation was purely against her son being trapped into marriage—she preferred him to be promiscuous rather than faithful, because it was less likely to lead to permanent ties. When she spoke of girls getting in the family way or men being forced into marriage to give them respectability, he remembered that it was always their foolishness rather than their wickedness which she criticized. In her world foolishness was a crime which admitted of no pardon. To throw away a career was deserving of nothing but contempt. Her confidence that her son would never do anything of that kind was almost complete. Almost . . .

But after all he was twenty-five, and he must marry some time. Gwen was a beautiful girl of decent family and he was fond of her. Why did he feel that he was committing some sort of indiscretion, even in some absurd way a betrayal? Well, he would think about it—there was no hurry. One of the advantages of being impecunious was that nobody expected you to be able to support a wife. No doubt he would suddenly receive a revelation of what was best to do. The smoke would clear and something would make up his mind. In the meantime he was finding that his present social life was even more exacting than the work it was beginning to replace. His job was busy, he was at work on his thesis, and he spent alternate week-ends at home. Christie still expected him to dinner once a fortnight, though these occasions had been getting rather stiffer recently. There seemed to be much less to talk about and Christie was tending to repeat his stories rather frequently. The rest of his time Gilling tried to spend with Gwen, but it was not very much. She grew restless and resentful, and on one or two occasions he was forced into cancelling Christie's evening. After the second cancellation Christie, without any explanation, ceased to invite him. Gilling became anxious. Fortunately Christie showed no great difference in his manner. He was as amiable as ever, if a little less playful. Gilling heard eventually that a new house physician was now receiving a cultural education once a fortnight. He was relieved. No offence had evidently been taken. Perhaps Christie had been just as anxious for a new face as Gilling had been for his freedom.

Summer moved into winter and Gilling's new Triumph, commodious as it was, had no heater. He and Gwen covered themselves with rugs and coats but there was no doubt that it was less than an ideal setting for making love. Gilling had now a sitting-room in the hospital with a roaring fire and it seemed foolish to crouch in a car in snowy ditches. They began to spend their evenings in his sitting-room. It was comfortable on his sofa before the fire and Gwen often stayed there until late—her parents seemed to have little interest in her movements and did not care if she returned at two or three in the morning.

They were there one Thursday just after midnight, when the

telephone rang. When Gilling answered it he heard a prim familiar voice. "Thomas—Christie here. I've just sent in a rather urgent emergency into the private wing. I'd like to have a word with you about it."

Gilling grimaced to Gwen and settled down back on the sofa to listen. "Yes, sir?"

His comfort was wrecked in a second by Christie's next remarks. "I'm in the lodge. Could you come along right away?"

He began to reach wildly for his clothes. "I'll be along in a few minutes."

"I'm in rather a hurry."

Gilling improvised wildly. "I just have to get dressed. I was in bed."

"Don't bother," said Christie curtly. "I'll come along and see you." As Gilling started to protest he put the phone down. Gilling turned distractedly to Gwen.

"For Christ's sake get dressed, Christie's coming. He'll be along in a minute or so."

She was suddenly infuriated by his peremptory tone. She flared up. "This is your room. Tell him he can't come in."

"I can't do that."

"Why not?"

"Because he's—who he is. I've got to let him in." He was pulling his trousers on, his hair dishevelled, his whole appearance ridiculous and undignified. She looked at him in disgust. He shouted at her. "This could ruin me. Oh Christ, Christ! You'll never do it in time. Could you hide somewhere?"

"I'm not going to act like a whore in a French farce," she said. She was more angry than he had ever seen her. She put her dressing-gown on and went to the mirror to arrange her hair. "If this room can be invaded by anyone who chooses, you'd no right to invite me here. As it is, you might try to retain a shred of dignity. You'd be better naked than the way you are."

It was true. His hair was uncombed, his shoelaces undone, his tie was in a knot and his shirt half unbuttoned. She lit a cigarette contemptuously. "I'd never thought to see you so afraid."

Suddenly he was terribly ashamed. He knew he was going to lose anyway and at least he should have lost, as she said, with dignity. As he tried to gather some shreds of his self-respect together there was a knock on the door. Before he could stop her, she said loudly and defiantly, "Come in!"

There was silence from outside. Gilling knew there was only one thing for him to do. Still crumpled and dishevelled, he opened the door and stepped outside. Christie, neat and dapper as always, looked him slowly up and down. His eyes took in the crumpled hair, the shirt half unbuttoned, the shoes unlaced. He said with supreme disgust in his voice, "Don't let me disturb you. I'll call my house physician."

Chapter 4

WHEN HE WENT into the interview room there were four men sitting on the opposite side of the long table. The only one he knew was Francis, and Francis showed no signs of recognition. Most of the questions were asked by a querulous little man in a double-breasted waistcoat. He was the type of man who gave the impression that there was some secret involved in the situation which he was determined to ferret out. Why was Gilling interested in a job at St. Vincent's? Was he not happy at Graftondale? Had he any particular object in coming to London? Did he want the job for its own sake or as a stepping stone to something else? Did he think he had sufficient experience to be a lecturer in medicine? Was his health satisfactory? Gilling answered in the conventional way. He was pinning his hopes on Francis. Once, at a medical meeting in Graftondale, Francis had taken him on one side and suggested that if he ever felt like coming to London there would be a good chance for him at St. Vincent's. But, of course, it might have meant nothing. Perhaps the present job had been fixed for someone else and Francis had been hopelessly embarrassed by the whole situation. When he left the interview room he was despondent and exhausted. It was quite a surprise to him when they called him back five minutes later and told him he had been appointed.

It was also a considerable relief. The situation at Graftondale had been deteriorating during the last few months at alarming speed. Since Christie had seen Gwen in his bedroom he had hardly spoken to him. He was obviously in great disfavour. It was plain, too, that a number of others had decided to take a prudent course and abandon him also. He was astonished at the extent of Christie's influence. He began to suspect that the word had gone round that it was dangerous to be seen speaking to him.

The sense of isolation was terrifying. He saw everything which he had spent his life working for leaking away from him. He had spent eight years clawing his way up the ladder, only to have it removed from under him because of one indiscretion. He realized now to the full the really terrifying power conferred by age and seniority. Christie might be laughed at, but when it came to the point his power was absolute. He had to fight with himself to resist the temptation to go to Christie and to abase himself, begging his way back into favour. It was only the conviction that he would be wasting his time that really prevented him from doing so. He dared not tell his mother—he knew the agony it would have caused her—and in his extremity he was bound ever more closely to Gwen. They made wild plans together. He would abandon the struggle, he would go into practice, he would emigrate to the Dominions—and always now these plans included marriage. Somehow the idea seemed more acceptable in the hour of defeat and tribulation than when the world had been there for the asking. Now it no longer appeared to him as a form of imprisonment but as a refuge and a consolation.

When the job at St. Vincent's was advertised, it had seemed like a possibility for the revival of his career. Francis had seemed well disposed towards him. If only he could get away from the atmosphere of Graftondale, which was now utterly hateful and depressing to him, he could make a start again with new people. He would no longer be resident—they would marry and settle in a flat in London. It would be an immense new world. He had no doubts that, given the chance, they could conquer it.

Well, here it was, he thought as he left the interview; he had the second chance he had prayed for, perhaps the last chance he would ever get. He must get back to the hotel and telephone Gwen. But as he was preparing to leave the building he heard a voice behind him. He turned round and it was Francis, now suddenly transformed back into the friendly cheerful person he had met at Christie's dinner party.

"Congratulations," said Francis. "I'm delighted."

"I didn't think I was going to get it," said Gilling.

"It was a near thing." Francis didn't explain why. "We just managed to get it through." He changed the subject quickly.

They talked about trivialities for a while and then Francis said, "Have you anything planned for this evening?"

"No—not really."

"Then you must dine with us." He waved aside the beginning of a protest. "No, really you must. My wife would like to meet you. We have a small party, absolutely informal. Just a few friends. Seven-thirty at my house." He gave Gilling an address in Sloane Street and left hurriedly.

Looking back, it seemed to Gilling that there were certain key moments in his life, punctuating, as it were, the gradual advance of his career, when he was suddenly shown a way of living quite outside his experience and his inner voice said to him urgently: I want that, I must have it. It had happened to him when he had first seen the grandees of Graftondale drawing up to the front door of the hospital in their limousines, when he had seen the consultants teaching the students gathered round the beds. It happened, more strongly than ever, on the evening after his interview, in the Chelsea flat of Gilbert Francis.

It was hard to pin down the essential quality of what he found there, the essence of a way of living that it was so essential for him to isolate, to capture, to keep. It was not mere opulence. The consultants at Graftondale were rich, possibly even richer than Francis. Christie's enormous stone mansion had a heavy magnificence about it which made Francis's flat seem positively frivolous. Yet it was something to do with more than just having wealth, it was a certain way of regarding it. In Graftondale, money and power were taken seriously. Here for the first time in his life, Gilling met people so utterly sure of their wealth and position that they could treat both with a sort of huge carelessness, a positive indifference. They lived extravagantly—they all had, it seemed, country houses, racehorses and boats and villas on the Mediterranean—it was accepted that most people had. It was also accepted that young people were frequently "hard up." That was amusing—though of course they would become rich later, either from success or because some member of their family would die and leave them money. It was rather embarrassing for people to be hard up once they became middle-aged, though if they were amusing or elegant or well-connected they were permitted to get away with it.

Gilling knew that it was trivial and unworthy to be impressed by all this. He nevertheless *was* impressed, and since he believed in facing up to his own motives he decided to admit it to himself. He knew that his fascination with the purely luxurious element of Francis's life was shallow and romantic and would quickly fade. The thing which struck deeper, which he knew he would never be able to forget, was the careless acceptance of power and influence. To Francis and his friends, Old Etonians almost to a man, it had been disclosed early on in life that God had placed them at the heart of things for His own special purpose. They had been born to run the Empire in all its aspects, to take charge by natural right in every branch of activity where they might find themselves. They knew everyone, they had a private line into every seat of authority. Over their cocktails they spoke intimately of ministers and peers and bankers and dukes and members of the Royal Family. Francis, as the representative of this set in medicine, was on easy terms with men who were no more than great names to Gilling. These were the men who really ran the profession, the presidents of colleges and associations and societies, the holders of Royal appointments, the personal physicians to the great. To these men, the courtiers of medicine, the grandees of Graftondale were like touchy provincial barons, to be wined and dined and flattered on their visits to the capital, fobbed off every now and then with grandiose but meaningless honours and appointments, and played off one against the other by the real rulers, the professionals.

Naturally, Gilling did not discover this in one evening at a dinner party of twelve people. What he did discover was a new atmosphere, a level of privilege wholly strange to him, one which he suspected might be almost the top layer of such privilege which he must explore if given the chance. And the strange thing was—it seemed incredible but one had to admit it—Francis seemed to have taken to him. One always knew. Francis treated Gilling, in fact, as he had never been treated by any of the Graftondale consultants, almost as if he regarded him as an equal. In Graftondale the hierarchy was absolute; the authority, though paternal, was rigid; and the barrier between the old who ruled and the young who submitted was complete. It was a formality built into hospital life, and even privileged individuals like Benson-Grey were not exempt from it. In their maturity, when they took the lives of patients in their hands each day, they were still treated by the consultants as if they were schoolboys. In all his relationship with Christie, Gilling had never been allowed to forget his position.

It was a heady evening. They drank martinis at the flat and Gilling was introduced by Francis to a variety of people whose names he instantly forgot. He met a pretty dark-haired girl, was stiff with her at first and then found himself, after the third martini, being rather bold and entertaining. She was interested, or professed to be interested, to hear that he was coming to London, and even gave him her address and telephone number. He had heard that London was a lonely city but it did not seem to him that he was going to be lonely. In some extraordinary way he felt more at home with these people than he did in Graftondale. Perhaps it was because here he was unknown. Here he existed in the way he longed to exist, not in the context of his family background or his education, but purely in terms of what he had to offer. His self-confidence increased throughout the evening. It seemed, now that he had observed one corner of it, that the great world would not be quite so difficult to conquer for a clever and pushing young man. He became suddenly aware of the vital importance for him of getting away from Graftondale. Graftondale was still wrapped in a provincial inertia which it liked to regard as stolidity, a sour pessimism which it dignified by the title of hard-headedness. In Graftondale anything but the conventional road of advance was sneered at, dreams were there to be ridiculed. In Graftondale he was a boy from a council house with second-hand boots, clever and hardworking no doubt, but condemned to wait his turn and touch his cap until his master saw fit to call him. Who was he to dream of greatness, to imagine a future beyond the confines of his northern muckheap? In Graftondale they would keep him back until he had learned to control his dreams, until he himself had begun to think they were absurd.

When he was with Francis, Gilling suddenly felt free from this spider's web of false and depressing assumptions. To these people he was like a man from a strange country, and they looked at what he had to show without preconceived ideas or prejudice.

They were familiar with greatness and it did not seem absurd to them that an eager young man should aspire to it. They might accept him or they might throw him aside and forget him. But they would not laugh at him.

Or so he thought, his mind racing under the influence of the martinis and the hock, the brandy and cigars, the laughter and conversation, the heady influence of being taken as an equal by distinguished, rich and elegant people. After dinner, as he sat by himself, dreaming of a future without limit, Francis came over to sit beside him. He said, "Tell me—I've been meaning to ask you—what did you do to Little Jesus?"

Gilling was puzzled. It was a little late in the evening for cryptic remarks. Francis laughed and went on. "Your reference, my dear fellow. It was terrible—unbelievably bad."

"Oh?" He sat up, appalled. Then he remembered that after all he had got the job. It didn't matter. Little Jesus was irrelevant from now on. It was quite a thought. But *how* had he got the job?

"I was completely thrown," said Francis. "You see, he told me in confidence some months before that you were the best man he had had in ten years. On the strength of what he said, I sold you to the committee. It never entered my head that he'd write something like that."

Like what? Gilling yearned to ask, but he knew it would be fatal, Francis couldn't be as indiscreet as that. Presumably it was one of those cryptically worded recommendations which are damning without being actually defamatory. The little bastard, Gilling thought, he never forgave me for that night when he caught me with Gwen—he never will. But what do I care now? Francis is the man from now on.

He laughed. "I'm not too surprised." He began to tell Francis the story. As he told it, he knew Francis was listening with delight, storing it away as an amusing anecdote to tell his friends, strictly in confidence of course. He obviously knew that Christie was homosexual. He was not outraged, merely amused by it. Gilling responded to his audience and told his story as an amusing hospital frolic, a bedroom farce. It went down well. But inside him was a tiny voice which told him that the story was a lie, it had not been a casual tumble in the hay, it was the girl he loved. It had not been amusing at all at the time, it had been squalid and humiliating for both of them. And afterwards, alone in his room, he had cried from shame, and from fear that his life was ruined and that he might lose his job and his future. He had contemplated begging Christie for mercy, apologizing and abasing himself. It had been a shameful episode. And there was something shameful now and insulting to Gwen in the way he was making a joke of it, and speaking as if she were a whore, a casual pick-up.

But Francis was roaring with laughter, drowning the small voice with his appreciation. Francis obviously thought that he was a great fellow, a valuable acquisition, quite a character beneath his quiet manner. Gilling was neither strong nor perverse enough to resist an appreciative audience and was also a little drunk. Francis poured him another brandy and said, "Well, you really ought to apologize to me. Your sexual escapades have put me to a lot of trouble. I had to fight tooth and nail with the committee—practically giving my word that Christie was going out of his mind. They came round in the end but it was a hell of a sweat. A few of them were for playing safe and appointing Keeley instead of you. He's a sound man—nothing against him. But a bit dull." Francis said casually. "Also he's married. That counted against him."

"Yes?" Gilling put his glass down on a side table very carefully. His brain fought its way through the alcohol which enveloped it. He knew suddenly that he was going to need a clear head. Gwen and he had planned to get married immediately if he was successful at the interview. However, this hardly seemed the time to break the news to Francis. He waited, smiling mechanically. The brandy was beginning to turn sour in his stomach.

"Yes. You see—I shouldn't really tell you and it's very confidential, understand." Gilling nodded, trying to look discreet. "But the point of this business today was really to try to find a new resident assistant physician. Marshall Scott is retiring in six months and Laidlaw will move up on to the consultant staff. That leaves a vacancy. And you—well——" He left the sentence unfinished. He grinned and patted Gilling gently on the arm. "So you see you were up at a fortunate time. The other thing is

165

that the hospital doesn't like resident staff to be married and particularly the R.A.P. They're thinking of bobbing off home all the time." Gilling could feel the pressure mounting against him. It was the usual story—the more they offered you, the more they owned you. He was, as Francis said, fortunate, unbelievably so by comparison with any of that hundred or so of young men who had started the long medical course with him nearly ten years ago. He was favoured, the great ones believed in him, they had selected him for the ultimate success, far beyond what Graftondale had to offer. Those limousines at the front door, once the summit of all ambition, now seemed trivial and provincial by contrast to what he might have. And in return they would take—what? His life perhaps. If he wished to protest, to demand a right to a personal existence, this was the time to speak. He said nothing.

Francis went on. "It's a bit of a bore, obviously. But it's not as bad as you might think. There's a decent little flat—you can entertain." He smiled meaningly at Gilling. "Nobody bothers you. I was R.A.P. myself for a time and I quite enjoyed it. And it makes you almost a certainty for the staff."

Gilling did not know what he was going to say to Gwen, but somehow he would have to make her understand. There was no possibility of turning down this quite staggering opportunity. Yet there was a fundamental question, a question he couldn't ask. Fortunately Francis was quite young and he knew what Gilling wanted to know. He said, "In case you're interested, the next staff vacancy is in six years' time."

"Six *years!*"

"I know it's a long time."

"It's impossible," she said, "impossible. For God's sake, you're twenty-six." Tears of outrage and mortification streamed down her face. "Who the hell do they think they are!"

"They know who they are," he said bitterly. "They're the men who make the rules."

"To hell with the rules. At your age—you're not a monk, you're not a schoolboy. You're not a convict. Rules!"

They were sitting in the car, parked in a little track leading into a deserted wood in the country just outside Graftondale.

Somehow there was no longer any happiness in being together in his room at the hospital. It was not so bad out here; sometimes they were disturbed by hikers or boy scouts and once a policeman had peered through the window, but it was fairly private once the darkness came down. Now it was dusk and raining hard. The rain streaked down the windows of the car, driving on to the roof from the branches of the black trees. It was utterly deserted, as if the whole world had gone off somewhere and left them behind.

"Tell me," she said fiercely. "Be honest. Do you think it's fair? Do you think it's reasonable?"

"Of course not."

"Then couldn't you tell them so?"

"Of course I could. And they'd see my point. They'd be very polite about it. But I should dish myself as far as St. Vincent's was concerned."

"And that would be the end of everything?"

"Yes," he said simply. "Yes, it would."

She said desperately, "There are other hospitals. Other jobs."

"Not like this," he said. "I should end up as a nobody."

"I don't believe that," she said. "You're brilliant. You could never be a nobody."

"Oh yes," he said with a conviction born of experience. "In the wrong job, in the wrong place——" He tried to explain to her the knowledge that ten years of experience of the machine had taught him. "You see, a career in medicine is a continuous thing. It's a pattern that has to be right everywhere, or almost everywhere; if you do something badly wrong at one time, it counts against you always. Most of the big men have done the right thing all the way through. Teaching hospitals, professorial units, the right kind of research, the right kind of qualifications at the right time, the right kind of impression on the right kind of people. They didn't let themselves be shunted into backwaters where they could have done the most brilliant thing in the world and nobody would know. Without anybody to push you forward, nobody listens to you. All this stuff about people coming out of country general practice and becoming famous is all eyewash. It doesn't happen. With very good connections perhaps

167

you can afford to make a mistake or two, but that doesn't apply to me. I can't afford to turn down chances."

He wondered whether she had been listening. She merely said, almost in a whisper, "Six years. You'll be thirty-two. I'll be thirty-one."

He said eagerly, "But we'd be home then. We'd be home. Just now I have to eat dirt. I have to do what they say. They can ask any damn' thing from me. I have to submit. But then, if I got on the staff, I'd be one of them. Surely it's worth it?"

Her voice rose. "It's humiliating. Don't you understand that?"

"It's an inconvenience——"

"An inconvenience! Six years!"

His failure to make any impression upon her exasperated him. "Please stop saying six years."

"I have to say it. Otherwise I can't believe it. That anyone could ask you—that you should ask me——" With an artificial brightness she said, "Tell me now, what am I supposed to be doing during this time?"

He loved her, he sympathized deeply, he was miserable too— but somehow he could not resist the impatience which arose within him. There was nothing to be gained from raving against the inevitable. Absurd and unjust though the rule might be, it was there, you had to live with it. And you had to do so without bitterness, without everlasting grievances and complaints, otherwise you would destroy yourself. You had to accept the reality of power. You might not like everything it did—well then, the answer was to get power yourself and change things, so that others in their turn had to accept your way. But acceptance of the structure was essential. Even secret rebellion would somehow come through to them in the end. They would know, by an accidental phrase or an expression on your face or an unguarded action, that your service was only lip service. They would remember—and they would strike you down. And by their law they would be justified. For the structure was essential to the profession. In a sense it *was* the profession. One day he would command the structure and he would have the right to say what should be done and what should not be done. He knew when that day came he would demand acceptance from others.

He said vaguely, "Perhaps you could get a job in London——"

"And live in a flat on my own? While you lived in the hospital? And see you once a week on your night off? For six years! Oh, Tom, be sensible——"

"Well then, stay here for a bit." He knew he was being unconvincing. "When I get settled there I might be able to make some arrangement——"

She laughed shrilly. "Let's be honest. Whatever else we lose, don't let's tell lies about it. You'll play it their way, I know that now. And it's them or me——" she said sadly. "Poor old me."

"That's unfair."

"The whole bloody thing's unfair." She switched on the light in the car.

"Why did you do that?"

"At important moments you should always see people's faces." All the violence and resentment had gone out of her voice. Now there was only a sad acceptance of the inevitable. "It imprints itself on your mind—like a photograph you can look at later. Once I saw you as a nice, rather exciting young man. Then a month ago I looked at you and I saw you, quite suddenly, as a husband. You looked quite different. You weren't a stranger, a separate person any more. You were part of my life, and I saw how you would be when you got older, the way your mouth and your eyes and your hair would change. I saw you the way I saw my clothes or my handbag or the furniture of the house I live in. You existed with me in time. Now you don't any more. You're just a bright, rather nice, rather exciting, and rather calculating young man, who would like to be kind within the limits of his self-interest. Not a man for the great sacrifice, the grand gesture. A bit of an opportunist, a bit of a cad. And nothing much to do with me really. Just a nice young man I'm seeing off on a journey." She looked away from him and began to tidy her hair in front of the driving mirror. "I won't wait six years for you, Tom."

He said, weakly and rather despicably, "If you really loved me——"

She replied with the dignity which he seemed to have lost. "I love you. At least I think I do. But I won't wait six years."

She smiled and then effortlessly removed the last remains of his self-esteem. "I wouldn't be so cruel."

The humiliation was all the greater because he knew what she inferred was true. For all his sadness there was relief in his heart. She knew him almost too well, she was right in suggesting that the sacrifice of six of the most precious years of her life would impose an obligation on him which he would find suffocating and unbearable. No one would ever be so kind to him again as she was being to him now, no one so unselfish. He felt a rush of tenderness for her, and a painful spasm of regret for what he was losing. He looked at her face. Even in the cruel light of the inside of the car she was beautiful and desirable; more desirable than ever now that he was free and was going to leave her. He put out his hand to touch her, wondering whether she would push him away in disgust. Instead she picked up his hand and stroked it for a while. Then, looking at his face, she laughed sadly and, unbuttoning her blouse, put his hand on her naked breast.

"The last time," she said.

The last time, he thought, half asleep in his chair, an old man, past sex, past love, with a distinguished wife and the respect of his profession, and £75,000 nicely spread in equities with a strong potential for growth. It was strange to think that Gwen would be sixty-two. What would time have done to that beautiful willing body, those large liquid eyes, that mountain of fair hair? Better not to think. He told himself that he was not ashamed of the way he had chosen. If he was an opportunist, God had made him so; in the last instance one could not act out of character. He had tried to be as good a man as he could be within his limitations.

Gwen had understood that. She had understood many things about him, including things he never knew at the time but only realized afterwards. She had said—the last time. And she had been right, it would never be like that again, not with anyone, not at any time. As she had said, there were moments like still photographs which you kept looking at again and again all through your life. To this day he saw the act of love in terms of one moment, in a car on a rainy night, when she lifted his hand to her breast and then made love for the last time, uncomfortably, agonizingly, and with infinite tenderness, in a wood on a hill which he would never see again as long as he lived.

There were other women, of course—but they were not part of his youth and his hopes any more. There was also his work. He found St. Vincent's smaller, more casual, less brutal than Graftondale. With Francis behind him he was able to make an impression and he found they were surprisingly ready to accept him. He did not, as it happened, even have to stay resident for six years after all, since a member of the St. Vincent's staff obligingly died early and he received his appointment two years before he could reasonably have expected it. He was only thirty, an unusually early age to become a London consultant.

It was soon after this when his mother died. He went up to Graftondale for her funeral. At least, he thought, she had seen the fulfilment of her hopes. She knew that he would be successful, even famous. His father walked silently by the coffin at the funeral, remote as ever, and then the two men went back to the house afterwards and drank tea and tried to make conversation. It was not a success and they both soon realized that they had nothing to say to each other. Gilling was conscious that his father had still not forgiven him for the earlier betrayal, probably never would forgive him. He wondered, as he left, would he ever see the old man again?

After that there were few real problems. The war came a few years later and he volunteered but was turned down on account of a small crater in his stomach which had been causing him trouble for some time. He realized afterwards that this was fortunate for him, since he might easily have been killed in those early dangerous, disastrous days. As it was, he carried on at St. Vincent's and made a great deal of money in private practice. After a year or two he became restless, fearing that a complete lack of war service might count against him in the future, no matter how genuine his rejection. In 1941, after an intensive course of treatment, he managed to get his ulcer healed up, and pulled strings to get into the army on a special research assignment concerned with battle fatigue. It was during his time in the army that he first met a plain, gangling Wren officer who turned out, surprisingly, to be the niece of a duke. She made little of her social connections, but there was a curious kind of unaffected dignity about her which fascinated him. He had never been sure, in fact he was not sure even to this day, how much of her supreme self-possession and disregard for appearances was due to birth and upbringing, how much to her own detached and independent character. From the first there had been something about her which he found at the same time impressive, likeable, and rather absurd. Her walk, her gestures, her voice were all a little odd and awkward. She was one of those natural eccentrics who did everything, even the most ordinary things, in a slightly odd way, not with any idea of attracting attention but because she reacted in a direct individual manner to all situations instead of following the paths laid down by customary behaviour. All the details of her life carried with them a certain quality of improvisation. Her clothes bore no relation to current fashion, she spent money in a bizarre and improvident way which fascinated and baffled the careful Gilling. She travelled everywhere with a variety of paper bags containing food for a multitude of pet animals.

There was a gentle tolerance about her, an enormous rock-like security which gave Gilling a sense of comfort which he had never known since the early years of his life when his mother had seemed all powerful and infinitely resourceful. And in her curious detached way, she fell deeply in love with him. It was not like Gwen, of course, the physical side of their relationship was unimpassioned to say the least. But he was middle-aged now and passion was fading in him too. After they married, Gilling discovered that there was another world for him to explore, one which was supposedly dying but which nevertheless retained a degree of power which startled him. He found himself, as a member by marriage of a great family, taken seriously by men who had never noticed him before. He had moved, he realized, from a ladder on to an escalator. There was no need for him to climb actively any more. The machine would carry him up automatically from now on. All he had to do was to make sure not to fall off.

He had worked too long and too hard to make foolish mistakes. When the Health Service came after the war he was already influential in the Royal College of Physicians. He was, in a current phrase, a "College man." While he had doubts about the Service and a profound dislike of Mr. Bevan, he made no inflammatory speeches, he was cautious and followed the College line. Afterwards he found the Health Service quite surprisingly painless. He had no financial worries, and there was still a plentiful supply of wealthy private patients for a man such as himself. There was also a great deal of administration and committee work. He had a clear head and a patient, amiable manner and he found himself much in demand on public bodies of all kinds.

He was constantly surprised by the easy successes of this last phase of his career. It seemed to him that as he grew stronger his competitors became weaker. There were so many ways in which a man could lose his place. In his time Gilling had seen a score of promising reputations wrecked by the most unlikely misfortunes. There was Craxted, who had taken to the bottle, and Myran, who had developed paranoid delusions. Olwen Hall the neurologist had been cited as co-respondent in that unpleasant divorce case; Wembleham had made an excessively familiar remark to a certain Royal Duke. All (except for Myran, who could hardly be blamed for his mental condition) were victims either of carelessness or of a kind of impulse towards self-destruction. Gilling had often wondered how they could risk the sacrifice of so much for so little. He had never been able to understand it, and he had often racked his brains to think how they could consider it worth while.

Now, he thought bitterly, his colleagues must be thinking the same about him. He looked back, trying to think of the point where he had suddenly moved into danger. He found it hard to pin it down. Each step had appeared to be safe. He had not started with the idea of risking everything—surely nobody did, except perhaps a man like Line. It was only later on, when it was difficult to draw back, that the risk appeared in all its horror. He wondered about Line. More and more he thought about his adversary these days. He could not resist a strange admiration for Line. Unlike himself or Craxted or Olwen Hall, Line had known what he was risking and had risked it deliberately. You could say what you liked, there was something rather grand about that.

Chapter 5

THE NEXT MORNING Groom began to get down to the details of his direct examination.

"Now Sir Thomas, in Professor Line's letter you are accused by inference of two things. The first is that you have taken an obstructive attitude towards scientific advance, demonstrated in particular by your attitude towards the work of Mr. Brook. The second is that this attitude was a contributing factor in the death of John Kincaid. We will deal with the more general question first. Sir Thomas, have you ever conspired with others to impede scientific advancement?"

"Certainly not."

"Would you consider yourself capable of taking up a dispassionate view about an important scientific discovery?"

"Certainly I would."

"Is it one of your functions, as a leader of the profession, to evaluate medical advances?"

"Yes."

"Did you write a review in the *Journal of Experimental Medicine* on this very subject?"

"Yes."

"What, in general, were the views you expressed?"

"I described the difficulties involved in distinguishing real advances from blind alleys. In my position, which I freely admit is influential, one is very conscious of these difficulties."

"In what way would you describe yourself as influential? How is this influence exerted?"

"Well, one sits on committees of one kind or another which have to decide whether work is supported with money or facilities or general encouragement. Bodies like the Medical Research Council, or the Royal Society, or the various voluntary foundations. Of course these are not the only organisations, and one person doesn't dominate them all. There is a collective influence exerted by the heads of the profession generally."

"And what, in your article, did you describe as the difficulties?"

"The first is that a vast number of projects are submitted to us and we only have money to support a minority of these. We naturally do the best we can to pick out those we consider the most promising and those which we think in the long run will bring the greatest advances to medical science. We also have to consider the expense of the project in relation to our limited resources. So it's a question of selection, and we are bound to disappoint a lot of very sincere and able people, who genuinely believe that their project is of the very greatest importance. We don't say we are always right, but we take a lot of trouble, we take the best advice available, and we think on the whole the results in the past have justified our selection." Gilling felt himself falling into his lecturer's style. He had thought and spoken of this so often that it was very easy to give oneself confidence by turning on a kind of gramophone record. But he knew that he must watch this. It would never do to give the impression of lecturing the jury. He pulled himself back to a less aloof and more intimate style of exposition. "It's really hard to see how we can be accused of being hostile to innovation, since research, by definition, is concerned with innovation, so if we didn't believe in it we wouldn't be serving on all these bodies. What we are engaged in doing is choosing one approach to innovation rather than another for support. As everyone knows, research is a very laborious and expensive business and most of it comes to nothing. It's a mistake to remember the great discoveries but to forget the vast mass of work which proves abortive. Nobody, not even the greatest scientific genius, could ever guarantee to pick just the few correct leads out of all those presented at a given time, and to reject the others as a waste of time and effort. All we can say is that we do our best to establish priorities. We don't claim to be infallible."

"In this article you wrote, did you give examples?"

"Yes I did. I claimed, and I sincerely believe this, that while we have often supported work which has turned out to be disappointing, we have always recognized the really important discoveries at a very early stage and have supported them to the limit. I gave several instances of this. The artificial kidney, transplantation of organs, the development of antiviral substances —and so on."

"Did you make any other special points in this essay?"

"Well yes, I did. I referred specifically to projects which I believed were simply not worth the expense and effort required to pursue them. I said that the temptation should be resisted to support such projects because they had an up-to-date or fashionable sound. I gave several examples of this, one of which was data analysis."

"This is the kind of work represented by the Brook-Halder machine and referred to by Professor Line in his letter?"

"Yes."

"Now, Sir Thomas, since this machine looms so very large in this case, I think we ought to discuss it in some detail. When did you first hear of the Brook-Halder machine?"

"I can't remember exactly. Of course, diagnostic machines of one kind or another have been under study for up to ten years now. The first claims for one which worked were in 1962. It's a fairly obvious idea, a development of the computer. Ever since then, people have tried to develop improved models. The Brook-Halder machine was one of these. I think I first heard of it about four years ago."

"Had these diagnostic machines achieved wide popularity?"

"They are used to a limited extent in large centres in the U.S.A. Not in this country."

"Would you say you had a prejudice against them?"

"No. But I think their value is extremely limited."

"Can you explain to us why?"

"Certainly." He hesitated for a moment and looked at Groom questioningly. "I take it everyone here understands the principle on which they work."

"Professor Line's letter contains an explanation of this principle. Would you agree with that?"

"I think, if I may say so, that it's a slanted and biased explanation. It's what I would call the explanation of an enthusiast.

The basic principle of the machine, as I see it, is that you feed in the data from your clinical history and examination, and the machine, which has already been programmed with all the data from the hospital records and the cases treated there over the last fifty years, compares the information from the individual case with that of the hospital records. Its diagnostic experience is claimed to be, not that of one person, but of the whole hospital. In other words it purports to do your thinking for you. It tries to fit in individual data with other data which have been fed into it regarding the nature of disease in general. If they fit in exactly, it gives you a diagnosis. If they don't, it gives you a series of alternatives and a list of investigations required to narrow the field down further."

"Does the machine ever find itself baffled? Does it ever have no further alternatives or investigations to suggest?"

"Well, in theory the machine always proceeds to the final diagnosis. But this is actually meaningless, since its final suggestions may be such suggestions as 'surgical exploration' or 'therapeutic test.' "

"What does therapeutic test mean?"

"It means that if you have two alternatives you should try the treatment for one of them to see if it responds. If it does, that's the diagnosis. If not, it must be the other."

A wintry smile flittered over Sir Frederick Groom's face. "That sounds rather like 'suck it and see.' "

"More or less. And surgical exploration is 'take a look at it and see.' In my opinion there is nothing very helpful about either of these suggestions. They are the last resort of baffled physicians since the beginning of medicine. They're obvious—and they may be dangerous."

"In what way?"

"Well, one of the objections to the diagnostic machine is that it can concern itself with nothing but diagnosis. It behaves as if diagnosis was the sole object of medicine, which of course it isn't. The object of medicine is the alleviation of human suffering. It may be better for the patient to leave the diagnosis in doubt than to submit him to a dangerous procedure—such as, for instance, surgical exploration. But the machine takes no account of this."

"I see. Now, Sir Thomas, would you mind summarizing for us your reasons, apart from the one you have just given, for believing the machine to be of limited value?"

"Yes. One has to think first of what the position is with regard to present methods of diagnosis. How often are mistakes made? And how often could such mistakes, when they are made, be rectified by the machine? Now as a matter of fact, an advisory committee to the Ministry of Health, under the chairmanship of Sir Horace Trimble, has gone into this very question. It was concluded that serious mistakes in diagnosis were on the whole uncommon on the part of experienced consultants, who were in any case the only people who would have the facilities to use the machine. Of these mistakes, most could probably be avoided by greater use of consultation with other experts. In the cases where a diagnosis was impossible to arrive at by a whole series of experts, these were precisely the cases where the machine would take refuge in such platitudes as surgical exploration or therapeutic test."

"So what you are really saying is this—that proper use of present consultation facilities would in general give you everything the machine could give you?"

"Yes."

"How much do these machines cost, Sir Thomas?"

"According to Professor Line's own estimation the Brook-Halder machine has so far cost £200,000."

"Two hundred thousand pounds." Groom paused for a moment to let the magnitude of the figure sink into the jury. "Are there any other disadvantages?"

"Yes, the really practical problems in medicine aren't dealt with by the machine at all. Supposing you had a pain in the back for four days. There might not be much in the way of other helpful information. Now if you fed this information into the machine, you would get a list of suggestions for investigations which would probably take three weeks to carry out and cost the Health Service several hundreds of pounds. In the meantime, your pain might very well have gone. An enormous amount of medicine is common sense and putting things in their right proportion, and this the machine cannot do. Since it is concerned completely with absolutely one hundred per cent diag-

178

nosis, it almost always recommends X-rays. Now the human body can only stand a limited number of X-rays—beyond that they may be harmful. The machine knows nothing of this. There may be many cases in which it is far better to be ninety per cent sure of the diagnosis on one or two investigations than one hundred per cent sure on twenty. The enthusiasts for the machine say that you can always refuse to do the investigations suggested. But if you do, what's the point of the machine? Also, human nature being what it is, many doctors would find it hard to refuse to make investigations."

"Why?"

"Well, for one thing, if anything went wrong, they would be afraid of being accused of negligence. The line of least resistance would always be to do everything the machine said."

"So it was on these grounds that you formed the opinion that the machine was not worth the very large sums required for its further development?"

"Yes."

"Had various other research committees been asked to support this project?"

"Yes."

"Committees on which you were not represented?"

"Yes."

"And these also had turned it down?"

"Yes."

"But I gather the work is still going on?"

"Oh yes." Gilling's voice held a note of contempt. "I believe they have finance from some newspaper."

"Sir Thomas, I would like to ask you a very serious question. Were there any personal considerations involved in your rejection of financing this project?"

"Certainly not."

"Did the fact that Dr. Brook was young and unknown have anything to do with it?"

"No. He was in any case no more young and no more unknown than most of our recipients of grants. In fact he had rather more powerful support than most."

"From whom?"

"Professor Line."

"Did you have any indication of the reaction to your refusal to support this work?"

"Not from Dr. Brook. I heard that Professor Line was very angry."

"Did Professor Line say anything to you directly on the subject?"

"Not at that time. He wrote urging me to influence the committee to think again."

"And what did you reply?"

"I said that I understood how he felt and I would certainly take this into consideration. I reported the matter to my committee but I'm afraid it didn't persuade us to reverse our decision."

"Was there any extra evidence in Professor Line's letter or was it just a personal plea?"

"It was a personal plea."

"How long ago was all this?"

"About two years."

"And were you approached for support after this time?"

"No."

"Very well," said Groom. "Now we come to the illness of Mr. Kincaid. How did you first hear that Mr. Kincaid was ill?"

"I received a telephone call from Dr. Barton, a well-known practitioner in the West End of London. He told me he was Kincaid's family doctor and that Kincaid had just come back from a very exacting foreign trip and wasn't feeling too well. He seemed to be suffering from strain and overwork. Barton asked if I would see him. So we arranged an appointment at my rooms in Wimpole Street. I saw Mr. Kincaid there two days later."

"How was he?"

Gilling was conscious of his first flutter of apprehension. Everything had been arranged and rehearsed beforehand, he knew precisely what he was to say, nothing could go wrong, and yet there was the sensation of moving into an area of danger from which he would not be able easily to retreat. Yet all had gone perfectly so far. He knew he was going down well with the jury. He had sufficient experience of himself in front of an audience to know when he had their sympathy, and he was convinced that he had it now. All he had to do was to continue in the same way and all would be well. Taking a firm grip on the gentle, reasonable voice and manner which had served him so well so far, he strode forward without flinching into dangerous territory. "Well, my first impression was in agreement with Dr. Barton's diagnosis. Kincaid seemed very tense and excited. Of course, I hadn't ever seen him before. So it wasn't easy to say how abnormal this was. He kept insisting that he was perfectly well, making jokes and so on. He was a man of great personality and charm. I had a long discussion with him about his life and his work and his recent activities. It seemed to me that he had formed the habit of driving himself too hard and I told him so. He laughed and said that he was probably too old to change."

He could see the fleeting affectionate smiles on the faces of many people in court. The picture of Kincaid had aroused in them a trace of that feeling of excitement and warmth which the man himself, even at his most perverse and exasperating, had always transmitted. Groom said, "Did you take his complete history?"

"Yes. I took very detailed notes of his medical background and any symptoms that he complained of. I was slightly limited by the fact that he kept saying that he felt perfectly fine and that he wouldn't be seeing me if it wasn't for the unnecessary fussing of his wife and family doctor."

"What kind of symptoms did he have at this time?"

"Very vague ones. He felt strung up, perhaps rather more than usual. He slept badly and tended to have nightmares. Sweating. Occasional palpitations."

"Was that all?"

Gilling was prepared for this and knew that it was vital that there should be no hesitation. He answered definitely, "Yes."

"Did you examine him at this time?"

"Yes."

"Thoroughly?"

"Yes. I gave him a complete physical examination, and also arranged a blood count, an X-ray of his chest and an electrocardiogram."

"Were there any positive findings?"

"Very few. His pulse was a little high, about ninety, but that could be due to excitement. There was a tremor of his fingers, his reflexes were a little brisk. That was all."

"Was his temperature normal?"

"Yes."

"What was your diagnosis?"

Gilling said rather diffidently, "At that time there wasn't a lot to go on. I thought he was suffering from a mild anxiety state caused by overstrain."

"And what did you prescribe?"

"I gave him advice about his way of life—to take it easier, not to work so hard. Rest and relaxation. Also a sedative for the night and tranquillizers for during the day."

"Did you make another appointment for Mr. Kincaid?"

"Yes. In a month's time."

"And what was his condition like then?"

"It was disappointing," said Gilling. "He certainly wasn't improving. He'd lost a few pounds in weight. His pulse was a little higher than the previous time, but not very much increased. He was paler. There was nothing very dramatic physically, but mentally he had changed quite noticeably. Instead of the febrile optimism he had shown at the previous visit, he was quite gloomy, almost depressive. He kept saying that he was breaking up, failing, feeling his age."

"What significance did you attach to this?"

Gilling paused. "It was hard to know. He was, as I knew from his family doctor, a man of mercurial temperament. He had always oscillated between great optimism and depression. This is known by the psychiatrists as the manic depressive temperament. My feeling was that this was a manifestation of his natural temperament aggravated by overwork and strain."

"Had he followed your treatment?"

"He told me that he had taken the drugs, but he more or less admitted that he ignored my advice to rest, which of course was the most important part of the treatment. I told him that it was very difficult to treat him if he didn't take advice and said that the only thing for him to do now was to stop work altogether. I didn't think that he needed to take to his bed because that might aggravate his anxiety and give him too much time to brood. But I thought he must have a complete holiday. I also said that I would like him to see my colleague Dr. Franks."

"Dr. Franks is a psychiatrist?"

"Yes."

"How did he take this?"

"He argued against me very forcibly. Indeed, if I'm to be honest, he became somewhat aggressive. He accused me of having no knowledge or understanding of his condition, of recommending rest because I couldn't think of anything else, and of implying that he was going out of his mind."

"Did you think he was going out of his mind?"

"No, I didn't think he was psychotic or anything like it. I thought he had an anxiety state. Dr. Franks has made a specialty of anxiety neurosis."

"How did the interview end?"

"He stormed out of my consulting rooms."

"What did you do then?"

"I rang up Dr. Barton and explained what had happened. He was naturally very upset, but there was nothing we could do. If Kincaid refused treatment we couldn't force him to have it. We had to leave the matter there."

"What was the next you heard of Mr. Kincaid?"

"It was about two weeks later. Barton rang me up to say that Kincaid had suddenly collapsed in the middle of a reception at the Czech Embassy. I said that naturally I would be very glad to see Kincaid if he wanted me, but that after what had happened at our last meeting I couldn't very well do so otherwise. Barton said it was quite all right and that Kincaid was asking for me. So I admitted him to a private bed at St. Vincent's."

"How was he then?"

"His condition had obviously changed for the worse. He was rather rambling and disorientated and highly agitated. He was very apologetic about his behaviour at the previous consultation and kept emphasizing that he had ignored my advice and that he knew that I had tried to do my best for him. His leg reflexes were a little enhanced on the left side, his pulse was still rapid, and for the first time there was a slight temperature. We carried out some laboratory investigations and kept him under sedation.

He now said that his headache was rather severe. The clinical picture was still obscure but it was becoming apparent that there was more than a purely psychological condition present. Over the next few days I called in several of my colleagues; Sir Horace Trimble, Lord Maxfield and Dr. Franks. Mr. Kincaid's condition remained fairly constant on the whole, though it varied from day to day."

"Was it about this time that you saw Professor Line?"

"Yes. Of course the news about Mr. Kincaid had received a lot of attention in the Press and everybody was talking about it. About four days after he had been admitted to hospital I was standing in the hall at the Royal Society of Medicine when Line came up and spoke to me. He seemed very agitated. He told me that he was a friend of Kincaid's and had been extremely distressed to hear that he was so ill. He asked me how he was getting on. I said that it was a difficult case but that we were doing our best to get to the bottom of it. He asked if we had made a diagnosis yet and I said no, not a precise one. I was perhaps not very forthcoming. It wasn't a question he should have asked."

"Why not?"

"It was a matter of professional confidence. One can't tell a patient's diagnosis to anyone who asks."

"How did the conversation proceed?"

"He said he had heard that we had had difficulty in arriving at a diagnosis and that this was the kind of case in which record analysis might be of some value. I said that I doubted it. He said that the Brook-Halder machine was at my disposal and they would be pleased to analyse my data in the case and see if they could help with the diagnosis. I thanked him very much and told him I would bear his offer in mind."

"And did you?"

"Of course. I discussed it with Sir Horace Trimble and Lord Maxfield. None of us thought that it would be of any help."

"I see. Now how did Mr. Kincaid's condition develop after this?"

"About a week later he had another attack in which he became unconscious. There was loss of power and sensation in the left

184

leg. His temperature and pulse were raised. He was very restless. It appeared that some kind of intracerebral episode had taken place."

Groom said dryly, "You mean that something had happened inside his skull?"

"Yes. It wasn't easy to know exactly what it was, but on the whole we inclined to the view that he had a cerebral tumour which had broken down and given rise to haemorrhage. That would have accounted for most of the findings, though the temperature was a little high. At this stage we called in Mr. Dudley, the neurosurgeon."

"What did he think?"

"He said he thought it was impossible to be sure, but that some further investigations were necessary. In particular a ventriculogram."

"What is that?"

"It's a procedure by which air is injected into a cavity in the brain and then X-rays are taken, to see if there is any deformity in the shape of the cavity."

"Was this done?"

"Yes."

"And what happened?"

"The procedure seemed to upset the patient to an unusual degree. A rather indefinite shadow was shown, but Mr. Kincaid first became very restless and then went gradually into a coma. It appeared that there was a serious and continuing rise in intracerebral pressure. Also his temperature went up to 101. Indications now were that we were dealing with an infected process, probably an abscess, which was increasing rapidly in size. We decided there was only one thing to do if the patient's life was to be saved. This was an operation to drain the abscess and relieve the pressure."

"And was this done?"

"Yes. Mr. Dudley operated immediately. There was an abscess there and he drained it. Mr. Kincaid's condition improved somewhat when the drainage was completed."

"Who was in the operating theatre at the beginning of the operation?"

"Mr. Dudley and his two assistants; theatre sister and her

three assistants; Dr. Parsons the anaesthesist; myself; Sir Horace Trimble; and Lord Maxfield."

"Was Professor Line there?"

"No."

"Was he there later?"

"Yes. Much to my surprise. I was looking round the theatre just after the main part of the operation had been completed, when I saw someone in a mask and gown whom I didn't recognize. I said to Sister, 'Who is that?' She said 'Professor Line.' I went up to him and asked him what he was doing here. He didn't answer, so I said, 'You have no right to be in this theatre.' He said, 'Dudley agreed to it.' I said, 'I am in charge of this case. You should have asked me.' "

"What happened then?"

"I didn't want to argue with him in front of the nursing staff and perhaps distract Mr. Dudley from his operation. I asked him if he'd mind coming out of the theatre into the surgeons' room so that we could speak there. When we got into the surgeons' room I told him again that I thought he should have asked my permission to attend the operation. He disputed this, and we were just arguing about the matter when one of the nurses came in and told me that Kincaid's condition had suddenly deteriorated. When I got back into the theatre I found that his pulse was difficult to feel and he was obviously extremely ill. We did our best to resuscitate him but unfortunately it was to no avail."

"I see. And Line?"

"I forgot all about Line. When I did remember, he'd gone."

"Yes. Now I believe there was an inquest on Mr. Kincaid?"

"Yes."

"And what was the final diagnosis of his condition?"

"It was discovered at the post-mortem that his brain abscess had been the result of spread from a relatively minor infection of his lung with an infectious fungus, an aspergillus."

"Is this an uncommon condition?"

"Extremely uncommon."

"Is this fungus a usual source of infection in this country?"

"No. It's a tropical disease. It was assumed that Mr. Kincaid must have picked it up on his world trip."

"Did Mr. Kincaid ever show any signs of a chest infection?"

"No."

"Is it unusual for a man to have a chest infection and show no signs?"

"It can happen. A small focus of infection without symptoms can sometimes lead to very serious complications."

"Can you think of any way in which this diagnosis could have been made earlier?"

"No."

"After the inquest, what was the next you heard of this matter?"

"It was when I opened my copy of *Medical Science* and read Professor Line's letter."

"And this was totally unexpected?"

"Totally."

"He had never told you beforehand that he was about to write such a letter?"

"No."

"These charges he made in the published letter, did he ever make those to you in private, as one professional man to another, to give you a chance of answering them?"

"No. Never."

"Supposing he had, what would have been your reaction?"

"I should have given him all the evidence to show that there was no basis for his statement."

"When you read the letter, what did you do?"

"Well, I first consulted with my solicitor and my colleagues who had also been involved in looking after Mr. Kincaid and we all agreed that the letter was obviously defamatory. I therefore called upon Professor Line and the publishers of *Medical Science* to withdraw the statements."

"And did they?"

"The editor of *Medical Science*, Dr. Gale, agreed instantly to put in a notice in the journal next week in the form I requested, apologizing for the statements."

Groom paused for a moment. Then he said, "And Professor Line?"

"He refused."

"And what did you do then?"

"I brought this action. I had no alternative."

Chapter 6

GROOM NODDED respectfully to Gilling and sat down. The easy part was over. Gilling braced himself for the ordeal of the cross-examination. He had a picture of Symons suddenly firing at him violent, unexpected, and hostile questions, for which he would be totally unprepared. But in fact the cross-examination started very quietly. It was really not very noticeably different from the examination in chief.

Symons said, "Sir Thomas, I'd like to question you in more detail about your views on this machine. Are we to understand you consider it entirely valueless?"

"I wouldn't say entirely valueless. It may be useful occasionally, but not often enough to justify its routine use." He added, "In my opinion it's a very crude substitute for the human mind. Since human minds are available, it seems hardly necessary."

"Surely it is regarded as an accessory rather than a substitute? An aid to the physician?"

"I can't see the point of an aid which is inferior to the physician himself."

Symons leaned forward eagerly. For the first time Gilling realized how dangerous he could be. "But the physician does use aids, doesn't he? A book isn't a substitute for a physician, but it may be indispensable to supplement a stock of information."

Gilling floundered a little. "I don't think that's a valid parallel."

"Wouldn't you accept the proposition that this machine is, in fact, a kind of enormously detailed reference book, which can check back to see whether any possibilities have been forgotten or overlooked?"

Gilling shook his head uneasily. "No, I wouldn't."

Symons worried at the point remorselessly. "You would agree that we can all forget things? We can all make mistakes?"

"Certainly."

"So it might be considered useful to have a check back of this kind? Just to see what the machine said?"

"I wouldn't consider its advice of value. It would necessarily only have access to information about the patient which I should give it, which would be less than that available to my own brain. And since the computer is neither as complex nor as flexible as my own brain, I would be in effect asking advice from something inferior to myself."

"Inferior to yourself?" Symons seemed to savour the phrase. Repeated, with the inflexion he gave it, it did indeed sound a little arrogant. He said softly, "Can you be sure, Sir Thomas, that there's not an element of vanity here? That you don't like to think that a machine could do something which you couldn't?"

"No, of course not. That's absurd."

"Is it? After all," said Symons, "there's a certain mystique about being a doctor, isn't there? Especially a very important doctor. Are you sure that there isn't something slightly distasteful about the idea of being corrected by a machine?"

"Quite sure," said Gilling curtly.

Symons frowned. "But the computer has certain advantages over you, surely? It has a more accurate memory."

"Perhaps. For information it receives. But it doesn't have anything comparable to my experience with patients."

Symons looked at him steadily. "Are you then saying that this machine is *never* any value in diagnosis?"

This was difficult, but Gilling had anticipated it. He was aware that Line was able to produce examples of success with the computer. He explained easily, "Well, of course anything or anybody can occasionally be useful. A junior student can occasionally offer a useful suggestion. But that doesn't mean that one should ask his advice as a routine."

Slightly to his surprise, Symons did not pursue this point. Instead, he asked, "Did you consistently oppose the spending of money to develop this particular technique?"

"On the occasions when I was asked my opinion, I came down against it. My personal opinion was that this was a very expensive field of research with few applications. Moreover, it was fundamentally not medical research at all but research in electronic engineering."

"Surely you wouldn't deny money to work in medicine based on engineering principles?"

"One has to judge every case on its merits. That was my opinion about this particular project."

Symons looked down and shuffled through some of the papers on the desk in front of him. "When you were asked to use the machine on Kincaid, there was no expense involved then, was there? The machine was there."

"It was my opinion, and that of my colleagues in charge of the case, that it would not be of any assistance."

"I see." Symons paused. "Perhaps now we could go into some of the details of Mr. Kincaid's illness. Would you at any time have considered him to be an easy case?"

"No. He was a very difficult case."

"More so than the ordinary run?"

"Yes."

"In an exceptional case like that, might it not have been worth while to try anything that might help?"

Gilling was prepared for this too. "There's a tendency for people to say 'try anything'—particularly in a difficult case. But one has to be selective. One can't subject the patient to every conceivable form of investigation."

Again Symons pounced on the weakness of the answer. "But you wouldn't have been subjecting Mr. Kincaid to anything, would you? All you had to do was to put the information into the machine."

Gilling was angry with himself. He had done the one thing which Groom had warned him against. He had talked too much and given the opposition an unnecessary opening. He covered up again. "I can only say, from my own very considerable experience, that I don't think it would have helped."

Symons looked again at the table in front of him. From a heap of papers on it he picked out a pile of foolscap sheets. "I have here a copy of the hospital case notes. Do they contain a complete background of Mr. Kincaid's illness?"

"Yes."

Symons looked carefully through them. "They're obviously very careful and detailed. There's just one part I don't quite understand. Under the heading Personal History, there are no details at all—simply the two letters W.S. What does that mean?"

"The letters stand for Wimpole Street. It means that any information regarding his personal life was kept in a special locked file at my rooms in Wimpole Street. This is usual with important public figures like Mr. Kincaid. One can't run any risk of such information falling into the wrong hands."

There was a slight pause. Symons was not entirely sure how to handle this. "Of course," he said, "your discretion is commendable, Sir Thomas, but it does seem that we have something less than the complete story here. It places us in rather a difficult position."

"I can assure you that this part of the history doesn't bear on the final diagnosis."

Symons was silent for a moment. Gilling could see him debating within himself the advisability of pressing the matter further. Finally he decided against it. "Well," he said, "I don't wish to be difficult. Perhaps we can see how we get on. Now, Sir Thomas, when did you feel that you had actually made a diagnosis in this case?"

Gilling relaxed. He had been worried for a moment when Symons had picked up that point about the personal history, but it seemed to be over now. "Medicine isn't quite so clear-cut as that," he said. "One tries to make a provisional diagnosis at the first examination. Then one tries to confirm or exclude that by laboratory tests. Sometimes it's easy, sometimes more difficult. The provisional diagnosis may be simply the most likely of several alternatives."

"After your first examination of Mr. Kincaid, what was your provisional diagnosis?"

By a sharpening in Symons's tone, Gilling could feel that the pressure was about to begin. He would have to walk warily from now on. "Anxiety state and overstrain," he said.

"And after the second?"

"The same. Rather more severe."

"And you were satisfied with that?"

"I thought it was correct—yes."

Symons's voice was soft but with an undertone of menace. "But it was not correct, as it turned out?"

"It was certainly not the whole story. I think he probably had an anxiety state, overlaid on his physical condition."

"You listened to his chest?"

"Of course."

"And you heard nothing, in spite of the fact that he probably had some, what did you call it—focus of infection—there?"

"Yes, that is so. The X-ray was also quite normal."

"He had no signs of brain abscess?"

"None."

"Now you say in your evidence that he had a raised pulse. Is that typical of an anxiety state?"

"It's quite a usual finding. A response to the strain and excitement of examination."

"And the tremor, is that common?"

"Oh yes."

"And brisk reflexes, is that common?"

"Not common. It can occur."

"Did he have any other symptoms of significance?"

"I don't think so."

"Tingling in his fingers?" Symons was reading from the case history.

"Oh yes—slightly. I remember now."

"What significance did you attach to this?"

"No special significance. People can complain of many small symptoms of this kind when they have an anxiety state."

"Headache?"

"Yes, he complained of headaches."

"You thought all these were neurotic symptoms?"

"I dislike the word 'neurotic.' It has disparaging undertones. I thought they were manifestations of anxiety."

"These are, of course, symptoms which can be associated with serious organic disease?"

"Sometimes, yes. But there was no indication from my examination or the laboratory tests that that was so in this case."

"I see." Symons turned another page in the case notes.

"So Mr. Kincaid received sedatives and advice to rest. Now, when you saw him a month later, he seemed worse—so you say. He had lost weight, he was pale, and his pulse was higher. One hundred and four per minute according to your records. That's quite high, isn't it?"

"Yes, quite high. He was really very agitated."

"You still thought it was nothing more than that?"

"Yes."

"Psychologically he was really acting very strangely, wasn't he?"

"Well—he was agitated."

"But surely in a different way from the previous time?"

"That wasn't too surprising, under the circumstances."

Symons said sharply, "Under what circumstances?"

Gilling was a little flustered. "The circumstances of the case," he said weakly.

Symons frowned. "You mean—anxiety neurosis?"

Gilling hesitated. He had a feeling of a situation moving, ever so slightly, out of his control. "Yes."

Symons regarded him carefully. "You seemed to hesitate a little there, Sir Thomas. Are you sure you considered this as an ordinary case of anxiety state?"

"That was my provisional diagnosis."

"Did you know of a certain occasion, three days before he saw you for the second time, when Mr. Kincaid had a rather distressing experience in the House of Commons? When he completely lost himself in the middle of his speech?"

"Yes. I knew of that."

"Is that a usual symptom in anxiety neurosis?"

"Not exactly usual. Possible. A manifestation of tension——"

"Even in a man like Mr. Kincaid, who had been in the House for about twenty years? It wasn't a very important speech."

"It could happen."

"It never occurred to you at that time that there might be some other trouble?"

Gilling had to fight back his irritation. There was something maddening about this incessant probing. It would have been bad enough if it had been an easy case and he had been proud of his handling of it. But in the present circumstances . . . all the pride of his profession rebelled against being exposed to criticism by a layman. He said shortly, "It's easy to be wise after the event."

"May I suggest to you," said Symons, "that this blackout, this very high pulse, this loss of weight, this striking psychological change in the two visits—were rather unusual symptoms for a run-of-the-mill psychoneurotic."

"There's no such thing as a run-of-the-mill psychoneurotic. Surprising symptoms are the rule in psychological medicine."

Symons looked dubious. "But the next time you saw him, he was even more surprising, wasn't he? He had a temperature, certain changes in reflexes, he was rambling, he imagined things, he had hallucinations. I believe at this point you abandoned your original diagnosis?"

"Yes."

"What did you diagnose now?"

"At this point," said Gilling, conscious of how weak it must sound, "we weren't quite sure."

"You weren't quite sure," repeated Symons deliberately. "And how long was it until you were—quite sure?"

"It wasn't until he had the further attack that we were able to narrow it down to a lesion in the skull."

"And it wasn't until after the operation that you knew it was an abscess?"

"No."

"And it wasn't until after the post-mortem that you knew the cause of the abscess?"

"No." Put coldly like that, it sounded dreadful. How could one possibly make them realize the agonizing difficulty of the whole affair? "As I have emphasized, it was a very difficult case."

"I think everyone in court appreciates that, Sir Thomas." There was a slightly triumphant note in Symons's voice now, as if he felt well in control of the situation. He said with some emphasis, "Surely that was a sufficient reason to use any help you could get?"

"I called in several of the best physicians in London." Gilling was beginning to feel alarmed. Somehow everything he said was beginning to sound shifty and defensive. There was a tiny moment of panic before he answered each question, a moment of terror that he might say the wrong, the dangerous, thing. He struggled to fight it down.

"But you weren't prepared to avail yourself of Professor Line's offer?"

"I couldn't see that it would have helped."

"It would have been no trouble, it would have cost nothing. Who knows, it might have come up with the answer?"

"I didn't believe it would."

"You think you and your colleagues got as near to the diagnosis as was possible?"

"Yes."

"And yet, Sir Thomas, with all due respect, there are certain odd and anomalous features in this case. You have said so. And for a week after Mr. Kincaid came into hospital you were really without a diagnosis at all. According to what you say, he had symptoms, he had signs, and yet with the whole battery of scientific investigation you weren't even able to make a *guess* at what might be wrong? You had no idea at all?"

The insolence of the man was intolerable. Gilling snapped, "I said we weren't able to narrow it down for a week. I didn't say we had no ideas."

"Very well, you had ideas." Symons's stocky figure radiated aggressive scepticism. "What were they?"

Gilling frowned. He felt a chill wind of danger blowing near him. He protested. "I can't see the point in going into this. These were discarded diagnoses. Some of them were mere guesses. What value could they be?"

Before Symons could press the point the judge intervened. He said dubiously, "Mr. Symons, is this really relevant?"

Symons turned away from Gilling to look at the judge. Instantly his manner changed. He became less determined, more conciliatory. "My Lord, we are proposing to show that this machine can add something to the process by which Sir Thomas arrives at his diagnosis. I submit that his methods of coming to a decision are relevant in this connection."

The judge still looked dubious. "I really have my doubts as to whether we can effectively analyze Sir Thomas's thought processes in this court. I think we must draw the line at discussing ideas which simply passed through his head. Is there anything about this in his notes at the time?"

"No, my Lord."

"Then, I think I agree with Sir Thomas. Could you find some more concrete line of questioning?"

Symons inclined his head. "As your Lordship pleases." He accepted the judge's ruling equably, almost, it seemed, with indifference. Gilling tried hard not to show his relief. It had been a near thing, the judge had saved him. He suddenly thought triumphantly, Symons is giving up, I've beaten him, he can think of no more questions, I'm home. There was quite a long silence as Symons leafed through the case history in a leisurely fashion. Then his eyes seemed to be caught by something on the first page. He looked up at Gilling and said casually, "Just one more thing. On this case sheet you have written in capital letters in one corner NO MORPHIA. Why was that?"

Gilling hesitated. After his initial relief, it was difficult to get back his earlier wariness, his concentration on what he was saying. He said, "I thought it might be dangerous."

Symons frowned. He gave the impression of a man who has a suspicion that he has stumbled on something important, but has no very clear idea why or how. Sensing by instinct the lack of confidence in Gilling's reply, he pressed the question. "Dangerous? Why?"

Gilling hesitated again. This was something he had not anticipated. He had forgotten all about that confounded note about morphia. Suddenly he realized that he was not safe at all, he was in danger again. Serious danger. "Well, perhaps inadvisable would be a better word. My registrar might easily have written it up—the patient was restless, one has to be careful."

He realized he was floundering.

Symons pressed again, obviously hoping desperately for some clue as to what he had discovered. "But why? What harm would morphia have done?"

Try as he would, Gilling could think of no satisfactory way out of the trap into which he had been led. "It's a question of general principles," he said vaguely. "If one isn't sure of the diagnosis. These drugs can be dangerous——"

"In what way?"

"Well—they can sometimes cause coma."

"Surely not in small doses?"

"That rather depends on the individual patient."

"I see." Symons was like a man solving a puzzle, laboriously, piece by piece. "So you thought Mr. Kincaid was particularly at risk with morphia?"

"Yes," said Gilling with some reluctance. "Yes, I did."

Symons picked up the case sheet and looked at it again very carefully. "Now when was it—on what date—that you wrote NO MORPHIA on the case sheet?"

It would have been too dangerous to lie about it. There would almost certainly be other witnesses. "At the beginning. When he came into hospital."

"Yes. That's how it looks." Symons thought for a moment. Then he looked up in puzzlement. Another piece of the jig-saw had fallen into place. "But surely he wasn't so very ill then, was he? He was conscious, he wasn't restless—was he?"

"No."

"Yet one of the first things you did was to write NO MORPHIA on his case sheet. Why?"

Cornered and desperate, Gilling tried wildly to repeat the method of his earlier reprieve. He looked up at the judge. "Really, I can't see the relevance of all this——"

He saw from the look on the judge's face that there would be no help from that quarter this time. As he searched for some kind of answer, a flash of illumination seemed to come over Symons's face. He leaned forward and said eagerly, "You had a reason, didn't you, Sir Thomas? What was it?" As Gilling hesitated again he said fiercely, "Was it anything to do with that part of the history you kept back in Wimpole Street?"

There was a silence. Gilling stood helplessly in the witness box. What was he to do? What could he possibly do? There was no possibility of holding out any more. They would get it from him now. And even if they didn't, everyone would be guessing, perhaps guessing things even worse than the truth. He made one last appeal to the judge. "My Lord, this is really very difficult for me. It concerns Mr. Kincaid's private affairs——"

The judge shook his head. "I'm sorry, Sir Thomas. This is

a court of law. The question is good. I'm afraid you must answer. Why were you so afraid of morphia?"

It was the moment of betrayal. Betrayal not only of Kincaid, but of his own honour, of his profession, of his special position as the repository of all the secrets of the great. "Kincaid was an advanced alcoholic," he said. "His liver was badly damaged. Morphia would have killed him."

Chapter 7

As he heard the murmur of astonishment which passed through the court, Gilling remembered his own appalled reaction when he had first heard the news. It was hard to describe the magnitude of the shock. He knew, perhaps better than anybody, how many discreditable secrets were hidden in the lives of the eminent, how many were drunkards or drug addicts or sexual perverts or subject to periodical attacks of mental derangement. He knew only too well that most powerful men were merely ordinary men to whom power had been fortuitously given, who ran the nation's economy or foreign policy with the same haphazard improvisation as they would have given in less fortunate circumstances to the management of a sweet shop. But Kincaid was different. When he had first appeared on the political scene, it had seemed that for once, by pure chance, democracy had managed to throw up a leader who possessed, not only imagination and administrative capacity, but the kind of integrity for which the electorate had now almost ceased to hope. He had presented the image of a Chatham, a Churchill, a Kennedy. His determined uncompromising character had not made him an easy colleague for conventional party politicians, and his career had been marked by a series of spectacular resignations on points of principle. These had led him into the position of a leader of a small but dedicated rebel group in the governing party. This group was well known to exercise an influence far out of proportion to its numbers. It represented, as did Kincaid's own personality, the only moral element in a political system where both main parties had sunk themselves in opportunism and electioneering. If Kincaid, too, was corrupt and degenerate, then night had truly fallen on British politics. There was nothing left.

Gilling had heard it first from Barton. Dr. Alastair Barton was a prominent member of that group of high-class fashionable Mayfair family physicians which, it had been predicted, would vanish without a trace from the face of the earth as soon as the National Health Service was introduced. In fact, they had flourished as never before. Gilling knew Barton to be pompous and stupid but painstaking and honest. His charges were high but he gave good value for it. He was a tremendous snob. He loved to let people know the names of his rich and important patients, but his discretion about their ailments and private affairs was absolute. He wore a black suit with a white shirt and stiff collar and shiny black shoes. He had a small neat moustache and his head was almost entirely bald.

He came through to Gilling one evening on the telephone. He was as self-important and heavily discreet as usual. He said, in a low, heavily significant voice, "I have rather an important patient I should like to consult you about, Tom. Do you think you could manage to pop in for a drink some time this evening?"

Gilling felt for his diary. "Well now let me see . . ."

"I can fit it in any time you are free. It's rather urgent. I'm afraid I can't talk about it on the phone. It's very confidential."

"I could manage seven o'clock this evening."

"Fine. Very many thanks." His voice became brisk again. "I look forward to seeing you then."

Cases of this kind from Barton were nothing new. Gilling wondered vaguely who it could be. Even now, if he was to be honest, he got a certain excitement out of this kind of thing. He had a normal human liking for being in the know, for being in possession of the innermost secrets of the great ones of the land. It was with a slight thrill of curiosity that he went that evening to Barton's house in Eccleston Square. Barton received him deferentially in his book-lined study. He poured out a glass of sherry.

"Well," said Gilling, "what's the story?"

"Rather a difficult one, I'm afraid." Barton gazed inscrutably into his glass of wine. "It's John Kincaid. You know him?"

"I've never met him personally." There was a silence. Barton seemed unusually hesitant. Gilling said, "What's his trouble?"

Barton put his glass down, turned slightly away from Gilling, and said abruptly, "He's an alcoholic."

Gilling felt not only startled, but in some way betrayed and let down. It was as if he had personally relied on Kincaid, as if Kincaid had promised him something, had raised his hopes and cynically cheated him. But it is not the job of a fashionable physician to take up moral attitudes. He pulled himself together and said in a matter of fact voice, "How long?"

"Off and on for about five years. Every so often he takes a grip on himself and goes right off it. Then under strain he tends to cave in again." Gilling felt a sudden pity for Kincaid. Perhaps he, too, like Gilling himself, was tormented by a sense of failure, a feeling of unfulfilled promise. Barton went on, "He's very careful in public and indeed he keeps it pretty quiet from his own family. Nowadays he doesn't drink much at all with other people, but he keeps a bottle in his bedroom and tends to go in and have a jolt periodically. He was off until three months ago, then his wife noticed he was beginning to act a little strangely in the evenings and she knew he was on it again. Then recently he went on a world tour—you may have read of it?"

"Yes."

"It was pretty strenuous. Australia, Japan, India, Pakistan, Egypt and so on. Anyway he came back looking rather shot and obviously knocking it back quite heavily."

"Did he tell you this himself?"

"No, that's the devil of it. I'm not sure about the best way to handle it. I had the story from his wife, Molly. She's been a patient of mine for years. She's desperately worried about him." He frowned solemnly and took a sip from his sherry glass. He was, thought Gilling, rather like one of those characters who appear in the first act of a drawing-room comedy and tell everybody the plot. "She can't get him to admit that he's drinking again, but she knows he is. She's here at the moment, as a matter of fact, waiting in the drawing-room. She'd like to talk to you if possible."

Gilling agreed. In the circumstances there seemed no reason to object to meeting her. When they went into the drawing-room he saw a middle-aged, handsome, controlled woman. She looked like the classical political wife, thoroughly trained to say the right thing at every occasion, to open bazaars and make minor speeches, to be always on duty. She said, "It's very good of you to see me, Sir Thomas. If you can help my husband you'd be doing a great thing. Not just for me but for many other people." Gilling nodded understandingly. "The real problem is that he won't admit he's drinking, even to me. I doubt whether he'd admit it to you either. But I can assure you that he is. I know him so well and I can tell when he's taking it even when other people can't. Also I've found bottles . . ." She flushed. "I put them back and don't tell him. It's terribly important—he's a very proud man, you see—that he shouldn't realize that I know he's lying. It would be a horrible humiliation for him. So I can't help him any more. I have to pretend it isn't happening. Yet if it goes on I know he'll break up. Or else somebody will spot it."

"If he won't admit it to you, how can we get him to come and see me?"

"He's prepared to agree that he's tired and overwrought following this big trip of his. I could get him to come to you for a check-up."

Gilling frowned. "But I could hardly raise the question of alcohol. He would obviously want to know how I knew about it."

"Yes, I know that. And if you did, I think he'd get very angry and deny it." She shrugged her shoulders. "But we've got to try something, haven't we? I just hoped you might be able to get it across to him."

"I suppose I could try." Gilling's voice was dubious. It sounded like one of the most difficult and unpleasant cases imaginable. But he was taken by Molly Kincaid. And in any case there was no alternative. He must do the best he could.

Looking back, as he had done so often since Kincaid's death, he had often thought that perhaps this was the point at which his whole management of the case had gone wrong. At that time his main worry was how he was going to tackle the problem without antagonizing Kincaid. It was a reasonable anxiety but he wondered now whether this distraction had not led him into a fateful error. Had he committed the ultimate sin which he constantly warned his students against; had he, that is to say, started out with a preconceived idea which had distorted his whole handling of the case afterwards?

It was, he thought suddenly with bitterness, this damned business of dealing with important people. The whole relationship with the patient was damaged somehow. Theoretically, he should have approached Kincaid purely as an individual, wiping everything else from his mind, and making his own assessment on the facts alone. But it was not so easy. One had to face the fact—important men *were* different. They thought of themselves differently, their problems were different, so much hinged upon their state of health that you couldn't treat them just like ordinary people.

Yet he could not absolve himself from blame. Difficult though it was, it was supposed to be his sort of problem, the kind he was specially skilled to cope with. And he had failed.

When Kincaid came for the first consultation Gilling had the usual feeling on first meeting a celebrity. The face and voice and mannerisms were so familiar that he had the sensation of being acquainted with Kincaid, yet not on a plane which was relevant to normal life. He was smaller than Gilling had imagined, dominant in a cheerful, off-hand way, and he projected an impressive vitality. His manner, though amiable, contained a certain resentment. This, in Gilling's experience, was normal in important men—in front of the doctor they felt themselves in an unaccustomed position of disadvantage. As Gilling examined him he was only half thinking of the diagnosis. His main preoccupation was the problem of how to introduce the question of alcohol. The results of his physical examinations seemed to fit in fairly well with what Barton had told him. When the examination was finished Kincaid put his jacket back on and grinned at Gilling.

"As you see, there's nothing whatever the matter with me. My wife worries. Then she goes and worries Barton. He's a pompous idiot, don't you think?" He laughed. "All right, you needn't answer that. I never thought he was very intelligent, but Molly has confidence in him. In my job it's my business to spot stupid men, just like it's yours to spot sick ones." He lit a cigarette; his hand trembled slightly as he held the light to it. "Now, what have you got to say to me?"

Gilling could not help admiring the way in which he managed to assume a degree of ascendancy even in these unfavourable circumstances. He knew that the difficult part of the interview was about to begin. He began very warily. "You've been doing too much. You're tired. Overstrained. You should take it easy. Cut down on engagements. Take plenty of sleep. We'll give you sedatives at night and tranquillizers by day. I'll write you a prescription for those. You ought to cut down on your smoking. As far as alcohol is concerned"—he spoke with a deliberate casualness—"I think you ought to cut that out altogether."

Kincaid frowned. "Altogether?" Gilling nodded. "I'm afraid that's quite impossible."

"Why?"

"Well—I go to a lot of functions, embassy receptions and so on. If I refuse a glass of sherry and start yelling for orange juice God knows what they'll think."

"Oh surely——"

"My dear fellow, you don't know what my life is—I live in a goldfish bowl. It would be all over Fleet Street in twenty-four hours that I couldn't trust myself."

All the amiability had gone out of his voice. What he said was quite sensible, but surely there was far too much emotional charge behind the words. He was ready to fly into a rage. It seemed to Gilling that if he pressed the matter any farther the whole situation might come into the open and perhaps do more harm than good. It might be better to leave it till a later consultation when he had gained Kincaid's confidence. He said reluctantly, "Very well then, as little as you can."

"Of course." The engaging smile flashed back on Kincaid's face. The tense moment was over.

"And see me again in a month."

He rang Barton afterwards and told him about the consultation. He suggested that Molly Kincaid should keep an eye on her husband and try to get him to follow his advice. For the moment one could only wait and see. Personally he was not too hopeful.

When Kincaid returned a month later Gilling saw immediately that his fears had been realized. Kincaid was plainly worse. His tremor had increased and there was an agitation about his manner which had not been present on the first occasion.

"Did you rest?" asked Gilling.

"How can I?" Kincaid was defensive. "I have a job to do. I can't just drop everything."

"That's what they all say," said Gilling easily. "Then they have a heart attack and they have to go to bed. They find that others can take over." He smiled at Kincaid but Kincaid did not smile back, he merely looked sulky. "How are you feeling?"

Kincaid seemed to wonder for a moment whether to tell the truth or not. Then he shrugged. "Rotten."

"In what way?"

He said in a staccato voice, "Headache. Can't sleep. Seem to be losing weight. Tired all the time." There was really, Gilling noted, a remarkable change in his manner. His easy dominance had turned to irritability, his confidence to depression. Plainly he was a manic-depressive type of personality, which was fairly common in drinkers. Just now he was in the down phase. "I just feel I'm breaking up. I've burnt myself out."

"You've been overdoing things, that's all."

"Last week in the House I had a sort of attack, went muzzy. Lost the thread of what I was saying. Never happened to me before."

"You can't account for it in any way?"

"No."

"What time did this happen?"

"About half past three in the afternoon. I had been at the Grocers' Company to lunch in the City. It went on rather a long time. I smoked a couple of cigars. That might have been it."

Gilling nodded thoughtfully. He had been to City luncheons in his time. It was not too difficult to guess what had happened.

Kincaid said rather anxiously, "Do you think it could be that? The cigars, I mean?"

"It's possible," said Gilling cautiously. He looked down at the case sheet on which he was filling details and said casually, "Did you have much to drink?"

Once again Kincaid lost all his amiability. He said acidly, "I wasn't drunk, if that's what you're suggesting." He looked up at Gilling as if hoping for a quarrel. But Gilling remained silent and eventually Kincaid said sulkily, "A few glasses of red wine, that was all."

He glared at Gilling aggressively, but Gilling made no comment. He put down his pen and said, "Now I'd like to examine you again."

The examination showed a definite deterioration in Kincaid's condition. Loss of weight was very noticeable. His skin was dry and the tremor was aggravated. His general depression of manner was a noticeable contrast to his behaviour on the previous occasion.

Gilling said, "You're obviously aware yourself that you're not at all well. I'm afraid I'm going to have to insist upon a complete rest."

"What do you mean by that?"

"No public engagements at all. You're to go away for a few weeks. Just you and your wife. You don't need to go to bed. If you do you'll only brood. Play golf or something like that. Good meals, sunshine, absolutely no smoking or drinking whatsoever——"

Kincaid turned and looked at him with great intensity. "Sir Thomas, has my wife been talking to you?"

It was an unpleasant moment. Gilling said evenly, "I spoke to her on one occasion. I advised her how to look after you."

"It's odd you didn't tell me about it." His hostility was now overt. He said with a shade of contempt, "I must confess I'm a little disappointed in you."

"Why?"

"Because I visualized this as a relationship between you and me. Barton is my wife's doctor and I always feel that they're engaged in a little conspiracy—in my interests of course, but just the same I resent it. I hadn't thought that you had involved yourself in this."

In face of this attack, Gilling retired as if by some natural protective reflex behind the patronizing platitudes of the medical adviser. He said soothingly, "Everyone is trying to help you, Mr. Kincaid. No one has any ulterior motive."

Kincaid was not soothed. He said aggressively, "Did my wife tell you that I was drinking too much?"

The violence of his manner was alarming, and Gilling judged it necessary to lie. "No. She said you were under great strain. She was worried about you."

Suddenly all the violence went out of Kincaid's manner. He

sighed despondently. "Everybody lies to me. That's the worst about being ill. You can't trust anyone. They feel justified in deceiving you. My wife lied to you. I'm not an alcoholic. Do you believe me?"

Gilling found himself treating Kincaid more or less like a psychiatric case. "Of course," he said. "But I still think your nerves are very upset. What I'd like to do is to call a friend of mine into consultation. He's a specialist in nervous conditions."

Kincaid's eyes narrowed. "A psychiatrist?"

"He's a neurologist and a psychiatrist——"

Kincaid laughed shortly. "First I'm drunk, then I'm out of my mind?"

Gilling said gently, "Mr. Kincaid, you're too intelligent to say things like that."

Kincaid seemed not to have heard him. "You're no use to me, I'm afraid." He stood up and appeared to pull himself together. Gilling recognized once again this remarkable quality he had of suddenly assuming the position of ascendancy. "I suppose I had exaggerated hopes of you. I was misled by your reputation." He grinned ruefully. "You'd think I, of all people, would know how little reputations really mean."

Gilling was too experienced to be drawn by this. He said, "I can only advise. I can't compel you to receive treatment."

"No, that's true." He shook hands with an almost jaunty manner. "Good-bye, Sir Thomas."

Gilling watched him through the window as he went down the steps of the Wimpole Street house. His chauffeur opened the car door and as Kincaid sank into the back seat he suddenly seemed to crumple. The effort required for that last exit must have been almost more than he could summon. Now he was ill, tired, and very lonely. Gilling turned away from the window and began to think about his next patient. There was nothing more he could do.

Later he made a telephone call to Barton. It was plain to both of them that his efforts had been a failure. So long as Kincaid was not prepared to admit the truth and was not prepared to accept treatment, there was nothing further to be done. Gilling thought it was likely that this would be the last he would hear of the case. But two weeks later Barton rang him again.

"It's Kincaid. He's collapsed at a reception at the Czech Embassy. Could you come and see him?"

"I'd be glad to, of course. But it's rather difficult. Last time——"

"He wants you. He keeps asking for you."

"Oh, in that case—of course I'll come. Where is he now?"

"I'm speaking from the Embassy. He's lying down in a room here. I think he ought to be in hospital."

"I'll get him a private room at St. Vincent's and see him there."

When Gilling went to see Kincaid in hospital he was shocked at the deterioration in his condition. Barton said in a hushed voice, "I think he has the D.T.s."

Gilling found himself becoming rather exasperated with Barton. There was something funereal about the man, as if he enjoyed these catastrophes. His irritation was increased by the fact that even after a full examination he had difficulty in coming to a decision about Kincaid. It wasn't really very much like D.T.s, and there was a temperature. For the first time he began to have a suspicion that he might possibly have missed something right from the beginning. But what?

The collapse at the Czech Embassy had been dramatic and unexpected and the papers were full of Kincaid's illness. Gilling set up a battery of laboratory investigations and called Trimble and Maxfield into consultation. Soon it became plain that there was something more than mere alcoholism involved. Kincaid's condition varied quite markedly from day to day. In contrast to the previous occasion on which they had met, he seemed to have developed a great confidence in Gilling. In one lucid moment he said, "It was good of you to come to me. I behaved very badly." The apology filled Gilling with guilt. He was conscious that he had deceived Kincaid. In his own interests, it was true—nevertheless he felt ashamed. Kincaid went on, "I lied to you when I said I hadn't been drinking. It was this awful headache and this feeling of tension. I just felt I couldn't manage without it."

"Don't think about it. It's unimportant."

"But this last attack couldn't be anything to do with it. I've taken nothing for a week."

"I know. Don't think about it."

"There's something badly wrong with me," Kincaid said painfully. "Something quite different from the drinking. I'm sure of it." By this time Gilling was beginning to think so too. The thing which caused him so much anxiety was that he had no idea what it was. His investigations had taken him nowhere. Neither Maxfield nor Trimble had been able to come up with any useful idea. And now the papers were beginning to report that Kincaid was very ill. Each time Gilling left the building he was photographed, and it had become necessary to put out frequent bulletins of progress. The journalists reported every word of these non-committal reports and brought in their own experts to analyze them. They could make little sense of them, which was not surprising. With increasing anxiety Gilling and his colleagues waited for some symptom or sign to show itself which would give them a clue to the diagnosis.

It was just after one of these fruitless consultations that he ran into Line in the hall of the Royal Society of Medicine. To his surprise Line stopped him just as he was about to get into the lift. "Sir Thomas." Gilling raised his eyebrows and said nothing. For years he and Line had avoided each other socially. They could hardly be regarded as being on speaking terms. But it was not possible to avoid him without pushing him physically aside. Line said, "How's Kincaid?"

Gilling said, "He's very ill."

Line seemed undeterred by the discouraging reception he was getting. He went on doggedly, "I asked because he's a friend of mine and I have the greatest admiration for him. I was very distressed to hear that he was unwell." He paused as if waiting for Gilling to make at least some slight overture of friendship but Gilling said nothing. "Could I ask you if you have made a diagnosis yet?"

"We're waiting for some investigations."

"I see." From Line's tone it was plain that he interpreted this as an admission of complete mystification. "I just wanted to say this. As you know, at the Metropolitan we have this very elaborate system for analyzing clinical data." If Gilling had not been so angry he would have been amused by the elephantine way in which he tried to avoid referring to the Brook-Halder machine. "Sometimes in a case like this it does help to process the available information. It's just possible that we may have had a similar case in the last thirty years and it would give you a line. If you'd like to avail yourself of it——"

Gilling was furious and his fury was aggravated because he was worried and at sea. He saw this as a crude attempt to exploit the Kincaid case to promote the Brook-Halder machine. If he agreed to use it, Line would go around saying that he had poured scorn on it for years and then been only too happy to try it when he was in a difficulty.

"Thank you," he said curtly. "It's very kind of you. I'll bear it in mind." He saw Line open his mouth to speak, but then fortunately the lift descended and several people came out. He was able to dodge smartly past Line and press the button. The impudence of the man, he thought. A charlatan. A self-advertiser. How had he ever managed to get a chair at the Metropolitan?

And yet, he thought as he made his way back to the hospital, it would be a relief when they found something which gave them a line on the case. Nowadays he was finding it hard to fight down a sense of panic. If only Kincaid would suddenly improve. He could remember so many cases where this had happened, and then suddenly afterwards nobody could imagine why they had been so worried. Then of course there were the others, when what seemed to be minor symptoms had turned without any warning into something quite disastrous.

He longed for a lucky break but nothing happened to help them. They worried and they conferred. Maxfield recommended endless complex laboratory tests. Most of these gave no information, and even when positive results were obtained he was disinclined to commit himself on their interpretation. Trimble, by contrast, had a habit of making wild guesses and retracting them the next day. Franks, the psychiatrist, had written an enormous case history, followed by a commentary phrased in incomprehensible jargon. He at least was in no hurry to make up his mind—any dramatic deterioration would mean that it wasn't a psychiatric diagnosis anyway. A letter appeared from Line, repeating his offer in writing. Gilling threw it angrily aside and did not answer it. Two days later, quite unexpectedly, Kincaid collapsed. He was now unconscious and paralyzed down one side.

Gilling said, "I think there must be something inside his skull. We shall have to call in a surgeon."

The other two looked at him in consternation. Trimble said, "But who——?"

Gilling said gloomily, "I'm afraid it'll have to be Dudley."

Dudley was a spare, sardonic, sceptical man. Though a sound and competent neurosurgeon, he had a reputation for plain speaking and offensive behaviour which had been consistently damaging to his private practice. This had left Dudley with an illogical sense of grievance which had made his manners even worse than before. He was the last person Gilling would have chosen to have called in for a patient like Kincaid, but this was one of the difficulties about using private beds in one's own hospital. Dudley was the St. Vincent's neurosurgeon, and it would have been a deadly insult to have used someone from outside. Dudley was well aware of Gilling's dilemma and derived a certain amount of satisfaction from bringing it out into the open.

He said, "I'm flattered that you should have asked me, but really you don't have to, you know. If you'd prefer to use someone from outside——"

"No, no, I wouldn't think of it." Gilling could hardly turn back now, much as he would have liked to. "There's no one in the world whose opinion I value more——"

Dudley cackled. "Don't overdo it, Tom. Just be honest. If you prefer Hartly or Shenker——"

"Nonsense, my dear fellow." Gilling brushed him aside. He was very worried and had no time for this sort of pantomime. "Now, he's pretty bad. How soon do you think you could get along and see him?"

After the consultation they all retired to the ward office for a conference. It was a fairly small room, hardly big enough for the five people present—Gilling, Maxfield, Trimble, Franks and Dudley. Dudley looked around at them with some amusement. He was well aware that none of them liked him.

He whisked through the case notes. "Well, this is a bit dicey. We don't know where we are." He turned over another page.

"I take it you're not expecting a diagnosis out of me. Not after all the big brains you have on the problem." He looked again at the notes. "You've been having some fun with him, haven't you?"

Dudley dropped the notes on the table. It was a slightly offensive, contemptuous gesture. Gilling picked them up, he hardly knew why. Dudley said, "Five different antibiotics, hydrocortisone, intravenous vitamin B12, low protein diet—he's really had the works."

He made no attempt to be pleasant about it. Certainly, Gilling had to admit uneasily, when you looked through the treatment sheet it didn't give the impression of a particularly well-managed case. He was fond of saying to his students that a careful study of the case notes could tell you, not only about the patient, but also about the competence and thoroughness of the doctor in charge. One of his favourite lectures was on the importance of the case history. He saw it as a logical progression, starting with the account of the patient about his illness, his response to expert questioning, then the objective information obtained by examination, supplemented by the laboratory and X-ray investigations. From these you made your primary diagnosis and initiated the correct treatment. It was how he liked to think he did it himself.

Now for the first time it occurred to him that all this was nonsense. If he was honest with himself, he didn't make a diagnosis in a precise logical way at all. The more usual process was that the patient's symptoms and signs reminded him in rather a vague indefinite way of something he had seen before; he then set about confirming or excluding this possibility. If he excluded it, he thought again, searching for the most likely possibility; he went on until his investigations confirmed this hunch. Sometimes, having arrived at an answer this way, he would take the students to the patient and give a teaching, pretending that he had made the diagnosis by the conventional method—by this time he often actually thought he had. It was the same with treatment. It was all supposed to be logical and scientific and carried out according to plan. If there was a bacterium you used the right antibiotic to kill it, if there was a deficiency you corrected it, if there was thrombosis you gave anticoagulants, if the blood pressure was too high, you lowered it. You were in charge, like the pilot of an aircraft, turning a knob here, pulling a lever there.

In simple cases it might work like this. But then anyone could treat the simple cases, just as anyone could make a simple diagnosis. As soon as difficulties arose, the whole plan went out of the window. You were back with hunches and guesses and vague memories of something which had worked on a previous occasion, you weren't quite sure how. Every physician had his obsessions, his favourite diagnoses and methods of treatment, just as every surgeon had his favourite instruments.

Looking through Kincaid's case notes he realized that he could have used them very effectively as an object lesson, a cautionary tale for beginners. For instance, he had not waited until his examination was finished before making his provisional diagnosis; he had in fact accepted it from someone else—from Barton, a man whose intellect he despised. In the interests of tact and diplomacy he had not even questioned Kincaid properly about his drinking habits. He had played for time, given useless wishy-washy advice, and hoped for the best. Then, when it became obvious that there was something more than alcoholism, he had been taken on the wrong foot, he had never been able to adjust himself properly to the changing situation. He had taken the easy way by calling in a variety of helpers, none of whom were any better qualified than himself. Each one, after a first examination, was full of incisive logic and suggestions for new investigations. Each, when the treatment obstinately refused to work, had retreated into his favourite method of management of a difficult case. Maxfield had favoured corticosteroids. Trimble had voted for antibiotics, the psychiatrist for tranquillizers. The whole thing was like a battle, planned neatly and precisely beforehand, but thrown into utter confusion by the refusal of the enemy to conform to the plan.

Well, he thought, that was medicine, just as real and important as the medicine he taught to his students. It was not his fault that it was like that. Medicine was difficult, you couldn't win all the time. His fault lay in the vanity and complacency, in that he had not admitted the truth to himself. He knew now that what he taught was at least in part a fraud. And as he accepted that fact, his mind turned by the natural process of logic to himself. Line thought him a fraud, he knew. Was it possible that Line was right?

Dudley said, "Like you, I think there's a lesion in his skull. I don't know what it is, but it seems to be getting bigger. Of course, the trouble with the skull is that you can't just open it up and have a look."

"Then what do you recommend?"

"We could stick a needle into his ventricles and pop some air in. An X-ray might show something. If it's a tumour there would be distortion. It could be an abscess, of course. If so, we might try to get a needle in, get some pus out. We'll have to see." He bared his teeth apprehensively. "Mind you, he looks pretty dicky. We can't do too much and get away with it, not the way he is. We can use a local anaesthetic. Give him a decent dose of morphia——"

Gilling said, "I'm afraid not."

"Why not?"

"His liver's in very bad shape. He couldn't take morphia. Some barbiturate perhaps."

Dudley sighed. "Oh well—if you say so." He rolled his eyes. "Happy days. Let's do it this afternoon."

Everywhere, thought Gilling, it was the same—there seemed to be far too many people. It was the same in the operating theatre; what with the attending physician, Dudley's assistants, theatre nurses and porters, the anaesthetist, it was difficult to move without bumping into somebody. Fortunately it was a fairly large theatre and Dudley didn't seem to be put off by the crowd. Kincaid was almost comatose, even without a general anaesthetic. It was oppressively hot and the tension was considerable. It was an atmosphere one grew to recognize, the sort of atmosphere which accompanied a case which wasn't going too well, when the doctors were in trouble. Everyone down to the most junior nurses knew it immediately. They all waited while Dudley towelled up, then made two incisions in the scalp and removed a small piece of bone with a burr. He put the needle through into the lateral ventricle of the brain and injected some air. X-rays were taken. Then there was another long wait while the

X-ray plates were developed. Dudley sat on a stool. "Everything takes a long time in neurosurgery," he said philosophically.

The X-ray films were brought back and they all had a conference with the radiologist in the surgeon's room. It was agreed that there was a distortion of the ventricle on the right-hand side. That tied in with the paralysis of the leg on the left-hand side. It looked as if something must be pressing on the ventricle.

Dudley said, "Well, there we are. There's something here. We still don't know what it is. It could be a localized abscess with this temperature he has. But where the hell does it come from? The antibiotics didn't help. It just might be a haemorrhage, I suppose, or a tumour——" He turned to Gilling. "We have to make up our minds now. Either we go looking for it, which is damn' dangerous, or we leave him and hope for the best. Personally I reckon he'll die if we leave him." He added sardonically, "What does the committee think?"

There was a slight silence, then Maxfield spoke reluctantly. "I think we all agree," he said.

"Right. Then let's go for it."

To the spectators Dudley's procedure seemed interminable. Gilling remembered from his early days that watching operations was almost more exhausting than performing them. He grew weary from standing in the oppressive heat in these stuffy clothes and he was full of apprehension at the outcome. He was overcome by the feeling of impending disaster. No good would come of all this. Everything had been wrong from the start.

He looked round, hoping vaguely to see an encouraging face. Everyone was in gown, cap, and mask and it was difficult to recognize one person from another. Trimble was easily identified by his magnificent belly, Maxfield by the curiously amateurish way in which he tied the strings of his cap—he was not used to operating rooms. The anaesthetist and Barton looked pretty similar. Gilling could not identify the exact moment when he sensed that there was an extra person in the theatre. At first he wondered if it might be a theatre porter or an assistant anaesthetist or someone from the X-ray department. But the man stood apart. He seemed to have no connection with anyone else present. All Gilling could see between the cap and the mask was a pair of cold blue eyes, intent on every detail of the operation. It was all very odd. He was wondering how to find out who the stranger was when Dudley said, "Ah ha."

Gilling moved forward. "What is it?"

"It's an abscess all right." He showed Gilling a syringe full of pale yellow liquid. "I got a needle into it."

"What are you going to do now?"

"I'll have to go down a bit. Get to the place where it's nearest the surface. Then we can open it and suck it out. But it's deep. It won't be too easy." He said to the anaesthetist, "How is he, Liston?"

"Could be worse. I'm giving him a whiff of gas to keep him asleep."

"It's when we open the abscess and let the pressure down—that's when we have to watch out for trouble. Everything's pushed over to one side at the moment. When it swings back suddenly you can get a collapse. See what I mean?" He moved out of the way to show Gilling the operating field. Gilling looked and then moved away; Maxfield and Trimble looked in their turn. Dudley still stood aside. He said, "Do you see it, David?" The man with the pale eyes nodded his head without speaking. Suddenly, with a choking sense of rage, Gilling realized who it was.

Dudley had turned back to his work. Gilling went up to the stranger and said in a whisper, "Professor Line?"

Line nodded.

"Might I have a word with you outside?"

Line hesitated for a moment and then walked out of the theatre. Gilling followed him. They went into the surgeons' room. Gilling said, "What are you doing here?"

Line leaned against the table and pulled his mask below his mouth. He said equably, "Dudley invited me."

"He never informed me."

Line shrugged and said nothing. He was not, his attitude seemed to say, responsible for Dudley's behaviour. Gilling said, "This is my case. I should have been consulted." Again Line said nothing. "This is most unprofessional."

"I'm sorry," said Line, without noticeable contrition.

"It's really outrageous." Gilling was trembling, with an old man's nervous rage. "We've enough problems as it is without

every Tom, Dick and Harry wandering in and out of the theatre."
He glared at Line. "This case has nothing to do with you.
Nothing at all. I haven't asked your advice."

"I know that."

"It's monstrous. You come pestering me with suggestions,
invading the theatre, writing me letters, interfering. I won't
have it. Please understand that."

"Kincaid's a friend of mine," said Line obstinately.

"If Kincaid or his family wanted you to treat him they would
have called you at the beginning. As it happens, they called me.
Please leave this theatre."

"I was merely trying to help. I have certain facilities. I just
wanted to put them at your disposal."

"I've already told you. If I want your help, I'll ask for it."

"It's common knowledge you're in difficulties——"

"Look, Professor Line, for the last time——" It was a dreadful
situation. This was the kind of agonizing personal confrontation
that he had been able to avoid for practically all his life. Now
he felt himself helpless against this man who obstinately refused
to take hints, to behave with common decency, to play to the
rules. He searched for some way of handling the situation with
dignity, a form of words which would leave him in charge of the
field. As he struggled there was a knock on the door. The ward
sister poked a frightened head in.

"Sir Thomas, I'm sorry to interrupt you but Mr. Dudley
would like you to come into the theatre." As Gilling paused to
put his mask back over his nose, she said, "Urgently." He knew
then, from the look in her eyes, that Kincaid was dead.

Chapter 8

It was not often, in Symons's experience, that one suddenly uncovered a completely new aspect to the case during cross-examination. Usually the weak spots of a witness were fairly easy to see in advance, and it was possible within limits to work out a strategy of attack and keep to it. He had tried to do this with Gilling. He had, according to his usual practice, pushed hard and hoped for the best. His considerable experience in the courts and elsewhere had told him that Gilling, like every other powerful man, must be constantly engaged in practices and compromises of which he was secretly ashamed. He knew that Gilling must be engaged in jobbery and favouritism because that was the way of all great men. He knew that Gilling's statements that grounds for research were always made fairly and sensibly must be a lie, since such statements always were. He knew that Gilling must be to some extent prejudiced and bigoted, and that he must occasionally mishandle a case and make foolish mistakes —because, after all, Gilling was human. He had hoped to convince the jury of all these less attractive aspects of Gilling's life and character. But what he had never expected was that Gilling would try to conceal some vital piece of information bearing directly on the case. It was not Gilling's dishonesty which surprised him. It was the fact that he should dare to take such a risk.

The discovery was so startling that he was at first disconcerted by it. It was hard, on the spur of the moment, to know how the fact that the folk hero Kincaid had been a secret alcoholic was going to affect the outcome of the case. Much now would depend on himself and the way he handled the subsequent cross-examination. The news, he could see, had dropped like a bomb into the press benches and the public gallery. There was a hub-bub of excited conversation. The delay while the judge called for silence gave him a few moments to gather his wits together. He was just about to resume cross-examination when he felt a tug at his sleeve. It was Bradwell.

The solicitor spoke in an anxious whisper. "I'm afraid this was news to us. And to Professor Line. He'd like to discuss the implications before going any further. Is it possible to get an adjournment?"

Symons thought for a moment. It would prevent him going for Gilling straight away, and would give the witness time to recover his balance, which was in theory a bad thing. On the other hand, heavy pressure on Gilling now might even have the effect of rousing sympathy. He had lied, it was true, but it might well be possible to present it as a gallant lie. A lie to protect the reputation of a great man. There was a danger of showing him in a heroic rather than in a discreditable light if one wasn't careful. Also this was the kind of issue on which the client had a right to be heard. He looked at Groom, who nodded almost imperceptibly in agreement. Both sides were anxious to regroup before resuming the battle.

He looked up at the judge.

"My Lord, this has come as a complete surprise to myself and my client. We were under the impression that we had been informed of all the clinical details about Mr. Kincaid. Would it be possible to have an adjournment for discussion?"

"Has Sir Frederick any objection?"

"None at all, my Lord."

The judge looked at his watch. "It's getting along for four o'clock. Perhaps it might be as well to adjourn the court until Monday."

Back in his chambers Symons poured Line and Bradwell a glass of sherry and said, "Well, that was a carry-on, wasn't it? You could have knocked me down with a feather." He said to Line, "And you had no idea at all?"

"None." Line was looking very thoughtful indeed. Symons regarded him with a certain anxiety. He found Line a slightly disturbing client. He could never be sure that Line was being entirely open with him—he always seemed to be holding something back. If Line had been the man to suppress an important piece of evidence, he would have been hardly surprised. The curious thing was that he thought of Gilling in exactly the opposite way; he had envied Groom his precise, hard-headed, sensible client, predictable both in his virtues and his vices, the sort of man you knew where you were with. He suddenly chuckled.

"What's the joke?" said Bradwell.

"I was thinking of Groom. He's a marvellous old chap—his face never moved an inch. But he must have felt the floor was giving way under him." Line spoke for the first time. "Kincaid," he said in an appalled voice. "My God, it's hardly believable."

Symons shrugged impatiently. He disliked these hushed tones. Line had spoken like a schoolboy who has just heard that the captain of the first eleven had been caught cheating in an examination. "I didn't know him personally, but I suppose he was a man like any other."

"He wasn't a man like any other," said Line. "That's the whole point. He could have been in the Cabinet any time he had wanted. All he had to do was to play in—just a little, just enough to show that he was one of them. And he wouldn't. Because he didn't believe in it. That makes him something special."

Symons shook his head. "Now that one hears it, I'm not too surprised to find that Kincaid hit the bottle. There's something a bit abnormal about so much standing alone and fighting the good fight." He could see Line frowning angrily. Plenty of identification there, he thought with amusement. Line saw himself, in his own way, as a kind of Kincaid, sacrificing himself for the right. "After all it's just another form of egoism. A rather self-destructive kind."

Bradwell cut in. He said to Line, "You mustn't take too much notice of Oscar's philosophy. To him virtue and honour are simply manifestations of neurosis. It's a consequence of spending a life in the Law Courts."

Line managed to force a laugh. "Yes, I can see that." My God, he thought, how could he have got himself involved with such men. Bradwell the tweedy do-gooder, taking up the case in the same way that he might take up vegetarianism or racial discrimination; Symons the cheap cynic, the hired hatchet man, the dog you set on your enemy to tear him to pieces. He longed to get back to Susan, to the boys at the hospital. He felt degraded in this office. He said, "I shall have to get back to the Metropolitan."

Symons nodded. "Then let's talk detail. The important thing here is to concentrate on the case and forget everything else. The papers are going to be screaming their heads off with all this stuff about Kincaid and it's easy to fall into the trap of attaching too much importance to it. My guess is that there wasn't anything particularly sinister in the concealment of this evidence. I imagine Gilling and the others got together and decided, as these important gentlemen tend to do, that there were certain things which the general public wasn't entitled to know, and this was one of them. The fact that it was a matter of extreme importance in the case didn't appear to them to matter. Now of course from a legal point of view that was very naughty indeed and we're all shocked. But juries haven't nearly as much respect for the law as the chaps who make their living out of it. They're liable to see Gilling as rather a gallant old gentleman, shielding his patient from dishonour until finally trapped into revealing all by wicked lawyers. So we've got to go canny here."

"All right," said Line. "So what's your plan?"

"We have to destroy that kind of picture completely—for good and for all," said Symons. His eyes narrowed; his bulldog face was wrinkled with determination. "We have to show that the reason Gilling held out on us was not out of gallantry but from fear. After all, why didn't he make the diagnosis? Isn't it possible that the main reason was his obsession with this problem of the alcoholism, which blinded him to other possibilities?" He said to Line, "As a medical man you could tell me that."

Line thought for a moment. "Yes, it's possible. Even likely. His early management of the case was curiously hesitant. I imagine he started off with the idea that they were all alcoholic symptoms—as indeed they could have been—and didn't start to consider alternatives until quite late on."

"Excellent." Symons was triumphant. "So we get him on that. The prisoner of a preconceived idea. It fits in beautifully

221

with his rejection of your machine—that also cut across his pre-conceived notions. We link the two together and get a picture of him as a rigid, inflexible old man who can't adapt his mind to new situations. My plan is to take him through the case again, in enormous detail, every little thing. We can do that justifiably since he's tried to deceive us about it. At each point we go for him on the basis of this preconceived idea. We'll hammer him with that. If we can really get it over he's beaten. He'll never get up again."

Line regarded him with distaste. "I don't think I can really accept that supposition. My feeling is that he kept quiet about the drinking to protect Kincaid. I would have done the same myself."

"Not on my advice, you wouldn't," retorted Symons.

Line ignored him. "In fact I can't help feeling that it's very unfortunate that it had to come out. I know it wasn't your fault that it did, but just the same—— After all, it doesn't really affect the main issues. It's a tragedy for Molly Kincaid. And it puts a very unpleasant atmosphere into the case." He brooded, "If only Groom had confided in us beforehand, we might have agreed to leave it out."

Bradwell said, "That would have been quite impossible."

"Would it?" said Line vaguely. "Well, it's too late now. But I can't help feeling that the less we say about it the better."

"The better for whom?" said Symons caustically. "It would suit Gilling very nicely."

"We're not in a mud-slinging competition," said Line. "We've got to draw the line somewhere."

"Don't you want to win the case?"

"Of course I do. But not at the price of my self-respect."

Symons said angrily, "I don't know about your self-respect or what exactly it amounts to, but I want to make it quite clear that you can't win if we go soft on Gilling. You can be certain of that."

"I didn't say go soft on him."

"You didn't like my plan for cross-examination. You thought it was too tough. Well, this is a tough business. After all, you threw the first brick when you wrote that letter. I'm supposed to prove you were justified. I can't do that if you tie my hands."

"I simply said I didn't think your theory was right. I think the reason Gilling didn't mention it——"

"Look, forget what you think or what you suppose. When Groom gets you on the stand he won't be giving you the benefit of the doubt. It's our business to put *our* case. They're quite capable of putting theirs."

Bradwell said, "I think one has to accept that, Line. It's the way the law's designed to work."

"Damn the law. We've got to be honest with ourselves."

Symons said disgustedly, "That kind of remark means nothing to me. What are you trying to say? If you don't like my proposals for conducting cross-examination, I want to know what your own are." He added menacingly, "Then I can tell you whether I accept them."

Line was beginning to detest Symons. Anyone might think that it was he who was under cross-examination and not Gilling. But he retracted a little. "Naturally I realize you're the expert. I'm not trying to teach you your job——"

"Aren't you?"

"But I have the right to express an opinion. To you this is just another case. To me it's—well, my whole life depends on it."

"My idea was to try and save your life."

"Your idea is to win the case. That's what you're really worrying about. A victory for yourself." He was no longer even pretending to be polite. "You mustn't try to humbug me."

For once he had Symons disconcerted. Bradwell stepped in. "I think you two are at cross-purposes here. I can sympathize with you, Line. I don't think we should ever be so keen to win that we use discreditable methods. On the other hand I don't believe Symons suggested anything of the kind. We can't deny ourselves a strong cross-examination of a witness who has already proved himself to be lying. That's what it really amounts to."

Line said, as if to himself, "I detest Gilling and everything he stands for. But there's such a thing as honour." Symons was about to speak but Line unexpectedly got up from his seat and made for the door. He said over his shoulder, "Remember that when you're cross-examining on Monday." Then, to their astonishment, he was out of the room.

The two men sat in silence for a moment. Then Symons said, "Marvellous, brilliant. Is he often like that?"

Bradwell said, "He's an emotional man."

"He's a crackpot, if you ask me. He doesn't want to be nasty to Gilling. On the other hand he doesn't want to interfere with my cross-examination. What am I going to do?"

Bradwell looked at him with something between fear and dislike, between admiration and disgust. If you employed a savage animal to defend you, you had only two choices, to imprison it or set it free. By leaving the issue in doubt, Line had made his choice whether he knew it or not. "Why ask me?" he said. "You know very well what you're going to do."

Susan said, "I'd like a drink."

Line threw himself into a chair. His face was wrinkled with a kind of sulky resentment. He said, "Help yourself. You know where the things are."

She did not move. Her mouth tightened. "I want you to pour it for me."

He said in an aggrieved voice, "Don't tell me you've chosen a time like this to get feminine."

"I haven't chosen anything," she said sharply. "I *am* feminine. The fact that I sleep with you doesn't entitle you to treat me the way you treat your——" She searched for an extreme example. "Your house surgeons."

His indignation was almost comic. "What the devil did you mean? I treat my house surgeons like equals."

"When you remember." She laughed. "Poor boys, I've seen them suffering. You know, they'd really be very much happier if you simply acted like the boss."

He put his hand to his forehead. "I really don't understand. What have I done to you? Just because I asked you to get your own drink——"

"Oh, don't be silly." Had she really hurt him with those remarks about the house surgeons, she wondered. Had it even registered properly? It was difficult to know with David. He obviously thought she was being bitchy, and perhaps he was right. But the day had upset her badly. And it was at least partly his fault.

"Then what is it?" he asked. "What's wrong? Why do you attack me in this way?"

She did not reply. She said, "Can I have a drink?"

"Of course you can." He got up from his chair. With a sudden change of manner he said, "I'm sorry if I was discourteous. What can I get you?"

"I'll have a Scotch on ice." As he went into the kitchen for the ice it occurred to her that they were on the verge of their first serious quarrel. The thought sobered her. When he came back with the drink she made an effort to be casual. "Thanks."

"Is that all right?" he asked.

"Perfect."

"I'm glad." He sat down. "Now perhaps you'll tell me what you're so angry about."

"You have no idea, I suppose?" She put down the glass quickly. She could feel her hand beginning to tremble.

"No."

She could see he was telling the truth and her anger returned. "You've perhaps forgotten that when you left me outside the court-room to go and talk to your solicitor, you said you'd come back and take me home."

"I did?" He was incredulous. "Are you sure? I could have sworn——" He passed a hand across his brow. "I thought I asked you to meet me here."

"You didn't. You said you'd come back. You left me there to be tormented by reporters and newspaper photographers. It took me almost half an hour to realize you weren't coming back." She was near to tears at the recollection of the incident. "If it hadn't been for Brook I might have been there still."

He frowned. "You're sure you didn't misunderstand me?"

"Certain."

"Well, if you say so." He was reluctantly prepared to believe her. "It must have just slipped my memory. Such a day—you've no idea."

She was resolved not to be so easily appeased. "It's not the first time."

He ignored this challenge to take the issue on to broader ground. It was true that misunderstandings of this kind were not uncommon with him. He had always been unpunctual and absent-minded, he was constantly busy, he forgot times and appointments. When there was trouble about it his usual reaction was to feel rather aggrieved. People should be more understanding. . . . In the hospital, for instance, if he came late to his operating list or his out-patients, as he not infrequently did, nobody was difficult or sulky. Everyone took it for granted that he had a good reason. It was tiresome of Susan to make such a fuss about it.

"I'm sorry," he said curtly. "I was busy and anxious. I evidently forgot. I'm sorry."

She sipped her drink without replying. He was suddenly maddened. "I've apologized. Isn't that good enough?" She said nothing. "You might come half-way to meet me—instead of sitting there—sulking."

"I'm not sulking." Her voice was not angry now. It was calm and rather speculative. "You don't understand, do you? You think it's rather unreasonable for me to be put out about this. To you it's a small thing. But it isn't to me." She paused and then said, "We should be quite clear about something, David. I regard myself as your equal. If you want me to stay with you you must treat me as such."

"You're being utterly absurd," he said, with genuine perplexity. "You couldn't have a man more easy-going than I am. Everyone treats me exactly as they please."

"That's your favourite delusion."

"I never have any trouble with the people who work with me. Good God, if I turn up late at the hospital, Sister knows she's perfectly at liberty to complain——"

"Except that she doesn't, does she? Obviously not, or you wouldn't get in such a state when I do. I suppose she just grits her teeth and says 'I quite understand, Mr. Line'—and Brook and Halder and the housemen and the probationers all crack their faces trying to smile about it. But supposing *they're* late. How about that?"

He said uncomfortably, "That's an absurd comparison. They're not so busy."

"Well, I am." She finished her drink. "That's all I have to say. Now tell me, what happened with Symons? How did it go?"

He said despondently, "Not too well."

"Why not?"

"Symons is an able man, but he's narrow. He cares for nothing but his own reputation as an advocate. He just wants to be a winner. The real issues of the case mean nothing to him."

"Wasn't that the sort of man you wanted?"

"Up to a point, of course, but—it's unsatisfactory talking to him. I don't seem to have any real contact. He has no"—he hesitated for a word and then said awkwardly—"no human sympathy."

"And Bradwell?"

"He's not much use either," he said irritably. "Too bloody home-knitted altogether." He burst out, "Christ, you've no idea how depressing it is to have no confidence in the people on your own side."

There was a silence. Then she said, "It wasn't really a good day, was it?"

He said defensively, "I suppose it didn't go too badly."

"Not for you perhaps." The real cause of her distress suddenly came back to her. She looked at him as if asking for an explanation. "But how about Kincaid?" When he did not reply she said accusingly, "What have you left of him? What about his wife and children? Have you thought what the case is doing to them?"

"You can't blame me for what happened."

"I didn't blame you. I just said it wasn't a very good day." She looked away from him. "I watched Gilling as he went out of court. Until then I'd seen the whole thing as a spectacle. It was slow going, it needed cutting a bit, but it had a sort of ponderous drama. When the court rose today I suppose I'd expected, in some absurd way, that everyone would take off their costumes and go back to normal life. Then I saw Gilling with his wife, just outside the court. He was hurrying, he wanted to avoid the photographers, he had his head down, his wife was almost holding him up. I saw his face, David—I saw his face——"

Her voice broke and he saw the tears in her eyes. She was an actress, he reminded himself, her emotions were superficial and mercurial, she cried and laughed easily. But his guilt would not be dispelled. He said, "It was his own fault. If he'd told me beforehand——" When she did not answer, he went on, "One has to do this kind of thing. If you go in you have to win. It's either him or me." He stopped suddenly. He realized he was talking like Symons.

"You wrote a letter two years ago," she said. "Did you think of this when you wrote it? I want you to tell me something." She looked at him painfully, her face contorted. The tears were rolling down her cheeks. "Would you have written it if you had known?"

"I don't know," he said hopelessly. "How can anyone know about a thing like that?"

Gilling made his way through the crowd and scrambled hurriedly into the car beside his wife. The chauffeur put the engine instantly into gear and forced his way through the busy traffic of the Strand. Gilling did not look directly at his wife. Instead he gazed out of the car window, watching the people hurrying across Waterloo Bridge towards the station, the coal barges forcing their way up the river against the tide. The lights were going up in the Shell building on the south bank. It was Friday and London was leaving, perhaps a little earlier than the rule required, for the week-end. In all the great stations, Waterloo and Paddington and Victoria and Liverpool Street, the commuters were pouring into the trains, each carrying his brief-case and umbrella and folded *Evening Standard*—each enduring his hour of purgatory as a price to be paid for the tidy trees and gardens, the golf and lawn-mowing and Perry Mason on Sunday evening. For the first time in his life Gilling found it in his heart to envy them. Though he would not have exchanged his life for theirs, for a moment he coveted their lack of responsibility, their innocence.

Neither he nor his wife spoke, but suddenly he felt her hand pressed against his and he knew that she had felt his loneliness and despair. Her hand was dry and bony, slightly swollen with arthritis; her rings hung loosely on the lean flesh around the knuckles. He pressed back gratefully, though the touch brought him little comfort. She loved him, he knew, but somehow she could not comfort him. Not as his mother or Gwen could have done. It was strange to learn as a man of over sixty the necessity of passion in a relationship with a woman. Without that, even friendship could be no more than superficial. He did not want a hand in his, he wanted a breast on which to pillow his head, the warmth and reassurance of the flesh.

She said, "You mustn't worry too much about this." She looked quickly at the partition to make sure that the chauffeur could have heard nothing. "I'm sure everyone understood your motives."

"Perhaps."

"Of course they did. And they sympathized. You were placed in an impossible position."

"I was wrong," he said. "I should have known we couldn't keep it secret."

"You could hardly be expected to make an announcement of it."

He voiced the thought that now lay constantly at the back of his mind. "Perhaps I should never have brought the action."

"You had to. You know you had to."

"I'm not so sure. If I ever had thought it would come to this——" She was good, he thought gratefully. She was kind and loyal, why could not her support give him consolation? "The trouble is——" He hesitated. "What happens to me involves the others."

"The others?"

He nodded. That was one of the penalties of a high position. Everything that happened to you sent out shock-waves like ripples in a pond when a stone drops into the water. There was no knowing how far the waves might spread, what they might touch, whom they might affect. But there were those so closely involved with you that they were bound to be affected. "Trimble. Maxfield. The Minister. This case has always been a worry to them. This may be the last straw. They'll be wondering how to get rid of me."

"Nonsense. You're tired and depressed."

"It's true," he said with conviction. "I'm becoming an embarrassment. In my position that's a great sin. Perhaps the greatest."

"You've done nothing wrong."

229

"That's not the point."

He tried to make her understand, but he could hardly explain it even to himself. He simply knew it—this was his world and he knew its ways by instinct rather than reason. But to his wife, he knew, it would always be mysterious. She was too simple and direct to comprehend the tortuous ways in which the world was managed. To her, people were good or bad, honest or dishonest; she believed in honour and virtue and service and loyalty— she was as medieval as the heraldic devices on her coat of arms.

"But they agreed with everything," she said. "They discussed it with you. Everything."

"Yes." She could not see that this was irrelevant—it was not what he had done, it was the fact of exposure which changed the situation. Power was founded on an illusion and the one thing which disqualified you from power was to be involved, whether by your own fault or by accident, in the destruction of that illusion. And the illusion was—what? Simply that one man was fit to be another man's master. His action might not have discredited him in the eyes of the public; indeed, it might have even made him popular. But it had humanized him. It had shown him up as capable of confusion, of conspiracy, of deceit. It was not permitted to a powerful man for his lies to be discovered. He tried to explain. "Those are the rules," he said. "They may be unfair but I've always lived by them. I can't complain if they go against me."

When they reached the house, he said, "I'm tired. I don't feel at my best." There was something drumming in his head and he could hardly get out of the car. A dreadful fear struck him. That tiny stroke that he had a year ago, that minor black-out, had it been a warning of something worse to come? Was he on the verge of another? He saw himself suddenly losing consciousness, crashing over on the path, with his mouth twisted and half his body paralysed. He saw the substance of his brain, the delicate cells smashed and torn by a tearing wall of blood, flattened and wrecked like a delicate field of grain in a hail-storm. Perhaps it might be his frontal lobes, and he would be affected in his speech and his memory, mumbling and gibbering, a helpless wreck of an old man, hidden in a wheel-chair behind the walls of his house, not even worth destroying any more. He had seen it happen to so many others; how could he have failed to visualize it happening to himself? Then he remembered the fear with which he woke up each morning. Perhaps below the level of consciousness something within him knew of the danger and feared it. Perhaps that was the source of his constant dread.

The fear was so great and so immediate that he was amazed to find himself walking normally from his car to the door of his home. Each movement of his legs seemed like a miracle. He felt his body as if it were an eggshell which might at any moment fall on to the floor and shatter into smithereens. If only he could get to bed and lie quietly in a darkened room, seeing no one, perhaps he might lose this precarious feeling. His circulation was like a bomb within him, prepared to burst and blow his brain to pieces. He said again, "I don't feel at all well. I must go to bed."

Patton said, "That's rather unfortunate. What's wrong with him?"

"They didn't say," said Maclaren. "Just that he was confined to bed. He wouldn't see or speak to anyone."

Patton shuffled the pencils in the rack on his desk. He liked the coloured ones in the front and the plain ones at the back. Would his secretary never learn? "Well, we shall have to confer in his absence." He scratched nervously at a rash on his left wrist. "What's your reaction to the situation?"

Maclaren had been a civil servant long enough not to answer silly questions like that. He lifted his eyebrows in a way that reminded Patton that his job was to give expert opinion and advice, not to react to situations. Patton flushed and said, "What I mean is, how much do you think Gilling has damaged himself?"

"Not too much so far. But in the end——" Maclaren shook his head. "He's going to have a tough day on Monday."

"He was less than frank with me, I'm afraid. They all were—even Trimble," Patton said with prim distaste. "It's very difficult to trust people who keep things back from you." Maclaren said nothing. A mournful expression came on to Patton's face.

"Poor Kincaid. Poor chap. Of course one had one's suspicions, but just the same——" He said with great solemnity, "I was talking to the Prime Minister about it earlier on."

"Yes?"

"It was a great shock to him. He used to be a good friend of Kincaid's at one time. Still regards him with considerable respect." Patton made a cipher notation on his scribbling pad. He must remember to enter that conversation in his diary. It would be good for his memoirs. *The tragic news about Kincaid was a complete surprise to me. I had no idea of the startling disclosure Sir Thomas Gilling was about to make in court. It was immediately plain that the whole position of Kincaid's group in the House of Commons was now thrown into the melting pot. Repercussions could be enormous. I immediately telephoned the Prime Minister. He said*——(Actually all he had said was, "Poor bastard, they might have spared him that"—but one could edit that a bit.) "He agreed with me that this was a very tragic and regrettable thing. Apart from the personal implications it destroys confidence in public life. A little of it rubs off on all of us."

"I suppose it will damage Kincaid's friends most of all."

"They were really finished politically as soon as he died," said Patton indifferently. "Between ourselves, some of them have been making overtures to patch things up for a little while, but the P.M. has been keeping them dangling." He had no sooner said it than he regretted his confidence. He always had a feeling that Maclaren secretly despised these political manœuvres. "But that's neither here nor there. Our task is to consider the Ministry. We've got rather heavily involved with Gilling over this Academy of Medicine. As things have turned out," he said reproachfully to Maclaren, "one rather wishes we hadn't. Not that I'm blaming anyone, of course."

Before Maclaren could reply there was a knock at the door. His secretary said, "Sir Horace Trimble and Lord Maxfield are here."

When the two men came in, Trimble was sweating more heavily than usual and Maxfield's gentle detachment seemed to have reached a point where it was hardly possible to make much contact with him at all. Neither of them looked like men with an entirely clear conscience.

Patton said, after the usual courtesies, "I think I must be frank. Sir Thomas's disclosure yesterday was a great shock to me. Until then I had the impression that I was completely in your confidence."

"Yes, yes, I quite understand," mumbled Trimble apologetically. "Most distressing for you. Can't say how sorry I am. Gilling thought it was for the best. I have to confess I agreed with him at the time."

Maxfield said dispassionately, "It was a conflict of loyalties. One didn't wish to cause unnecessary pain."

Patton nodded dubiously. "As it turned out, of course——" The Minister left his sentence unfinished. "I don't want to exaggerate the importance of this. Gilling hasn't lost the case yet, I appreciate that. But he didn't show up well yesterday and he's liable to have a rough passage on Monday. I have a feeling that whatever the outcome he's still not going to be an exact fit for Vice-President of the Academy of Medicine, not in the first instance. I don't know exactly how you gentlemen feel——"

Trimble said, "It's damn' difficult. I've had Miles Plant on to me about the same thing. But it seems a bit hard to make a decision before the case is even finished. Don't you think so, Maxfield?"

Maxfield said, in his most sepulchral voice, "I imagine that constitutionally a decision on the officers of the Academy can await its formation."

His face was impassive, his eyes half closed. Patton glanced at him sharply. What was Maxfield up to? To talk about the constitutional position was mere evasion—everybody knew that all the offices would, according to the usual procedure, be dished out beforehand. Did he think that Gilling was finished? Had he someone else up his sleeve for Vice-President? Time would show. In the meantime it was clear that the disposal of Gilling would present no difficulty.

"There's just one more thing," he said. "You gentlemen are going to be on the witness stand on Monday and Tuesday. I think you'll agree that I've invested enough of my personal reputation in this matter to be taken into your confidence. I hope there aren't going to be any more unpleasant revelations in court."

233

Trimble flushed. "Such as?"

"I don't know." He regarded Trimble unsympathetically. The fact was that Trimble's appearance alone was enough to sow certain seeds of doubt about his integrity—those jowls, that great belly, could hardly have been obtained by purely innocent means. Maxfield was rather more reassuring. One almost wondered how counsel was able to pluck up courage to question a man of such imperishable dignity. But then one might have thought the same about Gilling. . . .

When they had gone he said to Maclaren, "Do you ever get tired of these chaps?"

"Sometimes."

"I do." Patton got up from his seat. "They live their own life, they tell you nothing, they bow in and out of the room like fat Italian cardinals, then they go back to that bloody Vatican of theirs in Regent's Park and God knows what they get up to. I don't trust them an inch."

As he packed his papers carefully into his brief-case he said, "Sometimes I wonder if this Academy of Medicine is ever going to come to anything in the end."

Chapter 9

MONDAY was a bad day for Gilling. It was like one of the days of his boyhood when he had awakened in his cosy bed at home and realized with a sickening jolt that the week-end was over, safety was over, it was time for him to get up and dress and walk to Thorpe Hall to be beaten and humiliated. Since then, Mondays had grown easier for him. He had often felt sorry for men who were not so fortunate as himself; men who despised their work or feared their employers, or who started a week of drudgery without joy or hope. Now he felt sorry for no one but himself. Those curious agonies of apprehension in the moment after waking, from which he had suffered all his life, had not been meaningless after all. There had been many preparations for this moment.

In the face of a situation such as this, he knew, there was no real possibility of either flight or evasion. There was nothing you could do but to stand and suffer. That was what life told you from your earliest youth. You were like the men who were told to lay their heads on the block, to strip and climb up the table in the torture chamber, to put their hands in the shackles. Logically there was no reason why the condemned man should not at least struggle, bloody the nose of one of his executioners if nothing else; after all he had nothing to lose, you couldn't hang a man twice. But now Gilling knew that despair makes all other considerations irrelevant. Passion was spent, revenge was meaningless. His only function was to endure, with some shred of dignity, to the end of the punishment.

The cross-examination fully justified his fears. He had known that he would be attacked and had prepared his answers—he hoped at least to give a good account of himself. But he had completely miscalculated Symons's approach. He had imagined that this would consist of a serious, minute probing of the statements he had previously made, hostile and aggressive perhaps, trying always to catch him out in contradictions, but proceeding in an orderly logical sequence—the way, in fact, that he would have done it himself. But Symons used a quite different and profoundly disconcerting technique. He would ask questions on one subject up to a point and then, without warning, switch to another; after a little while he would work his way back to the original subject from a different angle, in the intention of catching Gilling out in a contradiction. It was not only confusing but also, despite the consistent courtesy of the questions, deeply insulting, since it was so obviously a technique which one employed in questioning a liar. The inference was that Gilling could no longer be relied on as an honourable witness. It would have been an exhausting ordeal at the best of times—in his present state of mind it was pure agony. Nor did he have any clear idea how well he was managing to stand up to the attack. Sometimes it seemed to him that Symons at least gave the impression of trapping him in contradictions. Incidents which had appeared clear in his mind beforehand became muddled as he described them. Some of his dates were slightly wrong. Certain things which he could have sworn he had remembered correctly had evidently not happened in precisely that way, since they conflicted with documentary evidence. As the questioning went on hour after hour, a kind of panic began gradually to overcome him. He found it hard to remember that he was the plaintiff in a civil action and not a prisoner in the dock on a criminal charge. Worse still, as the questions droned on, was the dreadful fear that perhaps in this ghastly reversed trial, he might not, after all be innocent. Somehow, during the time he had stood in the witness box, all the clarity and certainty had been driven out of his life. He no longer had confidence in the picture of himself which he had built up so painstakingly over the course of his professional career. It was as if the courtroom were a hall of mirrors in which he was constantly confronted with his own image from unexpected and frightening angles.

Could he really swear that he had done the best that could be done for Kincaid? Could he be sure that Brook had not been victimized? It was all very confused—so many factors had come into it. Brook was an unlikeable young man, there had been a general feeling that, clever as he was, his personality was such that he wouldn't really make it in the end. Could he be sure that the fact that Brook was a Jew had nothing to do with it? You could, of course, swear that it hadn't and no one could deny you. You could produce examples, any number of them, of very successful Jews in London teaching hospitals, but that wasn't the point. In a field like medicine, how the devil could you separate Brook's work from his personality, how could you separate his personality from his race? How could you view him apart from Line, his protector, who maddened and provoked everyone; deliberately, it seemed. And this confounded machine of his, was it really any good? How much had he taken against it on genuine scientific grounds and how much because it was such a repulsive mechanical idea; how much because Line had tried to ram it down their throats? How much had he been led into making this whole thing, this important matter of life and death, into a personal issue, a childish team game with himself and Trimble and Maxfield and the Minister on one side, and Line on the other?

He was wondering how much longer of the cross-examination he could possibly stand when, to his surprise, it was suddenly over. Subconsciously he had been expecting a dramatic development, a climax, with the victim driven to the ropes by a series of stunning blows and the fists drawn back for the kill. Instead, after a relatively innocuous question about a discrepancy in Kincaid's hospital records, Symons said "Thank you very much, Sir Thomas," and sat down at his table, shuffling away fussily at some papers. Then Groom was up for the re-examination, desiccated as ever but reassuring, picking up one by one the pieces Symons had chipped off from Gilling's public image and carefully, with professional deliberation, sticking them on again in the right places. Gradually Gilling began to feel more respectable, a little less like a card-sharper who had been caught red-handed without a hope of escape. He was able, when Groom had finished, to get back to his seat with a show of dignity.

But it was no more than a show. How he had appeared to the jury he could not know, but he was almost beyond caring. What had been irretrievably damaged was his own opinion of himself. In his own mind he had begun to accept Line's case. The career he had made for himself now seemed to him to be a sham, built on jobbery and conspiracy and the exploitation of others. It had led him to the point where he had killed Kincaid, as Line said he had, by incompetence and carelessness and pig-headedness.

He had never really considered this possibility before and the shock now was terrible to him. He looked at his wife. She smiled reassuringly and he smiled back. Now he felt ashamed before her as well. She was only another object which he had used to advance himself. Surely she must understand that by this time? Surely she must hate him too?

He heard snatches of the rest of the evidence. Gale, the editor of *Medical Science*, was explaining to Groom's junior just how the letter had come to be published. Gale was a thin, earnest man, with high magnifying spectacles and a wheezy voice due to chronic asthma. In the language of the police reports, he appeared to feel his position keenly. It had, he explained breathlessly, been an unfortunate series of accidents. He himself had been on holiday that week, the deputy editor had been called to a meeting, a relatively inexperienced assistant editor had been at the printers and had thought the letter had already been passed. . . . Later, when he came back from holiday and saw the letter in the journal, he was of course very distressed. At his meeting with Sir Thomas he had agreed to do everything possible in restitution. Sir Thomas had been very understanding, had accepted the journal's apology and had taken the matter no further. He had also telephoned Line and tried to persuade him to make a personal retraction. Unfortunately Professor Line had refused to do so. No, he certainly didn't consider any of the statements or inferences justified, in fact he would like to make it plain that he had the highest respect not only for the work but for the integrity . . .

He was overdoing it, thought Gilling, feeling slightly nauseated. Gale's eagerness to appease made him sound as if he were frightened to death, which was the last kind of impression they all wanted him to give. Why hadn't Groom anticipated this? It seemed as if Groom grasped the danger of the position at just about the same time as Gilling. He pulled his junior by the sleeve and whispered something in his ear. The examination ceased abruptly.

Symons rose for his cross-examination.

"Dr. Gale, the journal you edit is owned by a private company?"

"Yes."

"Do you have an advisory editorial board?"

"Yes."

"Composed of eminent physicians and surgeons?"

"Yes."

"What do they do?"

"They're available for advice on policy, on individual scientific papers, on recent developments in medicine and so on."

"They're valuable to you?"

"Naturally."

"Are Sir Thomas Gilling and Lord Maxfield members of this Board?"

"Yes, they are."

Symons paused for a moment to reflect. Then he moved unexpectedly into another area. "Now, you were away on holiday when the letter was received?"

"Yes."

"When did you first read the letter?"

"Not until the Saturday—when Sir Thomas telephoned me."

"You would have the journal for several days, though, before that?"

"Yes."

"But you didn't read it through?"

"Not all of it."

"Your own journal, for which you were responsible, and you didn't go through it between Thursday and Saturday?"

"Not completely."

"You're quite sure you didn't go through it, see this letter, and think—well, it's aggressive, but just good controversy?"

"Quite sure."

"Anyway, when Sir Thomas rang you up, you were shocked, you say?"

"Yes."

"And you took a taxi straight down to the Athenaeum Club—

where you were confronted with three of the big guns of the profession—Sir Thomas Gilling, Sir Horace Trimble, and Lord Maxfield.

"Yes."

"Two of these being members of your own Advisory Board."

"Yes."

Symons said, with a trace of contempt in his voice. "You were being put on the mat, weren't you?"

Gale flushed. "I wouldn't put it like that."

"Well, there you were, called to the Athenaeum, told that they objected to the letter and you must put it right. Is that so?"

"I agreed with them. We had made a bad mistake. I was only too anxious to make amends."

"Very commendable." Symons paused. "So that was all wrapped up. The more difficult question was Line. You were sent to telephone him?"

Gale said sharply, "I offered to do so. I hoped I could make him see reason."

"And what did he say?"

"He said, in effect, that he wasn't prepared to go back on what he had said."

"I see. And you argued with him?"

"Yes."

Symons looked down at his notes. Then he took up a piece of paper, walked towards Gale and paused again. He timed it perfectly so as to create a slight hush of expectation in the court to precede his next question. "Dr. Gale, did you say to Professor Line, 'David, try to think of me. I have to live with these people'?"

Gale blinked behind his spectacles. "Really—this conversation was two years ago. I can't remember every word I said."

"Surely you couldn't forget saying a thing like that? If not in those words . . ."

Gale fell into the trap. "Well, it's possible."

"I see. So it's not out of the question you said that—or something like it."

"No—I suppose not."

"This was obviously a very natural consideration in your mind. Here were these influential men, members of your editorial board, friends of your proprietors. . . . You had to consider the future of your journal, hadn't you?"

"Well, of course."

"Of course." Symons went back to his notes. He plucked another piece of paper out of the heap. "Dr. Gale, do you remember a scientific paper sent to you by Dr. Brook on data analysis four years ago?"

Gale smiled. "I'm sorry, Mr. Symons. We receive over a thousand papers a year——"

Symons was not disconcerted. "But this was rather unusual. The paper was rejected by you personally——"

"There's nothing unusual about that."

"It took you ten months to do so. Is that unusual?"

Gale said uneasily, "That is rather a long delay. I should have to know the details——"

"I'm surprised you've forgotten them. There was quite a vigorous correspondence with Professor Line about it, afterwards."

"Oh yes—yes. Now it comes back to me. He claimed that Brook had lost priority."

"Exactly. While Brook's paper was in your office a similar paper was published elsewhere."

"That sort of thing's bound to happen sometimes. Two people may be working on the same lines. It was just bad luck."

"But the paper was delayed ten months, Dr. Gale. Was that bad luck?"

"I can't say exactly why, not offhand."

"In your letter to Professor Line you say 'unfortunately this paper was held up for an unduly long time by referees.' What referees?"

"Well, I'm not sure."

"Could it have been Lord Maxfield?"

"I can't remember."

"Do you know who published the other paper—the one that robbed Dr. Brook of his priority?"

"No."

"Was it Dr. Charles Dean, one of Lord Maxfield's assistants?"

"Was it? I don't remember."

Symons nodded his head slowly. "You don't remember,"

he said with great significance. "Well, perhaps Lord Maxfield will be able to remember when he comes to give evidence."

Gilling's concentration on the trial was intermittent. At times he would listen with great intensity and then his thoughts would wander off to consider his own predicament or to indulge in irrelevant daydreams and reminiscences of his past life. In these troubled daydreams whole portions of the evidence passed him by. Throughout the re-examination of Gale and the examination of Sir Horace Trimble he hardly heard a word of what was being said. He was vaguely conscious of Groom sitting down and Symons getting up to cross-examine. None of it seemed to be very important. But then suddenly his mind was brought back to the court by a change in the atmosphere, one of expectancy. People were leaning forward holding their breaths. He knew instantly that it could be for only one reason. Sir Horace was in trouble.

Trimble stood in the witness box, huge, purple jowled, glaring at his tormentor through small eyes shrouded in fat. He was like a savage old bull, out of condition, puffing and blowing, blood running from a hundred pinpricks of the banderillas, yet full of rage and fight, backed up against the barrier and still dangerous. Opposite him stood Symons, a stocky, bewigged matador, twitching the folds of his gown in his determination to drive home his advantage.

"Now, Sir Horace, you said in evidence that you believed Dr. Brook hadn't anything to offer in the Kincaid case?"

"Yes."

"You said that there has never been any prejudice against either Brook or his machine?"

"Yes."

Symons waited for a moment and then snapped, "Do you know Dr. Brook, Sir Horace?"

"Not well. I've met him, if that's what you mean. He was a student of mine."

Symons leaned forward and asked, almost confidentially, "Did you like him?"

The question was unexpected and Trimble was disconcerted. He fumbled. "What do you mean?"

"I should have thought it was fairly plain. Did you take to him? Was he the sort of person you approved of?"

"I really don't know. He was just—a student. Nothing special."

"Nothing special?" Symons raised his eyebrows. "I was told he was a brilliant student."

"Well yes, I think he was, now you mention it."

"But when he qualified he didn't get a job at your hospital?"

"You say not. I can't remember."

"It's funny, if he was so brilliant." Trimble said nothing. Symons said, with deceptive casualness, "Was that about the time that your nephew got a job at your hospital, Sir Horace?"

"I honestly don't know."

"After passing his final examinations at the third attempt?"

"I really can't remember."

"You remember Dr. Brook writing a letter to the Hospital Committee? Protesting about this particular matter?"

"I remember there was some such fuss. As I recollect, it was all handed over to a committee of inquiry from outside the hospital, who decided he had no case."

"Who was the chairman of the committee?"

"Offhand I can't say——"

"Sir Thomas Gilling?"

"Yes, I think it was."

"So they decided that Brook, who had received the Gold Medal for Medicine, wasn't good enough for a job, and your nephew, who scraped through at his third attempt, was just the man for the job."

"There are other things to consider besides academic distinction."

Symons nodded with great significance. "Evidently." There was a short silence while he looked down at his notes again. "Now, Sir Horace, you are, I believe, the chairman of the Grants Committee of the Plant Foundation?"

"Yes."

"You give grants every year on a fairly large scale for medical research?"

"Yes."

"Has Dr. Brook ever applied to the Foundation for a grant?"

"I believe he has."

"On several occasions?"

"Yes, I think so."

"Was his application ever successful?"

"I believe not. The projects were never considered sufficiently promising."

"I see. Dr. Brook was applying for the Research Unit of the Metropolitan Hospital, I think?"

"Yes."

"Where he was doing work on diagnostic systems?"

"Yes."

"You are aware that when Dr. Brook was in America, this work had received support amounting to over fifty thousand dollars from the Rockefeller Foundation?"

"Yes. He drew our attention to that."

"It didn't influence you?"

"We had to decide about the project on its merits."

"You thought it valueless?"

"We thought, as it stood, it didn't justify the amount of money which was asked for."

"Was there correspondence about this, first with Dr. Brook, then with Professor Line?"

"Yes. They both seemed very bitter and resentful."

"But you didn't feel inclined to change your opinion?"

"No."

"You don't consider diagnostic systems important?"

"They have some significance, but not as much as Dr. Brook thinks, in my opinion. It's a question of priority."

"They didn't merit priority over other projects?"

"Exactly."

"I have here a list of the projects supported by your committee in that year." Symons began to read in an unemotional voice, "The Development of Pleural Tumours in Mice after the Inhalation of Asbestos Dust. Chromosome Patterns in the Australian Aborigine. Studies of Rabbit Myxomatous Tumours under the Electron Microscope. All these were considered to take priority over diagnostic systems?"

"With all due respect to you, Mr. Symons, medical research is a highly technical matter. You really have to understand what it is about before you can give a useful opinion of what may be valuable, and what isn't. The title of the research can be very misleading. Anyone can give his experiments an important-sounding title. It's the details of the subject that count. I'd also like to say that there were eight members of that committee, all men of distinction."

"But you were the chairman?"

"Yes."

"Your opinion would count heavily and so would that of Sir Thomas Gilling. It would have been surprising if the committee recommended a grant in the teeth of your opposition?"

"They could do so."

"Yes. But not very likely, I think." He paused. "Are you absolutely sure, Sir Horace, can you put your hand on your heart and say that you were not influenced in this matter by the trouble Brook had caused over the house job at your hospital?"

Trimble said steadily, "It never entered my head."

"You had totally forgotten it?"

"It was not in my mind at all. I was not influenced by it. I can assure you of that."

He was good, thought Gilling. There was something gallant in the way he stood there, lying away for the good of the cause. You might think Trimble flaccid and degenerate, sunk in sloth and rotted with loose living, but you could rely on him to keep his nerve in a crisis, to stand by you at whatever cost. It was all nonsense, of course. The original trouble with Brook had never been out of their minds. He had liked to think that they had not been influenced by it, he had persuaded himself that they had acted fairly. Until now he had always believed it. It was only when he had heard Trimble swearing that they had never even thought about it that he began to doubt his own honesty.

He tried to dig down into the recesses of his mind, beneath all the preconceived ideas, the pompous verbiage, the conventional platitudes. Was it really as simple as Symons made out, that Brook had been kept out of a job to which he was entitled simply to make a place for Trimble's nephew? He tried to think back to the committee of inquiry. It was true that they had been less than sympathetic to Brook's case. After all, he had placed them in an impossible position. This kind of juggling with jobs went

on at London hospitals, it always had done, they were almost
family institutions. Also there was a matter of principle involved;
once you let people argue about who was best for which job,
God knows where you'd end up. A sense of outraged authority
dominated the whole proceedings. Here was this boy, just
qualified, having the impudence to question the decisions of his
elders and betters. A consultant had a right to choose his own
houseman, surely. It was monstrous of Brook to embarrass them
in this way. They would have reacted in the same way whoever
it had been. The fact that he was a Jew had nothing to do
with it. . . .

Suddenly Gilling remembered that nobody had mentioned
that Brook was a Jew. What on earth had made him think of
that? Could it possibly be true what Symons was saying—that
they had pursued Brook throughout his career, denied him money
for his research, prevented him publishing his papers, robbed
him of his F.R.C.P., waged what amounted to a vendetta against
him, and finally killed Kincaid because they could not bring
themselves to accept his help. Surely it was too monstrous, surely
it couldn't possibly be true?

He wished Symons would finish with Trimble. Somehow just
the fact of him standing there in the box, his fat face gleaming
with perspiration, was bad for their case. Gallant he might be,
and loyal, he nevertheless looked altogether too much like a
crooked politician at a Congressional investigation. One expected
him at any moment to refuse to answer a question on the
grounds that it might incriminate him. This was a danger which
all of them had anticipated but found themselves powerless
to do anything about. If Trimble offered generously to give
evidence for you at the risk of his own career you could hardly
refuse him on the grounds that he looked like a sharepusher. At
least, thought Gilling, that was one thing about Maxfield. He
might not be exactly warmhearted and appealing, but his
respectability was unimpeachable.

Now Trimble was at last standing down, looking as if the first
thing he wanted to do was to take off for his club for a couple of
double brandies. Gilling didn't particularly want to speak to
him and he had a feeling that Trimble didn't want it either. The
court was adjourning. A bad day, thought Gilling again, they

couldn't stand one much worse than that. He wondered if he was expected to talk to Perrin or Groom. After all there was little enough to say. They were conferring together in the well of the court, looking very concerned, as well they might, and glancing occasionally in his direction. As he tried to pluck up courage to go and speak to them a messenger came to him.

"Sir Thomas Gilling? A letter for you, sir." Gilling looked at the envelope. The handwriting was vaguely familiar but he could not place it. When he tore open the envelope and took the letter out, the first thing he saw was the House of Lords crest. Then he recognized the writing.

My dear Gilling,

As I left court today I felt compelled to send you a note to express my sympathy with you in the wretched ordeal you have to undergo. As a friend and colleague of many years' standing I felt my heart going out to you in your rebuttal of those absurd innuendoes thrown at you by Line's counsel. Let me say at once that I believe you were completely successful in convincing the whole court that Line's attempts to cast a slur on your character were as baseless as they were cowardly. Gale also, I thought, spoke up well and clearly. I was unfortunately not able to hear all Trimble's evidence but no doubt he was as lucid and honest as always.

I am sure, from what I have seen, that your case is unassailable and that you are bound to win this action with enormous damages simply on the evidence so far given. This being the case, I wonder whether any really useful purpose would be served by my appearance as a witness. I could only, after all, confirm a few facts already amply established by yourself and Trimble. While, as I am sure you know, my first thought was always to do everything possible to help you in this case, it does seem to me that perhaps it might not be in the best interests of the profession for too many of its leaders to appear in the witness box in a case which is regrettably attracting a great deal of press publicity. I may say that the Minister, with whom I had a telephone conversation today, agrees with me that this might be more politic and would assuredly not damage your cause. He asked me to give you his kindest regards and his most sincere wishes for your success.

Yours ever,

Maxfield

Chapter 10

GILLING LOOKED fixedly out of the window of his first-class carriage, shading his face with his hand. There were two other passengers in the carriage and he was consumed with fear that one of them might recognize him. His photograph had been all over the national press for a week now. Everywhere he went he saw heads turn as he passed by—it had the effect of making him feel as if he were walking around naked.

As the fields flashed past he recognized an occasional landmark across the flat, featureless plain. He had travelled this way many times before years ago, when he was a young man, before he had a car and a chauffeur to seal him off from the rest of humanity. This railway between Graftondale and London had been the route of his forays on the capital. He had travelled south to take examinations, to receive distinctions, to attend meetings, to address learned societies. Curiously enough, all his memories of travelling south through this countryside were associated with a sensation of tension, of nerves strung up before an ordeal; his memories of travelling back north were associated with triumph. This was the first time he had taken the road home in defeat.

There was a brickworks he recognized, a cluster of farmhouses, an isolated factory—soon they would be in Peterborough. Then Grantham, which was half-way home. After Grantham the stations came regularly, and as you went north after Retford they became bigger and shabbier. Doncaster, Wakefield, Leeds, then a delusive stretch of country which almost persuaded you that you were out of the West Riding at last; after that the chimneys and the bald black-scarred hills of Graftondale, the valley sodden with a smoke-filled mist. Even the new white concrete towers were already streaked with dirt from the incessant drizzle.

The train stopped and he fumbled in the rack for his bag. The woman opposite him looked up curiously from her *Evening Standard* and he knew from her puzzled frown that she had recognized him. He stumbled out of the carriage on to the platform and then looked round helplessly. Now that he had left the woman safely in the carriage he felt frightened and exposed—he could not think what he was there for. He had a vague memory of taking a taxi back to the house after receiving Maxfield's letter, packing a small handbag and leaving immediately for the station. It had somehow seemed absolutely essential to cover his tracks, to see nobody, to avoid particularly his wife and anyone else who might ask him what he was doing. For it was a question he would not have been able to answer. Now that he had arrived he felt lost and frightened, yet at least the streets and buildings were familiar. As he walked out of the station he saw the Corn Exchange to his left and the Town Hall looming up on the hillside opposite. To his right was the Grafton Hotel where he always stayed. The commissionaire smiled and touched his hat. Gilling turned away across the street, walking as fast as he could.

There was a light rain falling, soaking through his overcoat and up through the soles of his shoes. He must find somewhere to stay the night. He saw across the road a commercial hotel where he had vague memories of drinking as a student. On an impulse he went in and booked a room. He remembered the hotel as a raffish place with plush seats and plump barmaids and gilt mirrors where bookmakers ordered double whiskies and told unlikely stories of long-forgotten race meetings. Since then some degree of modernization had evidently occurred. The bar had been redecorated and refurnished and some rather unsuitable furniture of Scandinavian design had been introduced into the lounge. But the new plaster was already chipped, the light veneers of the wood were crumbling. Somehow the renovated parts contrived to seem even more dilapidated than the old dining-room, where the original plush and mahogany panelling still remained.

It was too late for dinner, and in any case he was not hungry. He went to bed and tried to sleep. He wondered how long it was since he had last been in Graftondale. The last time was five (or was it six or seven?) years ago, when he had been invited to give the first Benson-Grey Lecture in the great hall of the university. It was strange to think of Benson-Grey, once so apparently invulnerable. Quite suddenly, in middle life, nothing had gone right for him. He had just missed election to the Presidency of the College of Surgeons, his wife had died suddenly, then there had been some trouble with his daughter and some young man. Finally he had fallen dead with a coronary thrombosis, struck down in the middle of a meeting at the age of fifty-five.

The next morning the maid brought him a newspaper with his morning tea. He opened it and caught a quick glimpse of a double-page spread about Trimble and his nephew, with a picture of the old scoundrel outside the court, towering over his solicitor, eyes hooded, lips pursed, watch-chain across his waistcoat, a debauched grandee, a dilapidated latter-day Tiberius. Even in defeat there was something magnificent about him. He had the inherent grandeur which comes from years of power fully exercised and enjoyed.

Gilling threw the paper in the wastepaper basket. It was nothing to him now. He felt a sudden conviction that he would never see Trimble or Maxfield or the Minister or any of them again. The party was over, the champagne was finished, it was time to be gone. The plausibility of the picture of himself as a great man, built up so laboriously over a period of thirty years, had collapsed. To him, it had never been entirely convincing. Even in the moments of his greatest triumphs he had often felt the sensation of being a fraud and an impostor. Whenever he had passed an examination as a young man he had always felt that perhaps it was a fluke, a lucky chance which he could never repeat; when in later life he examined others he felt uneasy, since he always doubted his own ability to pass the examination that he himself was setting. When he received honours and distinctions he was unhappy at the thought that they were unmerited. He had a nightmare that somebody would come out of the crowd and stop the whole ceremony, protesting that there had been a mistake, this was not a great man, it was merely Tom Gilling, a hard-working scholarship boy with no special claim to distinction except a fair intelligence and a certain dogged persistence. It was not so much modesty on his part that afflicted him with panic on these occasions. It was more a terror of being found out for what he really was.

Curiously, he felt no bitterness against Maxfield. If you were a fraud, you could not expect others to endanger their careers to save you from destruction. He visualized them all talking of him with disgust and derision, wondering what might be the easiest way of shaking themselves free of him. Charlotte, too, loyal though she had always been, must surely feel the same in her heart. After all, she had not married him as a young man, gambling her life on the ups and downs of his. She had married him as a distinguished, successful man of middle age, a public personality. It had been his obligation to her to maintain it.

After breakfast he fetched his overcoat and walked out of the hotel. It was a dull gusty day. He passed by the taxi rank outside the hotel door and waited in the queue for a bus. The ticket he had once bought for threepence (or a penny-halfpenny if he could persuade the conductor he was under fourteen) now cost a shilling. But the streets leading to the housing estate had not changed much, and the estate itself not at all. The wide featureless roads were just as empty, the tiny gardens as carefully tended, and the lace curtains and china dogs still graced the windows of the front rooms. Identical houses stretched in crescents, circles, rectangles, and arabesques for miles over the windswept hills, neat, solid, comfortable, low-rented, and unspeakably dreary. As he walked along the pavement of Wimborne Villas, a road distinguishable by name only from Wimborne Place, Wimborne Court, Wimborne Terrace, and heaven knows how many other Wimbornes, he suddenly remembered the first great passion of his life—to get away, at all costs, from this terrible place.

It did not occur to him that his father might be out. After all, at eighty-five there are not many places to go for a shy, lonely old widower. His father came to the door as soon as he rang the bell. It was many years since Gilling had seen him and he had not been quite sure what to expect. He was relieved to find that the old man, though scrawny and bent, carried his years relatively well. He did not seem so very much older than the last time they had met. Perhaps, thought Gilling rather sadly, it was relative ages that counted; perhaps eighty looked no more dilapidated to sixty than sixty looked to forty. But evidently the process didn't work the other way. As his father let him through the door he shook his head in astonishment.

"By shots," he said, "it's our Tom." And with a bluntness which took Gilling back to his childhood, he added, "Nay, lad, you're getting on."

"I suppose I am." Gilling winced. In the midst of his agony, it was strange that he could still be wounded by a pinprick like this. Well, he might as well face that, along with everything else. So far he had been successful in concealing from himself that he was an old man. Medicine was such an old man's profession, one gained authority so late and clung to it so far into senility, that there was a conspiracy to pretend that a man of forty was young and one of sixty still in the prime of life.

They went through into the kitchen and his father, without asking him, put on the kettle for a cup of tea. It was an integral part of any form of hospitality in Graftondale. While the old man fussily produced cups and saucers and biscuits from a tin in the dresser drawer, Gilling looked round the house. It was clean, if a little shabby. The curtains were darned and the surface was gone from the linoleum. Otherwise there was hardly any change from the way it had looked when he was a boy. The garden was better kept and there was a new tool shed; presumably this was how the old man spent the long days of his retirement.

As they sat together on hard kitchen chairs, sipping the hot strong tea, they seemed to have little to say to each other. His father did not seem particularly surprised to see him and made no mention of the case, but surely he must have been reading the papers. Gilling wondered whether he was shy about mentioning it. He certainly looked preoccupied, as if he had some problem on his mind. Perhaps the kindest thing was to break the subject for him. Gilling was just about to do so when the old man spoke. His words were filtered through a mouthful of biscuit.

"It's no use," he said. "I've done my best with them, but they're still not right."

Gilling felt a little bewildered. "What aren't right?"

"These teeth." The old man spoke impatiently as if he suspected Gilling of not having paid attention. "I've told him time and time again. He files a bit off here and a bit off there, but it makes no difference. They still rub my gums."

Gilling slipped automatically into his professional manner. It was somehow different from his ordinary manner, though he would have been surprised and shocked to realize it. He became rather more sympathetic, yet at the same time more aloof, less personally involved. He said, "Have you told your dentist?"

"He doesn't care," he repeated gloomily. "Just files a bit off here and a bit off there. I tell him I need a new set but he takes no notice."

It was strange to hear this senile bitterness from the lips of his father. All his memories of the old man were of an almost maddening good-tempered acceptance of life's injustices. The tragedy of senility was that it brought the same unhappy qualities to everyone; it took from a man not only health and energy but even his individuality. Gilling said, "Well, we can soon fix that. I know the professor of dentistry at the Royal——"

"No." The old man shook his head violently. "I don't want anything special. Don't trouble yourself."

"It's no trouble."

"I've never believed in privilege. I'll stick to my principles. The National Health is good enough for me."

"But if they're hurting——"

"I can stick it."

"But we can get them right. There's no virtue in sticking to something which can be improved."

"I don't want any professors. This fellow's good enough for me."

"He doesn't sound very good."

"He does his best," said the old man perversely. Gilling sighed and fell silent. He knew from experience the type of patient who preferred a grievance to alleviation of minor discomfort. The old man maundered on. "Everyone's the same nowadays. Trying to tell you what to do. I had it out with *her*." He jerked his head vaguely in the direction of the next house.

"Who?" It was like a guessing game.

"The woman next door. She comes in twice a week to tidy up." He sucked a crumb out of the corner of his plate. "I don't say it isn't good of her, but she interferes. I'll tell her straight one of these days."

"I should be tactful. You need somebody to help."

"I can look after myself."

"Are you all right for money?" Gilling knew the answer. For years he had insisted on paying a generous allowance into the old man's banking account. He was reasonably certain that most of it lay there unused.

"Don't worry about me. I'm all right."

Somehow the conversation was going all wrong. He had been looking for—what? He could not say exactly. Some kind of truth or consolation, some kind of relief for his aching sense of loneliness and self-doubt. Perhaps some relief from the sense of guilt which had always pursued him for his treatment of his father. But the conversation had become bogged down in trivialities. He tried desperately to pull it back.

He said, "You may have seen that I'm engaged in a law suit."

The old man nodded. He looked away, shiftily it appeared to Gilling, out of the window. It was as if he had hoped to avoid discussion of the subject. Did he perhaps believe that his son was in the wrong? "I don't understand a lot of it," he mumbled. "All that about—what is it—a machine."

"That's not too important. It's a question of my integrity. Particularly in relation to Kincaid."

His father was silent for a moment. Then he said, "I remember him as a young man. Put up for a constituency near here, he did."

"Did he?"

"Yes. Spoke well. I heard him. Afterwards when Ernie Bevin came up I asked him what he thought of Kincaid." The old man shook his head. "He said he'd never get anywhere. All piss and wind he said he was."

"Really?"

"Those were his very words. 'All piss and wind.' " He sucked thoughtfully at his plate. "He didn't mind calling a spade a spade, our Ernie."

Gilling began to feel a sense of hopelessness. He tried once again. "They're trying to say I killed him."

255

The old man blinked. "Killed who?"

"Kincaid."

The old man looked uneasy. "Nay," he said finally, "they can't believe that."

"What do you feel—reading the case yourself?"

There was a silence. Then his father said, "It's a bit difficult for me to follow, you know. And I've had a lot on. What with my teeth and needing new glasses and her upsetting me. I've missed it some days."

He fell silent. Gilling could have laughed aloud at his own foolishness. That was the cause of his father's uneasiness—he had not even been able to pluck up sufficient interest to follow the case. Curiously, his spirits lifted a little at this discovery—it was difficult to sustain a note of tragedy when it was made plain how little your affairs mattered, even to your own father. If he were to die tomorrow it would be no more than a ripple on the surface of a pond. There would be a handful of obituaries, some of his colleagues would write commiserating letters to his wife. Their sorrow would be tempered by a feeling of relief, indeed a sort of triumph that they had outlived him.

The old man said suddenly, "Don't you worry, Tom. You were always a good lad and you've done well. Your mother always felt I didn't do enough for you and happen she was right." So, thought Gilling, he lived in guilt too. Perhaps it was the fate of everyone. "Well—she'd have been proud of what you've done."

"You think so?"

"She thought the world of you."

There was a silence. Neither of them seemed to have very much else to say. The old man got up and began to wash out the teapot. As he did so Gilling saw him looking furtively at the clock. Finally he said, "Were you thinking of stopping?"

"I hadn't thought."

"It's just that——" He looked away. "I usually go down to the club for a glass of beer about now." He added hurriedly, "I don't have to if you want to stop."

"No, I was going anyway."

Childlike, the old man was unable to conceal his relief. Gilling saw, with a pang of regret, that he no longer meant anything in his father's life. His success, his failure, his approaching destruction, meant less to the old man than an ill-fitting plate, a bossy neighbour, a habitual glass of ale at twelve o'clock. Quickly he rose and took his leave, wondering how he could have ever imagined that there would be anything here which would give him an answer to his problems.

As he walked away from the house Gilling realized that his visit to Graftondale had been an absurdity. His impulse to cut himself off from his present life, to return to the womb of his upbringing, had been not so much a failure of courage or character as a failure of common sense. In any case the world of his childhood had been no more simple and uncomplicated, no less terrifying than the world he faced now. The fact that his agonies then had been over the wrong sort of boots rather than the killing of a great statesman made little difference in terms of his own personal suffering. His pain had been as great. And in those days there was no avenue of retreat. A child cannot take a train or a plane, he cannot hide, he must get up each morning and look suffering in the face. Somehow from his knowledge that there was no avenue of retreat had grown a desperate courage of its own, the heroism of despair.

If nothing else, he had been reminded of the lesson he had learnt as a boy, that there was nowhere to go, nowhere to hide. The human predicament was a simple one in essence. Man ran through his life like a fox, with the dogs baying at his heels. They would get him by the throat in the end, nothing was more certain than that. The chase must always end in the same way—death was the final disaster, the final lonely defeat which came to all of us. There was no way of winning, but one could at least lose with dignity, and dignity meant fighting all the way, until the breath was out of your body, and then turning on the hounds, snarling and snapping, before they finally tore you to pieces. Only one sin was unforgivable. That was to give up the struggle, to acquiesce in the determination of the world to destroy you.

He picked the bottle of barbiturates out of his pocket and dropped it down a convenient drain. He cared no longer about winning. He knew nothing awaited him except defeat, whatever happened in the case. But he must turn and fight—the hounds must pay the price for their quarry.

Chapter 11

THE BLACK LABRADOR whined querulously, padded around the room for a while, and then came back to her and sat at her feet. She scratched his ears in an abstracted way. Perhaps he missed Thomas. On the other hand perhaps he was simply disturbed by the change in his daily routine, and the coming and going of large cars and solemn self-important men in black overcoats. First it had been Trimble, then Sir Frederick Groom with Perrin in attendance, not only dressed like undertakers but wearing the appropriate expressions as well. She had handled them badly, she knew. She had been stiff and abrupt, fending off their well-meant attempts at commiseration. She had resented their assumption that the case was finished and that Thomas himself was a wreck of a man wandering through the country waiting to be picked up and put into a nursing home for mental breakdowns. That indeed was the best possibility they considered. The worst, and perhaps the most likely, was mentioned by nobody.

Groom, fortunately, supported her in the end. He agreed to ask the judge for an adjournment of two days, which would at least give him a chance to find Thomas and decide whether it was possible to carry on. But she had had to fight alone against all of them in her refusal to agree to a search for him, or to notify the police. No doubt, as they pointed out to her, she would be to blame if anything serious happened to him; well, it was a risk she must take. For them, she could understand, it was important to be covered. So far as she was concerned, if Thomas was dead her life was finished, and what the world might say about her was insignificant. If he wanted to kill himself in some distant hotel room, it was his choice and he must be allowed the liberty to follow it. If he were alive he must be left in peace. Above all, the decision to close the case must be his and his alone.

The doorbell rang and she ran to it, hoping for a moment that it might be Thomas, returning as suddenly as he had left. Instead she found on the doorstep a girl in her early twenties with a curiously defiant expression on her face. There was also something vaguely familiar about her appearance.

"Lady Gilling?" she said. "My name's Susan Cranmer. I wonder if I can have a word with you."

What on earth could she want? Some charity probably. Really it was too bad at a time like this . . .

"I'm sorry, I'm afraid I'm very busy . . ."

"It's extremely important."

It always was, of course. "You should have made an appointment." It was maddening that she had, in her eagerness, answered the door herself. She felt a sudden resentment against people who forced you to be rude to them. It was no mitigation that the girl was obviously going through agonies of embarrassment herself. She should have telephoned. "I'm sympathetic to charitable appeals, but I'm afraid I can't be pestered at the door——"

The girl interrupted. "You don't understand. It's about your husband."

She felt a momentary nausea. The girl was pretty—was it possible that Thomas had a mistress? "What do you mean? Do you know him?"

The girl shook her head. "Would you mind if I came inside?"

Without speaking, Lady Gilling led her through into the living-room. "You'd better sit down. Now then, what is it you want to say about my husband?"

The girl sat down with a surprising degree of poise, considering her nervousness. Her voice, even the way she moved, was vaguely familiar. Where *had* she seen her before? After a moment's hesitation Susan said, "You may very well object to my coming to see you like this. I'm quite prepared for you to be angry, but I had to try it." She paused. "I'm—a very good friend of David Line's." She looked up, hoping vainly for some encouragement from the aquiline figure which towered above her, seated on a high-backed chair. A tough audience, she thought nervously.

Well, she had played to them before. You just had to keep pushing ahead—it was the only way.

"I know this is unconventional but I felt—well, somebody has to do something. Otherwise it's going to go on just getting worse and worse. Neither of them can win, surely you can see that?"

"I'm sorry, I'm afraid I still don't understand. Are you speaking for Professor Line?"

"No. Not directly. But I know him—better than anybody." She shrugged her shoulders. "I know he's not an easy man but he's sincere. I do want you to understand that. Whatever he did—he had no mean, personal motives."

"Are his motives very important?"

"Yes, they are. Because I can't believe that this case couldn't be stopped if people really wanted to stop it. David and your husband aren't compelled to destroy each other."

"It's gone rather far, I'm afraid."

Susan nodded. "I never realized what it would mean. I hadn't any idea. To show you what a fool I was, I rather looked forward to it. I thought it would be exciting, a sort of game. A tournament. Lots of thrills and excitement but nobody really hurt." She went on painfully. "I didn't know how squalid it would be. Men hired to pick away at other men's lives, to show them up, to make them into liars and cheats. Nobody ought to have to put up with that. Nobody's life can stand it. We're none of us good enough. It's not fair." She paused, as if hoping for assistance, but Lady Gilling said nothing. She went on, "David feels miserable about it, I know he does. But there's that dreadful man Symons. He says if you're going to fight you have to do it this way. And since he's the expert——" She paused and then said, "How's your husband?"

"I don't know." Lady Gilling's face was rigid. "He left the court last night and I haven't seen him since."

Susan gave a cry of distress. "I knew there was an adjournment. I thought he was ill."

"He may be. I don't know."

Susan said nothing for a moment. Lady Gilling could see she was temporarily at a loss. Eventually she said weakly, "I do hope that he's all right."

"So do I."

There was another silence. Susan said, "I suppose you hate David. I suppose you blame him for everything."

It was surely time to put an end to this. Lady Gilling said, "I don't wish to be unkind, and I'm sure you came here with the best intentions. But do you think you're really doing any good?"

"If I can do something to make us regard each other as human beings——" Susan said defiantly. "Don't you think that's important? I expect you think David's a sort of ogre. Someone who's determined to ruin your life. That's true, isn't it?"

It was, of course. She had tried at the beginning to see Line as a person, but as the struggle became more violent and more uncompromising he had turned into a purely notional figure, a violent spiteful madman with whom any sort of normal contact was unthinkable. A dangerous animal to be destroyed.

She said, "He left us little choice."

"But he's really not like that," said Susan pleadingly. "He's much more complicated, for one thing. He doesn't dislike your husband. It worries him to do him harm—it really does. I can see it. But his mind's full of a lot of ideas about principles and what people represent. He got into a terrible state about Brook —about him being a Jew and victimized and all that—you know. Actually I sometimes think Brook would rather he didn't. Because, after all, the more David stands up for him as a Jew, the more people think of him as a Jew and that's bad for him— wouldn't you say so?"

"Perhaps." Lady Gilling's voice was soft and cautious and non-committal. This conversation, which she had regarded so far as nothing but a tiresome embarrassment which she could well have been spared, now appeared to her suddenly in a new light. The girl was obviously tense and overwrought, her judgment, such as it was, submerged in a flood of anxiety and guilt. She had just given away, evidently without realizing it, a very valuable piece of information. Her mission was, of course, quite pointless. She had plainly no permission from Line to negotiate. Mere goodwill, a desire to be friends, was valueless at a time like this. The case had gone so far, so much damage had been done to Thomas, that any compromise on his part would be defeat. Only a complete capitulation from Line could possibly restore the balance. It was evident that Line would never contemplate anything of the kind. He was in a frighteningly strong position. This girl could do herself and Line nothing but harm if she stayed and went on talking. There was a side of Lady Gilling which was tempted to warn her of that. It was a chivalrous, quixotic impulse, and if there had been less at stake she would have been tempted to follow it. But in this gangling, eccentric, rather absurd ageing woman there lay a violent protective passion for her husband. She could not bring herself to refuse information which might be of value to him in the struggle on which his life depended. She would not solicit the information, she would not encourage the girl. That would be dishonourable. But she would not refuse to listen.

She said, "Does Professor Line know you're here?"

"No."

"Do you think he'd approve?"

Susan said hopelessly, "I don't know. I suppose not. But what's the alternative? Nobody wants to go on with the case. Nobody's enjoying it. Nobody's getting anything out of it." She qualified bitterly, "Except the lawyers. They're having a marvellous time. It obviously ought to be stopped. But when I talk to anyone they just shrug their shoulders and say nothing can be done. I can't accept that. I suppose you think I'm very young and foolish?"

"I think you're very young," said Lady Gilling. "It's very difficult at times for young people to accept the inevitable."

"If you don't mind my saying so, I think older people often find it a damn' sight too easy. And why should it be inevitable? It's not an avalanche. It's not an act of God," she cried in an agonized protest. "You all act as if it were. Even David. I always thought of him as a man who made his own fate. Now— he just acts as if he were being carried on by the tide."

"I'm afraid that's how most of us end up," said Lady Gilling. "Situations get out of hand. They get too complicated. We lose control." The girl sat there stubbornly, refusing to accept it. Lady Gilling felt a pang of sympathy for her. "How long have you known him?"

"About six months." Susan gave way to a burst of confidence. "I met him at a party given by a friend of mine. He seemed to me to be the first person I'd met who really counted for something worthwhile. It may have been partly because I tend to meet a rather trivial collection of people. I'm an actress at the National Theatre." So that was where she had seen the face, thought Lady Gilling. "Most of my friends are theatre people. They're fun, of course, but there's no depth to them. Apart from being attracted by David I have a tremendous admiration for him. But I suppose I have a thing about doctors." She paused for a moment. "This may seem naïve to you, but I had the idea because they were doing something so important, they somehow acted and thought in a bigger way than most people. Especially if they were in very high positions." She paused again and added unhappily, "Now—well—I don't know what I think any more."

"You perhaps expected too much."

"Oh yes, I'm sure I did. And in a way I know it's good for me to have learnt what I have." Lady Gilling regarded her with a kind of fascination. There was something quite remarkable about the girl's self-absorption. She was able to come into the house of a complete stranger and discuss the most intimate aspects of her own life without a moment's suspicion that it might be inappropriate, or that the other person present could be any less interested than she was herself. She was like a child retailing details of her life at school to a casual acquaintance. "I can see now," she went on, "that my emotions were very superficial. I was looking for an experience. It's happened to me before with other men, and then afterwards when the experience was over there was nothing left. But with David it's turned out quite differently. I know he's not the person I originally thought he was. He's much more complicated and difficult to understand. And though he doesn't like to think it—much more vulnerable."

What she really means, thought Lady Gilling, is that she started to have an affair with him and ended up by falling in love with him. It was always the same when you fell in love with someone. Because they were so valuable to you they looked precarious—just as love was precarious. She said, "You're afraid for him."

"Yes." Susan pondered and then burst out, "And he won't let me help him. He's stubborn. I know he's miserable. He hates the case now. He'd like to stop it. He hates Bradwell and that ghastly Oscar Symons. And he can't sleep. He wanders about the flat at night. He won't tell me what he's worrying about." She sighed. "I wondered at one time if it was money. I suppose this case is going to be frightfully expensive."

"My husband's counsel says the costs are likely to be about ten thousand pounds."

"Ten thousand pounds!" Susan was genuinely appalled. It was a sum almost beyond her comprehension. "Just over a letter —I mean, it seems ghastly, doesn't it? And David's not rich. He doesn't see private patients or anything. He's just on a salary. And he's so proud. He won't accept anything. I gather Lord Frampton offered to pay but he wouldn't have it. The trouble is he hasn't any real interest in money at all." She said it with pride rather than with regret, and there was also, Lady Gilling fancied, a certain contempt for others who were less cavalier about financial matters. Her emphasis on the fact that Line did not treat private patients carried a perceptible sneer against Gilling, the rich, fashionable physician. In spite of her determination to remain calm, Lady Gilling was stung by this attack on her husband. She said with some acidity, "If he's not interested in money, that can hardly be what he's worrying about."

"No, that's true." The girl treated her remark at its face value, either ignoring or unaware of the malice in it. She was like someone trying to solve a problem. Her whole mind was on her task. "I don't know what it is. I don't feel the same contact with him any more. Sometimes I think perhaps it's something to do with me—and perhaps I've failed him in some way. Or that perhaps he's missing his children. I can't see how he could be missing his wife," she said rather naïvely.

There was a silence. Lady Gilling said nothing—she could think of nothing to say. This was not, after all, a conversation in any true sense. The girl was obviously desperate with anxiety and unable to stop talking about her troubles, no matter how unsuitable the occasion or the person to whom she was telling them. She had hoped, in some curious, ill-formulated way, to find an ally in the opposite camp. But in the last resort she had nothing to offer, no solution; she was a mere bystander.

Susan said, "All I know is that it was different before the case came on." She burst out violently, "It's wrecking everything, this bloody case. Your husband's life, your own, David's—and mine. Why won't you help me to do something about it?"

Lady Gilling looked at her without sympathy. She was somewhat repelled by this unorganized emotion, this playing for sympathy. It seemed to her that all this girl really cared about was herself and the future of her sordid affair. Nothing would come of that in the end, she could tell her now. Perhaps all this melodrama really meant that Line was tiring of her and that she was reaching for another excuse for his behaviour, or for some dramatic way of resuscitating the relationship by bringing him a spectacular solution to his immediate problem.

"I don't know what I can do," she said slowly. "I can tell my husband what you said, but it doesn't contain any definite proposals, does it? If Professor Line would care to make an official approach through his lawyers——"

Susan shook her head hopelessly. "If I thought he'd do that I wouldn't be here. But I did want to say this. If your husband isn't well and it's—too much of a strain for him to carry on——" She went on hurriedly, "David's a generous man. He wouldn't want to exploit the situation. I feel sure we could do something on a personal level——" Her voice trailed away, frozen by the look on the older woman's face.

My God, thought Lady Gilling, that I have to sit and listen to this. That his mistress should take it upon herself to come into my house and offer charity. It had really gone far enough —the girl must be shown the door. She was about to speak when the telephone rang. Without even bothering to excuse herself she left the room to answer it.

When she returned her face was still controlled, the grey eyes as implacable as ever. "That was my husband," she said. "You'll be pleased to know he's alive and in good health." A note of triumph came into her voice. "And he's determined to win the case at all costs."

III

Chapter 1

LINE LAY AWAKE. He often lay awake in the darkness, watching the deep shadows of the curtains, feeling the cool touch of the breeze through the open window. Somehow the dark velvet silence seemed to throw into sharp relief the crisp, clear pattern of his thoughts. It was in the night that inspiration spoke to him most strongly and vividly, that harsh imperatives washed away expediency and told him without doubt or hesitation what he had to do. Propping himself up on the pillows, he lit a cigarette. He inhaled deeply, treasuring the smoke, deriving a perverse enjoyment from the assault on his lungs. He felt no fear of cancer. Cancer was in the future, and the future had little meaning for him. His problems were all in the here and now.

Tomorrow (or rather today since it was almost daylight) Symons would open the case for the defendant. By any standards his position was strong—indeed Symons had thought it quite possible that Gilling might settle at this point, making a defence unnecessary. However, the old man had evidently pulled himself together. Line was not sure whether he was pleased or sorry. It would have been an anti-climax to have had a settlement— he would have missed the excitement of the witness box and the closing speeches, the tension of awaiting the verdict. And yet ... it would have been pleasant to be home, with a victory over his enemies. And there was always the possibility that something might go wrong.

During this last week he had noticed, with the interest which he always gave to his own psychological reactions, that his attitude towards the case was beginning to change. Very gradually, his initial excitement was being superseded by a complex mood which alternated between apathy and apprehension. It was absurd, when everything was going so well; but there it was. He was not sure what had spoiled the case for him—whether it was the unpleasant truth about Kincaid or the callous destruction of Gilling by Symons in the witness box, or the endless, tedious public washing of the profession's dirty linen—whatever it was, the case was beginning to go sour on him. He began to feel that the story in which he was now involved would never be adequately finished; the battle he was fighting would have no proper satisfactory ending, with virtue triumphant and wickedness appropriately defeated. Perhaps the only thing to do was to tear the whole thing to pieces and start afresh.

It had happened to him often before, that situations which he had planned and initiated were taken over by others, who tore them out of his hands and managed them in a way quite different from his expectations. Like Hartly at Cosenza, who had not let him destroy himself because it would cause a certain amount of inconvenience to others. But nowadays he was big enough, they could not rob him of control, he would do what he pleased. But what did he want? He was not sure.

The difficulty was to preserve the first image of the enemy. It was easy enough in the beginning—but in the fighting you grew too near, you saw the fear in his eye and the trembling of his lip; you saw him secretly holding his wife's hand for consolation. It would not have been so difficult if he had been dealing with Maxfield or that dreadful Minister—men who seemed to have been born without heart, undeserving of sympathy or human consideration. But it was hard not to feel some human warmth for Gilling. It was still true that he was a menace, an obstacle in the way of progress. The power in him must be attacked. But he was a man too. How could one attack the power within without attacking the man himself? There was, of course, no way. Whatever one might feel about the case now, it was impossible to do anything about it. It must take its course. After Symons's attacks on Gilling there was no possibility of compromise. The only way in which he could stop the case would be by giving in completely; quite apart from the disaster to his reputation, he could not afford such a defeat financially. He had to win or he was bankrupt. The thought caused him a slight sense of relief. There was no decision for him to make. He was carried on by the tide and there was nothing that he could do. The matter was out of his hands.

Susan stirred in her sleep. She looked at him for a moment and then said querulously, "You're awake." When he did not reply she added, "You're always awake now," and then, half conscious, dropping back into sleep, "I don't understand. You frighten me." Then she was asleep again, sighing a little. What dreams did she have, he wondered. Small dreams. A dress that didn't fit, an appointment forgotten, an argument with the director. Sometimes he envied her—but only sometimes. The large dreams were better, he thought, proud of the scope of his own personality. Then he frowned as he remembered what she had said. "You frighten me."

Brenda had once said something like that. It had mystified him then, and it mystified him now. Why should he frighten anybody? He tried to see himself with Susan's eyes. Was she, like Brenda, beginning to resent the fact that she could not live without him, like a parasite burrowing under his flesh? Did she want to be so bound up with him that he could not hurt her without hurting himself also? Was she frightened, in other words, because he insisted on retaining in fact the independence they both claimed in theory? She had complained on one occasion that he was complex and difficult to understand. Again, he found it hard to know why. He did and said what seemed good to him, and so far as he knew he was neither devious nor calculating. If his desires were a little inconsistent and the slave of his moods, there was nothing unusual in that. What was it that women resented so much? Perhaps, he thought, it was his lack of acceptance. Women liked to chart a map of the emotions round which they could find their way, a map which was founded on acceptance of given situations. If a man refused to accept the pattern they felt harassed and insecure, they could never be certain what he would be up to next. But for him every situation was provisional, there was always an alternative reaction to it, the map could be torn up and redrawn. When they said he was unpredictable, they merely meant that he retained the power of choice; that he was still alive.

271

Susan stirred again. He was suddenly overcome by tenderness. She seemed to him at that moment very young and defenceless. Whether he was right or wrong, the fact that she was afraid of him meant that he had to some extent failed with her, just as he had failed with Brenda. What was he to do? How could he come close to her and gain her confidence, without giving himself over to her utterly?

He moved, and his restlessness awoke her. She sat up in bed and said, "I'd like a cigarette too."

"No. Go to sleep again. I didn't mean to wake you."

"I'm awake." She took a cigarette out of the packet at the bedside and lit it. "I shan't get to sleep again now."

She pressed herself against him and they lay there together in silence. After a while she said, in what he recognized as her "serious," thoughtful voice, "David, do you love me?"

"Of course."

"No, it's not 'of course.'" It was rather touching, he thought— the more solemn she tried to be, the younger she appeared. When you grew older you recognized the impossibility of attacking situations in this direct, studious way. To define a human relationship was like gaining the confidence of a wild, suspicious animal. It had to be done gradually, gently, obliquely, always in the knowledge that the more eagerly you grasped at it, the less likelihood there would be of success. She went on, "There's a part of you I don't know at all."

"That's not really surprising. We haven't known each other for so very long——"

"It's more than that," she said stubbornly. "I have the feeling that you don't want me to know."

"I'm not hiding anything," he said. "I can assure you of that."

She was silent for a while. He had the feeling she was thinking over what he had said. Then she stubbed out her cigarette in the ash-tray. It was as if she had come to a decision. "David, do you remember—right at the beginning—we said we'd always be honest and truthful with each other?"

"Did we?" It didn't sound very much like the sort of thing he would say, but in love one said all kinds of things. You forgot

272

them afterwards and then the women mulled them over and reminded you.

"Yes. We have to trust each other. I wouldn't want a relationship with someone I couldn't trust, would you?"

He had a distinct feeling of artificiality about the conversation. Why did she ask him such questions? She would find out one day that no one could effectively make conditions of that kind. It was impossible to lay down rules about what you would tolerate in human beings.

He tried to explain. "It's not so simple. We're none of us entirely honest. If we like other people we make excuses for them."

"You don't believe that. I know you now. You're just trying to be clever." She was rather impatient, eager to proceed. She said seriously, "What would you say if I told you I'd been unfaithful to you?"

He switched on the light and looked at her. It was important to know, especially in view of the way she had phrased the question, whether she was speaking of something that had happened or merely playing some obscure theatrical game. She had a taste, which he found on occasions exhausting, for dissecting the details of their relationship in terms not only of real events but also of hypothetical circumstances. It was as if she were anxious to get a detailed three-dimensional picture of their situation in the shortest possible time. It was on a par with the way she and her friends would discuss the detailed lives and desires of fictional characters, the childhood of Romeo or Hedda Gabler's relationship with her father. Perhaps this Stanislavsky approach had some validity in terms of the stage, where one had to build up a character from the bare bones of a few situations lasting an hour or two. But real life was really complex enough without it. He said suspiciously, "Have you in fact been unfaithful?"

"Would you care if I had?"

Really, he thought, in the middle of the night—this was too much. "Oh, come off it, for Christ's sake——"

"Don't you see it's important?" she said obstinately. "Surely you must have considered the possibility? You must have wondered how you'd feel?"

"It never entered my mind."

For some reason this outraged her. "You mean you thought I was so much in love with you that——"

"No, no." It was hard not to be exasperated. "I just simply didn't think about it one way or the other." He said rather plaintively, "My life's crammed with things that really happen. I'm loaded down with genuine problems. I can't go around racking my brain about how much we love each other and what I'd think if you were unfaithful and all that sort of thing. It's all too indefinite for me. If you *have* been sleeping with someone else, say so and I'll consider it."

"All right then," she said furiously, "I have. What have you got to say to that?"

What had he got to say to it? It was really rather difficult to know. "Who is it?" he asked.

"I won't tell you."

She was really being extremely trying. He did his best to keep control of himself. "Is it anyone I know?"

"I won't tell you."

"Are you in love with him?"

"Stop asking questions." Her voice was almost tearful. "Is that your only reaction—curiosity?"

He said patiently, "It doesn't seem to mean very much unless I know who or why or the details. I don't have any hold over you. Obviously I can't stop you sleeping with another man if you want to. But there are certain things I'd like to know. Do you still love me, for instance? Do you still want to sleep with me? Surely these are things which matter."

She began to cry. "I don't believe you care for me in the least. You don't care if I sleep with other men. I'm just like a prostitute as far as you're concerned——"

He looked at her in utter bewilderment. "Really, women are astonishing. Now *you* have a grievance."

She went on crying. He was baffled. Real tears? Or stage tears? Had she really slept with another man? He couldn't be sure. She was quite likely to have invented it. But supposing she had? How much did he really care? Thinking it over, he decided that it depended on whether she actually preferred the other man to himself as a person. If that happened it would be the end for him. Perhaps it was vanity, but he knew himself to that extent. To be rejected in favour of another person aroused in him a sense of outrage, an almost physical revulsion.

But judging by the way she was crying she hadn't rejected him, quite the opposite. More likely and more frightening was the possibility that this was a gambit in a game to possess him. He thought wistfully of the early days of their affair. The gaiety and adventure of it, the physical and mental sense of discovery. Now they had entered the hothouse world of the emotions. How much do you love me? What are you thinking about? Do you care for me more than your work? Do you just want me physically? Do you despise me for being so much in love with you? It was endless and no good came out of it. He had seen the signs of it earlier in that absurd quarrel because he had forgotten an appointment at the Law Courts, but he had persuaded himself that she wasn't going to be like Brenda, since in the first place she wasn't married to him, and in the second she was young and an actress and everybody knew that actors went in for shallow flamboyant emotions. They didn't have the deep pertinacious capacity for unhappiness that made Brenda such a problem.

He said, with sudden roughness, "Come on, for God's sake let's talk some sense. Have you or haven't you?"

She said, through her tears, "Of course I haven't, you bloody fool." She pulled out a handkerchief from under the pillow and began to dab her eyes. "Don't you *know* when somebody's crazy about you?"

He looked at her in complete perplexity. "Then why——" He gave up. "I really don't understand you."

There was something about his tone which provoked her. "Well, you should try!" She said again, "You should try. I try with you. It's difficult but I do my best. But you——" She made a restless, despairing movement of her hand. "All you really care about is your own affairs."

The remark was so reminiscent of Brenda that he found himself moving into one of the stock replies from their recurrent quarrels. "Surely you must see that I'm under a great strain. Do you have to go out of your way to increase it?"

She said wildly, "If you're fed up with me why don't you tell me to go? You'd like to do that, wouldn't you? But you're ashamed to. It doesn't fit in with your picture of yourself." She taunted him remorselessly. "Isn't that right?"

"I do wish you'd stop talking rubbish."

"It's the truth," she said savagely. "I mean nothing to you. Nobody does. All you care about is yourself and your bloody lawsuit. Nothing else matters." When he did not reply she sat up in bed and looked down at him as he lay on the pillows. Her lips quivered. "You haven't time or energy for anything else. It means more to you than your ordinary work. It's more than sex, more than love—it swamps all the rest of your life. You're frightened to death by it, but it excites you. You don't want to stop it even if it may mean the end of you. Lady Gilling was right——"

He suddenly seized her wrist. "What are you talking about?" She stared at him without speaking, half frightened but half defiant. "What's this about Lady Gilling?"

There was violence in his eyes and his voice. She felt a sick confirmation of her deepest fears. When she had told him she had been unfaithful he had felt nothing. It had taken this to arouse emotion in him.

"Let go of my arm and I'll tell you." His fingers relaxed but his eyes still held her. She said, "I went to see her."

"When?"

"A couple of days ago. It was during the adjournment. When Gilling disappeared."

"What did you think you were doing?"

"I felt somebody had to do something. I thought—if I could make some contact—something might come of it."

"Why didn't you speak to me first?"

"Because I knew you'd be against it."

He nodded. The menace was still there, but he was more controlled now. "And what did you tell her?"

"Nothing important."

"What did you tell her?" His voice rose.

"Stop shouting. You're frightening me."

He made an effort to control himself. "I'm sorry. But this is very disturbing for me. You may have done serious harm, perhaps without knowing it."

"No, I didn't, I swear I didn't." Had she been indiscreet,

276

she wondered feverishly. Had she? She could hardly remember all the things she had said. "I just said I was worried about all the trouble and unpleasantness of the case. I asked her if she could think of any way in which we could get together and help settle it."

He laughed. "She must have thought you an absolute halfwit."

"As a matter of fact, she was very nice. She understood how I felt."

"Marvellous," he said sardonically. "And I suppose she promised to advise Gilling to withdraw from the case?"

"No, of course not. And I don't suppose I did any good. Evidently he's as stubborn as you are." She said, defying him, "But I'm not sorry I went."

There was a long silence. He looked past her at the shadows on the bedroom wall. She tried to read his face but the expression which passed across it was too complex for interpretation. Eventually, with one of his sudden changes of mood, he turned his attention back to her. Smiling, he stroked the place on her arm where he had previously gripped her so violently. He said softly, "So you were unfaithful to me, after all."

Chapter 2

Brook sat down at the breakfast table and carefully buttered himself a piece of toast. Today the lines on his long narrow face were even deeper than usual. His mouth carried its habitual wry, melancholy smile. He looked at his boiled egg as if it were a sad little joke that somebody had played on him, and then tapped it gently with his spoon. His wife came in from the tiny kitchen. She frowned as she poured him out a cup of coffee.

"You should have worn your good suit."

"I shan't be giving evidence. They'll never get to me today."

"You never can tell. They might finish with Line quite quickly."

"Not if he has anything to say about it. He's been looking forward to this for months."

She felt the tension in his voice and automatically adjusted herself to it. In a soothing maternal tone she said, "If the truth be known, he's probably dreading this just as much as you are."

"You must be joking." He took a spoonful of yolk. As he spoke he blinked violently, as he sometimes did when he was nervous. "I shall probably vomit all over the witness box."

"You'll be fine. I'm not worrying." She sat down to her breakfast. She was putting on weight, he thought, without censure—she would be fat in middle age if she wasn't careful. And her hair was almost always untidy these days. Well, it was difficult with the children to look after. . . . She added, "It'll be all over soon."

"Will it?"

"Don't be enigmatic, darling. You know what I mean."

"Of course I do. But I don't think you understand. This isn't just something that happens in a few days. Win or lose, we live with it for the rest of our lives." He said with some bitterness, "I can speak from experience."

"Experience?" Then she understood. "Oh—you mean Trimble and the house job."

"Yes."

She pointed out with satisfaction, "Symons certainly showed him up over that."

Brook laughed ironically. "Oh sure. That was good for me. My fortune is made from now on."

Christine didn't like him to talk this way, he knew, but sometimes the bile rose in his mouth and he couldn't stop himself. The truth was that he felt himself miscast in his present part but he had never been able to think how to get out of it. He had no desire to be a central figure in a *cause célèbre*. He had always been a quiet, industrious, sensitive young man, without any taste for the limelight and without even any great ambition. He had always known that he was not a powerful personality and was not destined to become a great figure in the world. He was not worried about this. All he wanted was to be left alone, to spend his life working at the problems which fascinated his precise, delicate intelligence.

At the time of the Trimble episode it had not occurred to him that he was taking a very momentous step. He was young at the time and he had felt a sense of outrage that a notorious duffer had been preferred to himself. Like most intelligent young men, he had vastly overrated the importance of intelligence in the world of affairs and the respect which the world paid to it. He felt that he had been defrauded of something to which he was entitled by virtue of his industry and capacity. While he had steeled himself to expect some discrimination throughout his life on the grounds of his race, he had thought of it in terms of golf clubs, schools for his children—you had to take such things and shrug your shoulders and find a way around them. This was different.

His friends agreed with him. They were outraged. He shouldn't sit down under it. He should protest, the whole thing was too flagrant to be ignored. He must at least make them feel ashamed of themselves. Brook was a serious, literal-minded young man and soon he began to feel that he had a duty to lodge a complaint. When others said they would have done so in his position, he was credulous enough to believe them.

So, as a matter of principle, he protested. And, also on principle—the principle that the hospital should have the right to employ who it pleased and not be bullied by students—the protest was thrown out. From start to finish the fact that he was a Jew was never mentioned. Often afterwards he had wondered whether the discrimination had been on a racial basis at all. It might have been simply that Trimble wanted a job for his nephew.

Whatever the truth of the matter, he had often bitterly regretted his protest. Since then he had been treated, to his great embarrassment, as a controversial figure. He found it difficult to know how people regarded him personally, and how much their attitude was conditioned by the symbolic aspects of his Jewishness. He would have liked people to forget that he was a Jew and that he had once been badly treated.

The support he had received from various quarters had worried him almost as much as the prejudice and distrust which he had felt from others. His relationship with Line, for instance, had always worried him. He found Line altogether too partisan and protective—Brook could never bring himself to feel that he merited so much interest purely on his own account.

"Anyway," said Christine, "there's one thing. After this, everyone will have heard of your machine."

"Whether I like it or not." He scooped a little moon of white carefully out of the top of his egg. "Some people have greatness thrust upon them. That's me."

"You need publicity for research these days," she said reasonably. "Otherwise how do you raise the money? You can hardly say it's done Line very much harm."

"He's safely home," explained Brook patiently. "They can't shift him. They'd like to, but they can't. With me it's different."

"He'll look after you."

"So long as I hide behind him. But just wait till I break cover." He aimed an imaginary shotgun. "Bang, bang." He sat back thoughtfully in his chair. "Shall I tell you something about Line?"

"What?"

"I don't think he likes me."

"Rubbish. Look what he's done for you."

He shook his head. "It's my machine he likes." He gave a short laugh. "Do you know—if I criticize it, he takes its part. Of course, he doesn't really understand it. He doesn't see its limitations—partly because he doesn't want to. If I point them out to him, he's angry."

"You're always worrying that people don't like you," she said. "It's your imagination. Line's very fond of you. I know he is."

"He's not fond of anybody. He's in love with ideas. The idea of the machine. The idea of my being persecuted by people like Trimble and Gilling. Most of all the idea of himself, so very chivalrous and gallant and progressive, fighting my battles for me." He smiled sourly. "We all know that he has only to offer to play in with them a little and they'd be happy to give him anything he'd ever want. All this he sacrifices for me. What a gesture!"

"Well——"

"But you can't go on making a gesture for ever, can you? And then what?" He was silent for a moment. Then he said, with great bitterness, "They're all the same. Believe me."

She looked up at him startled and anxious. "Who are you talking about?"

His long face was sad and reflective. "To be a Jew isn't the real crime. The real crime is to be young and powerless. To *them*—the people who really matter—you don't really exist, not in the same way as themselves. They decide your affairs and your future between them without telling you. They deal you out like cards in a pack. They don't hate you, they don't punish you. They just play with you."

"Line's different."

"So he says." He pushed away his plate and lit a cigarette. "But he never told me before he sent that letter."

"He explained that. He wanted to take the responsibility himself."

"If he'd thought of me as an equal he'd have shown it to me. You know that. There's more to equality than half-pints and

Christian names." With an unexpected spasm of rage he said, "I'm tired of being grateful to him for defending me! How does he know I want to be defended?"

"He's done so much for you. Where would you have been——"

Brook seemed not to hear her. He said, "He owns me. From now on I'm tied to him, I've no chance of support elsewhere. If he falls down dead, if he gets bored with me, if he decides to take up some other lame duck, where am I then?" His voice rose. "He owns us both. We do nothing but talk about him, day in day out. Is that healthy?"

She protested. "He's your friend. I know he is."

"I can't talk to him. Not about this anyway. We're on intimate terms—but only on anything he wants to talk about. On anything else he can't hear me."

The tears started in her pale blue eyes. "I wish you wouldn't be like this. It makes me so miserable."

He regarded her helplessly. It was a recurrent pattern in their relationship. First he would tell her his troubles and she would try to talk him out of them. When she failed to do this she would become depressed and he would end up by having to console her. He realized sadly that there was no escape here. Much as she loved him, she could give no answer to the problems which tormented him.

Who else could he talk to? Well, there was always Halder. He had known Halder for five years. They had worked together, they were close friends and had had no personal differences apart from occasional disagreements. He admired Halder. He also envied him—envied his robust vitality, his self-confidence, his easy assumption that most people liked him and that those who didn't were a minority of eccentrics who could be ignored. Most of all he envied Halder's independence. This was partly a product of his personality and partly of circumstances. Halder had money of his own for one thing; for another, people like him were in great demand in America. He would be able to go back in a year or so and pick his own job. While he made no pretence of being in the same class as Brook as a scientist, he had drive and organizing ability and would make a first-rate professor.

It was all right for Halder, Brook thought sadly as he travelled on the tube to Lincoln's Inn. He was unmarried and had no responsibilities. Brook himself had at one time thought of trying for a chair in the U.S.A. but the trouble was that Christine wouldn't have it. When they had been over there before she had never really settled down, and the idea of bringing up her children in a foreign country appalled her. Yes, it was all right for Halder. Brook felt a sudden spasm of envy for his friend.

Halder was waiting for him at the entrance of the Law Courts. He was wearing a pale, rather crumpled suit of the kind of material which one tended to associate with the lining of a suitcase. His plump, stocky figure appeared to be trying to burst out of it above and below the jacket button, and the trousers, held up by a leather belt, showed a perilous tendency to slide down the front of his incipient paunch. He was cheerfully eager to tell Brook of some girl he had picked up the previous evening. "She's really great," he said. "Long golden hair, a nice big mouth and a pair of knockers on her you could get lost in. This time it's love." He guffawed. Brook gave a thin smile. He had grown so used to these sexual fantasies that he hardly listened to them. Halder spent a great deal of his spare time in cheap dance halls picking up girls, whom he described afterwards in terms which made them sound, not like human beings at all, but like illustrations from *Esquire* or *Playboy*. He had a useful facility for concentrating all his attention on one physical feature which he found stimulating and suppressing the rest. He was able to see a girl as a pair of breasts, completely ignoring a pair of bandy legs or shapeless hips. If fascinated by her legs he could conveniently close his mind to a mouthful of blackened teeth. On the rare occasions when Brook had actually met the objects of these transient adventures, they had almost always turned out to be stupid, vulgar, and plain, if not downright repulsive. This was the only aspect of Halder's life for which he felt a certain pity. At one time he had been embarrassed at having to listen to these interminable lubricous anecdotes, most of which he was convinced were entirely the product of Halder's imagination. But he had soon discovered that no real reaction was called for on his part and he hardly paid attention. One had to put up with the peculiarities of one's friends. On any other subject he had a great respect for Halder's opinion.

Halder came to the end of his account of the various things he had induced the girl to do on their return to his flat; he made the whole episode sound more like an exercise in collective gymnastics than a love affair. At the end he lit a cigarette with a sigh of satisfaction, as if this—the talking about it—had been the real sensual experience. Then he looked at his watch.

"Not so long to go." He grinned expectantly. "Today's the day. Today we're really going to fix them."

"Do you think so?"

"Sure, what else? Hell, they've been in to bat, haven't they—and they're worse off than when they started. I bet David could practically get a verdict now. He hardly needs to give evidence."

"Perhaps it would be better if he didn't." Brook could see Halder regarding him with surprise. He tried to explain what he meant without sounding too defeatist. "The cross-examination might be dangerous."

"I can't see why."

"Perhaps because we all have more to be ashamed of than we have to brag about."

"Not David." Halder spoke with an absolute confidence which made Brook feel hopelessly isolated. It was the way everyone spoke on the Unit. Why could he never go all the way with this easy, comfortable loyalty, the assumption that Line was always right, that he carried some special aura which freed him from the rules which bound other people? The source of this pervasive belief was mysterious to him. While he accepted that Line was able and energetic, he knew that several members of the Unit, including himself, were more intelligent. Line's originality as a research worker was limited and his operative technique no more than average. The mere fact of his being famous and powerful could not by itself have given him such a hold on the minds of his subordinates. There was something more than that. Perhaps it was his supreme egoism which exercised an almost hypnotic effect on others. Brook wished that he could be more suggestible. Soon, he feared, Line would sense in him a lack of gratitude, of loyalty, of the reverence to which he was accustomed. And what would happen to him then?

"You only had to look at Gilling to see he was a shaky witness," said Halder. "But David's looking forward to this. He's all set to give them hell. Can you see him breaking up under cross-examination?"

Brook shook his head. He couldn't. Perhaps that was the intangible thing that Line had, the impression he managed to give that whatever the situation he found himself in, he was bound to emerge as a winner in the end. No, he couldn't visualize Line breaking. But what about himself?

As Symons began his introductory speech, Line settled back comfortably in his seat and glanced around the court, rather in the way of a performer scanning the house during the overture before his appearance. Halder had been right—he was looking forward to giving evidence. He was tense, of course, just as he was before performing a new or difficult operation, but it was the kind of tenseness that excited and exhilarated him. He had confidence in his ability to perform well. And yet the situation contained just sufficient hazard to make it exciting. This, he decided, interested as always in the details of his own reactions, was actually much more stimulating than a new operation. In a way, too, it was more respectable. In an operation the gamble was with somebody else's life. Today it was with his own.

When he was called into the witness box, he felt the atmosphere in the court suddenly sharpen. He knew he was the man they had all been waiting to see. He had looked at himself carefully in the mirror before leaving his flat and tried to visualize how he would appear to them. A very youthful figure by comparison with the witnesses for the other side, looking nearer thirty-five than forty-five, tall and slim, neat but informal, with that rather sincere lock of fair hair which tended to fall over his face as he leaned forward to make a point. . . . He had been slightly ashamed of himself for being so studied about his personal appearance, but one had to face the fact that it was important. Much depended on the kind of impression he made on the jury. Groom had done his best to paint a picture of him as a self-advertising irresponsible mischief-maker. He had hopes that one look at him would make the accusation seem implausible.

"You are David Line, of 16 Bray Mansions, London, S.W.5?"
"Yes."

"You are a consultant surgeon at the Metropolitan Hospital and a professor of surgery in the University of London?"

"Yes."

The routine questions went on. Gradually, between them, Symons by questioning and he by answering, they built up the picture of a man. It was a picture designed to fit in with the young, eager, progressive figure who stood physically before the jury. This was a man who had come from a solid, respectable, but by no means affluent family. He had been to a public school, and Oxford, had shown promise as a classicist, and had then become conscious of a vocation towards medicine as a result of certain harrowing experiences in the war. As a doctor he had had an unusually brilliant career. He had qualified with distinction, had passed his F.R.C.S. within three years of qualification, and had trained as a surgeon in a variety of specialist hospitals. In due course he had obtained a Fellowship at the Hemisphere Hospital in New York. Two years later he was made an associate professor there. During all this time he had worked not only as a surgeon but as a research scientist. He had published work on the transplantation of organs, on the possibility of the replacement of amputated limbs, and, in association with others, on data analysis. As a consequence of this work he had been offered the chair of surgery at the Metropolitan Hospital in London at the early age of thirty-four. He had worked there ever since.

Symons plodded doggedly on, taking his time at the risk of boring his audience. It was essential to create the right impression of solid professional respectability. The picture he painted was a fine one. A portrait of exceptional ability and success. But it was a portrait by a court painter, designed to flatter by skilful selection. Every detail was true, just as every detail which Groom had brought out in direct examination of Gilling was true. But in both cases the result was flat and idealized. For the third dimension of character, Line thought wryly, one had to wait for the cross-examination.

Symons began to move from Line's personal record to matters of more immediate concern.

"When did you first become associated with Drs. Brook and Halder?"

"I first met them six years ago on a visit to Chicago. They were developing an early version of their machine and I was convinced it had possibilities. I invited them to come to work at the Metropolitan and they accepted."

"Why did you do this?"

"I thought this was a very promising subject for research and I was sure we ought to encourage it in this country. Brook was himself an Englishman. He'd only gone over to Chicago because he couldn't get research money over here. I felt very strongly about this. In this country we have good brains and an excellent record for producing original ideas, but because the authorities are mean with money and rather suspicious of anything unconventional, the development usually occurs elsewhere."

"Did you think you could get the necessary money for Brook and Halder?"

"I was determined to do so. I promised them they wouldn't go short of funds and I intended to keep my promise."

"And what happened?"

"Soon after I got over here I knew I was going to have trouble. I found that the word had gone round that the whole idea was absurd and in any case far too expensive. Also that I had made a grave error in inviting them over here without first asking the permission of the people who control research funds."

Groom jumped to his feet. "My Lord——"

The judge nodded understandingly. "Professor Line, you must not quote gossip. Please confine yourself to facts."

"I'm sorry, my Lord."

Symons said, "Did you apply for money for this research?"

"Repeatedly."

"Did you get any?"

"Not from the usual medical sources. We were always turned down."

"And so what did you do?"

"We made direct appeals to the public and to any special bodies we could think of. We had some help from various American sources. But our most generous benefactor was the Frampton Foundation."

"And this enabled you to develop the machine?"

"Yes."

"Did you publish scientific papers about this work?"

"We wrote a number. We had the greatest difficulty in obtaining publication. It wasn't quite so bad if my name was on the paper. But if it was just Brook or Halder there were always great delays and often a rejection at the end of it."

"Can you give us an example of this?"

"Well, there was one particularly disappointing episode. This was when a paper was held up for six months by a journal and in the meantime some very similar work was published by Lord Maxfield's Unit. This naturally destroyed our priority."

"Are you convinced of the value of this machine?"

"Completely."

"Would you mind giving the court some evidence of this?"

There followed a long account of the various achievements and successes of the machine. At the end Symons said, "Did you ever offer to demonstrate the machine to Sir Thomas Gilling and his colleagues in the hope of convincing them?"

"Many times."

"Did any of them accept your invitation?"

"No."

Symons raised his eyebrows and looked significantly at the jury. Then he went on. "Now, about Mr. Kincaid. What was your special interest in his case?"

"I knew him and admired him. I couldn't claim to be a special friend of his but we had met on a number of occasions and he impressed me profoundly—as indeed he impressed a great many people. To me he seemed to stand far beyond any politician I had ever met, both in aptitude and in integrity. He really saw the necessity for breaking out of the ghastly strait-jacket which is wrecking the future of this country." He said with emotion, "I see his death as a really appalling tragedy."

"When you heard he was very ill, what did you do?"

"Well," said Line, "of course, I wasn't in the inner circle, and I wasn't told what was going on. But with experience it's possible to read between the lines of these official bulletins. It's not just what they say, which is usually pretty meaningless; it's the names at the bottom which are significant. When new experts from different specialities are being called in every day it almost certainly means that the people in charge are completely at a loss. It soon became plain to me from reading the bulletins about Kincaid that they were having great difficulty in coming to a diagnosis. So I approached Sir Thomas one day at the Royal Society of Medicine and offered him the help of my machine." Line shrugged. "Unfortunately he refused it."

"Then what did you do?"

"I wrote him a letter which he never answered. And I became more and more anxious and outraged at the situation. It was plain that Kincaid was going to die unless they could find out what was wrong with him. Then I heard that Mr. Dudley was going to do an exploratory operation. I rang him up and told him that Kincaid was a friend of mine and asked him to let me into the theatre. He wasn't too keen but he finally agreed."

"Why did you want to be present?"

"I don't know exactly. I really felt that something terrible was happening and I had a wild hope that I might be able to help. I suppose it was foolish of me," said Line ruefully.

"That was the only reason you went there?"

"Yes."

"And when you were there, did you see Mr. Kincaid's case history?"

"Yes, I did. And I naturally read it. Then it suddenly occurred to me that here was all the information which we would have put into the machine if Gilling had allowed us to. So, while they were in the theatre getting ready, I copied it down in my notebook. Then afterwards I got Brook to put it through the machine."

"And what was the result?"

"It gave eight alternative diagnoses."

"And from these possibilities it would have been possible to deduce the correct one?"

"Yes."

"What did you do then?"

"I wrote the letter to *Medical Science*."

"With what object in view?"

"I didn't see how I could remain silent. It was bad enough that we had met with obstruction from the moment Brook and Halder had set foot in this country. It was bad enough that we had been starved of money and met with endless difficulty in publication. But this affair of Kincaid was the last straw. I was convinced that if Gilling had given us the information we could have made the diagnosis. The exploratory examination would have been unnecessary. The infecting organism could have been treated with the appropriate antibiotic and Kincaid would still have been alive today. I wrote that letter in the interests of the medical profession of this country and of the public."

"Have you had any doubt about it since then?"

"None."

"You still believe the letter was necessary and justified?"

"I do."

"Do you regret your action?"

Line shook his head slowly. With great deliberation he said, "Not in the least. If it happened all over again I would behave in precisely the same way."

Chapter 3

Symons resumed his seat and Sir Frederick Groom stood up to cross-examine. He regarded the witness balefully for a moment, before asking his first question. Behind the impassive reptilian expression on his face lay a suspicion that the cross-examination was going to be uphill work. The case for the plaintiff, which had seemed so watertight at the beginning, was now leaking badly, largely due to the vanity and stupidity of the doctors. Though the discovery that Kincaid was an alcoholic was for all practical purposes irrelevant to the case, its concealment and subsequent discovery in cross-examination had created precisely that atmosphere of secrecy and connivance in high places which it was most important to avoid. Trimble, for all his courage, had hardly inspired confidence, while Maxfield . . . Groom found difficulty in maintaining his self-control when he thought of Maxfield. He had been associated with Gilling in the Kincaid case, he had been with him at the Athenaeum when they bullied Gale, he had advised him to take the action, and he had been involved both in rejecting the requests for grants for the Brook-Halder machine and in that unfortunate affair of the scientific article which had been delayed. His absence from the witness box had screamed to high heaven.

It had seemed at the beginning that Line had set himself an impossible task. To win the case he had, practically speaking, to prove both negligence and conspiracy against a group of the most respected physicians in London. In the event, with the aid of some effective cross-examination, his opponents had practically managed to prove it for him themselves before he went into the box. All Line had to do now was to emerge as an honest, sincere, and intelligent man and the jury were likely to believe his account of the situation and award him the verdict. The only hope was to discredit him in some way. The case must be won in cross-examination if it was to be won at all.

Groom had been watching Line very carefully during the examination-in-chief, hoping for a clue to his weaknesses. So far he had seen nothing to encourage him. Line thought and spoke clearly, he was neither over-garrulous nor suspiciously taciturn, he had a handsome open face and a diffident charm of manner. He appeared to be completely at ease in the public eye, with an absolute confidence in his own virtue in all circumstances. Like many controversial figures, he was no doubt used to being attacked, and cross-examination would not be such an unnerving experience as it was to men who had led more sheltered lives. His answers to embarrassing questions would have been well rehearsed. There was little chance of taking him by surprise.

Still, you never could tell. Perhaps he would be over-confident. There was always hope in that. And, Groom reminded himself, he had a few tricks up his sleeve. He doubted whether Line would emerge from cross-examination as quite the sympathetic upstanding figure that he presented to the world now.

"Professor Line, would it be reasonable to describe you as a controversial figure in the medical world?"

"It's hard for me to say."

"Well, let me put it this way. You have been involved in a number of controversies in the last ten years or so."

"Yes."

"In which you have usually been in opposition to the more senior members of your profession?"

"Yes."

Groom paused and then snapped, "Do you enjoy this kind of thing?"

Line was not disconcerted by the sudden attack. He said equably, "I'm not sure what kind of thing you mean."

"I mean controversy. Opposition to established authority."

"Those are two different things. Which does your question refer to?"

Groom made an irritable gesture, as if Line were trying to

evade the question. "I think you know what I mean, Professor. Do you enjoy controversy?"

"Sometimes. But not when the issues are very serious, as in this case. It merely distresses me."

"Yet you precipitate these conflicts, surely?"

"I don't accept that. I try to act in an independent way according to what I think right. If that sometimes causes resentment among those who like to control the behaviour of others, I can't see that the fault's mine."

"Isn't it true that you like to oppose authority? That you have always done so?"

"I haven't opposed authority as such. But when I thought it was wrong, I like to think I had the courage to say so."

"Did you not have trouble when you were in the army for refusing to obey an order?"

"Yes. I said there was typhus in an area and my colonel said there wasn't. I was afterwards proved to be right."

"Yet you were sent home to England?"

"The colonel's dignity had to be preserved," said Line sardonically.

"Did you at that time give information to the Press—against the regulations?"

"Yes. It was the only way to get anything done."

Groom said significantly, "You've used this same technique again more recently, have you not?"

"One of the functions of the Press is to inform the public of things which men in high places would prefer to conceal."

"That is not an answer to my question."

"I've given information to the Press when I thought it in the public interest. I'm not ashamed of the fact."

Groom bared his teeth. "Are you perhaps proud of it?"

"Neither ashamed nor proud. It seemed the right thing to do."

Groom paused for a moment, then he said, "Is it true to say that ever since you came from America to become professor at the Metropolitan, you have been running a campaign against Sir Thomas Gilling and his colleagues?"

"No, of course it isn't true."

"But you have been in repeated arguments with him, haven't you?"

"Yes."

"Why is that?"

"For various reasons. The most important is the question of research finance for the work of Brook and Halder."

"You felt very bitter about this, didn't you?"

"I was disgusted. It seemed quite outrageous to me that they should be denied money for their work."

"When you say money, you mean a sum in the region of two hundred thousand pounds?"

"That's the approximate total over a number of years."

"Not many young scientists can lay their hands on a grant of that size, can they?"

"The work was worth it."

"In your view. But others might think differently?"

"They might. Personally I think the case we put was incontestable. In any case the total amount of money was irrelevant. We were not even able to obtain small sums for minor aspects of the work."

"You invited Brook and Halder to come to this country on your own responsibility?"

"Yes."

"Promising them that you would obtain adequate money for their experiments?"

"Yes."

"You didn't discuss beforehand with anyone whether this money might be forthcoming from the usual sources?"

"No."

"Wasn't that a little rash?"

"As it turned out, yes. But you must remember that I had been in America for some years, where you can always find money for worthwhile research. I didn't realize what I would be up against over here."

"What do you mean by that?"

Line spoke without apparent heat. "A closed ring of elderly men who control everything," he said coolly. "If you get across with them, God help you."

Groom gave a disgusted frown. "Aren't you being rather melodramatic?"

Line shrugged. "It's the situation. If it weren't, we shouldn't be here today."

"I suggest that this situation exists entirely in your own mind?"

Line shook his head. "I wish you were right. But it's common knowledge. Everyone in the profession knows about it."

"And you see Sir Thomas Gilling as a dictator, a Machiavellian despot?"

"I think socially he's a very charming man. He just has the idea that nothing should happen in medicine without his permission."

"What motive could Sir Thomas and his colleagues have for the kind of victimization you are suggesting?"

"I don't know. It's possible that they objected to my inviting Brook and Halder over here without asking them. It's possible they have a prejudice against the whole idea of the machine."

"Why should they have that?"

"Well," said Line amiably, "it attacks the personal magic and ascendancy of the physician, doesn't it? It takes a lot of the glamour out of diagnosis. Naturally that might be alarming to people with a very traditional cast of mind." His mouth twisted in a faint smile. "It's as if someone invented a machine which could carry out a cross-examination better than a barrister."

There was a ripple of laughter from the court. Groom waited for it to die down. The expression on his face never changed. "In fact you have no evidence of what you've just said? It's mere speculation on your part?"

Line said reasonably, "It was you who asked me to speculate."

Groom was finding it heavy going. "But to get back to facts, what happened was this, wasn't it? You invited these young men over to do very expensive research without any money at all, gambling that you'd get it out of the Medical Research Council or other bodies over here?"

"I never thought at the time there would be any difficulty."

"And when there was difficulty, you were in a cleft stick, weren't you? Having given your promise?"

"It was a very distressing situation."

"So then you tried to blackmail Sir Thomas with threats of publicity?"

"Certainly not."

Groom picked up a piece of notepaper from his brief. "I have a letter here, written to Sir Thomas at the time. You say 'I cannot believe that if the public hears of this (which it surely must in the end) it will be to the benefit of your reputation and that of your committee.' That was a threat, wasn't it?"

"No. It was a warning."

"And later you gave the story to the Frampton Press, didn't you?"

"I needed money for research. When I couldn't get it in the usual places I approached other sources. One of these was the Frampton Foundation. They asked me why I came to them and I had to tell them."

"And you gave them permission to pass the information on to the newspapers?"

"It was the truth. Why should it be kept secret?"

Groom persisted. "You gave them that permission, didn't you?"

"Yes."

"It was a good story for the Sunday papers, wasn't it?"

"Perhaps. I don't know. I'm not a journalist."

"And they made you a grant, didn't they?"

"Yes."

"In fact most of the money for the Brook-Halder machine has come from the Frampton Foundation?"

"Yes."

"And in return you have given them sensational stories about the iniquities of Sir Thomas Gilling?"

Line flushed a little for the first time. "That's nonsense."

"And the letter which is the subject of this action was the last in a chain of such sensations, wasn't it?"

"Definitely not."

Groom wriggled his shoulders menacingly. "The jury must decide. Now, Professor Line, we've heard a lot about this machine. Have there been any other issues on which you have been in controversy with Sir Thomas Gilling?"

"Yes. There was the question of priorities for the Hospital Plan. And the programme for post-graduate training. But those were quite amicable."

"Was there any other disagreement that wasn't quite so amicable?"

Line seemed to show a little reluctance in answering. "Well"— he said slowly—"there was the row about distinction awards."

"Distinction awards." Groom seemed to savour the words. He said to Line, "Perhaps it would be a good idea if you explain to the court what these awards are."

"It's a curious arrangement we have in the National Health Service. Awards are made to hospital consultants—they're supposed to be awards for high standards of work. They're graded A, B and C. The highest awards are worth four to five thousand pounds a year. They are made by a committee of which Lord Maxfield is chairman. The awards are supposed to be secret. Nobody knows who gets them or how much."

"And I gather that you oppose these awards?"

"Yes."

"Why?"

"I think they're iniquitous," said Line. "In the first place, it's very questionable to what extent they're given as a reward for real distinction and not just simply to recognize seniority. In the second place, they're in the gift of a small group of influential old men. Everyone who wants several thousand pounds a year for doing nothing at all is tempted to play in with this group. It stifles criticism, it encourages conformity and time-serving. It's patronage, pure and simple. And being secret, there's no way of knowing to what extent it is abused."

"I see," said Groom pleasantly. He seemed not in the least put out at having given Line the opportunity to make a speech. "Obviously you feel very strongly on this point?"

"Yes."

"And you have expressed these views in print?"

"Yes. Six years ago I wrote an article for a weekly review."

"Was this signed with your own name?"

"No, it was written under a pseudonym."

"You made an anonymous attack on the Awards Committee?"

"Yes, but——"

Groom interrupted. "You've answered my question."

"Not fully—you didn't allow me——"

"You're simply required to answer the questions. Now, Professor Line——"

Line turned to the judge. "My Lord, I appeal to you. Surely I have a right to explain my reasons."

The judge said, "I think that's only fair, Sir Frederick. So long as the witness confines himself to the point." Groom shrugged irritably. "Yes, Professor Line?"

"It was anonymous because of the convention that doctors' names shouldn't appear in public." Before Groom could cut in he added in an offhand voice, "Unless of course they happen to be attending the royal family, in which case they can have all the publicity they like."

Groom's eyelids dropped to a half-closed position. With him, it was a sign of extreme irritation. He said, "You would have preferred to break this convention?"

"Yes."

"And you did shortly afterwards, didn't you?"

"Yes. When people accused me of sheltering under a pseudonym, I didn't see I had any choice. So when I was asked to answer questions about this matter on television, I agreed. I was sick and tired of all this nonsensical secrecy and I told the producer that he was quite welcome to give my name. Afterwards, of course," said Line contemptuously, "there was a hullabaloo."

"What do you mean by that?"

"Well, they were furious that I had attacked the distinction awards and the personal publicity I got was a wonderful stick to beat me with. So they shifted their ground completely and said that I was advertising myself."

"And weren't you?" asked Groom sourly.

"No, of course I wasn't."

Groom said in a disgusted voice, "Oh come, Professor. I'm not just referring to this one occasion. Since then you've written and given interviews and appeared on television repeatedly under your own name. You've invited parties of journalists to your Unit at the Metropolitan Hospital. Can you honestly say you haven't courted publicity?"

Line was not disconcerted. "Never for myself," he said. "For my Unit perhaps. I had to advertise my Unit to get money for research. Anyway the convention about personal publicity is obsolete so far as people like myself are concerned."

"I see," Groom said with great significance. "You feel yourself exempt from the normal rules of your profession. Is that it?"

"No. But this particular rule was formulated to prevent doctors picking up private patients. I don't see private patients. There's nothing else I could gain from publicity. After all, I've already got one of the best surgical chairs in the country."

He hesitated. Groom suddenly stepped in. "And what else, Professor?" For the first time Line seemed disconcerted. He delayed his answer as if momentarily off balance. Groom said, "Weren't you going to say 'and a top-level distinction award'?"

Line seemed to spot his slip just too late. He stopped and stood there disconcerted. Groom stepped in. "I was going to ask you about that, Professor." His voice was triumphant. "I believe you have a top-level distinction award. Worth over four thousand pounds a year?"

"Yes. That is so—but let me explain——" Line now seemed very obviously confused.

"You receive such an award, don't you?'

"Yes I do, but——"

"In spite of your conscientious objection to the scheme?"

"Yes," said Line awkwardly. "I thought at first of turning it down——"

There was a sneer in Groom's voice. "But you didn't?"

"No." Suddenly the awkwardness disappeared from Line's manner. A gentle smile spread about his lips. "I decided to take it and make it over towards the expenses of the Unit. I've never touched a penny of it myself."

There was a buzz of excitement in the court. Silently, impassively, Groom cursed his client, cursed the solicitor for not finding this out beforehand. He heard the frenzied scratching of the journalists' pencils behind him, saw the faint triumphant smile play across Line's lips. A lesser man would have been hopelessly thrown off his stroke but superficially at least Groom appeared unmoved. He managed a sinister twist of the lips, designed to suggest that he had anticipated Line's revelation and intended to use it to trap him in some later part of the cross-examination.

The main thing, he knew, was to keep going, to let the impression fade, not to leave the jury to savour Line's victory overnight.

"Yes," he said, "a very noble gesture. It will perhaps serve as a contrast to some of the less romantic matters we are now about to discuss." His voice was pure acid. "These concern your career as a television personality."

Chapter 4

LINE BRACED HIMSELF for the assault. In his preliminary discussions with Symons they had agreed that it was on this question of seeking personal publicity—particularly by television appearances—that he was most vulnerable. Line had no sense of shame about it himself. His conscience was entirely clear. Everything he had done had been for the sake of the Unit. If the old men created a state of affairs in which research could only be supported by publicity, then that was the way it must be. It was their doing, not his.

It was not that he had ever sought the public eye. In a curious way it had almost been the opposite way round—as if the public had been seeking *him*. And since the meeting had taken place, it had been a love affair, a relationship so perfectly appropriate that it seemed almost divinely ordained. It had been woven like a thread through his whole career, even indeed through his marriage. It would have been difficult now to visualize his life without it. Yet—like most momentous events—it had been precipitated by an accident.

It was during the time when he was working at the Hemisphere Hospital on a research fellowship. He had been very pleased about the fellowship when he had obtained it. It had been achieved in the face of a good deal of competition and was thought by everybody to be a magnificent opportunity. The Hemisphere was more than a hospital, it was an enormous comprehensive medical centre with limitless wealth and a world reputation. It was staffed by medical celebrities and ranked with the Mayo Clinic, Johns Hopkins, and the Massachusetts General as one of the spectacular achievements of American medicine. To have been chosen to work there was an achievement in itself. If he could do more than that and make any kind of mark for himself, his fortunes in England when he returned should be assured.

Neither Line's personality nor his record to that date had inclined him to false modesty or lack of self-confidence. He knew that he had abilities which were out of the ordinary, and at his teaching hospital in England this had been instantly recognized. It was clear to him that nowadays the only way to make use of outstanding gifts was through research—the mere performance of routine surgery was a job for competent technicians, not for members of the élite. At the Hemisphere research was king. He would have the time and the facilities and the necessary atmosphere of stimulation. The competition would be great, of course—the hospital was full of brilliant men from all over the world. But Line was confident that he could give a good account of himself.

After six months he was not quite so sure. There was something rather terrifying about the Hemisphere. Its sheer physical size was intimidating—it was like a small town on its own. It lacked the reassuring family atmosphere of even the larger British teaching hospitals. The multitude of different special units lived lives of their own and contact with doctors in different specialties was rare and intermittent. The units themselves had vast polyglot staffs, most of whom divided their time between the wards and the laboratories. At times it seemed that the hospital contained more doctors than patients. They clustered round the beds, they attended clinical conferences in their hundreds. And they were all picked men, the cream of the medical schools of Pittsburg and San Francisco, of Tokyo and Manila, of Sydney and Athens and Delhi and Zurich and Paris and Manchester. It was difficult to be outstanding in circumstances like these.

Line was one of a number of research associates attached to the Unit of Professor Sheehan, a bustling white-haired man who lived his life as if he were in a fever to rush off to some other place, to start a different conversation or turn his mind to another problem from the one with which he was presently confronted. He was followed everywhere by a crowd of assistants who completed his operations, pacified his patients, and frequently kept appointments in his place. After welcoming Line effusively on his arrival, he turned him over to one of his lieutenants and appeared to forget about him completely. Line found himself with a generous allocation of laboratory space and clinical responsibility for a tiny number of Sheehan's patients.

He started on a series of experiments he had planned beforehand, to expand some work he had already begun in London on the restoration of amputated limbs in animals. His constant feeling of isolation made the work depressing rather than stimulating. There was little social life in the hospital itself. The colleagues he met were hospitable, but he was used to the more complex interlocking society of Oxford and London and the restriction of social contact was irksome to him. They drove him out to their houses in Westchester or Long Island and introduced him to their wives and children, but somehow conversation soon languished. He fancied they regarded him as stiff and reserved. He made few real friends.

In compensation for this he tried to direct all his energies towards his work. He spent all day in the laboratory and then retired in the evening to a small service flat which the hospital had found for him in a vast property development on the East Side. The flat was comfortable and convenient but the massive complex of identical tower blocks oppressed and bewildered him. Everything around him seemed designed to convince him of his own insignificance.

He began to worry about things which had never concerned him before, to wonder whether he had over-estimated himself and his own potentialities. Perhaps he was indeed, as this great city appeared to be trying to tell him, a mere atom, nobody of the least conceivable importance. He worried, too, about his experimental work. He began to lose faith in its value, to wonder if he had any real talent for research. What had once seemed inspired to him now looked, in his mood of despondency, hackneyed and banal.

After twelve months he was tempted to throw in his Fellowship and return to England—it was only the impossibility of giving a satisfactory explanation of this to his chief in London which deterred him.

And then he had a stroke of luck. It happened one night when he was on emergency duty. A drunken, semi-conscious man was brought in from a bar-room brawl with a severe injury to his left arm. When Line examined it more closely he found that the limb was almost totally severed, being attached to the upper fragment only by a relatively narrow strip of skin. His luck lay in the fact that this was the kind of situation that his animal work was designed to investigate. Ordinarily speaking the arm would have been amputated. Instead of this, using the perfusion technique he had designed for his animal work, Line spent the night reattaching the arm. It was a long tedious job, involving careful stitching of nerves and blood vessels, and he had little hope that it would be successful. Almost certainly the blood supply had been lost for too long and the arm would become gangrenous. He went to bed at five o'clock with the conviction that he had performed an interesting but basically futile experiment.

But at least he had a feeling of significance and excitement about it. When he went back to see the patient again after a few hours' sleep he felt positively cheerful for the first time in months. He was surprised to find one of the interns who had assisted at the operation lying in wait for him outside the ward.

"Is something the matter?"

The intern looked up at the ceiling. "Man, you don't know. You really don't know. They've been practically tearing the clothes off me in there."

"Who have?"

"The reporters." His eyes were sparkling with excitement. "Do you know who that guy is in there? The one we spent last night on?"

"He gave his name as Jack Francis."

"Correct. But not entirely correct. It seems his real name is Jack Francis Connolly. Otherwise known as Frankie Connolly." He paused dramatically.

Line was baffled. "Well?"

The intern was incredulous. "You've never heard of him? He's the star pitcher for the Yankees."

"Oh." Line felt his stomach turn over. This might be very good or very bad. "And his arm?"

The intern tapped him delightedly on the shoulder. "I'll tell you something. I think it's going to work."

It was by no means the first time that such an operation had been done successfully. Nor had the arm been entirely severed, as the newspapers insisted on saying. However, there was no doubt that it was the first time it had been done in such dramatic circumstances on someone who was such hot news as Frankie Connolly.

Line gave a short, non-committal statement to the journalists and then went to see Sheehan. For once he found no difficulty in getting hold of the Professor—the news, it seemed, was already round the hospital. Suddenly, overnight, he found himself transformed from a nonentity into a person of consequence. When he saw the evening papers he was alarmed to find that they had all printed his name and that some of them had even managed to procure a photograph—in England that would have meant trouble. But Sheehan telephoned to congratulate him. The news stories were all doing great work for the hospital. Connolly, whose every word carried an authority which would have made Moses tear his beard in frustration, was pouring out columns of praise and hero worship for the young genius who had saved his arm. Within a week the hospital received offers of donations amounting to several millions of dollars.

Line was surprised and rather touched to find that his American colleagues were neither censorious of the publicity he received, nor jealous of his good fortune. He gradually realized that he was expected to go along with the newspapers for the sake of the hospital. When he was asked to give an interview on television, he hesitated at first, but then on advice from Sheehan, accepted.

When he appeared he was interested to find that he was hardly nervous at all. Indeed, he had to admit to himself that he enjoyed the experience enormously. The contrast between his melancholy obscurity only a few days ago and his present celebrity amused and excited him. Throughout the interview he knew he was performing well and his confidence was confirmed when he saw the playback. It was immediately obvious that he had a natural knack for that kind of thing. He was photogenic. He spoke fluently and without pomposity, and there was a youthful eagerness about him which was hard to resist. There was also, to New Yorkers, an exotic quality about both his voice and his appearance. He represented a rather idealized American picture of a European—elegant and cultivated, with an indefinable touch of decadence.

After this his rise was startling. In the hospital he found himself now treated as a person of consequence. Some of the larger donations offered to the Hemisphere had fortunately carried the condition that it should be used on his particular kind of work, and one of the donors suggested that the money might be spent to provide a special unit under his direction. The conditions were accepted gladly and within a matter of months he found himself an associate professor with a staff of his own and almost unlimited finance.

It was a startling change, but one of which he was fortunately well equipped to take advantage. He found he was able to accept success and fame much more easily than he had adjusted to obscurity. Nor was his success confined to the hospital. His first television appearance had been such a success that he was constantly invited to take part in other programmes, and he became in a very short time a minor celebrity. Even after Connolly was discharged from hospital (the arm survived, but with considerable damage to muscle and he never actually got back to pitching), he was still called upon to take part in discussions on the future of surgery or the problems of medical research.

There was one particular show—a panel discussion called "Where Are We Going"—in which he was a regular participant. It was an attempt to project serious discussion on advances in science and the arts to an audience of serious "thinking" people. The sponsor was a manufacturer of breakfast cereals called Jorgensen. Line met Jorgensen, a tall, melancholy figure with an earnest belief in progress, on several occasions. On the last of these he was accompanied by his wife, a handsome dark athletic woman at least fifteen years younger than himself.

Line had always been attractive to women and he could sense instinctively when a woman was interested in him. His mind registered the fact that Brenda Jorgensen had looked at him in a certain way and spoken to him in a particular tone of voice.

He was not at all surprised when she turned up to watch a later recording of the same series—this time alone. They had drinks afterwards in the producer's office and he could feel her eyes on him. He was amused and mildly excited. Later she came across the room and spoke to him.

"Congratulations, Dr. Line." She shook the ice around in her glass. "You're a natural for television."

He had developed a standard modest response to this particular approach. "I'm naturally garrulous," he said.

She laughed shortly. She was evidently not taken in by his mock modesty. She said, "How's your Unit coming on?"

"Well enough. It takes time."

"I believe my husband made a contribution."

"A generous one." Automatically he said what he knew Americans loved to hear. "That's the nice thing about working in your country. No problems of money. Nowadays, unfortunately, research needs so much equipment. A new artificial heart arrived only the other day. It's magnificent. You should see it."

She lifted an eyebrow. "Is that an official invitation?"

He smiled back. It was almost like a password. "Of course."

The following week he showed her round the Unit. It was a fairly common request from generous donors or influential supporters of the hospital. He had developed a standard conducted tour for them—interesting but not too exacting or too long. There were one or two demonstrations which went over rather well and he had a gift for making technical details comprehensible. As soon as their initial enthusiasm showed signs of giving way to fatigue, they were instantly whisked off into his office and given excellent dry martinis. Rather too much of his time was taken up by this kind of thing but he recognized that it was necessary. It was a small enough irritant compared with the frustrations of his life a few months ago.

She was an unusually acute and intelligent visitor and he enjoyed showing her around. Afterwards she said, "It's going to be quite something, isn't it?" She studied his face carefully. "Doesn't it frighten you a little?"

"Why should it?"

"So much success, so quickly."

He considered. "To be honest, not very much. I think I know

307

what to do with it." It was true he had always been prepared for success. Only the time and occasion had been unknown to him. The only time when he had nearly lost his head was when the possibility had occurred to him that it might pass him by.

As if anxious to prick his complacency, she said, "Let's face it, you were lucky."

"Of course." He admitted it without resentment. "One has to have luck at some stage. I always knew I needed a break to get started."

"It may not continue."

"I'd be surprised if it did. But once you're going, you don't need it quite so much. From now on I think I can manage with just average good fortune."

"Doesn't it worry you that perhaps you may not be up to all this? That you might not be good enough to make the best use of it?"

He shook his head. "You don't really understand about research nowadays. The really big discoveries are few and far between—and so are the really big men. Even with them, a lot of their success is due to chance. Ninety per cent of research nowadays isn't done in that way at all. Everybody knows what the possible growing points in science are. Everybody knows the various ways in which these big outstanding problems may be tackled. For every advance made in this country you can bet your boots that there's a Japanese or an Englishman or a Russian or a German working more or less on the same lines. It's largely a question of luck who gets there first. So if you have the financial backing and an intelligent grasp of the subject, and you can get good people to work with you——" He made a gesture which took in himself, the handsome suite of laboratories, the staff of white-coated doctors and technicians—"you have as good a chance as anyone."

She frowned. "You make it sound too damn' much like a marketing campaign for breakfast food."

"Organizational problems have a certain similarity, whatever field they occur in. So do the solutions. A lot of research is organization nowadays." He laughed. "I can see I've shocked you. You expected something more romantic. You think that because I'm realistic about the means I'm cynical about the end. I'm not. I'm as starry-eyed as you could possibly wish about the object of what we're doing. I believe that medical research is just about the best cause we can possibly spend our time and effort and brains on. That's why I gave up another career and qualified as a doctor in the first instance. But this is a modern war we're fighting. We need tanks, not cavalry." He gave her a warm companionable smile. "So you see, I'm not such a cold-hearted bastard as you thought."

"You worry me a bit just the same."

He was genuinely surprised. "Good heavens, why?"

She stubbed out her cigarette. "I don't know quite. You're sort of intense and yet detached at the same time. It's a little bit unnerving. Not that I mind. After six years of Harvey Jorgensen I can do with some stimulation."

He laughed. Another password had been given. "You must bring him along," he said.

"Must I?" She was telling him as blatantly as only a rich, self-confident woman could, that she was bored with her husband and would like to have an affair with him. It was impossible not to be excited by the situation. She added, "Anyway, he's usually out of the country. He's decided that the United States isn't enough. The whole world deserves to know about Krumbleweet."

"What's it like, incidentally?"

"Sawdust with a dash of malt. It's one of those great mysteries. You never meet anyone who can stand it, yet there's a fortune in selling it."

"Like stout."

She gave a puzzled frown. "What in hell's stout?"

Line smiled. "Really," he said, "you must let me educate you."

There followed several months of extraordinary happiness. It was something he had never known before—or indeed was likely to know again, since it is impossible to repeat the unique experience of first love. The love affair was not, as he thought at the beginning, with Brenda, but with success, with public admiration, with the sight of his own image on a screen a few feet wide, living for a short while each week in the homes of a million strangers. It was an intoxicating sensation, as if he had begun to live on a vastly more significant plane than he had ever known before. His affair with Brenda was little more than a component of this brilliant dream. It gave him many things he badly needed, things which even success was unable to provide. All through life Line had been accustomed to feminine admiration, and he had come to need it as much, if not more, than sensual pleasure itself. At the same time he had always been wary for fear women might use this need to possess him. He was himself intermittently affectionate with women, but never passionate, and never dependent. He was not jealous and had no interest whatsoever in women who did not admire him. It seemed to him in the early stages that his relationship with Brenda was as near perfect as he could hope for. She was fascinated by him, but her appreciation was shrewd enough not to be cloying; she was amusing in company; she had an arrogant directness which made her a constant stimulation to him; she was beautiful to look at and magnificent in bed; and there was a pride about her, a detached independence which freed him from the sensation of being smothered.

The fact that she was very rich he found amusing rather than impressive. He was very happy to make use of all the conveniences of wealth when she put them at his disposal, even to use them with a careless lavishness which surprised her. But he was not dependent on money. He had no fear at all of being possessed in this way. He was like a man who is so sure of his complete independence of alcohol that he has no fear of getting drunk now and then when the mood takes him.

Neither of them made the slightest attempt to be discreet. They used her apartment when Jorgensen was away and dined together at the kind of restaurants which appeared to be run almost entirely for the benefit of the society section of the newspapers. They were both of them news, to the extent of being worth a mention in the notes of the gossip columnists. It was merely a matter of time before Jorgensen sued for divorce.

It was a divorce without rancour. They arranged the details with Jorgensen over dinner one night and got married in Reno two months later. They spent two weeks on a honeymoon in Mexico and then moved as man and wife into Brenda's apartment, which Jorgensen had given to them as a wedding present. It took Line three months to realize that Brenda's feeling for him had developed into something which had alarming implications for both of them. She had fallen deeply in love with him. He, on the other hand, was not in love with her at all.

They were still trying to sort this out when Line was offered, and accepted, the professorship of surgery at the Metropolitan Hospital.

Chapter 5

GROOM WAS a painstaking man. He went through Line's American career at considerable length—every telecast, every personal appearance, every signed article. At the end, the cumulative effect of this began to achieve the impression he was after. In the cold light of the Law Courts, those days in New York seemed a little high-pitched and febrile, exciting to take part in no doubt, but hardly the kind of thing one expected of a man who aspired to influence a great profession. Several members of the jury were frowning a little, in a way which suggested a readjustment of their mental attitudes towards the witness. Groom's spirits rose a little. He prepared to move the field of questioning gradually towards Line's present circumstances.

"It was this period in America which laid the foundations of your subsequent career?"

"Yes, I think one could say that."

"And your fame at that time was largely founded on personal publicity?"

"Not at all. All that mattered to me was my reputation in the profession. Personal publicity had nothing to do with that."

"But you'll admit that you did have a great deal of publicity?"

"Yes."

"Which you didn't go out of your way to avoid?"

"I've already explained the situation about that."

"And after you returned to this country," said Groom sourly, "didn't you immediately manage to get yourself into the public eye over here?"

Line looked up at the judge. "Is that a proper question?" he asked.

The judge inclined his head sympathetically. "I think you'd better rephrase it, Sir Frederick."

"Very well, my Lord." Groom wriggled his shoulders in his gown. He spoke as if humouring a child. "Professor Line, is it true that remarks of yours were published in the national Press soon after you took over the chair of surgery at the Metropolitan Hospital?"

"Yes, they were."

"What was the subject of these remarks?"

"They were about the research facilities at the hospital. I'd been given to understand when I accepted the chair that the necessary equipment would be made available for me to carry on my work. I was promised that during the six months before I could take over the department, everything would be made ready. In fact nothing was ready and the work came to a standstill."

"Did you protest to the hospital?"

"Yes. They simply said the delay was unavoidable and they would do what they could. Nobody seemed to care very much. In the meantime I and my staff were hanging around, completely idle. It was a fantastic situation."

"So you decided to publicize it?"

"No. It's impossible to keep a thing like that secret for very long. It was bound to leak out. When journalists came and asked me questions I told them the truth. After all," he said reasonably, "I could hardly tell them I was working when I wasn't."

"So there was a great fuss in the Press?"

"Yes. It was a time when there was a lot of anxiety about the number of scientists who were emigrating to the U.S.A. Naturally people wondered whether this kind of muddle wasn't a contributory factor."

"You thought it was?"

"Yes."

"And said so?"

"Yes. I couldn't see any reason for concealing my opinion."

"And as a result of this furore, you got your equipment?"

Line smiled. "Well, it certainly arrived very soon afterwards."

There was a burst of laughter. When it had died down Groom

said, "This made you realize that the Press could be very useful, didn't it?"

"There's an inference in that question that I made use of the Press. I didn't. I simply told them the truth when they asked me."

"As you have done many times since?"

"I'm not sure what you mean by many times. It's happened on a number of occasions."

Groom pressed on. "I suggest that this experience made you believe that whenever you had problems with authority, the way to win was to give them as much publicity as possible."

"No. That's not so. There was no such policy."

"H'm." Groom looked sceptically at the jury. "Be that as it may, you've seldom been out of the public eye since then. We have heard of your appearances on television in the United States. Tell me, when did you first appear on the television screen in this country?"

"About a year after I returned to England."

"What kind of a programme was this? Was it like the ones you did in America?"

"Oh no. It was much more elaborate. In my opinion it was a very exciting idea. It was called 'The Other World.' The idea behind the programme was that sick people live in a different world from the rest of us. They're cut off from everybody, and particularly from those who look after them. There's a barrier there which everyone knows exists, but nobody so far has been able to do very much about. We hoped to do something about it with this programme."

"You took part in all these programmes?"

"Not all of them. They went on over a period of several years. I introduced many of them and took an active part in some."

"And as a consequence, you became quite well known."

"My face did. I appeared anonymously."

"But after a while, a great many people knew who you were—especially in the profession?"

"I don't know. I should imagine that quite a number of them did. It could hardly be avoided."

"Did this programme, and your appearance in it, attract unanimous approval among your colleagues?"

Line smiled again. "I'm afraid nothing attracts unanimous

approval among medical men. I hope most of them thought I was doing a good job. Some of the older members disapproved."

"Why should they disapprove?"

"You'd really have to ask them. My impression was that they thought I was telling ordinary lay people too much about medicine—that I was damaging the mystery, as it were. They still wanted the doctor to be a rather remote, powerful figure. Personally I think that's out of date."

Groom picked up a journal from the desk in front of him and opened it at a marked page. "Do you know that it was said by a certain very eminent doctor—I am quoting here—'These programmes may well be a considerable source of anxiety and suffering—even actual physical danger—to those who listen to them without special medical knowledge.' "

"That sounds like Lord Sandray," said Line with unruffled good temper.

"Yes. Would you disregard his opinion?"

"Of course I wouldn't. He's probably the most famous and experienced physician alive today. He has a unique position in medicine. But that doesn't mean I have to agree with him on everything. And after all," he added amiably, "he was over seventy, even then."

"What you are really saying is that you think you know better than the heads of your profession?"

"As the holder of one of the most important surgical posts in this country, I think I have a right to make up my own mind. That is the way I'd put it."

Groom said, "The jury will decide which interpretation is the more reasonable." He went on, "And the upshot was that you went on with your television appearances in spite of these weighty manifestations of disapproval?"

"Yes."

"Yes, of course you did." It seemed to Groom that he was getting somewhere. Line's point of view might sound plausible on each individual issue, but any man who was perpetually in conflict with authority ran a considerable risk of being regarded as a crank. Juries, in his experience, were composed mainly of conventional people with a healthy respect for established authority and were prejudiced in favour of conventional attitudes. Even

Line's action in giving away the distinction money might not be entirely in his favour so far as they were concerned. Certainly none of the jury would have done the same. It was bound to make him seem a little eccentric in their eyes.

With the dogged persistence for which he was famous in the courts, Groom pressed the point home. "So here we have quite a lot of issues on which you differed from your senior colleagues. Research facilities, press and television publicity, distinction awards, the Brook-Halder machine, the management of Mr. Kincaid's illness . . ." Groom's voice trailed away as if there many other points of disagreement which he could list if he were not afraid of boring the court. He bared his teeth and said with sudden venom, "You're the only man in step, aren't you?"

Line was unmoved. "No. There are many who think as I do. Unfortunately most of them are afraid to speak up."

Groom raised his eyebrows theatrically. "Afraid? Really, Professor——"

"It's quite true," said Line evenly. "The hospitals under the Health Service are nothing but a vast machine of patronage. A few men control everything—qualifications, jobs, research money, distinction awards, honours. Nobody dares to speak out of turn."

"Except you?" said Groom with a perceptible sneer.

"I was lucky enough to achieve a very high position very early in life. They can't do much about me. That's why I feel an obligation to say these things."

Groom sighed wearily. "This is all very melodramatic. I suggest to you, Professor, that what we are dealing with here is not, as you imagine, a sinister conspiracy, but simply a group of hard-working medical men, trying to do their best for the profession?"

Line's answer was unexpected. He appeared to think over the question very carefully. Then, half turning to the court, he said with an air of great sincerity, "I think, in a curious way, they're both—at the same time."

It was impossible to know what the effect of this answer might be on the jury. Groom glanced quickly at them and felt reassured. They did not look like a particularly intelligent collection of people. Some of them were frowning in a baffled way. It was

316

always a mistake to try to be too subtle. He said cheerfully, "I'm afraid that's rather too clever for me. No doubt the jury will know what to make of it."

Soon after that the court adjourned for lunch. In the afternoon Groom began to cross-examine on the details of Line's letter. He said, "Now your defence, Professor Line—let's have no ambiguity about this—is that these statements are true in substance and in fact. That the allegations you have made about Sir Thomas Gilling are justified?"

"That's correct."

"Let's see what these allegations are in respect of the treatment of Mr. Kincaid. You implied, in effect, that Sir Thomas Gilling was negligent in omitting to make use of the Brook-Halder machine?"

Line side-stepped. "It's not for me to decide on a definition of negligence. My implication was that if Sir Thomas had used the machine he might have had a better chance of making the diagnosis."

"Wouldn't that convey, to an ordinary medical man reading this letter, the meaning that he had been remiss in not using the machine?"

"It might."

"And that he had therefore not done everything that he might be reasonably expected to do for his patient?"

"It might," Line said reasonably. "Obviously I can't predict other people's reactions to a letter."

"But that was your own feeling, wasn't it? That was the meaning you were trying to get over?"

"I thought he should have used the machine. Otherwise I wouldn't have asked him to do so."

"And you thought the reason he didn't was because he had a prejudice against you and Brook and the machine?"

Line said cautiously, "I can't say what other people's reasons are. In my opinion Sir Thomas's behaviour was suggestive of prejudice."

"Are you saying that if he'd used the machine, Mr. Kincaid would have been cured?"

"That's impossible to say. All one can say is that with a

correct diagnosis, the chances would obviously have been better."

"Now," said Groom heavily, "in your early answers to my learned friend, you contended that when the available information from the case sheets was put into the computer, the correct diagnosis emerged."

"Not as such. It emerged as one of eight possibilities."

"That's quite a lot of alternatives."

"Yes," said Line. He spoke like a man on firm ground. "But it would have been possible to exclude five of the others by specific tests. That would leave three. Two of these were completely incurable conditions in our present state of knowledge. The obvious thing would therefore have been to give the correct treatment for the third possibility in the hope that it was the correct answer. This would have given at least a chance of saving Mr. Kincaid."

"In fact," said Groom, "this computer doesn't make a definite diagnosis at all, does it? It makes a number of guesses."

"I don't know what you mean by a guess. It gives a series of alternative explanations for the facts fed into it," Line said in his lecturer's voice. "This is actually pretty much what we do ourselves when we think about things."

"You're hardly going to say that this machine is a substitute for a human mind?"

"Good heavens, no. It's used as a supplement, a cross-check. But that doesn't make it less important. To say you don't need it because you've got a mind is like saying that you don't need books because you've got a mind."

The words were spoken almost contemptuously, and Groom could see that Line was coming to despise his intelligence. What Line did not understand was that a barrister was not in court to appear clever. He was there to influence the jury, to ask the questions and voice the doubts of the common man. Part of Groom's job was to ask questions to which he already knew the answers, in the hope that these answers might seem unconvincing to the jury. He went plodding on. "As I see it, this machine is only valuable if it has all the facts?"

"As many facts as possible. I don't suppose anyone knows all the facts about anything."

Groom nodded significantly. "Perhaps that's worth remembering." He paused. "Well, how did you get hold of these facts about Mr. Kincaid which you fed into your computer?"

"From the case sheet in the surgeon's room during the operation."

"Why did you go to this operation?"

"I was a friend of Kincaid's. I was anxious about the case. I asked Mr. Dudley if I could attend and he agreed."

"You didn't ask Sir Thomas Gilling?"

"No."

"Don't you think you should have done so?"

"Strictly speaking, yes."

"Why didn't you?"

The light-heartedness had gone of Line's manner. This was obviously a subject on which he felt ill at ease. "Frankly, because I didn't think he would have agreed to my presence."

"Do you consider that to be a very honourable way of behaving?"

"I didn't like to do it that way," said Line apologetically. "It was just that I felt I had to be there and I couldn't see any other way."

Groom said in a shocked voice, "You deceived Sir Thomas and ignored the normal professional decencies to gratify your own curiosity?"

"It was not for curiosity. There was a man's life at stake."

"Are you really contending that your presence could have saved Kincaid?"

"No," Line said defiantly. "But I do claim that what I found out then may in time be the means of saving others."

"I see," said Groom with heavy scepticism. "And this information you obtained—you took it back and fed it into the computer, you say."

"I didn't put it in personally. I gave it to Dr. Brook. He then put it into the machine."

"Dr. Brook had never actually seen the patient?"

"No."

"And in fact neither had you?"

"No."

"So this wasn't a human being at all, this was a problem in arithmetic." Before Line could speak he went on, "And you got

319

eight possible answers. Now at that time, when you got those answers, did you know, from the post-mortem examination, what the correct answer was?"

"Yes, I did."

Groom said scornfully, "That made it rather easy to pick the correct one out of the eight, didn't it?"

"No. It didn't affect the matter."

"Oh come, Professor. You can hardly expect the jury to believe that."

"Certainly I do," said Line with some heat. "By a logical process of deduction——"

Groom cut in on him. "Surely this is like solving a clue in a crossword puzzle. Once you know the answer, the process of thought leading up to it becomes infinitely simpler."

"I don't accept the parallel," snapped Line.

"I'm suggesting to you that if you hadn't known the right answer all along, you couldn't have deduced it from these eight alternatives the machine gave you."

"I don't agree."

"Surely if you really wanted to test the machine, you should have done so without knowing what result you wanted out of it?"

"That was impossible. By the time the machine had given its alternatives, the correct answer was already known."

Groom frowned. "Was it?"

"Yes," Line answered steadily. But was there a moment of hesitation? Groom could not be sure, but on general principles he pressed his point. He said, "When was the post-mortem?"

"The following day."

"And when did you hear the result?"

"That evening."

"Who told you?"

"Mr. Dudley."

Groom was fishing wildly. He had no real idea what he was looking for; just a vague instinct, derived from Line's manner, that there was something not quite right about his story here. "And by this time the machine had not processed the information?"

"Not completely."

Again he felt a hesitance in Line's answer. Surely there must be something there. "What do you mean by that exactly?"

"It's difficult to explain without the machine," said Line rather loftily. "There are various checks and counter-checks to be carried out. It's a highly technical business, you understand. I'm not myself an expert on the details of the machine."

"Then who is the expert?"

"Dr. Brook."

"Very well." Groom decided that there wasn't very much further that he could get with Line on this point. He was obviously going to hide behind his expert. He tried to inject an undertone of menace into his voice. "I shall put this to Dr. Brook when he comes to give evidence."

It was as good a point as any to wind up a rather unsatisfactory cross-examination. Perhaps he might be able to get somewhere with Brook using this particular line of attack. He was not too optimistic, however. It was on the face of it unlikely that he would be able to catch out an electronics expert on the workings of a machine which he had himself invented. But at least he was able to imply that he had something up his sleeve for later on. Inscrutable as ever, he sat down.

Chapter 6

THAT EVENING Groom held a conference in his chambers. He sat behind his desk, looking strangely diminished without his wig and gown. His wrinkled face was unsmiling as ever as he regarded his three guests through the top half of a pair of bifocal spectacles. Gilling and Lady Gilling sat in high-winged armchairs at the opposite side of the desk. Perrin had placed himself with instinctive self-effacement in the shadows at Groom's right hand. This was Groom's performance, not his.

Groom said, "We've just been notified that there's an adjournment until next Monday. The judge has an important funeral to attend. That gives us a slight breathing space before we come up to the last lap. I thought this would be a good time to review the situation."

He sat back in his chair, removed his spectacles, and began to swing them casually in his right hand. He regarded Gilling without obvious emotion. "I'm sure it's quite plain to you, Sir Thomas, that our position at this point is not so secure as we might have hoped. It's my duty to be honest with you and it's best for you to face the facts. While I will obviously do everything I can to secure a verdict in your favour, I certainly cannot guarantee it. To be blunt, the situation is by no means free from risk."

Gilling was nettled by Groom's apparent lack of concern. "At the beginning you were confident enough."

Groom was unperturbed. "At the beginning," he replied, "I was unaware of a good deal of important information relevant to the case. Perhaps if I had been more fully briefed I might have been able to give you a more accurate assessment of the possibilities. The original case we presented has been weakened by various points which emerged in cross-examination: notably the facts about Mr. Kincaid, the general impression Sir Horace Trimble made under cross-examination—and perhaps most of all by the refusal of Lord Maxfield to go into the box. It's to be expected that the counsel for the defendant will make a great deal of this last item when he comes to make his closing speech." He paused as if waiting for Gilling to produce some reply to this oblique attack. When nothing was said, he went on, "But there's no use crying over spilt milk. I asked you here because I thought there might be certain aspects of the case which hadn't occurred to you. You see"—he leaned forward over the desk—"it's very easy in an action such as this, when a great many matters are discussed, to lose sight of the real points of importance. We've been talking for about a fortnight now about all kinds of things—like Dr. Brook's house appointments and who advised on the publication of certain scientific papers, about Line's television appearances and Trimble's nephew and so on. It may not have occurred to you that so far as the verdict is concerned, these points matter hardly at all."

Gilling found it hard to conceal his irritation. Groom's attitude was altogether too reminiscent of the detached, analytical approach used by medical consultants to discuss the technical details of an interesting but almost certainly fatal case. He wanted to remind Groom that, so far as he was concerned, this was not a question of legal technicalities—his whole life was at stake. He said sharply, "Then why did we spend so much time on them?"

"Most of them were mentioned in the letter—that inevitably brought them to the attention of the court. If we had tried to avoid talking about them, people would have thought we were frightened of them. Others were raised to give general background—or because they would be relevant to the way in which the jury might regard your evidence or Line's—or because they would affect damages. But my experience is that juries think in very simple terms. This case will be decided on one issue only: could the use of that machine conceivably have saved Kincaid's life?" Groom sat back again. "If you think about it, it's obvious. If the machine is good, all Line's other points are automatically established—your opposition looks like conspiracy. If it's bad"—he shrugged his shoulders—"your opposition is a prudent concern for public money."

Gilling calmed down a little. The point was obviously valid. "Yes, I accept that."

"So really, in a sense, the case has hardly begun." Groom smiled sourly. "After all, what direct evidence have we had about the machine? You say its value is unproved. You have produced experts to support you. Line says it's a great scientific advance and no doubt he will be calling one or two experts to agree with him. But when you come down to it, Line didn't personally use the machine on Kincaid, as he admitted in evidence. What he did was to hand over some information which he took from the case sheet to this young man Brook. Then Brook came back later with eight alternative diagnoses. Isn't that right?"

"Yes, but I can't see——"

"Wait a moment. That means that the only evidence that really counts about the reliability of the machine is what we shall receive from Dr. Brook on Monday morning. It's on his evidence that the whole case rests."

"He'll presumably say just the same as Line."

"Perhaps."

"And after all, he's an expert on electronics. You'll have difficulty in breaking him down."

"Yes, I know that." Groom paused. "Do you know this man Brook personally?"

"No. Only by sight."

Groom looked down at his desk and began to make patterns on the blotter with a pencil. "It seems likely that he has—unjustifiably no doubt—a sense of grievance against you."

"Evidently."

"You sat on a Court of Inquiry which found against him, you're supposed to have conspired with your colleagues to hold back his research work——" He tilted his head to one side, looking carefully at the patterns he was making. "He might have the feeling that you were destroying his career."

"He might," admitted Gilling. "It would be quite untrue."

"Of course. But he might feel it. It's just possible, isn't it, that he might become quite obsessed about this. He might conceive the idea of hitting back——"

Gilling was startled. It was an idea which had never occurred to him. "Oh no, surely——"

"We mustn't discard the possibility," said Groom. "After all, as a physician you're accustomed, as I am, to seeing people behave in very strange ways. I don't say it's the action of a completely stable person. On the other hand, are we sure he *is* stable? For instance, would you say it was an entirely usual thing for him to demand an official inquiry because he failed to secure a job?"

"Good heavens, no."

"So he's obviously a rather odd fish, this Brook." Groom frowned. He looked past Gilling, focusing his eyes on a far corner of the room, as if trying to imagine his way into the young man's mind. "I wonder if it's possible for him to have become so dominated by a sense of grievance that he actually faked the computer readings."

Gilling was genuinely horrified. "No—I really couldn't believe it. It's quite out of the question."

Groom looked back at Gilling. "I was about to propose it," he said, "as a line of cross-examination."

"Oh no. No, I really think we must stop short of that." Gilling was suddenly overcome by a sense of the indignity of the whole proceedings. He burst out angrily, "All the rest of us have been torn to pieces. There must be a limit somewhere. When all is said and done, we are medical men—colleagues——"

Groom frowned. "I take your point. However, I'm not sure I can think of an alternative approach. As you said yourself, it's hardly likely that we could convince him that he made a mistake."

"But he would never have deliberately faked the result. I'm sure he wouldn't."

"You don't actually know, do you?"

It seemed to Gilling that there was something not only distasteful but also slightly insane about this conversation. Surely they could not really contemplate attacking a man's character on the basis of an inference that they didn't even believe themselves. He looked fixedly at Groom. "Can you say to me—honestly—that you believe he did that?"

Groom was not disconcerted. "As a lawyer it's not my job to

325

say what happened or what didn't. My job is to explore those possibilities which are favourable to your case. This is one of them."

Gilling shook his head. "No. We must stop somewhere."

He remembered ruefully his earlier determination to fight it out to the finish, to use any method, to be even more ruthless than his opponents. He knew now that while it was right to fight back to the end, one must fight with dignity and honour or the fight was worthless. Others might degrade him—he must not degrade himself. He could only act within the bounds of his own nature and he was not, when it came to the last, a ruthless man. Though it might destroy him, he felt a sudden pride in the discovery. But he felt the need to justify himself to Groom. "Brook is still a young man," he said almost apologetically. "What happens to Line or myself is one thing. We both asked for it, in one way or another. And we've both had the best out of our lives. If we're broken now at least we had something. But Brook——" He said again, "One has to stop somewhere."

Groom shrugged his shoulders. "Don't be too hasty. You have several days. In the meantime, anything you can remember about him, anything you can find out—let me know. It might be valuable."

As he drove home, Gilling said gloomily to his wife, "Well, that was cold comfort, wasn't it?" Before she could reply, he went on, "I understand Groom's position. He wanted to warn me that I shall probably lose the case. That's really what the meeting was about."

"He didn't give up hope."

"One would hardly expect him to." He laughed shortly. "You must remember that I spend a lot of my life preparing people to face the worst. There's a certain form for these things."

"I'm not pretending the outlook's good. That would be foolish. But I think you're reading too much into his words. And there's this point that he made about Brook——"

He said impatiently, "Oh, I didn't attach much importance to that."

"Why not?"

"At first—when he said it—it sounded plausible that there

might be some weakness there. But when I thought it over afterwards, I realized it was all nothing. Whistling in the dark. It's a hopelessly long shot."

"I can't see why." She looked at him anxiously. "Tom, you do still want to win, don't you?"

He was momentarily outraged. "What do you mean?"

"Well—your case is that the machine isn't any good. If Line and Brook say it was successful—then there must be some flaw in their evidence somewhere, mustn't there? It's as simple as that."

Gilling was silent for a moment, shaken by the inference behind her words. Could it be that she was right, that he was weakening in his conviction—tacitly admitting the strength of Line's case to himself? For what she said was true. If his own case were right, Line's evidence must be flawed somewhere. If he once admitted the possibility that it was not, he admitted his own guilt. Now, when she raised the matter, he realized this fear of being in the wrong had been in his heart from the very beginning, destroying his will to fight. Yet never for one moment had it been in hers. She believed in him as he had never been able to believe in himself. He touched her hand gratefully. "What would I do without you?"

They were not a sentimental pair. Amiability, respect, even a detached affection were the common currency of their lives. Tenderness was rare between them. She felt the tears come to her eyes. She gripped his fingers and said, "I never doubted you, Tom. I know that you're right and that he's wrong. I know that you're honest and that he's a liar. He's out to destroy you. I won't let him."

Perversely he began to defend Line. "I think he's probably sincere. He has a point of view——"

"I hate him," she said with suppressed violence. "I've never hated anyone quite so much. I'd kill him if I could."

"No—no," he protested. "I understand how you feel——"

"I really mean that. If his death would save you, I'd kill him without a thought." She did mean it, he knew. There was something total, almost terrifying about her loyalty to him. It was a side of her which he had never previously suspected, which only suffering had revealed. He found it immensely touching but a

327

little frightening. He had never held such absolute commitment to anything. Always with him there had been a trace of caution, of reservation. Sanity had always governed his attitude in the end, no matter how deeply he might feel. She said, "I didn't tell you this before. A week ago a girl came to see me. Line's mistress. Susan somebody or other. She was in a great state. Anxious to know if there was some way we could work out together of stopping the case. She was worried to death about him."

"Why?"

"I couldn't find out. I thought it was odd because—well, at that time it looked as if he was pretty certain of winning. Yet she said he was anxious—he couldn't sleep and so on——"

"What did you tell her?"

"What could I say? I said any approach would have to come from Line himself—through his lawyers." He nodded agreement. "So it meant nothing, in practical terms. Yet the more I think of it, why should he be worrying like that?" Gilling made a hopeless gesture. "We ought to try to find out."

Gilling said rather testily, "Unfortunately Line's already given evidence."

"Brook hasn't."

He was growing irritable. "You mustn't take too much notice of Groom. He may be an excellent lawyer but he doesn't understand medicine. He thinks, because Brook invented and worked the machine, that he's important. In fact he's nobody—a mere boy—a creature of Line's."

She protested, "He's over thirty."

"That doesn't matter."

"I think it does."

It was very rare for them to snap at each other like this. She went on, "I know it's customary in your profession to treat grown men as children. But it's possible that Brook may regard himself differently. After all," she said pointedly, "he has a record of protest."

He was momentarily outraged that she should take Brook's part against him. He said, in his iciest voice, "You sound quite sympathetic to him."

"I'm trying to understand him. This idea of Groom's that he

might have faked the machine out of revenge—I don't think one ought to dismiss it completely. Alternatively he might have made a mistake and been afraid to mention it until it was too late—or something. Either way, he's a person on his own, not just a projection of Line. For all we know he may resent Line just as much as he resents you and Trimble."

"Don't be absurd. If it wasn't for Line, nobody would ever have heard of him."

"He did the work," she persisted. "He was the one who invented the machine."

Gilling sighed. "I'm afraid you don't really understand," he said patiently. "Line holds the chair. It's his department. It's his business to take the responsibility for what happens in it."

"You don't think Brook might resent that?"

"Why should he? That's the way it works."

She saw that he was genuinely puzzled. The principle of seniority was so rooted in him that he had become incapable of visualizing how anyone could refuse to accept it. The rebellion of Line was outrageous and indefensible in his eyes, but at least Line was a professor. He had bought an entrance ticket to the power game. For a man in Brook's position to consider himself fit to take part in the game was quite simply an absurdity. It was presumption gone mad.

As she looked at his set, rigid, unhappy old man's face she realized that for once there was no contact between them. He would fight on because he must, but to him it was a fight without hope of victory. His mind was closed to the only avenue of hope by the rigidity of his caste, which denied him the chance of seeing Brook as a man in his own right, with the power to think and act independently of his master. Yet Brook was the only hope they had. If they regarded him as an automaton, a mere projection of Line, then the case was already at an end.

There was only one possibility left and she would have liked her husband's support for it. But she knew now that this was impossible. She would have to act on her own.

Chapter 7

"IT'S NICE OF YOU," said Lord Sandray enigmatically, "to come and see an old man like me."

Indeed, she thought, he *was* old—almost alarmingly so. His face was parchment, his thin stooped body looked like a skeleton which had been carefully swathed in layer upon layer of Hawes and Curtis clothing. He must be well over eighty. That was one of the most distressing aspects of high medical politics—the age of everyone. Yet that was where the power was. The corridors of senility.

"I have to be honest with you," she said stiffly. "My visit wasn't entirely social."

Suddenly he was shaken by a spasm, like a dreadful suppressed cough which threatened to choke him. It worked its way through his body, and brought a momentary colour to his cheeks and tears to his eyes. But it passed away, leaving something like a smile on the aged cracked face. It was not until then that she realized that he had been laughing.

He dabbed at his eyes. "I didn't really imagine it was, my dear," he said. "But I admire your honesty."

"I came to ask your help."

"Yes." His voice said that he knew perfectly well what she was going to say. After all, he had been a king himself for twenty years. He knew the custom of the court. He teased her a little. "What makes you think I can help you?"

So she must flatter him. Well, it was a small price to pay. "After all, you're the greatest man in the profession, aren't you?"

"Am I? One wouldn't think so nowadays," he said peevishly. "I think perhaps I made my contribution at one time. But people soon forget. I'm a nobody now. Just a back number. I think most of my colleagues will be pleased when I'm gone."

Was there no end to man's vanity, she wondered. Did he really expect, aged and infirm as he was, to occupy the same position as he had ten years ago? "I can't believe that," she said briskly. "Tom has always said you'd be one of the great men of medicine of this century—and not just in England."

"Very kind of him," said Sandray grumpily. "Just the same, they all wanted me out at one time—Tom included. They intrigued against me, you know. I suppose he wanted to be President of the College." He glared at her through bright beady eyes. He had a long neck and a little ruff of hair, which made him look like a buzzard waiting for its victim to die. "They thought they could do without me." He gave a short, dry, cackling laugh. "Academy of Medicine indeed! They think they invented the idea. Why, we were talking about that before the war. Do you know that? Before the war." She nodded politely. The only way was to let him ramble on until an opportunity appeared to get him back to the point. "It wasn't practicable then and it won't work now either. You can tell Tom that."

"Yes, I will. I'm sure he'll be most——"

"No, he won't. Or he'd have asked my opinion before. I suppose they thought I'd be against it because I haven't done it myself." That sounded likely enough, she thought. "Well, they must try their own way and see how they manage." He spoke as if these eminent greybeards in their sixties were a group of callow adolescents peddling theories of revolution. "I hardly see any of them any more."

"Tom said he saw you at Comitia a month or so ago."

"At the College? Yes, I still go to Comitia. I'm the oldest Fellow, you know. The oldest past President. It's up to people like me to see the old customs are kept up."

The ritual, she thought, the mumbo jumbo; old men carrying swords and lances, dressing up as masons or heralds or medieval courtiers, covering their heads with scarlet mobcaps and their bony shanks with knee-breeches. Parading up and down corridors intoning ritual from dead languages they had long ceased to understand. God help England.

He said inconsequentially, "And how's your cousin?"

"Which one?"

"Adrian." He spoke impatiently as if she should have known he could only have meant one cousin. "I haven't been down to the Castle for many years. Not since the old duke died."

Did he want an invitation, she wondered. It was strange, even when a man had spent a lifetime peering at the bodies of the great, these minor snobberies still evidently counted for something. Well, it might be possible to arrange. Adrian was a vague, easy-going man. Often he had only the haziest idea of who his guests were.

"Adrian often asks after you," she lied. "Only recently he was asking me if there would be any possibility of getting you out to Marlowe for a weekend."

"Very kind of you. But I don't go out very much these days." It would perhaps give him even more pleasure to refuse an invitation from a duke than to accept one. He changed track again. Cheerfully, almost as if it had been she who had been procrastinating, he said, "You said you wanted my help."

"Yes." Perhaps now he had had his fun she might get somewhere with him. "It's about this lawsuit."

"A mistake," said Sandray. "An obvious mistake from the beginning. If he'd asked me——"

He was certainly making her pay. Well, she would pay. "Perhaps he should have done——"

"I could have told him. Libel actions between medical men— always a mistake."

"It was difficult at the time to see an alternative."

"That's what people always say when they lose their heads," he said glumly, chewing at his false teeth. "They may think I'm an old has-been, but at least I never lost my head." He paused but she said nothing. At least *she* would not lose her head. She would be polite to this vain, pompous old fool at all costs. It was the one thing she would do for Tom that he would never do for himself. The beady eyes glared at her. "So now he's in difficulties?"

She nodded. "No doubt you've read the newspapers."

"Some of them. I'm still very busy, you know. I'm writing my life. It should be finished very soon." He cackled. "Yes, I

332

know what you're thinking. But I think I shall finish the book first," he said smugly. "The publishers are very keen about it."

"Yes, I'm sure."

"I met a great many very interesting and remarkable people in my time. A great many." Her heart sank. He was off the point again. "Mostly dead now, of course."

"I suppose so." She could not be certain whether his mind was genuinely wandering or whether he was doing this on purpose to torment her. Either way she would suffer it.

There was a slight pause. Then he said impatiently, "Oh come on, what is it you want?"

She was finding it desperately hard. It was not possible to say in so many words what she wanted from him. What she had vaguely hoped was that in the course of an amicable conversation his experience might give a pointer to what should be done. But it seemed impossible to develop a conversation. This sequence of vainglorious monologues, punctuated by sharp, hostile questions such as a testy examiner might direct at a student, was hopelessly disconcerting.

"I don't know exactly," she said, trying to disarm him with frankness. "I just feel it's a desperate situation, and yet there must be a way out. I thought if anyone could think of one, it would be you."

"Why didn't Gilling come to see me himself?"

She sighed. She had been afraid he would ask this. "He's very proud——"

"And you're not?"

"Not in these circumstances. I want to win. That's all that matters to me."

He chuckled. "*Sancta simplicitas.*" Suddenly she knew what he looked like, in this heavy dark room in his sombre clothes, with his pale claw-like hands and antique face. He was like some ancient prince of the church, full of years and cunning, the decrepitude of his body emphasizing rather than detracting from the reality of his power. She said, "I hope you won't refuse to help me."

He was silent for a while. Then he said, in an altogether stronger and more serious voice, "What matters here isn't you, or me, or Gilling or any of the rest of them. It's the structure. It goes back for hundreds of years, you know. It's been handed on generation after generation from Linacre and Harvey to people like myself and your husband. It's our job to preserve and strengthen it. I think I did my part. Whatever I may think of the foolish and wrong-headed things my successors have done, I still can't afford to see it destroyed." He brooded for a moment. "What's more, he sneered at me in court. Line did. About that business of the television. Said I was an old man—out of date." He said with great malevolence, "I haven't forgotten that."

She thanked God for Line's casual indiscretion. It probably weighed at least as much if not more than all that stuff about Harvey and Linacre and the precious heritage of the centuries. She said, pressing on the tender nerve, "What's your judgment of Line?"

He managed to surprise her again. The resentment died suddenly from his face. His voice became careful, judicial, and free from passion. She saw now one of the sources of his strength. He was a true professional. He had been assessing medical men all his life. It was his interest, his business, his hobby. He spoke with the confidence and the pride in his own special skill of an expert judge of bloodstock.

"He's clever," he said. "A very fast thinker and a good talker. He has an attractive personality and great drive—a natural publicist. It takes you quite a little time to realize that there's nothing beneath it."

"You think he's overrated?"

"Who by? The newspapers?" He laughed dryly. "They'd say anything to get an interview. None of the people who matter rate him very highly. As I see it, his whole position is largely a confidence trick. But he's been playing it so long that he's begun to believe it himself. He really thinks he's a great man. I'm afraid he's quite mistaken," he went on thoughtfully. "Great men are few and far between, you know. At my age you can look at people from a distance. Take your husband for instance. He's good, sound, not brilliant but a first-rate clinician, the sort of general consultant one could always trust in every circumstance. People of that quality are pretty rare in my experience. Trimble, of course, is awful. Maxfield was an exceptional man up to the age of forty; but he ran out of something—I'm not quite sure what. Line's more difficult to place. He looks and acts like a genius. He'd terribly like to be a big pioneer, a scientific surgeon. But when you come down to it, what has he done? He's a painstaking surgeon but his spectacular achievements are all newspaper stuff. Any fool can transplant limbs, you know. He made his name by chance—because he happened to have the best heart-lung machine in the world at the time at the Hemisphere Hospital. He didn't invent it—somebody else did. This later work with the Brook-Halder machine—that isn't his either. That's probably what's wrong with him, behind everything—disappointment. He so badly wanted to be a great man but he hadn't the spark. Few are chosen, you know. Rex Hartly has done more original work in the last three years than Line did since he qualified."

She became restive. This was interesting, and perhaps at another time she would have been fascinated by it, but where was it getting her? Well, at least it had put the old man into a good mood. She tried gently to bring him back to the point.

"And Brook—what do you think of him?"

"My dear, I don't know him. I don't even properly understand his work. All these mathematics——" He made a grimace.

"You see, as Sir Frederick Groom points out, he's the only witness to come. My husband's future really hangs on what he says."

Sandray looked grave. "Not just your husband's future, believe me. The implications of a victory for Line would be disastrous—quite disastrous."

She said tentatively, "Do you think it possible—Groom suggested this but my husband doesn't believe it—that Brook might have planned the whole thing—and faked the computer reading —out of spite because of what happened to him earlier?"

Sandray said dubiously, "I don't think so, do you?" As if afraid he might be accused of an excessive faith in human nature, he added in amplification, "In my experience revenge on its own is a very uncommon motive for action. It's too unproductive. It takes an enormous amount of time and energy and doesn't bring you much in return. On the occasions when people do act out of revenge, it's usually combined with self-interest—

it gives an extra impetus to the desire to defeat somebody who's standing in your way." He thought for a moment. "Actually Brook hasn't very much to gain if Line wins the case. His machine would get vindicated, it's true—but at the price of antagonizing everyone who could help him in the future. And it would make him an outcast in the profession. He'd be a slave to Line from then on. It seems a high price to pay."

"Do you think he realizes that?"

"Perhaps. Perhaps not." Suddenly his eyelids began to droop, as if he might fall asleep at any moment. Then he pulled himself together and forced a wintry smile on his face. "I suppose it might be worth while to make it clear to him."

Since the court was not sitting on Friday, Brook decided to go to work. At home there was no peace. The house was too small and it was impossible to get away from the children. They made a noise, which was natural at their age but nevertheless irritating. His wife said she liked him to stay at home, but really he had a feeling that he was in the way. There was dusting and polishing and vacuum cleaning to be done. Also her anxiety about him, ineffectually concealed beneath a crust of optimism, was unnerving.

At least the laboratory was quiet and private and he could distract himself with other problems. Mathematics had always had a soothing effect on his mind, rather akin to the way in which others were affected by music. It was something to do with the balance between complexity and symmetry, he imagined. Even the sight of the machine was reassuring to him, though it really looked like nothing more exciting than a bank of elaborate filing cabinets with dials on the front. It represented reason and sanity, a world free of messy emotions. It had no motives, no interests, no desires, no temptations. It was not distracted by conflicting pressures. It existed simply to give the right answers to questions. One of the most familiar and most vapid criticisms of the machine was that it was hopelessly limited and uncreative, that it could never give you back more than you put into it. Couldn't they see that it was exactly this quality which made the machine so enormously valuable?

The problem he was working on at the moment concerned

cancer of the female breast. For twenty years or more the surgeons and the radiotherapists had been arguing about the correct method of treatment. There were two main schools of thought—the first favoured radical surgery and limited X-ray treatment, the second believed in limited surgery and radical X-ray treatment. It had always been impossible to gain agreement as to which method was best, because when the second method was introduced, its supporters had introduced with it a different scheme of classification of severity of the disease. The consequence was that the results produced by the two schools were never mathematically comparable. Each school contended that its results were better than those of the other and neither would agree to change its system of classification. It had occurred to Brook that the machine, on the basis of the case histories of reported cases, would be able to re-classify the reported series so as to make them comparable with each other and finally demonstrate which treatment was more effective.

He had run into a difficulty, however. The machine, on his instructions, had re-sorted the data and had finally come out with figures which had shown Treatment 1 (radical surgery) to be more effective. On the other hand, the more he looked into the details the more uneasy Brook became. The reason was that the difference between the results of Treatment 1 and Treatment 2 was not very great. You had only to remove one fairly large series from the equation and it gave exactly the opposite result.

The series in question was known as the Wymark series. It had been published by Ernest Wymark of Illinois, in the early 1940's, and was quite the most powerful evidence ever produced in favour of radical surgery. The results were outstanding. The only difficulty was that no one had ever been able to produce anything comparable to these since. Why not? Brook ran over the various possibilities in his mind. Firstly, were the cases really cancer? It seemed certain that they were. They had all been confirmed under the microscope by Dr. Levay, one of the best pathologists of his time. Had Wymark lied about his results? It seemed hardly credible. He had followed up his patients meticulously and had published in association with four colleagues, all of unimpeachable probity. Were Wymark's gifts as a surgeon so remarkable that he could consistently achieve eradication of a growth where others failed? Just possible, but extremely unlikely. Brook was no believer in brilliant surgeons with miraculous powers. Anyway, even if it were so, perhaps one shouldn't include Wymark's series in the analysis—if the operation needed a superman to do it, it was hardly relevant in working out a standard treatment to be carried out by people of ordinary ability.

It was really very difficult to know what to do. Either way, he thought gloomily, there would be the most fearful outcry when he published the results. He had no real hope that the side which came out worst would seriously consider modifying their method of treatment. If experience was any guide, they would simply publish letters vilifying the machine.

He heard the door open and looked up to see an old man standing in front of him. The face was vaguely familiar, but he could not place it. Before he could speak, the old man said, mildly but with an air of authority, "Good morning."

Brook found himself standing up. There was something in the old man's manner which seemed to demand it. He had no idea who this person was, but it was as well to take no chances.

"You must excuse my intrusion. I used to be a physician in this hospital." The old man smiled benignly through his spectacles. "My name's Sandray."

Brook was pleased that he had behaved respectfully. So this was the old bastard in person. It was really quite a thrill to be talking to such a noted figure. Although he knew in theory that Sandray was still alive, he had always regarded him more or less as one of the eminent dead. He had never expected actually to meet him. "Oh—how do you do, sir?"

"Of course, in those days one could be on the staff of many hospitals. I was just a clinical physician, I'm afraid. A period piece." He chuckled and then said, "You're Brook, I imagine."

"Yes."

"I've heard about you. And this, of course." He waved his hand vaguely at the machine. "I still try to keep in touch with what's going on—as best I can. That's one of the great things about medicine as a career. It never ceases to fascinate. Don't you agree?"

You old humbug, thought Brook, you spent most of your time on medical politics. "Oh yes, indeed."

Sandray looked round the room as if surprised to find Brook alone. "I really came to see David Line."

"I'm afraid he's not here."

"What a pity." Before Brook could think it strange that he hadn't found out beforehand that Line would not be there, he went on, "I wanted to ask him about this machine. I've been following the court case very closely, and I really wasn't absolutely clear how it worked." He shook his head sadly. "I'm afraid medicine's become very complicated in recent years."

"It's not really a complicated machine."

"Oh surely——"

"No." This was one of Brook's hobby-horses. "The principle's quite simple. If you're interested I can show you——"

"That's extremely kind of you."

Brook began to explain. As he did so his natural awkwardness gradually left him. As always on his own subject, he became happy and confident. Sandray let him talk without interruption. He had the politician's gift of listening with apparent interest to the exposition of facts which he already knew. He was also aware that the surest way to win a man's confidence was to invite him to give you a lecture. After a while Brook began to warm towards him. The old man must be well over eighty but he was still sharp-witted. He picked things up quickly enough.

At the end Sandray looked him over like a trainer putting a value on a racehorse. He said, "How old are you?"

"Thirty-two."

"You know," he said with a trace of envy in his voice, "you chaps are very fortunate these days. Tremendous opportunities. You've no idea how difficult it was in my day to make a name if you were under forty. Nowadays if you're over forty you're senile. We hardly ever appoint a man of over forty to a chair any more. Quite right too, I should say." Unexpectedly he said, "You're Jewish?"

Brook flushed. "Yes."

Sandray seemed unconscious of his embarrassment. He had the natural insolence which comes from a lifetime of age and power. He had no inhibitions against asking personal questions. "I'm half Jewish myself—on my mother's side. I must confess I kept it quiet in my young days. You've no idea what it was like—the prejudice of those days. It used to upset me sometimes. But then I thought—if I worried too much about it it would hurt me more than it hurt them. If you want to do things in the world you have to put up with injustice and try to forget it. A grievance is a heavy burden to carry. I decided I couldn't afford it." He said pointedly, "In my experience martyrdom is a full-time job. It's difficult to combine it successfully with a career."

There seemed to be nothing much to say to that. Brook remained silent. Fortunately the old man did not seem to expect an answer. He switched the conversation again. "You know," he said, "you're a very intelligent young man. It's obvious you have great possibilities. If I were still a person of importance, I should offer you a job." Brook still said nothing. "I think perhaps you've been misunderstood. Because of all this business, people are beginning to think of you as just Line's man. That's bad for you. You can't feed on him all your life."

"I don't intend to."

Sandray smiled at him. It was an intimate, conspiratorial smile. "I'm sure you don't."

It was all so obvious, thought Brook, and yet somehow it worked just the same. What flattered a man was that you thought him worth flattering. He could see through the whole act and Sandray knew he could. That obviously wasn't important to the old man. The message had been passed. The vague promise, the veiled threat. Again Sandray did not bother to change the subject delicately. He turned his attention back to the machine. "Now tell me," he said, "what exactly are you using this device for just now?"

"A study of cancer of the breast." Brook was relieved to get the conversation away from himself and back to the machine. Happily he began to describe his problem in detail. Sandray listened carefully. At the end, he said, "Yes, that's most interesting. Fascinating." He gave a reminiscent smile. "Of course you won't have ever met Wymark?"

"No."

"He died—oh, fifteen years ago, I should think. A remarkable fellow."

"You knew him?"

"Oh yes. I was in the States when the series was published. It created quite a sensation. A tremendous piece of surgical research. It was his life work, of course. Naturally people questioned the results. But there was no doubt about his integrity or his methods. None at all."

This was invaluable information. Brook said eagerly, "You believe the series is valid?"

To his surprise Sandray shook his head and said sadly, "No, I'm afraid it's absolute rubbish." He contemplated with some pleasure the astonishment on Brook's face. "You see, I knew Levay too. He was a first-rate pathologist, as you know. But a depressive. As everyone knows, there isn't a very clear line between what you call a benign cell and a malignant cell. As Levay grew more depressed he began to regard more and more of these border-line cells as malignant. Naturally Wymark operated on such cases as cancers—and naturally they did awfully well. I'm certain that quite an appreciable number of the patients in his series didn't have cancer at all." He smiled gently. "I've always said that the most useful equipment for a successful surgeon is a pessimistic pathologist."

Brook looked away from him. He felt very tired and very discouraged. "Did many people know this at the time?"

"A few. There was some gossip, of course. But obviously it wasn't possible to make an open attack on Wymark's results on those grounds. And nobody wanted to be unpleasant to Levay. After all, he was depressed enough as it was——"

Brook said, in an agonized voice, "So really all the breast cancer figures are nonsense, and the whole argument that's been going on for twenty years has been based on a series which is worthless?"

"You could say that."

"And it's quite possible that thousands of women have been killed by getting the wrong treatment—simply because nobody wanted to upset Levay?"

Sandray nodded placidly. "Yes." His dark eyes regarded Brook beadily through his spectacles. "Dr. Brook, you've been very kind and told me a lot about your machine. I'm most grateful. Would you mind if I made a comment myself?"

"Of course not."

"Well, it's just this," said Sandray with an unconvincing show of diffidence. "I would have thought the trouble with your machine was its dependence on outside factors. Levay, for instance, was in his way a much better machine than yours. Unfortunately he was more delicately balanced—he went wrong. Wymark was an excellent machine too. Unfortunately he relied on Levay's answers, so he went wrong too. Then you put Wymark's answers into your machine, and your machine went wrong. I think you follow what I'm trying to say."

"Yes," said Brook. It was a doubt which had been in the back of his mind for years—perhaps from the earliest days when he started to build the machine. The machine worked logically and objectively. It moved in a straight line. But in the end it had to be aimed by men. If it was aimed in the wrong direction, it would move away from the truth instead of towards it. Sad about Wymark, thought Brook. His life work, Sandray had said. He thought also—sad about me, too.

Sandray said, "Now I really must go. It's been very kind of you to spend so much time with an old man like me."

As he walked out of the building he smiled benignly and passed the time of day with several surprised nurses and hospital porters. He felt invigorated. It was really like old times. He was glad to feel that age had not really blunted his capacities. When it came to the point they needed him. They had to call on him. They couldn't get away from that.

The trouble about people like Gilling and Trimble was that they had no sensitivity, no imagination. They could not improvize. He chuckled to himself. What was the name of that pathologist? Levay—Levay, he must remember that. Idly, but without any real concern, Sandray wondered what kind of man he had really been.

Chapter 8

Susan awakened gradually and reluctantly. She lay in bed for a while afterwards, hoping for something pleasant and encouraging to think about, so as to give her a good start for the day. Usually this exercise was successful, but today it failed. Her thoughts kept returning to problems which she had been hoping to forget. Ultimately she got out of bed, put on a housecoat, and went into the kitchen. She put some coffee into the pot, filled it up with water, and put it on the gas stove to percolate. Then she inserted two pieces of toast in the toaster and prepared herself a tray while the coffee was heating. When it was ready she took the tray into the living-room.

When she had finished her breakfast she poured herself a second cup of coffee and lit a cigarette. It was after ten o'clock but there was no hurry. Line had gone to the hospital an hour ago for his Sunday morning ward round. This was a special feature of his unit, a formal affair at which the more difficult cases were discussed at length; it was intellectual medicine on a high plane, with no concession for the dull-witted or the ill-informed. It was held on Sunday because he claimed that this was the only day on which he could give it sufficient time. Susan knew that there was more to it than that. Like so many of Line's habits and arrangements, it had a symbolic content. It was designed to show his independence of normal working hours and the total commitment which he expected from his staff.

It was all part of the flamboyant side of Line which she ordinarily rather admired. Today it suddenly seemed to her merely pretentious. As she sipped her coffee she forced herself to face the fact that she and Line were becoming increasingly out of sympathy with each other. She could count at least three serious squabbles in the last fortnight. He was under a strain, no doubt. But then so was she. Playing Nina every other night was a great tax on a young actress. She felt emotionally drained afterwards. She had repeatedly explained to him how much it took out of her but he was utterly indifferent. The truth was that he cared for nothing but his own affairs.

Last night she had tried to get his advice on a particular problem of her own. *The Seagull* was a success and her notices had been good. Landauer was delighted with her. Now he wanted to cast her as Desdemona, then perhaps try her out in Restoration comedy. Desdemona wasn't too intimidating but she was frightened of comedy. She was afraid that she might have no natural flair for it, and it was possible to flop in those Restoration plays in a way which could obliterate anything you had done before. On the other hand, she didn't want to funk it. To add to the confusion, her agent had been tentatively approached by a film company. Was she interested . . . ?

It was all very exciting and yet very worrying at the same time. It was plain to her that she had come to a crucial point in her career. If she did the right thing now she had a chance of going the full distance. The wrong decision could easily sink her for ever. Though she would obviously have to make the final choice herself, she needed someone to sympathize, someone to talk the whole thing out with. Her agent wasn't really very satisfactory. He simply wanted to take the film contract because there was more money in it. Surely this was the very point where Line could have been a comfort to her.

In fact he had not been a comfort to her at all—quite the reverse. When she had tried to explain the situation he had nodded absently as if he had his mind on something else. Then —the crowning insult—he had begun to turn over the pages of the evening paper. When she had attacked him for this, he had as good as told her that by comparison with his own problems her affairs were trivial and unimportant, that he wasn't interested in stage gossip and had far more important matters on his mind. They had quarrelled all the way home from the theatre and then for two hours into the night. As usual after a crisis, she hadn't been able to get to sleep and had ended up taking three grains of Nembutal and a glass of whisky. This morning she felt terrible. Exceptionally for her, her anger had not burnt itself out—her night's sleep had in no way diminished her resentment at his egoism. He was monstrous, callous, intolerable. Who did he imagine he was? Did he think she couldn't do without him, that she would put up with anything? It was outrageous to upset her like this. She needed her sleep. If she didn't get a good night's rest she would break up. She really couldn't stand any more scenes like last night. She would end up by being exhausted before she even went on stage.

The doorbell rang. When she went to answer it she found to her astonishment that it was Halder. His suit was even more crumpled than usual and his jacket seemed to be in the process of working its way off his left shoulder. His tie had come loose and nestled shyly under one side of his collar. His face was blotchy and his eyes bloodshot.

Seeing the surprise on her face he flapped his hand in an embarrassed gesture. "Hello," he said awkwardly.

"Hello." They stood gazing at each other in the doorway.

"I'm sorry to burst in on you this way. I hope it isn't too inconvenient."

"Come in," she said. "I was just finishing breakfast." When they were in the living-room, she said, "A cup of coffee?"

"Thanks," he said gratefully. "I surely need it." He ran a hand over his face and then yawned. "I feel rough this morning."

It wasn't difficult to imagine why. "A bad night last night?"

"Uh-huh."

He sipped eagerly at the coffee. She waited for him to speak but he seemed to have difficulty in getting round to what he wanted to say. Finally she said, "Shouldn't you be at the hospital?"

"For the ward round?" He nodded. "I guess so. But I wanted to talk to you alone—without David. I thought this would be the best time." He crossed his plump thighs and sat back in his chair. His socks hung in folds over his shoes. Between them and his trouser bottoms he showed several inches of hairy calf. Reluctantly he came to the point. "It's about Brook."

"What about him?"

"I was out drinking with him last night." Defensively he added, "Somebody had to. If he was going to get crocked it was better not to do it on his own. Isn't that right?"

"I suppose so."

"He worries me, that boy, I can tell you." He looked at her earnestly. "He's cracking up."

"Cracking up?"

"Right. Something's really got into him. He goes rambling on, to and fro, saying the same damn' thing over again in different words. You think you've got him straightened out and then a couple of drinks later he's back at the starting gate again. I've known him a long time as you know. We're old friends—I guess I understand him as well as most people. He has this melancholy streak. Up to now I could always jolly him out of it. But last night he won. I ended up as depressed as he was."

"What's his trouble?"

"Well," said Halder, "that's why I came to see you." He paused. His embarrassment was obvious. "I think it's David mostly."

"David?"

"Yes. You see, you may not know this, but Brook's always been a little mixed up about David. He admires him and he's loyal to him but—well, he has an idea in his head that David doesn't really like him. I tell him he's crazy—after all, we're all friends, aren't we? I tell him it's just imagination. But——" He shrugged. "I don't know. He says David's lost interest in him—hardly speaks to him any more. The way he feels, David cares about the machine and the work and all that. It's just that he doesn't care for him as a person." He ended lamely, "Well, that's what he says . . ."

Susan was suddenly aware that this was something serious. She knew, as no doubt Halder also knew in his heart, that it was not simply imagination on Brook's part. Line had these curious moods, when an exaggerated interest in another person was for no very obvious reason abruptly succeeded by an indifference amounting almost to repulsion. This phasic side of his character was by now well known, but it was nevertheless a very distressing experience for those who were dependent on him in any way. If he had indeed lost interest in Brook, he had certainly chosen an unfortunate time to display the fact. She said, "I take it Brook's very upset about it?"

"Yes." Halder writhed in his chair. "You see, he's a little scared. After this case he's liable to be out on a limb. Without David his situation will be pretty critical. So naturally he feels very insecure."

"How long has this been brewing up?"

"Some weeks, I think. But it got worse these last three days. Naturally he was worried about giving evidence on Monday. Then on Friday morning evidently some old character came into his lab." He halted. "Does the name Sandray mean anything to you?"

"I think David's mentioned him to me. And didn't his name come up in court?"

"Yes. Evidently he's two hundred years old and used to run the whole medical works over here in his day." Halder said, with a half ironical, half respectful emphasis, "*Lord* Sandray. Well, he came in and did a de-conditioning job on poor old Brook, who was in poor shape to start with. By the end the poor bastard didn't know which way he was pointing."

"You don't know what he said to him?"

"I don't know exactly, but as I get it he managed to frighten him pretty effectively." He brightened for a moment. "Maybe we could get him for intimidating a witness?" Seeing the expression on her face his optimism ebbed. "Well, maybe not. Also, of course, he got Brook on a tender point. Between ourselves he always thought David tended to overrate the machine."

"Did he?" She was puzzled. She said, almost aggressively, "But why? I mean—it works, doesn't it?"

"Oh sure. Sure it works." He retreated rapidly. "You don't have to argue with me. I'm not the one with doubts. But then I'm not your star witness." He brooded for a moment. "It's all rather complicated. Frankly I think there's something more to it than he actually told me. Something much more specific." He paused. His whole manner was vaguely apologetic. "Something to do with the Kincaid case."

He stopped suddenly, almost guiltily. She looked at him in puzzlement and then she heard what had distracted him.

It was the noise of a key in the lock. Line had come home.

As he entered the room and saw them both sitting there, Susan still not dressed, Halder crumpled and slovenly, Line recognized in a kind of detached way that he was very angry. The detachment gave him a certain satisfaction. It reassured him that he was not suffering from the kind of emotional spasm that he so despised in others. His anger was rational, he could record it, work out its reasons and chart its course, perhaps curb its manifestations if the need arose. This seemed to make anger more justifiable somehow. One could not be expected to be entirely free from emotion—but at least one could make sure that reason was in final control.

His present anger resulted from an accumulation of different causes. On the deepest level was his increasing conviction, difficult to formulate in exact words but none the less compelling for that, that the case was going wrong, that everything was turning out quite differently from what he had hoped. This conviction persisted in spite of the obvious fact that on a purely superficial level he was obviously winning hands down. It was reinforced by a curious sense of spiritual isolation, as if his whole world were sliding away from him, quietly and politely detaching itself from contact, and destroying his own reality in the process. He had not been so surprised that this should happen with Susan. Women were notoriously unpredictable emotionally. His gradual estrangement from her was worrying, but it made some kind of sense in terms of his previous experience. Life had already taught him that he was not the kind of man to enjoy peaceful relationships with women. He had no illusions about that. But he had always prided himself on one thing—his capacity to elicit affection and loyalty from those who worked with him.

What alarmed him now was the realization that this loyalty was beginning to ebb away. Looking back, he was compelled to admit that there had been indications of trouble nagging away at the back of his mind for some time. Ever since the beginning of the case nearly two years ago he had been plagued by a suspicion that Brook, and possibly even Halder, were not really as involved in the situation as they should have been. At times he thought he had noticed a certain restlessness in their manner when he was talking about Gilling and the Minister; when he paused to develop his argument they would occasionally cut in and ask him some question about one of his cases—almost as if they were looking for an opportunity to change the subject. They appeared to have no real understanding of the enormously important issues involved in the case, no appreciation of its implications. It was particularly exasperating of Brook to behave in this way, since when all was said and done the case was more or less for his benefit. Line had often wondered whether he was genuinely grateful for everything that was being done on his behalf.

And now it was something more than indifference—it was a positive insult. At a time of great crisis in his life, he found time to hold his regular Sunday morning ward round—and nobody turned up. Well, that wasn't quite true, Macpherson turned up. Macpherson would turn up if the building was on fire and would stay there until somebody told him to leave. The trouble was that Macpherson wasn't an entirely satisfying companion—there was something rather dispiriting in the way he always agreed with you, even sometimes before you had finished developing your point. And he hadn't much sense of humour—eager though he was to laugh. Still, he was loyal. . . .

It was bad enough that they should have deserted him in this way. But even in his gloomiest moments he had not visualized that he might find one of his assistants sitting in his home drinking coffee with his mistress. It seemed to Line that he was being subjected to a really outrageous humiliation.

He said coldly to Halder, "I expected you at the round."

"Yes—I'm sorry." Halder flushed. He was hopelessly disconcerted. He made an indecisive effort to rise from the easy chair in which he was sitting.

Line waved him back. "No, don't get up." He turned to Susan and said with exaggerated politeness, "Would it be possible for you to produce another cup of coffee?" As she picked up the pot he said, "A fresh one."

She was about to say something, and then changed her mind. "I'll see what I can do."

Line bared his teeth in an artificial smile. When she had gone out, he said, "Brook didn't turn up either."

"No?" Halder added hesitantly, "Look, David, perhaps I ought to explain——"

Line cut in. He was not interested in explanations. He found it hard to visualize any possible excuse which could appease him. He had been made to look ridiculous in front of the ward sister and the junior members of the Unit. The whole semi-mystical conception of the Sunday morning round—which was tied up with the idea that nobody was forced to attend but somehow everyone always did—was destroyed.

"There's no need to apologize," he said. "As you know, these Sunday morning rounds are completely optional. You don't have to come if you have something better to do. I think perhaps you missed something—we had one or two very interesting cases —and of course it was a disappointment to the rest of the Unit." He explained, "Without either you or Brook it hardly seemed worth while organizing a discussion."

"I really do feel badly about this. I guess I should have notified you——"

Line said carefully, "It would perhaps have been courteous." He saw Halder flush. He wondered uneasily if he had gone a little too far—after all, Halder and he had been until now on pretty easy terms. But really he could hardly be expected to put up with bad manners of this kind without lodging some sort of protest. It was nothing to do with the fact that Halder was his subordinate, he insisted to himself—nothing at all . . .

Halder plodded on, determined to produce some kind of an explanation. "The truth is that something very serious has come up."

Line registered no sign of interest. He held out a box of cigarettes. "I believe you smoke?" He made it sound like a dirty habit. Halder craved for a cigarette but he shook his head. Line looked at him without speaking. On his face was an expression of polite disgust. For the first time Halder began to understand why certain of his countrymen detested the British.

"I spent last night with Brook," he said.

"Really?"

Line looked pointedly at Halder's bloodshot eyes and battered face. "I hope you enjoyed yourselves?"

"O.K., so we got drunk," said Halder defiantly. "I know you

don't much care for people who get drunk but that's what we did. He needed some kind of release."

"Please," Line lifted a restraining hand, "spare me the psychiatry."

"Well, he did. He was in bad shape, I'm telling you."

"If your appearance is anything to go by, he's in an even worse shape this morning."

Suddenly Halder lost his composure. "Look, do you want to hear what I have to tell you, or not?"

Line thought for a moment. "I'm not sure that I do. You see"—he turned suddenly on Halder—"this is all rather a shock to me. I had the impression that there was a certain degree of frankness and loyalty in the Unit. I had confidence in you and I thought you had confidence in me. Now what do I find? In the middle of a time of great crisis, my two principal assistants walk out on me." Halder tried to protest but Line brushed him aside. "Oh yes," went on Line in an aggrieved voice, "that's what happened. Then, when I come home unexpectedly, here you are talking to Susan—behind my back——"

"Will you please listen?" said Halder desperately. "If Brook cracks up tomorrow——"

"Cracks up?" Line was incredulous. "I don't understand you. What on earth are you talking about?"

"That's what I'm trying to tell you. He's lost his self-confidence. He doesn't know whether he'll be able to hold up——"

Line's voice rose. "If he's in trouble, why doesn't he come and tell me himself?"

"I don't know." Halder looked away. "He's a little mixed up about you."

"Mixed up?" said Line incredulously. He began to pace about the room in his agitation. "I don't understand this. Not a word of it. This place is a madhouse. Here we are, with the case as good as won. All Brook has to do is to go into the box and give answers to some perfectly simple questions. Now you say he's cracking up. But nobody will talk to me directly. He talks to you, you talk to Susan. The only way I can find out anything is by coming on you by accident——"

"I wasn't sure how to handle it."

351

"Well, I'll tell you how," said Line angrily. "It's very simple. Get Brook here. Then he can tell me himself."

As soon as the telephone rang Brook guessed who it would be. There was no real way, he knew, of avoiding this moment. Beneath his fear of confronting Line there was a certain relief that at last it was going to happen—the reality, though frightening, had at least a natural termination. He knew, indeed, that this was what he had intended. When he had spoken in confidence to Halder, he had secretly hoped that somehow it would get back to Line and precipitate a crisis. Now there was nothing he could do. He couldn't turn back. He knew Line enough to be aware that his attitudes towards people were founded on certain rigid assumptions of what they were like and what they thought about him. Once he got the news of this present development from Halder, this whole artificial structure would collapse. The relationship between them would never be the same again.

Brook had felt increasingly over the two years since the letter had been written that this relationship was a fake. It was Line who was responsible for destroying their friendship, not he. Line had thrown it out of the window the day he had written that letter without consulting him. With that act he had demonstrated that there was no true equality between them. And strangely, it was after this act that Brook had felt Line's attitude beginning to change towards him. Almost as if it were he, Brook, who had done something discreditable. The change was nothing very tangible, but a coldness had appeared in Line's manner which someone as sensitive as Brook could not possibly mistake. It was as if Line now, instead of liking him naturally and easily, needed to force himself to do so against his natural desires. Perhaps Line felt shame about the letter and disliked him because he was the occasion for it. Perhaps . . . But after all, he reminded himself, what did Line's motives matter to him? Why should he rack his brains trying to interpret them? He felt a sudden revulsion against the whole unequal situation—a regret for all the wasted time and effort he had spent in trying to understand and play in with the unpredictable whims of this man. Was there anyone in the world, he asked himself savagely, who was racking his brains to interpret *him*?

When he got to the flat he was let in by Susan. She smiled sympathetically at him, and he wondered for the first time what sort of a girl she might be. It was a sign of his previous servitude to Line that until now it had never really occurred to him to think of her as a girl, someone he might speak to and laugh with as an individual—she had been a possession of Line's and, as such, remote, inviolate, almost inhuman. Now he wondered what she herself thought of the present situation. There was something about her which convinced him that she was at least not against him. Was it even possible that she was on his side?

He was slightly disconcerted by the way Line greeted him. The fears in his mind had led him to expect open hostility. But Line smiled amiably and motioned him to a seat.

"Sit down, Sam," he said. "I'm sorry to drag you out on a Sunday morning."

Brook mumbled something. Line continued to smile amiably. Beneath his smile anger mounted within him. The bastard, he thought, the rotten, treacherous, Jewish bastard, after all I did for him. He looked at Brook's long face, the eyes blinking a little with nervousness, the skin sallow after last night's debauch. "A drink?" Brook shook his head. "Oh come—a glass of sherry at least." He poured it out without waiting for Brook's agreement. As Brook picked up the glass of sherry his hand shook and he put it down again without bringing it to his lips. For a moment Line felt a spasm of pity for him, remembering a day at Cosenza when Hartly had poured him out a glass of beer and he had held it furtively in two hands. But the pity left him as he thought of what he had done for Brook. At Cosenza he had been alone. No one had stood by him. Nowadays these boys were incapable of standing alone. Not only that—they betrayed the ones who tried to help them.

"Now," he said, settling back in his chair. "Let's talk. What's the trouble?"

"Well," said Brook hesitantly, "I'm not quite sure what you mean——"

"Oh come." Line's amiability gave way to impatience. "You must know what I'm talking about. Everyone tells me we have a problem. Let's find out what it is and see if we can solve it."

Brook still remained silent. "I believe Sandray came to see you on Friday?"

"Yes."

"And threatened you?"

Brook said hesitantly, "No, not exactly."

"Of course not. I know Sandray—he's too clever for that. He just implied that there'd be a mark against you for the rest of your life." Line exploded. "Good heavens, surely you must know we have to expect that kind of thing. They're not going to go down without some kind of struggle. Naturally they'll do us all any harm they can—we knew that when we went into this thing." You mean when *you* went into this thing, thought Brook resentfully—but he had not the courage to say it. "We can't turn back now," said Line. "What's more, it wouldn't be any good even if we did. Do you think if we backed down at this point they'd simply forgive and forget?" He laughed derisively. "I'm surprised at Sandray. Surely he couldn't have expected you to believe that?"

"He didn't actually say that."

Line ignored him. "Of course you have to remember he's senile. He still thinks he's in charge. In point of fact he's nobody —he has nothing to offer, nothing to threaten with. And that will go for the others, too, once this case is over. He was bluffing you."

"Yes, I know." Brook was overcome by the difficulty of making contact. Couldn't Line realize that he was perfectly capable of working out all this for himself? He seemed to have the idea that being the boss gave him some special degree of insight into the situation. From experience, Brook knew that his own intelligence was more complex and subtle than Line's. This conversation reminded him of those embarrassing occasions which sometimes cropped up in the Unit when Line claimed by some master stroke of analysis to dispose instantly of a problem which had been baffling them all—only to discover that he had merely failed to see the full implications of it. Brook pulled himself together and tried to explain.

"There's more to it than that," he said. He spoke slowly, trying to clear the ideas in his mind as he went along. "I think it's perhaps time that I told you some of the things that are in my mind about the case as a whole—things which somehow I haven't been able to tell you before——"

"I can't imagine why," said Line tartly.

"No?" Brook sighed. "Believe me, it isn't easy to talk to you, when you're running hard for something. Perhaps I should have stuck out at the time but——" He shrugged his shoulders helplessly. "You have a tendency to assume somehow that we all agree with you. Everyone looks up to you, no one likes to disappoint you or make you feel they're letting the side down, as it were—so they go along. When you told us that you'd written that letter——"

"Are you going to tell me now, at this time," said Line icily, "that you were against it?"

"I don't suppose I'd have done it myself. But once the letter was sent——" Brook shrugged his shoulders. "Well, it was done, wasn't it? I couldn't see much point in going against you then."

"Better then than now, I should have thought."

Brook suddenly tired of being on the defensive. He burst out indignantly, "The trouble is, you won't listen! You get an idea and that's it. You don't want to hear a thing against it. When I try to talk to you seriously, you just switch off."

"Believe me," said Line, "I haven't the least idea what you're talking about."

"I'm talking about the machine," said Brook in desperation. "It's about time somebody did. We've got so damned involved with it that we don't think about it any more. It has to be perfect. Otherwise——" He left the sentence unfinished. He picked up his glass and drank from it. His hand was steady now. "You know that breast cancer investigation?"

"Yes."

"You may be interested to know that we've been wasting our time." He blinked furiously. "The Wymark series is a load of nonsense."

"What makes you say that?"

"Sandray told me. Wymark's pathologist was a depressive. He classified all the border-line cells as malignant."

Line looked at him incredulously and then laughed. "You don't tell me you believe that old humbug?"

"It's possible," said Brook stubbornly.

"He's a notorious liar. He lied himself in and out of the College of Physicians for close on twenty years."

Brook weakened a little. "I don't necessarily say it's true." He recovered. "But then, it doesn't have to be, does it? I mean, even if it's a possibility, it's an obvious weakness in the machine. If we put one human error into the programme——"

Line regarded him with increasing alarm. Halder was right—Brook was breaking up. You could see it happening before your eyes. It had to be stopped somehow or other. "Now listen to me, Sam," he said harshly. "All this is very interesting, and we must have a long talk about it some time. But just now I have a lot of other things on my mind. Let's win the case first—right?"

Brook said obstinately, "But it's relevant to the case."

"Nonsense. They don't want to hear a lot of theoretical stuff——"

"This isn't theoretical."

Brook's voice was suddenly decisive. For a moment he was in charge. Seeing this, Line strove desperately to restore his position of domination. It had always been easy before. "I'm telling you it is. What we're interested in is facts." His voice rose. "Facts. About Kincaid. We got the right answer. Are you denying that?"

"On the second run."

Brook almost shouted the words at him. The effort needed to speak them had been so great that when they finally came out they carried a violence far greater than he had intended. Instinctively, he stepped back, as if he could somehow physically retreat from the situation he had created. It occurred to him now that for two years he and Line had lived with this knowledge and yet the words, the fact, had never been mentioned. For a moment he had a panic fear that Line would deny the whole thing, would claim that he had invented it.

But Line said nothing. His silence was in a way even more unnerving than threats or bluster, or even ridicule. It was not a guilty, confused silence. It was more the kind of silence you got from the machine when you fed into it some extremely complex and difficult problem that required a rapid readjustment of innumerable facts, assumptions, and patterns of activity. It was as if he was simply giving himself the necessary time for adjustment to a whole new situation. The others remained totally immobile, waiting for him to speak. After about thirty seconds he suddenly smiled. All the muscles of his body seemed to lose their tension. He perched himself gracefully on the arm of an easy-chair.

"What of it?" he said. "I can't see how that matters. There was a small error in the information we put in the first time, so"—he waved a hand in a gesture of indifference—"we did it again."

Brook was determined not to be waved aside. After all, if it was nothing, why had it never been mentioned in all these two years? Everything else had been discussed in endless detail—but never that. He knew, too, that he was finished now so far as Line was concerned. He had committed one of the least forgivable of offences. He had reminded a great man of something he wished to forget. He knew he had nothing to hope for any more, nothing to lose by standing up for himself. He said, "Groom noticed there was something wrong about the time interval. He couldn't understand why the machine took so long to get the answer. He's going to ask me—tomorrow——"

"Nonsense." Line's ease of manner began to crack a little. "He's not interested in all that kind of stuff. I told him it was purely technical——"

"You left it to me to explain it."

Line jumped up from his seat. His self-control had now almost totally disappeared. "It's your machine," he shouted. "It's your job to explain how it works. God damn it, am I expected to do everything for you?"

"Listen," said Brook. He was trembling again now. "Just listen. That's all I'm asking. You talk about facts. Let me remind you of what happened. On the first run we didn't get eight answers—we got seventeen. Do you remember? And there were some possibilities it would have taken a month to exclude——"

"We've been into all that," said Line furiously. "You made a mistake in the programme."

"I did what you told me."

"Do I have to tell you this again?" said Line. "You made a

357

childish, elementary error. Instead of putting in 'severe occipital headache' you put in 'headache—no qualification.' "

"I took it from the case history."

"If you'd checked back to the Wimpole Street examination ____"

"You didn't tell me to do that."

"Do I have to tell you everything? Are you incapable of initiative?"

Suddenly Brook fell silent. It was like the occasional quarrels that he had with his wife. He could fight and hold his own for a while but the effort for him was much greater than for most people. After a while he felt drained and helpless—he had not the vitality to carry on. He could now no longer be entirely sure what happened on that day two years ago when he had fed the information into the machine. He had thought that Line had given him the symptoms with instructions to feed them into the computer. Then, according to his memory, when the first run had turned out so unsatisfactory, they had both gone back and seen that they had overlooked the extra detail when the headache had first been described at Wimpole Street. It was hard to remember now whether the fault was his or Line's. Line seemed to have absolutely no doubt at all that it was his. But what worried Brook was not so much the fact that they had made an error. It was something more fundamental, something born out of his ebbing confidence in the machine. Would they ever have done the second run if they had not known the right answer beforehand?

Now, so long afterwards, the whole episode was fogged over with confused recollections, devious motives, and unanswered questions of one sort and another. About one thing only he felt certain—that a court case of this kind was the worst possible background for the evaluation of scientific data. And for this, surely, Line had to take the blame. It was Line who had introduced passion and partisanship into the argument, who had turned defence of the machine into a crusade, so that anyone who dared to consider its deficiencies was made to feel like a traitor to the cause. For some time now Brook had begun to wonder whether the very force of the crusade had not to some extent created its own opposition. If Line had been more accommodating, might there not have been a chance of an agreement with Gilling years ago about the financing of the machine? Gilling in court had given the appearance of being a mild, reasonable old fellow. He might well have responded to tactful handling. If that were so, all this need never have happened. It came to Brook that he had reached a point where he now hated and distrusted Line. He resented his determination to think of the whole affair in terms of melodrama, to fight to the end on every point of principle, whatever the cost, not only to himself but to others. It was all very fine for Line—it was stimulating and exciting, it gave his life the heightened quality which seemed to be a necessity for him. Moreover, thought Brook bitterly, whatever Line might say, the cost to him would not be prohibitive. He was a professor, he was fireproof. Whatever happened in the case, he would still be left with his chair at the Metropolitan. Others might not be so fortunate.

But Line was now forcing him to the point towards which the conversation had been inexorably leading, asking a question of which he was afraid, since he did not know of a satisfactory and honourable answer. "What is it you're trying to tell me?" Line said. "Do you want to back out of the case? Is that it?"

Brook did not answer immediately. As Line and the others waited for his answer he realized how impossible it all was. He was trapped within a web of events. The performance of the machine had not been the simple, unqualified triumph which Symons and Line together had presented to the court. On the other hand it had been a great deal nearer to that than to the failure which Groom and Gilling had made it out to be. The absurdity of the whole argument was in taking such a delicate, complex matter into court at all, to be presented in the kind of black and white terms which could be understood by an audience of twelve ill-educated laymen. But it was too late to do anything about that.

"I'm not trying to back out," he said wearily. "I'm going to give evidence tomorrow. I'll do the best I can. But I think I'm entitled to explain my point of view." He became suddenly defiant. "I think this case was a mistake. I don't think you should ever have written that letter. To win the case we have to overrate and over-simplify our work. I can see why we have to, but it's a bad thing just the same. We shall win the case all right. But we shall win simply because we're the only people who understand the machine. If they knew as much as we do about its limitations—they could beat us. I think we need to remember that." He got up from his chair, smiled wanly at Halder and Susan and then turned to Line. The smile faded from his face. "Thanks for the drink," he said.

Chapter 9

The two old people sat stiffly erect in the black limousine as it made its way ponderously across Wimbledon Common. Separated from them by the glass partition, the rigidity of the chauffeur's back showed his consciousness of the significance of the occasion. They might have been going to Buckingham Palace for an investiture instead of to possible ridicule, failure, and disgrace.

Gilling shot an anxious glance at his wife. She had been withdrawn in silence these last few days, ever since the conference in Groom's office. He did not ask her why—it was their custom to respect each other's privacy. But he was worried about her. How would she stand up to defeat? It would be easier for him—after all, the position he would lose was one that he had never in his heart really felt that he deserved. It would merely be a question of going back to the obscurity from which he had originally come. For her, born as she was to dignity and distinction, the blow would surely be more brutal. She had a right to resent him for exposing her to it.

He contemplated dispassionately the end of the career on which he had lavished so much energy and ambition, for which he had made so many sacrifices. He felt that somehow it should have been possible to avoid this disaster, yet, try as he might, he could not think how. From the beginning the whole affair had carried a kind of inevitability. Just as everything until now had gone right, on this occasion everything, in a way which almost seemed predetermined, had gone disastrously wrong. Fate had raised him, and fate had struck him down. Accepting this, he found that he no longer hated Line. They were both trapped in the same inevitable tragedy. Like men of opposing armies hopelessly exposed in the firing line, they derived a fellow feeling from shared suffering. All their hatreds were saved for their allies, their friends and supporters, who took part in the struggle but were excluded from the necessity of paying the price.

He even found it possible to wonder whether, when the case was regarded from a distance, Line might not appear to be in the right. No one could deny that he had come out of the case astonishingly well. Was it really possible, Gilling wondered, that he was as Line saw him, a prejudiced, bigoted, ruthless old man? He did not feel conscious of being such a man, but perhaps nobody ever did. How could one ever be really sure? Unless one were like Line, gifted with an assurance of being always totally and completely justified in all one's actions. This confidence had obviously impressed the jury, and he had a feeling that Line had shown up better as a personality than he had. More honest and straightforward. And he had been able to keep the loyalty of his friends . . . Gilling thought again about Maxfield. It was a strange thing about being betrayed—you felt a sense of shame, as if you were the one who had done something discreditable.

If he lost, it would perhaps be best to retire. He was over sixty now—it would only mean the loss of a few years, and he could do a certain amount of private practice to keep him busy. Or he might leave London altogether—live in the country, or even abroad. On the other hand, that might look as if he regarded himself as disgraced. . . . Well, there was no point in meeting trouble half-way. He would decide when the time came.

They were met at the Law Courts by Perrin.

"Good morning, Lady Gilling. Good morning, Sir Thomas. Well, today's the day——" He laughed nervously. There was a high shine on his face and the strips of hair across his bald patch were like bootlaces stuck down with Sellotape. He detested occasions like this. They should have managed somehow to have settled the thing honourably out of court, though he still couldn't think how it could have been managed. It was really outrageous bad luck to be trapped in an action with a maniac like Line, who was not even prepared to consider the possibility of compromise. It made you realize what poor old Neville Chamberlain must have gone through with Hitler. He said to Gilling, "Groom asked me to extend his apologies. He's been called over to his chambers. He'll be back in a few minutes."

Gilling nodded absently. He had nothing to say to Groom anyway, and was rather relieved that his counsel was absent. It would only have been an occasion for more excuses about the difficulty of making bricks without straw and the possibility of an unfavourable verdict. He could do without that. He turned away from Perrin to walk into the courtroom. As he did so he found himself suddenly face to face with a tall, pale young man in a well-brushed but rather shiny blue suit. Behind him was a plump blonde girl with a soft, anxious expression.

At first, in the dingy corridor, he failed to recognize who it was, but then the man moved forward into the light and he saw it was Brook. It was an exquisitely embarrassing moment. This was the young man of whom he had once disposed in a rather cursory fashion in a court of inquiry and forgotten—but who was now, it seemed, to be his executioner. Convention laid down no standard greeting between the two of them. Perhaps they should behave like belligerents meeting by accident on neutral territory in wartime, showing neither hostility nor friendliness but simply acting as if the other person did not exist. But the encounter had occurred too quickly. Gilling saw Brook standing there in his best suit, like a student waiting for his viva in the examination hall. And because he had always liked students and sympathized with their nervousness he behaved as he always did on such occasions. He smiled reassuringly and passed on.

Christine said, "Why did he do that?"

"I don't know," said Brook. Yet somehow he did know. A nervous, sensitive man himself, he shared Gilling's revulsion from the actual expression of hostility, his instinctive tendency to behave, at least superficially, as if this ghastly situation had never arisen. He would probably have done the same in Gilling's position.

But his wife was busy reading significance into the incident. "He seemed—almost ingratiating." She laughed shortly. "I suppose he's afraid of you."

"I don't think it was that."

His contradiction made her more definite. She said positively, "He's scared to death. He knows he's going to lose."

Brook replied in his melancholy voice, "We're all going to lose and we're all scared, if it comes to that——"

"I don't know how he dares. How he can look at you after the way he's treated you——"

He took her by the arm. He thought of how much easier today would have been for him if she had not felt she ought to come with him. He was sad that it should be so. He must be gentle with her. She would be heartbroken if she knew that she was no real help to him in a crisis, only an extra responsibility. He took her arm and said, "Let's go inside now."

The court had been full every day, but today there was a noticeable increase in tension. There was only one witness left, then the closing speeches and the summing up. With luck there might even be a verdict. The reporters from the evening papers hoped that either it would be finished very early (which was unlikely) or else carry over until the next day. The morning papers hoped it would end too late for the story to be printed in the evening. The judge was anticipating a tricky summing up, in which he would have to watch his step if he wasn't going to be criticized in the Court of Appeal, and the lawyers were beginning to think of their next cases. As for the jury, seven of them were still enjoying the case and would be sorry when it was over. Three were overcome by the responsibility of making up their minds when the time came to give a verdict, and two were small shopkeepers who spent most of their time worrying about what was happening to their businesses while they were away. The whole court had that curiously stale sated atmosphere which hangs over any contest that has gone on long enough, which cries out to be resolved one way or the other.

Brook heard his name called and walked to the witness box.

"Are you Samuel Francis Brook?"

"Yes."

They went through the paraphernalia of identifying him and taking the oath. Symons then moved at a brisk pace through the examination-in-chief. Most of it had come up before in one form or another in previous evidence. The main object of the questions was to present Brook to the court as a reliable witness. This, said the examination-in-chief, was Samuel Francis Brook. A keen student, a young man of promise, a research worker of outstanding talent and integrity. When treated with injustice early in his career he had been courageous enough to protest and had in consequence been victimized ever since. Despairing of justice in his own country, he had emigrated to America and then later been brought back under the protection of Professor Line. On his return the victimization had started again. His work with the machine had been frustrated and his career stunted. Throughout all this he had remained calm and unresentful, bearing injustice with patience, carrying within him the conviction that in the end his work would finally receive the recognition it deserved.

From Groom's cross-examination a different Brook emerged— emotionally unstable and tormented by delusions of persecution. The man Groom saw was a scientist of very pedestrian abilities, who had latched on to a good thing in the States and tried to build it up by shrewd publicity. A weak man, utterly dominated by Line, who had persuaded and flattered him into over-estimating the value of his own work and then led him into a conflict with Gilling which had its true origins, not in any genuine scientific disagreement, but in Line's neurotic hatred of any form of established authority. Even as he resented the implications behind Groom's line of questioning, Brook knew that they contained at least a grain of truth. These seemingly incompatible people, Symons-Brook and Groom-Brook, were merely two different mirror images of the same personality. There was a side of him, he was well aware, which was weak and opportunist, which had deliberately not argued with Line when he had grown over-enthusiastic about the machine—which had never forgotten that this was his best chance of building a great name for himself and that it would be foolish to miss it by excessive caution. A side which had been so excited by the support of a great man that it was prepared to overlook uncomfortable facts, at least for a while. And when he had faced these facts and spoken up to Line about them, could he claim that it was for purely honourable reasons? Or was it, if he was to be brutally frank with himself, because he felt that Line had withdrawn his favour and turned away from him? If Line had continued to flatter him, would his present doubts have been so difficult to suppress?

Yet somehow even now he could not see himself entirely as a scoundrel. The truth was that he was neither a hero nor a genius, he was a timid man with a wife and two children and no private means. He had neither power nor influence. Within the limitations of his character and position, he was an honourable man. So perhaps were they all—Gilling, Line, Maxfield, Trimble, the Minister. All honourable men. . . .

"Now, Dr. Brook, I am going to go through Professor Line's letter with you. Because after all"—Groom looked at Brook with intense seriousness—"you're the expert here. This is your machine. The jury will naturally be anxious to hear your views on some of the claims made for it."

Brook fought against the impulse to give the menacing old man a nervous, placatory smile. It was Groom's business, he realized with a tremor, to destroy him. That was what he was paid enormous fees for. There was no possibility of getting round him and inducing him to go easy, so why bother to be ingratiating? He set his face into a blank rigid stare. The court usher then passed up to him a copy of Line's letter. He pressed it down on the rail of the witness box so that Groom should not see his hand trembling.

"The machine is first referred to in paragraph three." Groom began to read slowly from the letter. " 'There are machines available which are equipped to consider all alternative possibilities.' He then quotes your own machine. Would you agree with that statement?"

Brook read the sentence through. He was going to have to be very careful here. If there were any traps, it was important that he should spot them in advance. Fortunately his kind of precise intelligence was well equipped for intellectual games of this kind. "One needs to define the word 'all,' " he said. "The machine can obviously only take into account the information which has been fed into it. We have tried, and I think with success, to programme it with a very complete background of information about diagnosis in general. However, it's conceivable that information may exist somewhere in the world which we're not aware of."

"So in fact the machine may not consider *all* alternative possibilities?"

"To the extent I've mentioned, it may not. But I'd like to make it clear that these deficiencies in knowledge are likely to be very marginal."

"But so long as they exist, the machine cannot be considered infallible?"

"I don't think we ever said it was infallible."

"It can be deficient in knowledge, just in the same way as a human being?"

"To a much less extent. We can give it a degree of knowledge of facts which no human being could successfully memorize. The machine records these and never forgets them."

"Isn't it true that your machine can occasionally go wrong?"

"Oh yes. All machines can go wrong."

"In that event, it can produce results that are absolute gibberish?"

"Yes."

"Or even worse—results that are inaccurate and misleading?"

"That has occasionally been known," admitted Brook. "But we've never contended that the machine should be used completely uncritically. It's not a substitute for the human mind. It's a mechanical aid. After all," he said, "X-rays and electro-cardiograms can produce misleading results now and then. But one doesn't discard them because of that."

"But it might be a good reason for being cautious about using the machine?"

"I don't think it's a good reason for refusing to make use of it."

Groom turned back to the letter. "Now later on, in the fourth paragraph, Professor Line makes a rather startling claim. He says, 'Theoretically, within its terms of reference, it is impossible for the machine to make a mistake.' " He snapped at Brook, "How does that tie in with your statement just now that the machine is not infallible?"

Brook had anticipated this particular line of attack. The sentence in the letter had been a particularly silly one—the kind of statement that made him wonder whether Line was really a scientist at heart. "In fact," he pointed out, "Professor Line's statement is quite heavily qualified. I would say that, assuming the machine is working properly, it is bound to arrange the new facts you give it in accordance with its stored information. I imagine this is what Professor Line really meant. I don't think the phrase 'make a mistake' is very meaningful in this connection."

Groom said sourly, "You disagree with Professor Line's phraseology?"

"I think it's simply a rather vivid way of saying that the machine does what it's designed to do."

Groom turned back to the letter. "He says later, 'This is confirmed in practice.' Is that so?"

"Yes, I would say so."

"And then, 'There is no doubt that it is more reliable than even the most experienced individual diagnostician.' Is that correct?"

"Well, I'd like to put it this way——"

"I'm not interested in the way you'd like to put it, Dr. Brook," said Groom irritably. "I'm interested in the way Professor Line *has* put it. Would you say it was correct?"

Brook said carefully, "I would say it was a little too abbreviated to be absolutely precise."

"In what way is it imprecise?"

"One shouldn't compare the machine with a physician. One should compare a physician who uses the machine with one who doesn't. I would say that a physician aided by the machine has a very definite and statistically significant advantage."

"That's a much more modest claim than Professor Line made, I think you'll agree?"

Brook shrugged. He would do his best for Line, but after all Line had not consulted him on the phraseology of the ridiculous letter. He could hardly be expected to defend it. "I think that's what Professor Line really meant."

Groom gave a sceptical grunt. "Now in one of your articles, you said, 'When mistakes have been made, they have almost always been found to be caused by inadequate or misleading data either about the patient or about the disease.' "

"Yes, that's quite true."

"Can you tell the jury exactly what that means?"

This was another sticky question, but again he was prepared for it. It was in fact one of the fairly well-worn objections to the machine. Whenever he lectured about it, there would always be somebody in the audience who raised it. "Yes. All the data for the machine comes either from the patient, as an account of his symptoms, or from the physician, as a result of his examination. The patient may omit information, either purposely or through forgetfulness. He may be suffering from a psychological condition which leads him to invent symptoms or distort the ones he has. The physician in his turn may fail to observe certain physical signs or he may fail to define them accurately, so that the machine does not get a sufficiently precise description of them."

"Is it really possible to describe symptoms precisely?"

"It's not always easy," said Brook. "We've spent a good deal of time trying to work out accurate methods of description, so that the machine can classify them. It's obviously most difficult with the purely subjective symptoms—defining the intensity of pain, for instance . . ." He felt surprisingly at ease, considering how near he was to the most dangerous ground of all. The fact was that he had always been at his most confident when he was dealing with theoretical and impersonal issues. He had confidence in his own intellectual powers and on this level he felt he could cope with anyone. There was also something reassuring in the fact that Groom was attacking the cross-examination in this way, more as if he were asking advice from an expert than trying to break down a hostile witness. As he continued to explain the intricacies of the machine his spirits began to rise. Groom did not interrupt him. Indeed he listened almost apathetically, as if he was aware that Brook's evidence was bound to fade away in a cloud of technicalities which the jury had no chance of understanding. It occurred to Brook that he had really been worrying about nothing. One always underestimated the astuteness of barristers. No doubt they were like most other professional men—competent hacks for the most part, playing the game according to the rules and relying on the ignorance of their clients and the mumbo-jumbo of their cult to cover up their own mediocrity.

He came to the end of the description of a recent modification of one of the classification systems and waited for the next question. There was a short silence as Groom looked down at his notes. The tension in the court-room had slackened perceptibly. Groom looked up. His face was expressionless as ever. He looked like a chameleon measuring its distance before snapping up a fly. He said, "Did you know Mr. Kincaid personally?"

"No."

"You never saw him?"

"No."

"How did you first hear that he was ill?"

"From Professor Line."

"And who suggested the possibility of using the machine?"

"Professor Line. When it was obvious that they were having difficulty with the diagnosis."

"You also thought that this would be a good idea?"

"Oh yes. If there were any chance of Sir Thomas Gilling agreeing to it."

"Since neither of you had seen Kincaid, was it really possible for you to know whether the machine would help?"

"On theoretical grounds we thought it should."

"Did you really?" Groom's voice was sceptical. "Or did you just see a heaven-sent way of embarrassing Sir Thomas Gilling?"

"Definitely not." Though, thought Brook uncomfortably, one couldn't deny there had been a certain atmosphere of triumph on the Unit when they'd seen their old enemy in such difficulty.

"But you never thought at that time that you'd be able to use the machine on Mr. Kincaid?"

"No."

"When did you learn differently?"

"The day Mr. Kincaid died. Professor Line told me that he'd obtained the necessary information from the hospital and I was to put it into the machine."

"And you did?"

"Yes." Brook's palms were beginning to sweat. He no longer felt so confident. How could he ever have imagined that he could get away without being questioned about this? Still, he could hold on. It was his machine, after all. And he had been there when it had been used, which Groom had not. He should be able to take care of himself.

"Now," said Groom, "we come to a very important point in your evidence and I want you to answer very carefully, remembering all the time that you are on oath." His manner had ceased to be detached and his voice had taken on a distinctly threatening note. "At what time on the day Mr. Kincaid died did you receive this data?"

"About five o'clock in the afternoon."

"And you put it into the machine immediately?"

"We started work immediately. There was some preliminary work to be done before we could put the information in."

"How long does it usually take the machine to come up with an answer to a problem of this kind?"

"It's difficult to say precisely. The machine itself works very quickly indeed, but the preparatory work, and the work afterwards on sorting the information, takes a certain amount of time. The whole process might take four to five hours."

"Yet Mr. Line told us in his evidence that you did not have your answer until after the post-mortem result was known. That was twenty-four hours later." Brook hesitated before replying. Groom went on, "Professor Line referred vaguely to checks and counter-checks."

"Yes." Now was the time to blind him with science. "It's all rather technical. If I might explain——"

To his surprise Groom held up his hand. "Not just yet, Dr. Brook. I would like to ask you a direct question." He leaned forward. "This successful answer you got out of the machine—the one with the eight alternatives—was it the first answer you received?" He gazed very intently into Brook's eyes, as if trying to tell him something of enormous importance. Brook had the intangible feeling that behind Groom's words and the strange intensity of manner, was a feeling of obligation towards him, a warning to be careful. As he paused before replying, Groom cut in again to prevent an answer. He said, in the deliberate tone of a man quoting the words of a code, "Or was there a second run?"

The significance of what he said was impossible to escape. Not only the fact of the second run, but the technical term to describe it, was known only to those familiar with the machine. Brook stood gripping the rail of the witness box like a man paralyzed. It was like one of those ghastly moments in a dream, when something which was too horrible to happen to anyone was suddenly happening to him, and there was nothing he could do to stop it. It was impossible for Groom to know—yet obviously Groom *did* know. He had made no preparation for this, and for a moment he was incapable of formulating an answer. As he looked speechlessly into Groom's face, he saw for an instant something approaching compassion in the hooded eyes. Groom said, with surprising gentleness, "Was there not in fact a previous run in which you got not eight answers but seventeen?"

At least he had been saved from perjury. Groom was telling him, as explicitly as he could, that he had the whole story. Line had been betrayed. In his present state of near-collapse, Brook could not bend his mind to wonder who could have done such a thing—how such an unthinkable treachery could have occurred. He could only think of his own immediate predicament. Plainly there was nothing more he could do. For his own safety he must tell the truth. A great weariness came over him as he thought of everything that had gone into the case—the expenditure of time and brains and will and reputation, the pride and achievements of a lifetime, torn to rags by two weeks' argument about a forgotten scrap of paper. Perhaps this was how it inevitably had to end—in an action as futile and ignoble as the one that began it. He said sadly, "That's correct."

"And you were only able to get the second answer by changing the material you put into the machine?"

Brook nodded. "We made a mistake the first time."

"But you wouldn't have known that, would you, if you hadn't read the post-mortem report?"

Brook's reply was hardly audible. "No."

Groom waited for a moment. When he spoke again his voice was very soft and fatherly. He was more like a man hearing a confession than conducting a cross-examination. "In the light of these facts, can you really claim that your machine would have saved Kincaid?"

Brook knew he was beaten, so beaten indeed that he hardly heard the question, and did not notice that Groom had substituted "would" for "could" in describing their claim for the machine. In any event he could not be accused of betraying Line now. Someone else had already done it before him. He was prepared to say almost anything to get out of the witness box. "No," he said. "I don't think I can."

Chapter 10

AFTER a hearing lasting two weeks, the costs of which may well reach over £10,000, a jury of nine men and three women yesterday reached a verdict in the case of Gilling v. Line, a libel action between doctors which arose out of the treatment of a fatal illness of the late John Kincaid. Judgment was given in favour of the plaintiff with damages of £20,000.

The action was brought by Sir Thomas Gilling, Senior Physician to the Royal Household, against Professor David Line, a surgeon at the Metropolitan Hospital, with regard to a letter written to the journal *Medical Science*. It was alleged that this letter contained allegations against Sir Thomas's medical skill and honesty which could not fail to cause serious damage to his professional reputation.

Yesterday evidence was given by Dr. Samuel Brook, assistant to Professor Line. He was asked in cross-examination by Sir Frederick Groom . . .

Gilling's attention began to wander. He looked up from the papers piled beside him on the window seat and watched his wife striding away across the common. Occasionally, she would call sharply to one of the retrievers as they ran eagerly about her, leaping through the long grass and sniffing at rabbit holes. It was the regular after-breakfast walk which she had only missed at times of the greatest crisis. Already, for her, the normal routine had been re-established.

The case had formed a part of his life for so long that it was hard to believe it was over. He was like a man who had been watching for two years the spinning of a roulette wheel, with his life bounding like a tiny white ball on its circumference, knowing that one day the wheel must stop and the ball find its final decisive resting place—red or black, victory or disaster, triumph or ruin. Now the game was finished. He had won. He could collect his winnings, receive the congratulations of his friends, and return home.

Yet, in the end, what was his victory worth? The money, if he ever received it, would be of no real value to him—he had already more than he could spend. The vindication of his name, which had once seemed so vital to him, now appeared of little consequence. A certain allegation, long forgotten by most people, had been shown to be untrue. But was the truth about him very much more flattering than the lie? Did he appear to himself or to others, a better man than he had before the action was brought? He sighed, an old man's sigh. Perhaps it was not all loss. Perhaps all men of his age and position should be stripped naked before the world, just once, for the good of their souls. It was not everyone who was privileged with a dress rehearsal of Judgment Day.

He knew now that it was the trial that mattered, not the verdict. From what anonymous source Groom had received the information which had given him victory, he did not know. He was not even very curious. It seemed appropriate enough that in the end Line should have been betrayed as he himself had been betrayed by Maxfield and the Minister, as Line and he had, in their time, betrayed others. . . . He felt a vague pity for Line which was somehow part of a larger, more embracing pity for himself and Kincaid and his father and Gwen—for all those who had been sacrificed in the name of conflict and principle and ambition. It was the price exacted by a life of action. He realized quite suddenly that he had known this in his heart since the days of his childhood. It was the source of the fear with which he had awakened every morning of his life. Well, now the price was paid. Perhaps he would rest more easily.

He turned back to his paper. For Charlotte's sake he ought to read it to the end. *Sir Frederick Groom for the plaintiff* . . .

*　　*　　*

Sir Frederick Groom, for the plaintiff, said that this was one of the most serious libels in his experience. The jury was fortunate in being exempted from the task of deciding on the meaning of the words or whether they applied to Sir Thomas personally. Both these points had been admitted by the defendant, who based his defence entirely on justification and fair comment. This placed the onus squarely on the defendant to prove the truth of his accusations. It was not for the plaintiff to prove damage but for the defendant to prove that the damage was justified. If there was any doubt in the jury's mind about this, it should operate to the benefit of Sir Thomas.

What were these statements which Professor Line had taken on himself the burden of proving? Sir Frederick said that each member of the jury had a copy of the letter in front of him. He would go through it slowly, phrase by phrase. . . .

Line stopped reading for a moment. God, the letter again. If he'd only known when he composed it of the minute dissection and interpretation to which it would be subjected. Surely no man's words, written or spoken, ought to have to stand up to that kind of thing. It was like those ghastly sessions at school, when you had to discuss and analyze individual speeches of Shakespeare—speeches he probably scribbled off in the green room between hangovers to make time for a scene change.

A great deal of dust had been raised throughout the action about a great many issues. Many of the accusations made by Professor Line might well seem to the jury, not only unproven but also irrelevant to the main issue. The real point on which everything hinged was the value of the machine. Professor Line contended that it was so valuable that it could be regarded as negligent not to use it. He claimed that it could and indeed did give the right answer in the Kincaid case. However, as Professor Line admitted, it was not he who worked the machine. It was Dr. Brook, who had indeed actually devised it. And Dr. Brook said something quite different. He said . . .

Line began to skip. He ran his eye farther down the page.

The plaintiff's case was that the machine was by no means infallible, that it was still in a crude experimental stage and would not have helped in the management of Mr. Kincaid's illness. If the jury accepted this, Sir Thomas Gilling had been grossly libelled. He had been unjustly accused of negligence and also of conspiring to suppress valuable research. The damage to a man in his position of such an accusation hardly needed emphasis. The jury might think that it would merit very high damages indeed. . .

Farther down there was Symons's closing speech, in which he tried to play down Brook as much as possible, and to emphasize the absence of Maxfield, the unsavoury affair of Trimble's nephew, and the suppression of Kincaid's alcoholism. But it was plain on reading this, just as it had been plain in court yesterday, that these were peripheral issues. They had been important so long as Line's own front had held, and might well have tipped the scale in that event. After Brook's evidence they meant nothing. Symons had fought hard, but he had fought like a loser; and the summing up had been catastrophic. Mr. Justice Kerr-Thomas had been careful—when you read it in the *Telegraph* every word was scrupulously fair—but to anyone present in court, the emphasis given by his tone of voice and facial expression had made it plain what he thought the verdict should be. It had surprised Line at the time. When he had been in the witness box, he had felt waves of approval warming him and giving him confidence, and at the same time discouraging Groom, so that there was never any doubt as to who would win the battle of the cross-examination. It had felt at the time like something strong and permanent. It was incredible that a few sentences from an insignificant young man could destroy it so utterly.

He came to the end of the *Telegraph* report and turned to the other papers. *The Times* report was much the same, the *Guardian* similar, but shorter. The *Mail* and *Express* gave it a full page with pictures; Frampton's *Post-Telegram* reported it, but played it down and hid it between the motoring page and the small ads. They were presumably already haggling with Groom about the settlement of Gilling's action against them. One of these days there would be a small note to say they had apologized to Sir Thomas and paid a considerable sum in damages. And the whole affair would be forgotten.

With a spasm of disgust he pushed the papers aside. He was suddenly repelled by their obvious indifference to the case except in terms of its news or sensation value. They cared nothing for people or for principles—farce and tragedy were all the same to them. You could not blame them—in their callous indifference they merely reflected the attitude of their readers. It had been amusing to watch for a time—there had been a temporary thrill in the sight of victory turned into defeat, of proud men humbled, of a quick glance through a peephole at the discreditable secrets of the great. But it was over now. Tomorrow the crowd would turn its attention to other delights—a suicide, an air disaster, a society divorce.

He knew this was inevitable—yet somehow it was hard to accept, when he had lived with the case for so long, when for two whole years it had never been out of his mind. From the beginning he had never for a moment questioned its importance or genuinely contemplated the possibility of compromise or retreat. No material ambition, no research project, no love affair had ever so obsessed him. Now that it was removed from his life he was like a man who has suffered amputation of a limb— his balance distorted, his whole life disorientated. How long would it take him to learn to walk again?

He heard the sound of a latchkey in the door. He knew it must be Susan—apart from himself, she was the only one with a key to the flat. He fought back an impulse to get up and meet her, to ask her where she had been. When she entered the room he looked up from his breakfast and nodded casually.

"Good morning," he said.

She did not reply. Her face was very pale and her movements curiously artificial. She was like a woman who had just seen a street accident and had not yet managed to get over the shock.

Without looking at him, she sat down in an armchair and took off her gloves. She carefully inverted the fingers one by one, as if it were an important operation on which a lot might depend. The silence became increasingly oppressive. Eventually she was the one to break it.

"I suppose you're wondering where I've been?"

He shrugged his shoulders. He was determined to control himself. When she had not returned from the theatre on the previous night he had been at first anxious and then furiously angry. Now the ferocity of his emotion had burned itself out, leaving only a sick feeling of betrayal. He said, "It's no business of mine." When she did not reply he went on, unable to keep the bitterness out of his voice, "After all, you're free to come and go as you please." He added, as if stating a creed, "I don't want to own you—or anybody."

"Don't you?" She looked up at him. He was startled by the unhappiness in her eyes. For once she was not acting, she was not dramatizing herself—the pain was genuine. "I think you do." Before he could deny it, she went on quickly, "Oh I know you make a great fuss about making no demands on people. Can't you see what a fraud it all is? Can you really deceive yourself——?"

The accusation outraged him. It was like an attack on his religion. "What are you talking about?" His voice rose. "What demands have I ever made——?"

"It's not what you demand," she said sadly. "It's what you expect of people. Your terms of service." She faced up to him. "Because that's what it is really. There's no equality in it. It's the same for me as for your people at the hospital. We have to love and admire and trust you one hundred per cent. That's the contract. It isn't written down but it's there just the same. If we find we can't, you're not resentful or jealous. Oh no, not in the least. We just repel you, we stink. You've lived off the smell of admiration so long that if it isn't there you can't breathe."

She saw the flush come to his cheek. But he remained calm. He said very quietly, "What's happened to you? Why are you doing this to me?"

She looked at him in astonishment. "You don't know?" He shook his head. "No, I really believe you don't." She added, as if it were a discovery she had just made, "You're a very strange man."

"I don't think so."

"Oh yes." She rubbed her forehead with her left hand. It was a weary gesture and it came to him for the first time that she was near to exhaustion. She said, "I've been talking to Halder."

"At this hour?"

"Yes. I rang him up from a call-box. We met in a coffee bar over a couple of Espressos——" She began to play with her gloves again. "Have you ever been in one of those places in the early morning?"

"No."

"There's something rather nasty about them. It's funny how they start off trying to be continental and end up just giving you a feeling of Finsbury Park——"

"What were you talking about?"

Her lips twisted in something that tried to be a smile. "It wasn't sex, if that's what you're thinking. He's not really my type." She paused and then looked up at him. "I wanted to know who told Groom about the second run."

He had a curious way, when anything very distasteful to him was mentioned, of completely switching off all response. It had happened when Brook had first dared to rebel against him and it happened again now. It was as if he had shut himself away from the whole of the outside world. There was something unnerving about such a sudden and complete withdrawal. But she forced herself to persist. "After all, there were only four of us in the room when it was discussed. It wasn't me and it obviously wasn't Brook. So it had to be Halder, hadn't it?" When he made no reply she pressed the question again. "Hadn't it?" He still remained silent. "But it wasn't Halder—I know that now. It was you, wasn't it, David?"

He looked at her for a moment without expression. Then unexpectedly his glacial calm began to disintegrate. He pushed back his chair and got up clumsily from the table. A knife clattered to the floor as he knocked it with his elbow. Walking away from her towards the window, he said, "This is something you don't understand——"

His voice shook a little. Such a revelation of weakness from him was so surprising, so rare, that she was moved by it against her will. The tears came into her eyes. "Oh, David, why did you do it? Why?"

It was a cry of hopeless incomprehension. It was impossible, he thought—there was no way of telling her. He stood with his back to the room, gazing out of the window. The rush-hour traffic was building up in the Brompton Road; the small busy figures scuttled along the pavement, fearful of being late for work. He felt very far away from them, with their tiny problems and their anxieties—the gas bills and the income tax demands, the rebellious children and frigid wives. You could live in one of two worlds—the world of great decisions or the world of small ones. Each man had to choose his own world and accept it without complaint. "It was a matter of conscience," he said.

There was an arrogance in his tone which destroyed at a stroke all her sympathy for him. Even in total defeat his egoism was still intact. *His* conscience. Just as it was *his* lawsuit, *his* mistress. He turned round to look her in the face and she saw for the first time the cruelty in the pale blue eyes, the self-indulgence in the set of his mouth. "And Brook?" she said. "Did you tell him what you were going to do?"

"It wasn't possible."

"Don't you think you owed him that?"

"It was my decision. I had to take it."

"Then shouldn't you have taken it before?"

"Perhaps." There was no real remorse in his voice. He spoke as if repeating a rehearsed statement. "I always took the view that that whole business of the first and second run was irrelevant to the case. I still think it probably was. I assumed that Brook agreed with me. When he told me he had his doubts about it I decided it was my duty to inform the opposition."

She said ruefully, "Poor old Brook. So it was his own fault."

"It was nobody's fault. I did what had to be done." The implied reproach stirred him to indignation. "I might remind you that it was *I* who lost the case."

She shook her head wearily. "You didn't lose the case. You

gave it away." It was really quite simple, she thought, once you had the clue. Once you realized that for him it was only his own problems that mattered; the rest of humanity must make do with the crumbs left over after he had fed his own ego. "That makes everything fine, doesn't it? You're still in control—that's all that matters to you. You don't care about people. You use them, and if they don't like it there are plenty more where they came from. You don't even care about things—you can always get more of those too. All you care for is yourself and that bloody inner voice of yours." She rose and faced him. "Shall I tell you why you gave the case away?" He did not reply. "Because you couldn't bear to be dependent on Brook. He was supposed to be your slave. Once you found he'd started to think for himself, you hated him."

"Don't be absurd."

"You had to be free of him. And to prove to yourself that you were a great man." She threw out the words like an accusation. "I know you now, David. You get something out of proving yourself that other men get out of love. I can see it in your eyes this morning." She paused, looking closely into his eyes. "Beneath it all, you feel good, don't you?"

He turned away. The very sight of her had suddenly become distasteful to him. He said impatiently, "I'm sorry. I can't play this game."

"No?" Her anger faded. When she spoke again it was with something like regret. "I don't know that I can play yours, either, David."

"There was a time," he said bitterly, "when you asked nothing better."

"Perhaps I've grown up since then."

He struck violently back at her. "You mean you've sucked me dry." She was startled. He went on, "I was an experience for you, wasn't I? It was about time you had a love affair with somebody older than yourself—preferably somebody a little out of the ordinary. As you just said, it was part of your growing up. And because you're an actress you arranged every scene you could possibly think of. Love—jealousy—indifference—possessiveness—anything that came into your head." He said bitterly, "I hope you found it amusing."

She picked up her gloves and began to put them on. "I loved you, David, I really did."

He shook his head. "You're like all the rest," he said. "You fed on me. I gave your life strength and excitement and significance. All I asked from you in return was loyalty."

"You don't want loyalty," she said. "You want servility. Then if you get it, you despise it." She spoke sadly, without rancour. There was a maturity in her voice that he had never heard before. It occurred to him that in the very moment when they might have begun to understand each other, he was going to lose her. She explained, "So I have to lose anyway, don't I, in the end? If I leave you first, at least I keep my self-respect."

He put a hand on her arm to detain her, but she shook her head. "It's no good," she said. "It never was. I don't really know what you want, but it isn't me." She could see pain in his eyes, under the pride and the consciousness of rectitude—she knew at that moment that for him this was the cruellest defeat of all. It was the first time that she had seen him quite at a loss. There was a baffled frown on his face and as she looked closely at him she could see the first lines of middle age, the first grey hairs on his temples. A moment more, she thought, and she would be pitying him. "You know," she said gently, "I really think you should go back to your wife."

She kissed him lightly on the lips and then she was gone. He made no effort to stop her. He was overcome by a violent wave of depression, which seemed to him almost too heavy for one man to bear. He was utterly deserted. Was there no way he could find loyalty? She had battened on him, with all the selfishness of her youth, all the shallow curiosity of her profession. She had used him. Then, her purpose accomplished, the experience completed, she had no more time for him. It was the same with Brook, whom he had raised up from obscurity and who had repaid him with betrayal—if not betrayal in action, betrayal in thought. From the beginning of the case, Brook had held back, he had doubted the cause. Even Halder had hedged in the end, had shifted his feet and looked for compromise.

As he thought of them all, his bitterness gradually hardened into determination. They would not beat him. It was time

382

to be rid of all of them. Make a clean sweep on the Unit. Macpherson could be first assistant. He was dull, of course, one had to admit that—hardly in the same class intellectually as either Brook or Halder. But at least you could rely on him.

The thought of hitting back cheered him up a little. There was nothing like action for banishing depression. They would soon find he could manage without any of them. The true springs of his greatness were still intact. If he had lost the case, he had lost it in his own way—he had remained in control to the end.

Then he looked round the living-room of the flat and felt its emptiness. During the day he could seal up the walls of his life with work to keep out loneliness and isolation, but the working day had to come to an end some time or another, no matter how you prolonged it. And after that the empty flat, the long evenings, the weekends, the nights ... It would be like that dreadful time in the apartment in Peter Cooper Village in New York. He had little taste for social life and he had neither the time nor the inclination to chase around London after a new mistress.

It came to him suddenly and painfully that he was a middle-aged man. That was the reason, lying buried beneath all the others, why Susan had left him. "You should go back to your wife . . ." Perhaps—— He needed somebody and so did she. And there were the boys. He missed them, he was conscious of having neglected them. Perhaps it wasn't too late to make up to them for it.

With his usual impulsiveness, he picked up the idea and began to develop it. He would drive up to the Vicarage, talk to Brenda, see what could be arranged. Perhaps they could go over to the school and take the boys out to tea, stuff them with ham and eggs and listen to all their prattle about housemasters and practical jokes and apple-pie beds, or whatever they talked about nowadays. Happy family pictures passed rapidly and implausibly through his mind. Yes, he would do it. Today. But first there was the operating list. He must appear there quite normally. Calm, smiling—they would be watching him. Then afterwards it would all be added to his legend, how the day after the disaster he came in and operated as usual, utterly unconcerned, not giving the slightest sign that anything out of the ordinary had happened.

He looked at his watch. It was nine o'clock. He would be half an hour late for the list. Well, it would do them no harm to wait.